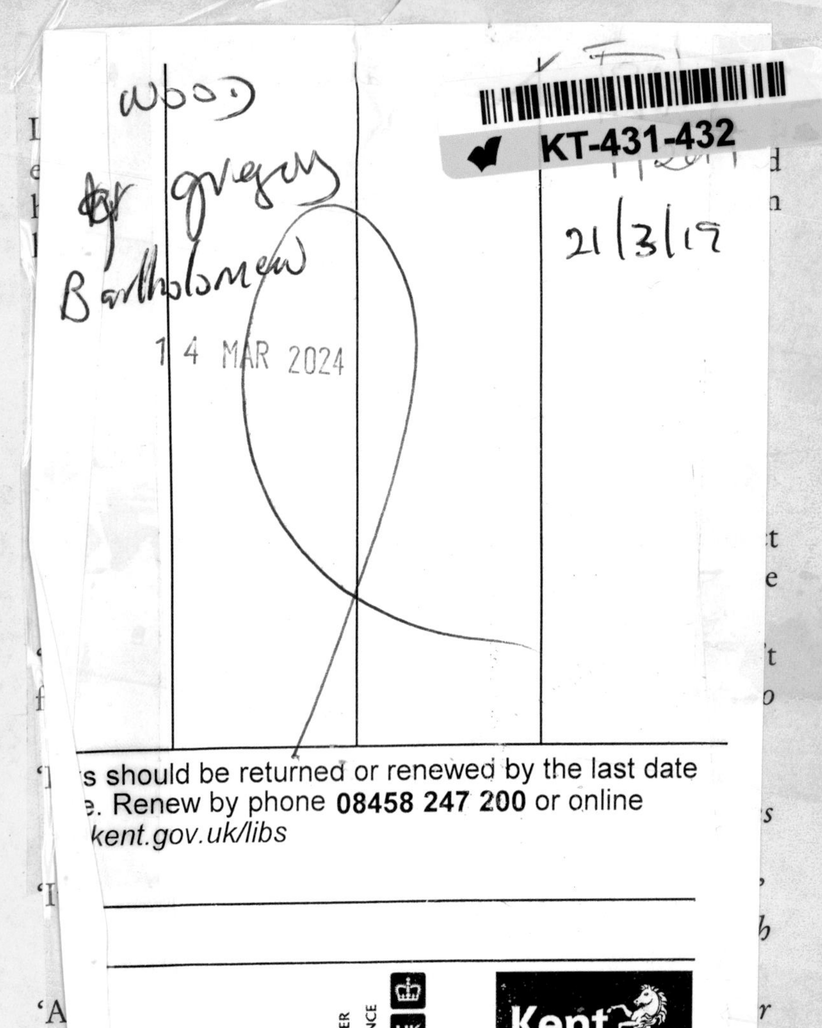
KT-431-432
21/3/19
14 MAR 2024
s should be returned or renewed by the last date
e. Renew by phone 08458 247 200 or online
kent.gov.uk/libs
s & Archives
CUSTOMER SERVICE EXCELLENCE
UK
The Government Standard
Kent County Council

C333577539

By Lynda Page and available from Headline

Evie
Annie
Josie
Peggie
And One For Luck
Just By Chance
At The Toss Of A Sixpence
Any Old Iron
Now Or Never
In For A Penny
All Or Nothing
A Cut Above
Out With The Old
Against The Odds
No Going Back
Whatever It Takes
A Lucky Break
For What It's Worth
Onwards And Upwards
The Sooner The Better
A Mother's Sin
Time For A Change
No Way Out
Secrets To Keep
A Bitter Legacy
The Price To Pay
A Perfect Christmas
The Time Of Our Lives
Where Memories Are Made

LYNDA PAGE

Where Memories Are Made

headline

First published in 2014 by
HEADLINE PUBLISHING GROUP

First published in paperback in 2014 by
HEADLINE PUBLISHING GROUP

1

Cataloguing in Publication Data is available from the British Library

ISBN 978 0 7553 9848 5

Typeset in Stempel Garamond by
Palimpsest Book Production Limited, Falkirk, Stirlingshire

Printed and bound in Great Britain by
Clays Ltd, St Ives plc

Headline's policy is to use papers that are natural, renewable and
recyclable products and made from wood grown in sustainable forests.
The logging and manufacturing processes are expected to conform to the
environmental regulations of the country of origin.

HEADLINE PUBLISHING GROUP
An Hachette UK Company
338 Euston Road
London NW1 3BH

www.headline.co.uk
www.hachette.co.uk

For my precious daughter Lynsey Ann Page –

No words are strong enough to express my deep love for you, my admiration for your achievements, my respect for you. Without you by my side I would never have survived the things that life has thrown at us. I could never have wished for a better daughter than you.

All my love as always

Mum x

CHAPTER ONE

Hard rain lashed down from an angry black sky, stinging the faces and soaking through the clothes of the three people gathered at the base of the ferris wheel in Jolly's Holiday Camp.

Shouting to be heard over the scream of the gale-force wind blasting in over a furious sea, fighting to keep herself upright, Rhonnie Buckland grabbed her husband's arm and shook it frenziedly. 'Dan, please wait for the Fire Brigade! They said they'd be here as quickly as they could. They shouldn't be long now.'

Dan shook his head, not by way of an answer but in an effort to clear his face of the streams of water running down it. 'Listen, love, there's no telling when they'll get here. This storm is bound to have blown a few trees down or else the brigade received a more serious call out after they got ours. That poor woman and child up there will be terrified. All I'm going to do is climb up and assure them we're doing everything we can to get them back down safely.'

Blind panic filled Rhonnie. 'Please, Dan, no. To climb up there in this weather . . . it's sheer madness. I know you mean well, but I couldn't bear it if something happened to you . . . especially not now,' she emphasised meaningfully.

He pulled her to him, hugging her tightly. 'You know there's nothing more important to me than my family – and now more than ever. I've climbed up the wheel more times than I've had hot dinners, my darlin', know every rivet and bolt better than the back of my hand. I'll be fine.'

Another voice cried out, 'This is all my fault! I should be the one to go up . . .'

Dan cut in resolutely, 'This isn't your fault, Adam. You didn't know that belt was going to snap. Even I couldn't have foreseen it. I checked the wheel thoroughly myself only the day before yesterday and it looked as sound as a bell then.'

'Yes, but if I hadn't let the little girl persuade me to give them another go round as it was the last night of their holiday, they'd be safely down now. You'd sent word that a storm was coming and for us to close the fair early and get the campers back up top . . .'

Dan interjected again. 'Not even the weather station realised how quickly the gale would reach shore or how bad it'd be, Adam. When all's said and done, you were doing what we all try to do at Jolly's, and that's giving our visitors a holiday to remember.' He glanced up, his face wreathed in worry. Although the wheel was lit with an array of colourful bulbs he was unable to see the topmost seat that held the stranded campers. The wind was driving the rain into shifting veils. 'That little girl won't forget this holiday in a hurry. Nor her mother neither,' he said grimly.

Despite feeling duty bound to help the campers until

they were rescued, the welfare of his beloved wife was the most important thing to Dan. 'Rhonnie, there's nothing you can do here so why don't you go and join the rest of the campers and staff undercover?' he urged. 'You're soaked to the skin and I'm worried you'll catch something nasty if you stay out in this weather much longer. And you'll need to update Drina and Artie . . .'

She cut in, 'When I leave here it'll be with you by my side. Until then, I stay.'

He knew there was no point in arguing the toss with her. He wouldn't be able to rest either if it was Rhonnie about to attempt such a dangerous act.

She urged him, 'As soon as the brigade arrive you'll come back down and leave them to it, won't you? Promise me, Dan?'

Cupping her wet face in his hands, he kissed her and replied, 'I promise.' Then added softly, 'I love you.'

She replied without hesitation, 'I love you too.'

Rhonnie watched Dan step over to the side of the wheel and begin to climb up the spars of one of the two towering metal towers that held the eighty-foot wheel between them. She wasn't religious but nevertheless said a silent prayer now for his safe return along with the two stranded campers. She felt a presence by her side and turned her head to see that Adam had joined her, his eyes fixed on Dan, obviously as worried as she was. To make him feel useful she ordered him back to the main entrance to the camp, telling him to wait by the gate to give the fire crew directions once they arrived.

Dan was a quarter of the way up the tower by now and she saw him place his foot on the next metal spar, ready to haul himself up, when it slipped and left him clinging to the framework to either side while he firmed his foot hold again. She gasped in horror and screamed, 'Dan, for God's sake, be careful!' Her plea was carried away on the wind. Suddenly the funfair was plunged into darkness as all the lights went out. The storm had taken down power lines. What had already been a dire situation had taken a turn for the worse. Dan had no light whatsoever to guide him up the tower and she had completely lost sight of him so had no idea how he was faring.

Unexpectedly something touched her arm and she jumped in alarm, spinning round to see her father, Artie Fleming, shining a torch at her.

'Oh, Dad, Dan's climbing up the wheel to reassure two campers – a mother and her daughter – until the Fire Brigade arrives. I begged him to wait until they got here but he wouldn't listen.'

Artie immediately shone the beam of his torch upwards, fanning it around, trying to locate Dan's whereabouts, but the torrential rain and ferocious wind were too much for the wavering beam.

Artie greatly admired Dan's compassionate nature but inwardly damned it now for making him immune to Rhonnie's distress. He shouted reassuringly, 'Dan'll be fine, love, stop worrying. He'll be back down before you know it, wanting you to tell him what you're cooking for his dinner.' Artie only wished he felt as confident as he sounded.

Forty feet up in the air, Dan's strength was beginning to ebb. He flattened himself against the metal frame while he paused for breath. He knew he still had a way to go before he reached the top. Several times, as the wind and rain blasted him so hard he'd feared he would be blown to certain death, he'd wished he'd listened to Rhonnie and waited. But he had a responsibility to the two terrified campers above, and so Dan kept going.

It seemed an eternity to him before he finally reached the top of the tower. He was mortally relieved to find that the cab holding the stranded campers had come to its abrupt halt as it travelled past the support tower, which meant he'd be relieved of the task of working his way around the actual wheel to locate it. The wind seemed to be far more turbulent up here and was violently swinging all the cabs backwards and forwards. The two people he'd come to reassure were visibly terrified, both clinging to the flimsy metal safety bar in front of them for dear life, their frantic screams carried away on the wind.

He'd manoeuvred himself around the tower support and was now on the inside face. His sudden appearance had the woman scream piercingly, obviously having trouble deciding whether she was seeing an apparition or if in fact it was a real person. Finally she made up her mind and called to Dan: 'Oh, thank God, thank God! You've come to save us. I thought we'd been forgotten about. I thought we were going to die up here.'

Sitting at the far side of the seat, she was barely five feet away from Dan but the wind was preventing him from hearing everything she said, though he did manage to make out that she was glad to see him. Then, to his horror, he saw her flip back the safety bar and encourage her terrified daughter to stand up and stretch out her arms towards Dan. The mother obviously believed he was part of a rescue team. But even if he could have managed to anchor himself safely and lift the child over to the tower, there was no way a little girl could climb back down in any weather, let alone a gale. He'd be left fighting to keep her from being blown away as they descended, as well as looking out for himself. She was far safer staying in her seat until the rescuers arrived. In desperation Dan hollered at the woman to explain this, but couldn't make her understand him.

Sobbing in terror, the young girl was now standing on the short footrest, wobbling precariously despite her mother holding on to her legs, arms outstretched towards Dan. Panic engulfed him. It was inevitable that the wind and lashing rain, which at the moment the slight-framed youngster was miraculously managing to brace herself against, would knock her off balance – and then there was nothing between her and the ground eighty feet below. Somehow he had to make the mother get her child seated again and the safety bar pulled back. The only thing he knew he could do to achieve that was get closer to her so she could hear what he told her.

Under normal circumstances, jumping from the tower on to one of the wheel-support bars spanning the middle of two perpendicular spokes, a distance of a yard or so, then swinging himself monkey-like across the gap between the wheel and the seat, was something Dan wouldn't have thought twice about, but conditions now were anything but normal. He would need to time his jump with the unpredictable swaying of the seat, and it was vitally important that he didn't brush against the child or he'd be responsible for sending her crashing to her death.

He was preparing to launch himself when, to his utter

shock, he realised the woman was now actively urging the reluctant girl to jump across to him. Panic rushed through him. Any second now she might just do it. Without another thought, he took a leap over to the wheel-spoke bar, just managing to keep a grip on the wet, slippery metal. So far so good. Then, with a huge effort, he swung his body against the relentless wind to give himself momentum and launched out towards the cab, praying that its forward swing would coincide with his landing.

As he made to grab the cab's bars, though, the wind blew it backward. The bars were suddenly out of his reach. He found himself grasping at thin air, and the next thing he knew he was plummeting downwards.

Dan's last vision was of his beloved wife; his last thoughts that he would never gaze into her beautiful blue eyes again, hold her in his arms, feel her lips on his, be a father to their children. His last emotion was one of indescribable sadness that the long life together they had planned had been cut so cruelly short.

CHAPTER TWO

In deep concern Artie Fleming watched Drina, the woman he dearly loved and hoped some day to make his wife, as she paced back and forth on the kitchen floor, her homely face wreathed in worry, wringing her hands together. Shaking his head in utter helplessness, Artie said to her, 'I've no idea what to suggest, love. I'm at a loss, I really am.'

Drina Jolly stopped her pacing and turned to face him. 'So am I. But there must be something we haven't tried yet to make Rhonnie see that her life is still worth living. I was so hoping for an improvement in her today, but in fact she's worse. I've hardly had a word out of her. She didn't attempt to eat any of her breakfast, and when I called in late this afternoon she hadn't touched the lunch I had made for her either. How did you find her when you went in today?'

He sighed heavily. 'Same as you, love. Lost in her own world, hardly acknowledging I was there. It's like she doesn't feel she has anything left to live for, and is willing her own death so she can be with Dan.'

Drina came over to the table and took a chair opposite him. She fiddled anxiously with a button on her pink twinset. Fixing her eyes on him, she said with conviction, 'In Rhonnie's defence, if I lost you so unexpectedly then I'd feel life wasn't worth living either.'

Artie leaned over, gave her hand an affectionate pat and tenderly told her, 'The same goes for me too.' He sat back and rubbed one hand over his chin thoughtfully. Artie had vowed to himself on the day they first got together that he would do everything in his power to give her a happy and contented life from then on – to try and make up to her for the misery and betrayal she'd endured from her late husband Joe Jolly.

He had been a destitute travelling Romany who had seen his chance to better himself by marriage to an heiress. Artie couldn't deny that Joe had used his wife's legacy to build a profitable holiday camp business, and had given her a lavish lifestyle. Through hard work and determination Joe had come to be perceived as a pillar of the community and a respectable family man, above reproach – though he was anything but.

In material terms Joe had been generous with Drina; emotionally he had been withdrawn and a serial philanderer who had deceived her with a succession of women, though only one had meant anything to him. The worst thing of all was that Drina had known all about his infidelity, and had been forced to turn a blind eye as Joe kept a stranglehold on the family finances and business. Their son Michael bitterly resented his father's authoritarian stance and they had fallen out. Michael had been banned from the family home at the time of Joe's death – though this hadn't stopped Drina's son from returning to the camp and robbing the safe and walking away from his father's fatal heart attack without lifting a finger to help him.

Until the reading of the will neither Drina nor Michael had had any idea that Daniel Buckland, the child of Joe's deceased cousin and his wife, had in fact been Joe's all along and neither had Daniel himself either. His mother had been the true love of Joe's life, he having persuaded her to stand back and go along with his plan of bettering life for the three of them by marrying a wealthy girl.

Dan had grown into a handsome, capable and popular young man who had stolen Artie's daughter's heart and married her two years ago. He had discovered the truth about his parentage at the same time, on being named sole beneficiary of Joe's estate. Michael had vowed revenge on him, and had been determined to gain possession of what he saw as rightfully his. Dan, though, a young man of high principles, had insisted on signing over his inheritance to Drina, feeling it rightfully belonged to her. She had only accepted his generosity on proviso that she, Dan and Rhonnie became equal partners in the holiday camp, and had stipulated that on her retirement or death the estate would be passed lock, stock and barrel back to Dan and Rhonnie and any children they may have by then.

Dan's shocking and untimely death had deeply affected everyone who had known him, but life went on. There was a demanding business to be run, but Rhonnie would play no part in it.

Her grief at her loss of her soulmate was as all-consuming now as it had been the moment she had first cradled his crumpled body in her arms. From that moment on she had no choice but to accept that something inside her was dead, and nothing either her father or her surrogate mother Drina had tried had succeeded in making her reconsider. From the night of Dan's death Rhonnie had not left the cottage, except to attend the funeral where she had to be supported throughout by Artie and Drina. Immediately it was over she had insisted on returning to the cottage and nothing had persuaded her to venture out of it since.

After the funeral she had stripped off her clothes and redressed herself in a pair of Dan's old pyjamas and his dressing gown. Drina managed to coax her into taking the odd bath, but Rhonnie had refused to allow Dan's clothes to be washed, no matter how much Drina pleaded with her. Nor would Rhonnie allow her to launder the bedclothes. The clothes and the bedding still smelled of Dan, and for as long as that lasted Rhonnie felt he was still with her.

If she wasn't in bed, weeping into Dan's pillow, Drina or Artie would find her huddled in his favourite armchair, clutching the teddy bear he had won at the fair on their very first date together. She spoke very little; conversation was limited to barely more than yes or no. It was doubtful she would bother to eat unless Drina stood over her and bullied her into at least a mouthful or two of the tempting meals that were made for her. Rhonnie had lost more weight than her previously slim figure allowed; she was beginning to look gaunt and hollow-eyed. She was locked in a deep, dark hole of despair. After a month of trying everything they could think of to help, the people who loved her had begun to despair of ever finding a way to rescue her.

Tears were glinting in Drina's eyes as she uttered, 'Oh, Artie, why did Him up there have to pick on Dan when he had such a bright future ahead of him? It's said God moves in mysterious ways but I defy anyone to understand just why, in His infinite wisdom, He saw fit to end the life of a good man like that. Dan will be missed dreadfully by all who knew him, and Rhonnie's life is shattered into the bargain. Why couldn't He have chosen any number of those who are nothing more than a blight on society?'

Artie gave a shrug and sighed, 'I don't know, love. Only He can answer that, and I'm sure you'll be tackling Him about it when your time comes.'

Drina responded with conviction, 'I certainly will be. I hope he's got a good answer for me or else I will be questioning His so-called wisdom.'

They both lapsed into silence for a while, each willing themself to think of something they hadn't yet come up with to help Rhonnie on her road to recovery.

Finally Drina said, 'I think the time has come for us to be cruel to be kind, so to speak.'

Artie frowned at her quizzically. 'And by that you mean . . .?'

She heaved a sigh. 'Well, I very much fear that if we don't take matters into our own hands, force Rhonnie into doing something by not taking no for an answer, we'll end up burying her too.'

His face ashen at the very thought, he said vehemently, 'We can't have that.' He then looked dubiously at her. 'So you're suggesting we drag her out of the cottage bodily, are you?'

'Yes. Unless you can come up with another way to get Rhonnie dressed and out of the house? Even a walk round the garden would be a start.' Drina frowned worriedly. 'But that's just it, isn't it?'

Artie pushed aside his half-eaten dinner. Drina had barely touched hers, he noticed. 'What is, dear?' he asked.

'Well, everywhere she looks there are happy memories

of Dan, aren't there? Constant reminders of her loss. The cottage where they lived together; the garden where they sat on a warm evening after work; the camp . . . well, every corner of that place holds memories of Dan for Rhonnie.' Drina paused for a moment before she went on, 'I think we need to get her well away from these constant reminders. It's not that I expect her to forget him for one moment, but at least freed from memories of him around her she'll be able to concentrate on accepting that there is a life for her without Dan in it.'

Artie remembered his own loss. He nodded and said grimly, 'When I lost Hilda, I faced the same problem. Rhonnie insisted that me moping round the house wasn't helping me to pick up my life again so I agreed to go out for a pint. But I couldn't face the memories the local held of my wife and the many good times I'd had with her there, so instead I opted to go to another pub nearby. Had I known what that decision would cost me, I would never have gone.' He added ruefully, 'I met Mavis there that night.'

Drina smiled affectionately at him. Artie was well padded and ordinary-looking, but to her he was the most handsome man she had ever seen. She leaned forward and tenderly stroked his hand. 'Yes, well, my dear, there is another way of looking at it. If you hadn't met Mavis that night then you wouldn't have arrived here in search of Rhonnie after Mavis had driven her out of her own home – and then you and I would never have met and been living happily together now. So, for you, Mavis was in fact a blessing in disguise! I know *I've* a lot to thank her for. I never thought I would know what it feels like to be loved and cherished, but since you've been in my life every moment is a joy to me. When Joe was alive things were very different.'

Artie looked at her in surprise. 'I've never looked at it like that. I really do have a lot to thank Mavis for, don't I? So what's the plan for getting Rhonnie away from here? Only God knows how we do, considering that we've already tried everything we can think of to get her up and dressed, let alone out of the house.'

Drina gave a secretive smile as she pushed back her chair and got up, saying, 'I'll make us a cup of tea and then I'll tell you what we'll do.'

The small kitchen in the two-bedroomed white-washed cottage Drina now lived in with Artie was a far cry from the four-bedroomed, lavishly furnished Victorian villa in its acre of grounds that she had lived in with Joe. This was definitely not the sort of dwelling where people would expect the owner of a thriving business to live, but Drina didn't care what others thought – she wouldn't swap her little cottage for the world. Unlike her last husband, Artie adored Drina for herself . . . not her money.

She had met him when he'd arrived at the camp in a terrible state, in search of his daughter Rhonnie. Mavis, the woman who had taken the place of his dead wife Hilda, had totally fooled Artie, playing the part of the loving, dutiful wife while he slaved away as a long-distance lorry driver in order to keep a roof over her and his step-daughter's head. Rhonnie had known what Mavis was doing but had been unable to break her father's heart by telling him so had left home in disgust. Then Artie had discovered that Mavis was deceiving him with other men while he was away working, and had arrived at the camp in search of his daughter, a broken man. Dan had given him a temporary job on his maintenance team while he recovered from his ordeal, which was made permanent when he decided to stay on.

What had started out as a friendship between Drina and Artie had developed into deep love, which would have remained unrequited on both sides had Joe not died. After her husband's death, though, having been deprived of love for so long, Drina hadn't wanted to risk losing this chance of happiness. Not caring what others thought of her, she did nothing to hide how much Artie meant to her, and he'd been only too happy to go along with her wishes, barely able to believe that after his recent disappointment with Mavis, this wonderful woman was his.

Drina was astute enough to know that once Artie was legally free from his marriage to Mavis, he would not necessarily ask Drina herself to marry him. He would consider it a comedown for the widow of a successful businessman to attach herself to an odd job man. But Artie's love for her had boosted Drina's low self-esteem, and her newfound self-confidence gave her the courage to tackle him about the situation. She left him in no doubt that she was perfectly willing to give up all she owned and live in a shed with him. This gave Artie the courage to return to his home town of Leicester. With the help of a solicitor he got Mavis and her latest man out of his house there and sold it, enabling him to buy this cottage. The merciless Mavis, though, would not agree to a divorce unless he settled a sizeable amount of money on her. She wasn't entitled to it and Archie did not have it, but pride would not allow him to accept Drina's offer to pay his ex-wife off, so until either he had the money or Mavis relented Artie and Drina were content just to live together, not caring that some considered it a sin.

Drina happily sold the huge house that held so many miserable memories for her, and the money from the sale was put towards the building of an indoor swimming pool for the campers to enjoy when the weather wasn't being kind. Providing a roof over her head, paying the bills and putting food on the table was enough to satisfy Artie's pride. He wasn't averse to Drina using money she earned from her job heading up Jolly's to pay for extras for them. This enabled the two of them to live together in perfect harmony, outsiders remaining unaware of their turbulent background and assuming they'd been together several decades.

Having made the tea, Drina put the pot and cups, milk and sugar, on the table. As she poured, she told Artie how she planned to aid his daughter.

After she had, he looked at her askance. 'Getting Rhonnie back in the land of the living is the most important thing to me, but can we just go swanning off on this so-called holiday like you're proposing? After all, you're the boss of a very busy holiday camp. Without Dan and now Rhonnie to fall back on, who will look after the business while we're away? I'm in charge of maintenance and we're coming up to our busiest time with the start of the summer holidays just around the corner.'

She petted his hand. 'We're lucky enough to have good staff working for us. I'm sure the main day-to-day running of the business won't suffer in the slightest while we're away . . . not with the likes of Jackie in charge of the office. Nothing gets past that young girl. If she sets her mind to something, she sees it through to the bitter end. She can be impulsive at times, she can forget to keep her thoughts to herself, but I have great faith in her. As for someone to stand in as figurehead for me . . . well, as he's the next in seniority, I have no choice but to put Harold Rose in temporary charge. He's got his faults but he's honest and reliable. At least the company's finances will be in safe hands while we're away.'

Artie's eyebrows shot up in surprise. Harold Rose was the very last person he would consider putting in charge of a firm like Jolly's, but as Drina had said the man had been there a long time. Artie just hoped she didn't live to regret her decision.

Drina was asking him, 'Have you any idea who you will put in charge of maintenance while we're away, dear?'

He thought for a moment. 'Sid Harper is the obvious choice. He's been on the team the longest and he has the men's respect. This ought to make up to him for having his nose put out of joint when Dan made me his second-in-command last year. Sid always thought I was given the job out of favouritism. He thought he should have had it because he'd been employed by Jolly's for longer.'

Drina said with conviction, 'Dan gave you that job because you were the best man for it. Favouritism or family connections never came into it.'

'Well, I could see why Sid might think so. Dan was married to my daughter and it was public knowledge then about my relationship with the boss,' said Artie, winking cheekily at Drina before carrying on, 'but thankfully, over time, Sid's accepted I got the job on my own merits and we've a good working relationship now.' He then eyed her keenly. 'So now we've sorted out who will step up in our absence, are you going to let me in on this miraculous plan you've come up with to get Rhonnie to come away with us?'

Drina heaved a sigh. 'Well, it's obvious desperate measures are called for. We'll make sure we're ready for the off, then go and see Rhonnie like it's just a normal visit. I'll make her a cup of tea and something to eat, like I usually do, while you chat away to her whether she's listening or not. When she drops off to sleep, you carry her out to the car and I'll make her comfortable in the back with a pillow and blanket. Hopefully she'll stay asleep for a good while, at least until we're well on our way to . . . well, I actually have a fancy for somewhere in Devon. I'm sure we'll have no trouble finding a place to rent in a little village somewhere for a couple of weeks. But hopefully, with the two of us to hand, coaxing her along . . . like she did with you when her mother died . . . she'll get sick and tired of being nagged into going for a walk or whatever and do what we're encouraging her to, just to shut us up. Once she's taken that first step, she'll soon be back to her old self again.'

Artie looked impressed. 'Well, as you said, it worked with me. It's certainly worth a try.' Then he eyed her quizzically. 'But how can you guarantee that Rhonnie will fall into a deep sleep?'

Drina grinned mischievously. 'With a couple of crushed sleeping tablets in her tea, I can! Come on, you wash and I'll dry. Then we'll go and see to our packing so we're ready to leave about mid-morning tomorrow.'

CHAPTER THREE

Jolly's Holiday Camp was situated on what had once been farmland about six miles from Mablethorpe, edging a wide beach of golden sand. Holidaymakers came there from every corner of Great Britain, travelling by coach, train, car, some even on pushbikes, excited at the prospect of escaping their regimented lives in th concrete-and-brick jungles of England's towns and citie to spend their well-earned, painstakingly-saved for tw weeks of freedom breathing in the fresh air of countryside. They enjoyed taking advantage of the fun-packed programme of events Jolly's offered or else just relaxing in the warm sunshine. The choice was theirs. The camp could accommodate up to ten thousand people in its colourfully painted wooden chalets edged with beds of summer flowers and shrubs. An army of four hundred or so staff were kept busy from morning until night, their mission to ensure that the campers went home after their stay having had a holiday to remember. Foremost among the staff were the Stripeys, named for the striped blazers they wore. They organised all the entertainment in the camp.

Among its array of facilities were an outdoor and a

heated indoor pool, plus a huge dance hall called the Paradise. This had three bars, one of them a carousel, and its own resident band, the Paradise Boys, catering for the older campers. In the basement was a separate discotheque, Groovy's, catering for teenagers and people in their early twenties. It had its own resident DJ and pop group. There was also a cinema styled in the fashion of an old theatre, which had three showings a day. There was a session for children in the morning, an afternoon matinee of vintage films for the older generation, and a recent release in the evening. Adjoining the ballroom were two quiet lounges vith their own separate bars, also offering coffee and tea; ames room with pool tables, dartboard and table-tennis s, and a television room. Sports contests were held on playing field, and nearby were several tennis courts, ng and putting greens, and a roller-skating rink. around the camp were several children's play areas ings and slides. Down by the beach was a funfair an assortment of stalls and fairground rides. A team of ten donkeys provided rides on the sand, while a miniature railway skirted the perimeters of the camp.

A nursery gave hard-pressed mothers a break from their youngsters for up to four hours a day, and two qualified nurses provided a twenty-four-hour medical service for the camp, soothing fevered brows and dressing cuts and grazes. Anyone needing hospital treatment was quickly despatched there. A camp photographer captured special moments, the prints being displayed for sale from a small kiosk. There was a hairdresser and a barber; gift, sweet and ice-cream shop, a cigarette kiosk, further kiosks for fish and chips and hamburgers, and a launderette.

The flat-roofed administration building adjoined the

Paradise. Downstairs was the reception area where staff checked campers in and out and dealt with any problems they encountered during their stay. A booth held the Radio Jolly equipment and several times a day forthcoming events would be announced. On the floor above were the offices, which were accessed through a door inside reception. The general office was a large light room which held two desks, one for the office manager, the other for the junior and switchboard operator. There was a row of filing cabinets and a large metal stationery cupboard, plus a table with a printing machine on it. A door at the back of the room led into a corridor from which two further offices could be reached: a side room for the accounts manager, and one off it for his two assistants and the toilet facilities. At the end of the corridor another door led out on to the fire escape up to the roof. In warm weather the reception and office staff would sometimes sit up there during their dinner break.

Jackie Sims was a pretty, bright and bubbly twenty-one year old. Today she was dressed in a colourful thigh-length print shift dress, with a matching band in her thick, dark shoulder-length hair. She wore lime green sling-back shoes on her dainty feet. Jackie had started working as an office junior at Jolly's on leaving school at fifteen and was now Rhonnie's assistant.

A capable and ambitious girl, Jackie had often daydreamed of one day being in charge in the office, but would never have wanted it to come about in the way it had. Dan's death had deeply affected her. She felt that if she ever landed herself a man with half Dan's physical attributes, personality and integrity, then she would have won the jackpot. But it was Rhonnie's reaction to her husband's death that was affecting Jackie the most. It deeply distressed her not to be able to comfort her. They had worked together for three years and Jackie was very fond of her.

Several times since that dreadful night, despite Drina's telling her that she was wasting her time, Jackie had gone to the cottage, hoping Rhonnie would let her in, even just for a minute, but the door had remained firmly closed. Only Drina and Artie saw her now. How on earth they had managed to persuade Rhonnie to go away with them, considering she refused even to get dressed and poke her head out of the door, Jackie had no idea, but all credit to them they had. She prayed that Rhonnie would return well on her way to recovery. Jackie believed she could best help by keeping the camp running as efficiently as it had done when Drina and Rhonnie were at the helm. In order to do that, though, she needed someone she could rely on to work alongside her.

As there was a tap on the door of the general office, Jackie took a deep breath and crossed her fingers, praying that this would be third time lucky.

The first person sent by the agency at eight-thirty that morning had been a middle-aged, matronly type, dressed in a staid brown tweed suit, high-necked blouse, thick stockings and stout flat brogues, her iron-grey hair pulled into a tight knot at the base of her neck. The moment it became clear to the woman that she was to work for a slip of a girl less than half her age, and not be in charge herself, the candidate marched out in extreme indignation. Jackie had been relieved, not having taken to the austere woman nor having fancied working alongside her.

The person who had turned up at ten-thirty had been

as totally different from the first as it was possible to get: a plump sixteen-year-old girl wearing a skirt that barely covered her ample backside, with a top stretching perilously tight across big breasts. Her moon-shaped face was plastered in a thick layer of pale panstick; white eye shadow and thick black eyeliner plus spidery false lashes did nothing to enhance her beady grey eyes, and pearly white lipstick covered her thick lips. Jackie felt positive she had copied her look from a Hammer House of Horror film. She seemed a nice girl and willing enough, but typed using only two fingers and had never clapped eyes on a PBX switchboard before.

Jackie hadn't time to waste teaching someone the basics. She needed someone skilled enough to get down to what was required of them straight away, so that she herself could get on with the more important tasks involved in running a busy general office for a thriving company. And all that besides the extra work she suspected Harold Rose was going to push her way, judging by what he had already done this morning. And he'd only been in his role of temporary manager half a day! Therefore the unskilled girl went the same way as the older woman . . . back to the agency. Jackie had wasted no time in telephoning them to give them a piece of her mind for sending two such unsuitable candidates that morning, wasting their time and hers. They promised they would send her someone suitable the next time, if she'd give them another chance. She really had no choice as this agency was the only one to operate in their vicinity.

A while later the agency informed her that another temp would be with her shortly. When there was a tap on the door Jackie thought this must be them arriving. Expecting a woman to walk in, Jackie's eyes widened in surprise to see a tall, slim young man in his early twenties, boyishly good-looking with shoulder-length thick, wavy fair hair. He was smartly but fashionably dressed in maroon coloured trousers and matching jacket, plus a pink shirt with a frill running down the front, a long pointed collar and wide frilled cuffs.

Jackie's heart gave a flutter. He was just the type to tickle her fancy. If she wasn't already involved in a serious relationship of two years' standing with Keith Watson, a twenty-four year old from her home town of Mablethorpe, then she would definitely have let the newcomer know that she liked what she was seeing.

As his eyes settled on Jackie he smiled, showing a set of even white teeth. 'Miss Sims?'

'I am. What can I do for you?'

'I believe you're expecting me. I'm from the agency, come to temp for you.' He made his way over to stand before her desk. 'I'm Alan Stanhope. I like to be called Al, though, it's more hip.' Her surprised expression had obviously registered with him. 'You were expecting a woman? Well, I might be a man but I can produce office work as good as any woman can. I type sixty words a minute. The last PBX switchboard I operated had ten outside lines and thirty extensions, and unlike most temps I actually enjoy filing and make great tea and coffee.'

Oh, this man is going to be a Godsend! thought Jackie. From sheer curiosity there were many questions she would like to have asked Al about himself, but as he wasn't going to be working here for long, and technically was employed by the agency, it wasn't her place to delve into his personal life. She responded straight-faced, 'You could be a dog with two tails for all I care as long as you can handle the work. Just do me a favour, though, and slow your typing down a bit . . . I can only manage forty-five words a minute and I don't want you showing me up.' Then, standing up and grinning as broadly as he was, she held out her hand to him and added, 'Deal?'

Al inwardly sighed with relief. It had been a tricky time at home for him recently, with both parents dead set against his plans for the future. Al knew that if he was ever going to follow his dreams then he needed to gain his independence from his parents and considering how his parents had reacted to his plans he dreaded what his friends would say, so that meant them too. After walking out of their house and his job running the office of his father's engineering firm, he'd been using up what little savings he had on paying for cheap lodgings and food while going after any job he saw advertised. Without a reference, though, no one seemed willing to take him on. The agency had seemed very doubtful about his prospects, but had agreed to keep him under consideration. Down to his last couple of pounds, this morning he'd been sitting on his uncomfortable single bed, huddled inside thin blankets in the damp, cold rented room, not daring to put a shilling in the gas meter as he didn't know where his next was coming from. It seemed to him then that he had no option but to forget his plans and return cap in hand to his parents, begging them to take him back and promising to become the son they expected him to be.

He had almost jumped out of his skin when there was a thump on the door of his room. Without waiting for a response, his elderly landlady had barged in, obviously annoyed at being disturbed, telling him he was wanted on the telephone downstairs in the hall. Having been turned down for all the jobs he'd applied for so far, Al couldn't imagine who would be telephoning him. No one else knew where he was staying. When he'd heard the clipped tones of the owner of the employment agency, informing him that in this instance she was waiving her rule about sending someone without references after a good job, Al wasn't fooled. He knew she was in a tight spot and he was her last resort. He didn't care, though; he was at last being given the opportunity to earn some money, and provided the firm he was being sent to was pleased with his work, he'd receive a favourable report and then hopefully the agency would keep him in work and he'd be able to earn money at last to put towards his plan.

Al accepted Jackie's hand and shook it enthusiastically. 'Deal,' he said. Before she gave him a quick overview of his duties, out of courtesy she felt she ought to introduce him to Harold Rose. Though why Drina had put the likes of him in temporary charge was beyond Jackie's reasoning. Mr Rose was very abrupt with people and had as little to do with them as he could get away with. He never looked anyone in the eye while conversing with them, which was always on work-related matters, never personal ones, and he possessed no sense of humour. He would arrive for work at eight-fifteen prompt and leave on the dot of five-thirty. He liked his morning coffee and two Digestive biscuits at precisely eleven, and afternoon tea and two Rich Tea on the stroke of three. He only approached his staff when he needed them to do something for him, and at all other times would work away behind the closed door of his office. This morning, apart from when he'd installed himself in the boss's room, there'd been no sign of him.

Asking Al to come with her, Jackie went over to the boss's office and tapped on the door, politely waiting until she heard Mr Rose's summons before she led Al inside.

Harold Rose was sitting behind Drina's desk, the accounts ledgers open before him. He was forty years old, slightly built and of medium height, with an ordinary face obscured by horn-rimmed spectacles. He wore his thinning mousy-brown hair cut in a short back and sides.

Jackie announced, 'I've brought Alan Stanhope in to meet you, Mr Rose. He's from the temping agency and will help me in the office.'

Harold flashed a quick look at Al then dropped his eyes back to the ledger he was working on. 'Er . . . pleased to meet you, Mr Stanhope. Thank you, Miss Sims.' Harold Rose never addressed anyone by their Christian name, only their formal title.

It was apparent the interview was over.

Back in the general office, the boss's door firmly closed again, Jackie said diplomatically, 'Mr Rose is a man of few words. He's the same with everyone, so don't take offence. Right, there's plenty to do here so I hope you're prepared to be busy. First things first, though. While you settle yourself in, I'll make you a cup of tea. Or would you prefer coffee?'

He eyed her in astonishment. 'But surely I should be seeing to chores like that, Miss Sims?'

'Apart from showing respect to the likes of Mr Rose, we don't stand on ceremony in the general office, Al. And there's nothing I would ask you to do that I wouldn't do myself. Now, is it tea or coffee?'

Al knew he was going to enjoy his time working at Jolly's.

CHAPTER FOUR

At four-thirty the following Saturday afternoon, Jackie and Al were standing at the window in the general office, both supping on a much-needed mug of tea, looking down at the scene below. They had a bird's-eye view of the camp's high wrought-iron entrance gates with letters welded into them spelling out 'Jolly's Holiday Camp'. Directly beneath the office was a huge forecourt with a twenty-foot-high fountain complete with four mermaids and dolphins spouting water. The camp's row of single-storey shops lined one side of the courtyard. Today the whole area was teeming with holidaymakers, coming and going in the late-spring sunshine.

Every Saturday morning the administration staff always joined the four receptionists in dealing with the hordes of campers checking out and in. Coaches to ferry those departing home or to the railway station started to arrive at about seven-thirty, and it was non-stop from then on for the staff until they had checked in the last arrival around four in the afternoon. The latest changeover had just proved as hectic and problematic as always, and now the staff involved were glad it was over, for another week at least.

As Al supped on his tea he was thinking that he would have felt he had died and gone to heaven had his parents brought him to a place like this for a holiday when he was young, instead of to a rented cottage in an isolated location in the Welsh countryside where his only playmates had been cows and sheep. His parents still spent their annual fortnight's holiday in that cottage, but thankfully a few years ago, he had reached the age where he had the right to choose whether he accompanied them or not.

As she sipped her tea, Jackie wasn't looking at the new intake of campers below but at the steadily growing queue outside the camp surgery. Everyone there seemed to be in a degree of discomfort as they waited their turn to see the duty nurse, Sister April Stephens.

Al noticed Jackie's expression and asked her, 'Anything wrong?'

'I hope not,' she mused. 'But something isn't right, judging from that queue of people waiting to see Nurse.'

Al looked over at them. 'Oh, I see what you mean. Most of them are clutching their stomachs. Oh, dear, a kiddy has just been sick . . . and now that man too.'

Jackie thrust her half-empty mug of tea at him, saying, 'Hold the fort. I'm going to find out what's going on.'

Easing her way politely through the crowd of at least thirty men, women and children, all looking tense and pale, she entered the surgery. Sister April Stephens, a very pretty blonde thirty-five year old, was busy in the treatment room, looking extremely concerned as she informed an obviously sick young woman with a crying four year old in her arms, and her equally ill husband who was holding another miserable young child, what to do to ease their suffering.

After they'd left, before April asked the next patient to come in, Jackie enquired, 'What's going on, Sister? In all the time I've worked for Jolly's, I've never seen such a queue at your door before.'

April sighed. 'And I hope we won't ever do so again, especially given the cause, Jackie. I dread to think what damage this could do the good name of Jolly's.'

'Why, what do you mean?' asked a worried Jackie.

'It seems we've an epidemic of food poisoning on our hands.'

The significance of this instantly struck Jackie. 'Food poisoning? Oh, my God, this is dreadful! But Chef Brown keeps his kitchen immaculate . . .'

'Clean enough to eat off the floor,' April agreed. 'Judging by the symptoms it's my opinion that the cause is from eating poultry or dairy food contaminated at source. Thank goodness it seems to be a mild outbreak. No one I've yet seen is seriously ill, just in a lot of discomfort. Twenty-four hours on water and bed rest should see the back of it. I've had about fifteen cases so far and all those were on the first dinner sitting at twelve. I've not had anyone yet who was on the second sitting at one,' she frowned. 'Strange that. Anyway, that's management's look out. Mine is to convince the folks stricken with this bug that they're not dying. Tomorrow they should feel as right as rain and be able to enjoy the rest of their holiday. On the handover at six, I'll inform Sister Pendle of the situation so that she's prepared when she comes on duty later. Hopefully everyone who's been struck down with this will be on the mend by then, so she'll have a quiet night.'

As nothing like it had ever happened before while

she'd been working for Jolly's, Jackie hadn't a clue how to go about finding the cause of the outbreak. This was a job for Harold Rose, considering the severity of the situation and the possibility of repercussions.

Back upstairs in the office, after quickly updating Al on what was going on, Jackie went to inform Harold Rose.

All the time she was explaining things, he seemed to be looking over her shoulder at the door behind her. When Jackie had finished talking, he slid his glasses higher on his nose, ran his hand nervously over his thinning hair, then finally responded. 'Oh, er . . . well, I'm sure it's nothing you can't handle, Miss Sims. Now I . . . er . . . really need to concentrate on these accounts.'

Jackie gazed at him incredulously. She couldn't believe he was expecting her to deal with this serious situation on her own, deeming the accounts to be more important. Drina Jolly and Rhonnie would have dropped everything and joined forces at once to deal with this potentially very serious situation. If this was Harold Rose's idea of being in charge then Jackie was glad it was only going to be for a short time.

It was glaringly obvious to her that the outbreak must have originated in the restaurant. She needed to inform Chef Brown at once and ask him to try and uncover the source as he was the one who oversaw all the food that was prepared and consumed on the premises. It was a prospect she didn't relish. Sixty-year-old Chef Brown was ex-army. After his twenty-five years of service there he'd left the Catering Corps and been with Jolly's ever since. He was a huge bear of a man, nearly as wide as he was tall which was just under six foot. He was good-natured and tolerant; unlike the stereotypical chef he did not swear and shout at his army of forty staff, ruling them with a rod of iron, but treated them all with respect. He was, however, fiercely proud of the way he ran his kitchen and didn't take kindly to criticism in any form. Jackie knew he wasn't going to enjoy being accused of poisoning forty-two campers.

After asking Al to hold the fort, she set off to do battle.

She was down in reception heading for the kitchen block when one of the receptionists, Anita Williams – or Ginger as she was affectionately called due to her curly mop of carrot-red hair – called out to her. Ginger was the girl who had first introduced Rhonnie to the camp, and the two girls had stayed friends ever since – not that Ginger had been able to help her either since she'd been widowed.

Jackie called back to her, 'Sorry, Ginger, but I've something really important to deal with. I'll get back to you.'

She was stopped in her tracks by a brusque voice shouting over, 'And we don't need to guess what that important matter is!'

Jackie turned back and saw that the voice had come from a middle-aged woman, well-padded arms folded under her ample bosom, who was looking back at her combatively.

Wagging a fat finger at Jackie, the woman went on, 'This camp came highly recommended, and me and me friends and neighbours saved all year so we could come. Some went without to keep up the weekly payments so as not to disappoint their kids. We were all expecting a good time, not to find ourselves at death's door.'

The woman had every right to be angry but despite appreciating that, Ginger, who wasn't best known for her tact and diplomacy, was having difficulty keeping her tone pleasant and polite. Regardless she did manage to say evenly, 'Jackie, this is Mrs Evans. She wants to know what we're doing about the situation?'

With a smile on her face, Jackie responded, 'Mrs Evans, first may I express Jolly's sincere apologies for what's happened? We really are dreadfully sorry. Secondly, may I assure you that we're going to investigate the cause of the outbreak and make sure it doesn't happen again.'

'That's all well and good, but where are we expected to eat in the meantime? Not in *your* restaurant or any of the other eating facilities you offer, I'm sure you can appreciate that?'

Jackie stared at her blankly for a moment before she replied, 'Well, yes, of course I can, Mrs Evans, but we haven't anywhere else but the restaurant, the fish and chip and hamburger kiosks for you to eat.' She then added with conviction, 'But please let me assure you that Chef Brown has been with Jolly's for years and nothing like this has ever happened . . .' she prayed it hadn't before she had come to work here '. . . and whatever is the cause . . .'

Mrs Evans cut in, 'There's no "whatevers" about where this was caught. Apart from individual sandwiches we all made ourselves to eat on the journey here, the only other place we've eaten together was in your restaurant.'

Jackie was caught on the back foot. 'Mrs Evans, I assure you . . .'

The woman was unstoppable. 'You keep assuring me

of a lot, young lady. But why am I dealing with a chit like you over this serious situation? Where's the management? Skulking in their offices, are they, afraid to face the music?'

Jackie privately agreed with Mrs Evans that it should be management dealing with this serious situation. 'No, not at all, Mrs Evans. Mr Rose . . . he's our temporary manager as Mrs Jolly the owner is away at the moment on family business . . . well, he thought it was important to get to the bottom of this quickly. That's what he's doing now, making his investigation, and he's asked me to deputise for him in the meantime, letting you know how we're handling the situation.'

The woman took a deep breath, puffing out her chest before announcing, 'Well, let me assure you, young lady, we'd better receive a satisfactory answer and a cast-iron assurance this is an isolated incident or we'll be demanding that we all get our money back and you meet the expense of a coach to take us back home. Hopefully it won't be too late for us to organise bookings at another holiday camp that isn't hell-bent on killing us and then we can enjoy what's left of our summer holiday.' She pushed her face close to Jackie's and snapped, 'And let me *assure* you, we won't be recommending Jolly's to anyone, just the opposite in fact.' Her face suddenly contorted in pain then and she clutched her stomach, wailing, 'Oh, God, where's the nearest convenience?'

Jackie's thoughts were racing. It would be just terrible for Drina to return and find the business in ruins. Jackie had to get to the bottom of this matter quickly and somehow restore the camp's good name. Mrs Evans and her party would need to be convinced not to leave but to stay and enjoy the rest of their holiday.

Ginger asked, 'How are Mr Rose's enquiries coming on? Has he found out anything at all that could shed light on the outbreak?'

'Well, he's only just started so it's a bit early for that yet. Look, I have to go. See you later, Ginger.'

'Yeah. You and Keith still coming to Helen's birthday bash at Groovy's tonight?'

'Yes, looking forward to it.' And she was. Jackie, like most twenty-one year olds, loved a night out dancing into the small hours, despite having work in the morning.

She made to leave again but Ginger stopped her with, 'Oh, just a minute, Jackie.' Flashing a look around to make sure none of her other colleagues could hear, she asked, 'Have you managed to find anything out for me yet?'

Jackie stared at her non-plussed. 'About what?'

Ginger snapped, 'Oh, Jackie, how could you forget? You know how keen I am to find out about Al. Whether he's got a girlfriend or not, and anything else about him.'

'Ginger, give me a chance! He's only been with us a couple of days.'

'Four days and . . .' she looked at her watch '. . . five hours twenty-two minutes.'

Jackie chuckled. 'Oh, Ginger, you are a case. Look, I'm doing my best, but it's quite difficult as we're so busy with work and I'm . . .' She was about to say 'doing work that should be Harold Rose's', but stopped herself from speaking out of turn about him. Ginger had many good qualities but discretion wasn't one of them. 'Al doesn't seem willing to talk about anything that involves his family or friends,' Jackie added.

'Well, try harder for my sake, Jackie. I really fancy

him but I don't want to show myself up if he's already got a girlfriend. But if I don't make my move soon, someone else could get in before me.'

Jackie conceded, 'Okay, I'll see what I can do.'

Ginger beamed her infectious smile. 'Then I'll let you get on. Oh, before you go . . .'

Jackie had already turned away. Now she spun back, declaring, 'Oh, what now, Ginger?'

'No need to snap. I was only going to ask if you'd heard anything from Mrs Jolly about how Rhonnie is getting on?'

'Not personally. I know she has spoken at least once to Mr Rose but she's always called straight through on the private line. I presume she's just checking how things are going here, but he's not told me anything about the call. I only know she telephoned because I happened to be taking his morning cuppa in to him when he was speaking to her. Now I really do have to get on.'

Jackie found Chef Brown wedged in the captain-style chair before the small desk that spanned the entire width of his office. He was adding to a list he was making, when Jackie appeared in the doorway. Sensing a presence, he turned round. Seeing who it was, he smiled warmly at her. 'Oh, you've saved me sending over one of my staff tomorrow morning with the list I've just finished of foodstuffs to be ordered. Anyway, I'm always pleased to see your pretty face, Jackie. What can I do for you?'

He seemed to be in an unexpectedly congenial mood, considering the crisis they faced. Then a thought struck Jackie and she asked him, 'Chef Brown, have you been here in your office since second sitting finished? Not been out into the camp at all for anything?'

He looked at her curiously, obviously wondering why she had asked him that. 'Well, not exactly here in my office. Between you and me, I did pop out the back for a crafty fag, and after that I've been in the dry food store, checking what I was running low on to add to my list. But other than that, yes, I have been here.' His brow furrowed quizzically. 'Why?'

'Oh, then you won't have heard.'

He shrugged his massive shoulders. 'Heard what exactly?'

Jackie took a deep breath, wishing she wasn't the one to be breaking the bad news to him. 'Well, er . . . you see, Chef Brown . . . er . . . forty-odd campers have been struck down with food poisoning after eating their lunch in the restaurant. Sister Stephens confirms it. She says it's not serious, they just need plenty of water and rest so that's good, isn't it?' Jackie forced a smile, sensing the outburst to come.

Through her blabbering Chef Brown had been staring at her frozen-faced. Then his expression darkened thunderously. He began to rise from his chair and instinctively Jackie took several steps back as though afraid his angry words would blast her off her feet.

Towering over her, he furiously bellowed, 'And my kitchen is being blamed? Well, I won't stand for it! The whole place is thoroughly washed down after each service is finished, and scrubbed from top to bottom every evening. Not one single crumb is ever left lying about. It is germ-free. I inspect the hands of every staff member before each shift. If I find one speck of dirt then they're sent off to wash them again, and again if necessary.

'All the food I buy in is from suppliers I've been using for years, and all are regularly government-inspected. All meat is immediately frozen or put in the cold store as soon as it's delivered; we never refreeze uncooked meat that's been defrosted, and never leave it lying around for any length of time before it's cooked. Dry goods are stored separately. All food waste is put in pig-swill bins kept outside, which several farmers around here regularly collect. Today's dinner-time menu was pork chops and mashed potatoes, with jelly and tinned fruit for afters. Now you go back and tell that gutless prat Rose . . . who, by the way, should be here himself confronting me with this, not hiding behind your skirts . . . to look elsewhere for the cause of that outbreak because it never came from my kitchen.'

Despite Jackie knowing that his bark was far worse than his bite, Chef's behaviour was still coming across as very frightening. Tremulously she responded, 'I will, Chef Brown. And I'm sorry to have bothered you, I really am.'

With that she spun on her heel and fled.

Back outside she flattened her back against the wall, her thoughts racing. If the campers hadn't eaten contaminated food from the kitchen, they had to have eaten it somewhere else. But Mrs Evans had told her they'd eaten sandwiches prepared by themselves, and it was highly unlikely they'd all had the same filling bought from the same source. Jackie heaved a despondent sigh. She had no idea where to proceed from here. There wasn't an avenue left to explore. It seemed to her that they had no choice but to give Mrs Evans and her party their money back and pay for a coach to take them home, then just pray that the backlash against the camp's good name didn't prove as damaging as Jackie feared it would. She couldn't help but feel that she had let Drina Jolly down badly the first time she had been entrusted with the responsibility of running the general office.

Al could tell by Jackie's expression that her investigation had been fruitless. As he handed her several message slips from people who had tried to reach her on the telephone while she'd been out, he said, 'No joy, I take it, on finding the source of the food poisoning?'

She accepted the slips and shook her head. 'Chef Brown is adamant his kitchen is not at fault so I've completely drawn a blank. I suppose I ought to go and report my findings to Mr Rose, get his authorisation to hire a coach to take Mrs Evans and her party back home. And they must have their money back too. While I'm doing that, would you please telephone around a few local coach companies and get some quotes? I suppose we should be thankful it's only going to be one coach we need, them all being from the same party, and we're not having to ferry them back to different parts of the country.'

As soon as the words were out of her mouth something struck Jackie. Nearly ten thousand other campers had eaten the same food as the stricken campers had, and all the forty-two affected people were from the same party. There was no getting away from it. Those campers *must* have all eaten something in common, and whatever it was it had not originated from the camp.

To Al's bemusement she announced, 'Hold off on

getting quotes for the coach. I need to check something first.'

Jackie dashed out again.

Having found out Mrs Evans' chalet number from reception, Jackie rushed over there and purposefully knocked on the door. It was answered by a harassed-looking middle-aged man. 'Yes, love?' he said.

Jackie introduced herself and asked, 'I wonder if I could just have a word with Mrs Evans?'

'Oh, you've come to update her over this food poisoning business, have yer? Well, I'm sorry, love, yer'll have to come back as she ain't well enough. She's not long got back from the toilet after being stuck on it for the last hour, and now she's resting . . .'

A voice from inside called out, 'Who is it, Cyril?'

He turned his head and answered, 'It's the girl from the office. She's after seeing yer, but I've told her you're . . .'

Mrs Evans barked, 'Let her in. I can't wait to hear what cock and bull Jolly's are going to try and fob us off with to get out of paying up for the suffering they've caused.'

He stood aside so that Jackie could enter. Mrs Evans was lying on one of the single beds, propped up on pillows. She looked pale and drawn. When Jackie was standing at the side of her, Mrs Evans looked up beadily and snapped, 'Well, come on then, let's hear whatever management suggests to wheedle their way out of this and avoid paying up.'

'I'm not here to spin you any cock and bull, Mrs Evans. I know you're insisting you and the rest of your party became ill after eating Jolly's food, but you couldn't have.'

Despite her weak health, Mrs Evans barked, 'But we did.'

'But you couldn't have,' Jackie insisted. 'You see, it's only your party who are ill. Other campers ate at the same sitting and are not. I just wondered what else you'd eaten today? I know it's a long shot that forty of you had the same filling in your sandwiches, but I don't know how else to explain this.'

The woman snapped with conviction, 'Poppycock! We all brought different food with us and ate different breakfasts too. Me and Cyril had toast for breakfast, and cheese and onion in our sandwiches. Mrs Roberts and her sister Tilly never had time to make any as they'd overslept. They caught the coach by the skin of their teeth. Mrs Davis shared her tongue sandwiches with them because she'd made too many. Cissy and Bert Matthews had bacon sandwiches for breakfast. I know that because I live next-door to them and could smell the bacon frying. They had potted meat and beetroot in their sandwiches. Cissy was berating Bert for dribbling beetroot juice down the front of his shirt, loud enough for all the bus to hear.

'What breakfasts or sandwich fillings the rest had I've no idea, but isn't that enough for you? It won't wash, my girl. Just tell your boss to give us our money back and pay for a coach to take us home, because everyone I've told you about . . . except for my Cyril who's always had the constitution of an ox . . . has suffered food poisoning.'

Just then a knock sounded on the door. Without waiting for any response, another middle-aged woman bustled in. Ignoring Jackie, she addressed Mrs Evans.

'I'm doing the rounds and you're the last. How are you, Martha?' She pursed her lips and shook her head. 'Got to say, you don't look great. As green around the gills as my Arnold is. Anyway, all the others are asking me if you've had any news yet on getting our money back and a coach home? *And* there's the problem of where we're going to eat tonight . . . well, I know food will be the last thing on *your* mind, and all the others struck down with poisoning, but the two of us who weren't will be starving again soon. I mean, dinner was a while ago now, so I hope Jolly's have made arrangements to have food bought in for us from outside. They'd better have as the only food we have left between us is those two slices of cake that me and Cyril never had on the journey because we were full from our sandwiches. A slice of cake isn't going to keep me going until I get home. So have you heard anything from the management yet, Martha? Oh, and by the way, how are you feeling?'

Mrs Evans gave a snort of derision and said, 'Well, you telling me I look fit for the knacker's yard doesn't help me feel any better, Marion! And neither does talking about cake when just the thought of food is turning my stomach at the moment. Anyway, I'm glad you're here because this young lady has been sent by Jolly's to try and convince us we're to blame for the outbreak, so they can get out of seeing us right.'

Marion seemed to see Jackie for the first time. She gave her a stony glare and said, 'Is that right? Well, you go back to your boss and tell him that it *is* Jolly's fault and if they don't settle matters with us to our satisfaction then we'll . . . we'll . . .' She flashed a look at Martha Evans. 'What will we do, Martha?'

'Well, er . . . we'll . . . Yes, that's what we'll do. As soon as we're all back on our feet, we'll be outside the camp restaurant warning all the other people that they're risking their lives eating in there. And then you'll be facing a mass evacuation, with them all demanding their money back.'

Marion gave Jackie a push towards the door. 'Now go and warn your bosses what we'll do if they don't do right by us. Eh, and don't forget some food for me and Cyril. Fancy fish and chips, mushy peas and pickled onions, do you, Cyril?'

He licked his lips. 'I do. I'm getting a bit peckish, I must say.'

She told Jackie, 'Then that's what we'll have. Oi, and not from that kiosk! Have it brought in from Mablethorpe.'

'Oh, will you stop talking about food, Marion?' Martha Evans moaned. 'You're making my stomach churn, and it was just beginning to settle down.'

Her friend looked ashamed and mumbled, 'Sorry, Martha.'

Jackie sighed inwardly. It seemed that the cause of the food poisoning was a mystery that was never going to be solved. And the camp was going to bear the brunt. She just hoped the damage was minimal. Hopefully Harold Rose would agree to the injured parties' demands . . . in fact, she couldn't see how he'd be able to refuse. By settling with them he might persuade the sufferers to look a bit more favourably on Jolly's and decide not to spread bad publicity about them.

Jackie had just shut the chalet door behind her when she got the overwhelming feeling that something had been said inside the chalet that was the key to solving this whole mystery. She felt positive of it. If only she could remember what it was . . . She tried to recall all that had been said, then suddenly it came to her. Surely it couldn't be a coincidence that out of the party of forty-two who'd all had their dinner in the restaurant, there were two who hadn't been struck down by food poisoning and two slices of cake left? Spinning around, she tapped on the door and, in her need to explore this latest piece of information, forgot to wait for a response.

The three occupants looked surprised to see Jackie back so soon.

After apologising for bursting in on them, she addressed Marion. 'That cake you told me was eaten on the coach . . . two of you didn't have any and there are two pieces left. Well, I . . .'

Marion snapped, 'Cyril and I were full from our sandwiches or there wouldn't have been a crumb left. I'm famous for my Victoria sponge. The recipe has been passed down from my great-grandmother. I've won numerous competitions at church fêtes . . .' She suddenly stopped in mid-flow, narrowed her eyes and wagged a warning finger at Jackie. 'Oh, I see where this is heading. You're desperate to palm off the blame. Well, I won't stand for it. Three of them I made to go round all the party, with my own fair hands. Each of them good enough to be eaten by the Queen herself, let me tell you.'

Martha said under her breath, 'Well, the piece I had was on the dry side, if you ask me.'

Marion shot at her, 'What was that you said?'

Martha Evans gave an innocent shrug. 'I never said anything, Marion. You're hearing things.'

Regardless of her friend's denial Marion still looked at her suspiciously for a moment before she returned her attention to Jackie. 'Now you get out of here and don't come back unless . . .'

But Jackie wasn't going anywhere until she had answers to questions she needed to ask and cut in, 'I wondered where you got the eggs from that went into your cakes?'

It was Martha who answered. 'From the Co-op, same as we all do in our street.'

'Yes, that's right,' Marion backed her up. 'Going to blame the Co-op for poisoning us now, are you?' She began herding Jackie towards the door. 'Now once again, out with you, lady, and don't come back . . .'

Cyril Evans, who had been sitting on his bed all this time listening to proceedings suddenly piped up, 'But you didn't get the eggs for the cake from the Co-op, Marion.'

She stopped and turned back to face him, looking puzzled. 'I never get eggs from anywhere else, Cyril, so what are you blabbering on about?'

'But last night you called round to ask if we had any spare because when you went shopping earlier for your sandwich fillings you forgot to get the eggs for the cakes and the corner shop had shut by then. Martha was upstairs packing at the time so it was me that answered the door to you. I went off to look if we had any in the pantry, only we didn't as we'd had the last two that morning for our breakfast and Martha didn't buy any more, what with us coming away for a week on our holidays, so we couldn't help you.'

Jackie could have sworn she saw a flash of worry in

Marion's eyes before she said matter-of-factly, 'Oh, yes, that's right. I'd forgotten about that.'

'So where *did* you end up getting the eggs for your cakes?' Martha asked sharply.

'Oh, er . . . I can't remember.'

'Marion, we're talking about something you did less than twenty hours ago. 'Course you can remember. Now where did you get those eggs from?'

She started shuffling her feet uncomfortably. 'Well . . . er . . . after trying a few others who didn't have any spare either, I . . . er . . . went to see Nelly Brown. Miserable old bugger could see how desperate for them I was and charged me more than the Co-op does.'

At this news Martha shut her eyes and let out a loud groan of despair. 'You bought eggs from her? Marion, no one buys eggs from Nelly Brown because people have got ill from eating her eggs before. Only those that don't know that buy from her.'

Marion said defensively, 'Well, I didn't know.'

Martha eyed her suspiciously. 'Well, if you didn't, why didn't you have a slice of the cake?'

'I've already told you, because I was full from my sandwiches.'

'I don't believe you. I think it was because you did know and didn't want to risk eating it. Well, you'd better go and tell everyone that it's you to blame for poisoning them and nothing to do with Jolly's. They're not going to be very happy with you, just like I'm not, so for the rest of the holiday you'd better make yourself scarce.'

Marion almost choked as she cried, 'Well, there's absolutely no proof it was the eggs in my cakes that caused the poisoning. They looked all right when I cracked them open and didn't smell off, so it's not fair I should take the blame.'

Martha said, 'Well, we'll just have to prove it one way or the other then, won't we? Go and get the tin with the remains of the cake in it.'

'Why?'

'Because you're going to eat a piece, then you're going to stay put here where we can keep an eye on you and see what happens.' Martha said to Jackie, 'And you'd better stay too, so you can be a witness. If Marion becomes ill then it's the cake that's the cause. If not then it has to be something prepared by Jolly's and we get our money back and a coach home. Is that fair enough?'

Jackie nodded. 'It is.'

It didn't seem that she was going to have her night out with Keith, Ginger and some of the other staff, dancing the night away at Groovy's celebrating Helen's birthday. But this had to be settled one way or the other.

Marion almost choked on the cake, but under the watchful eye of Martha Evans, Jackie and Cyril had no choice but to finish every crumb. While they all waited to see what happened, sitting on Cyril's bed, he and Jackie played game after game of knockout whist while Marion sat anxiously on the other end and Martha dozed on and off in her own bed. It was approaching eight o'clock and Jackie was just about to lay down a winning hand when Marion's face suddenly turned pale and she clutched her stomach, issuing a low painful groan. Then as fast as her rotund body would carry her, she made a dash for the door, yanked it open and disappeared in the direction of the toilet block.

Martha roused herself from a doze just in time to

witness Marion's departure. She looked over at Jackie shame-faced and said quietly, 'Well, it seems we have our answer. I can only apologise for blaming Jolly's without considering for a minute that it was something we'd had before we arrived here.'

Jackie smiled at her. 'I'm just glad we've got to the bottom of it, Mrs Evans. I hope you all recover soon and enjoy the rest of your holiday here with us.'

The woman smiled. 'Thanks, love. One thing is for sure: Marion won't be getting any more eggs from Nelly Brown!'

Mortally relieved that the situation was resolved, Jackie had arrived at the camp's row of shops on her way back to the office when it struck her that she really ought to go and inform Chef Brown that his kitchen was no longer under suspicion. She might still catch him before he finished his shift.

The staff entrance was still open so she knew Chef Brown was about. Bracing herself, she went inside. She found him in the process of locking up his office.

Hearing footsteps clicking across the tiled floor, he spun his large body around to check who it was invading his kitchen at this time of night. Seeing it was Jackie, to her surprise, instead of clouding with anger his face filled with shame. As she reached him, he said, 'Ah, Jackie love, before you say anything, I want to apologise for my behaviour towards you earlier. Of course, the first place that would be under suspicion when there's an outbreak of food poisoning is the kitchen. I just took the accusation personally, that's all, because I pride myself on running such a tight ship that nothing like this is allowed to happen. After you left and I'd calmed down, I felt terrible and wanted to come and apologise straight away. But I couldn't get away and by now I thought you would have gone home. I was going to come and see you first thing in the morning. Please accept my apologies. What I should have done, instead of blowing my top, was told you to get the health people in to check the kitchen over and for them to clear it or condemn it, as no matter how diligent I am . . .'

She interjected, 'There's no need for that, Chef Brown. I've found out where the contaminated food came from and it wasn't your kitchen.' Jackie told him about the suspect eggs.

He looked relieved. 'Well, to be honest, despite doing all I can to prevent anything like this happening, I was worried I'd let myself down somewhere, so I'm really pleased to hear that. I appreciate your coming to tell me. I'll sleep well tonight. I expect you will too.'

Jackie smiled at him. 'I certainly will. Goodnight, Chef.'

He responded accordingly before turning back to finish locking up his office for the night.

CHAPTER FIVE

It was well after eight-thirty by the time Jackie arrived in the office to collect her belongings before going home. She was most surprised to see Al still sitting behind his desk. 'What are you doing here?' she asked him. 'Your mother must be worried out of her wits and your dinner will be shrivelled up with keeping hot for so long.'

He told her, 'Oh, I don't live at home. I've got a room with an old lady in Skegness.' He then added jocularly, 'Believe me, the evening meal she cooks me always looks shrivelled up and is never hot, no matter whether I'm on time or not.' He then very obviously changed the subject. 'Mr Rose left as usual on the dot of five-thirty and I didn't like to leave until you came back, just in case you needed me for any reason. I kept myself busy clearing up the filing.'

Naturally inquisitive, Jackie had to stop herself from asking why Al didn't live at home. One of the very valuable lessons she had learned from Rhonnie was that some people took offence at having their private lives queried. If there was information they wanted made public knowledge they would voluntarily impart it. To

Jackie's mind that was all well and good, but if they didn't volunteer the information this only opened up a lot more questions, one being . . . what were they hiding? Come to think of it, Al had worked with her for over a week now and she knew next to nothing about him. He had listened to her while she had chatted away as they worked, all about her widowed mother, brother and boyfriend Keith, and happenings at the camp during the years she had worked here, both hilarious and tragic, but had never once reciprocated by telling her anything about his life outside Jolly's. Maybe that was because he felt he had nothing of interest to tell her. Jackie felt it unlikely that she would ever discover the reason, though, as Al had only a few more days of working here before Drina and Rhonnie were due to return and then his temporary placement with Jolly's would be over.

She smiled at him. 'I appreciate your staying behind tonight, Al. Make sure you put down the extra hours you've worked on your agency time-sheet.' In light of the fact that he had stayed behind for her sake, she felt it only right to offer him a lift back to his lodgings on her scooter, despite the fact that she was desperate to get home herself because Keith would be waiting for her.

She knew he'd be upset that her having to work later had scuppered their night out as he'd been looking forward to it, but was sure he'd be understanding once she told him the reason. She pictured Keith in her mind's eye. He was four years older than Jackie at twenty-five years old, five foot ten in his stockinged feet, fair-haired, handsome in a rugged way, with an easygoing nature. He was a qualified mechanic and worked for a local garage. He had no idea who his father was as he had been born illegitimate to his then seventeen-year-old mother who had abandoned him at six months old, stealing off in the middle of the night, leaving him with her own widowed mother to raise and never being heard from since.

Jackie's own mother had only been fifteen and her father seventeen when they'd had to get married as a baby was on the way. They had lived from week to week as her father hadn't earned a great deal from his job as a builder's labourer, but regardless they had been extremely happy together, their family complete when Robby had arrived four years later. But when Jackie was only six the happy family was ripped apart by the untimely death of her father, when scaffolding that had not been properly erected had collapsed and toppled him fifteen feet on to the hard ground below. He'd lived for four days until internal injuries had killed him. Her mother, a petite, extremely pretty woman of only thirty-six now, had never looked at another man since, but devoted her life to raising her children as best she could, doing whatever menial low-paid jobs she could land, mostly cleaning. Life had eased for her once both her children were at work and contributing to the family finances. Instead of having to labour all hours, now it was eight until five-thirty in the local bedding factory, in the packing and dispatching department.

Jackie therefore had experienced growing up without one parent and felt deep sympathy and understanding for Keith who had grown up with neither. Very importantly to Jackie, who adored her mother, Keith got on with her like a house on fire and treated Robby like his own younger brother. When she had first met him at a local pub one night while she had been out with her friends and he with his, Jackie had instantly taken a fancy to Keith and made it her business to wangle her way into conversation with him. She had asked him why someone hadn't snapped him up before now and he'd told her that it was because he'd never met anyone he'd thought enough of to feel serious about. She was hoping that now he had. After eighteen months of going out together, she felt it was only a matter of time before he would ask her to marry him.

Al was a very well-spoken young man and from the way he conducted himself it was obvious he'd come from a good background, so Jackie was shocked when he prodded her in the back to prompt her to stop on the corner of a crumbling street of terraced houses in a run-down area of Skegness. Although he had told her he lived in lodgings, she had expected them to be in a far more salubrious area than this one.

Having thanked her for the lift home, Al went off down the street and Jackie was in the process of turning the Lambretta around when a man coming out of the off licence on the opposite corner caught her attention. He was tall and thin, shaggy-haired and thickly bearded. Shabbily dressed, he was clutching a brown carrier bag which obviously held bottles of either beer or spirits. She did not recognise him yet he was still vaguely familiar somehow. She watched him as he turned the corner and disappeared. For the life of her Jackie couldn't place him and so put his familiarity down to the fact that the man just reminded her of someone else, whoever it might be.

A while later Jackie entered the back door of her home

to be greeted by the sight of a pan bubbling away on the stove, keeping the meal on the plate sitting above it hot. She could hear the sounds of her mother's and Keith's laughter coming from the sitting room. As Jackie stripped off her coat a warm glow filled her. She had friends whose parents did not get on with their boyfriends for various reasons, mostly because the young men weren't considered good enough for the girls, and it put a strain on the young couples' relationships. Jackie felt herself fortunate to have a mother who thoroughly approved of her boyfriend and a boyfriend who thoroughly approved of his girlfriend's mother.

Using a cloth to take her plate of food off the pan, and collecting a knife and fork, Jackie went in to join them.

The next morning when she updated Harold Rose over the food poisoning incident, all the response she got from him, while he stared over her shoulder as if at someone else, was a cool thank you and then a prompt dismissal back to her work. Jackie felt her contempt for his idea of how to manage a business rising several notches.

CHAPTER SIX

It was not surprising that Jackie hadn't recognised the man she had seen coming out of the off licence. The last time she had seen him he'd looked completely different. Then he'd been a lardy, heavy-jowled young man. Now he had no spare fat on him. Twelve months in prison, for trying to sell back a gold cigarette case and lighter to the police inspector whose house he'd unwittingly stolen them from, was the cause of the change in him. Encarcerated with hardened criminal types who terrified him, Michael Jolly's blubber had melted from him. But all those long nights spent staring up at the ceiling from his top bunk had afforded the deeply unpleasant man plenty of time to formulate a plan that would see him successfully carry out his threat to reclaim what he felt was rightfully his: Jolly's camp and all the profits it generated.

Michael hadn't come up with the plan completely by himself; he didn't possess the intelligence to plan anything more involved than a simple burglary. He'd almost despaired of ever coming up with anything that stood the remotest chance of success, when while he was swabbing out the bathrooms one morning he was privy to the conversation of two old lags who'd come in to use the facilities . . . each thinking it extremely amusing to urinate all over his clean floor while trying to outdo the other with details of the best scam in their illustrious past. What one old lag told the other had struck a chord deep within Michael and every night since then he had lain awake thinking about it, and how he could adapt it to suit his own purposes.

After months of thinking of nothing else, he finally felt positive he had the ideal scheme. He couldn't do it on his own, but one thing he'd learned in prison was that there were always others willing to do anything, no questions asked, if the price was right. All Michael had to do was pick the right people for his purposes, get the money to pay them, and then he could put his plan into operation. And that's what he was doing now: amassing his working capital by ways that had stood him in good stead before, but this time doubly conscious he must not get caught. He begrudged the time he was having to put his plan on hold; he wanted to be living the high life right now, the kind of life he should always have been living had it not been unjustly denied him. But he'd waited this long so a while more would not kill him. And then, when he did finally get his hands on his inheritance it would be doubly sweet.

People would think him witless to return to an area where he'd been notorious in the past for his criminal activities and which he'd had to leave in a hurry while he readied himself to carry out his plan, but he knew he was safe coming back to this area due to the dramatic change in his appearance. Sometimes he himself did a double take before the mirror, not yet having grown completely used to the thin face that stared back at him instead of the old grossly fat one. He was positive no one else would recognise him. The main reason he'd come back was that he knew the locals gossiped and that way he could find out everything that was going on in Jolly's. Forewarned was forearmed. He had already discovered to his great delight that his half-brother Dan had recently been killed in an accident. This was going to make Michael's quest so much easier.

CHAPTER SEVEN

By the following Friday, much to Jackie's relief, nothing more catastrophic had happened than a rotund camper getting his face wedged tight in the hole on a photo board depicting comic cowboys and it taking several staff and jars of vaseline to free him. All talk of the food poisoning incident had died down.

Pulling a letter confirming a future booking and the receipt for a deposit out of her typewriter, and separating the carbon papers from between its copies, Jackie complained to Al who was in the process of typing out envelopes for her, 'I do love my job but there are some bits of it that are repetitive. You'd think there was a genius out there somewhere who could invent a machine to duplicate a letter or form so that it appeared to be an original and we didn't have to type out each one individually. It would make our lives so much easier, and the time saved . . . I'd kiss his feet in undying gratitude!'

Al laughed. 'I'd settle for an automatic filing machine. Mind you, I do like filing as then I can let my thoughts wander and dream about the future.' He added hurriedly, in case Jackie should ask what that dream was, 'Oh, while at the same time keeping my eye on the files, of course.'

She chuckled. 'I do the same when I'm filing only I don't need to dream about my future, I already know what that is.' She told him confidently, 'I'll be happily married to my boyfriend Keith, looking after our children.' Then she asked him the question Al had hoped she wouldn't. 'So what future are you dreaming of?'

He looked at her blankly for a moment before saying dismissively, 'Oh, I've nothing particular in mind.' A light on the switchboard lit up and a buzzing sound began. As Al responded to it, Jackie wondered if it was her imagination that he'd seemed glad of the diversion. She felt he knew exactly what future he had in mind for himself but for some reason didn't want to share it with her. She wondered why?

Having put the caller through to the girls on reception, Al replaced the receiver and returned to sorting through the pile of filing. He had something to ask Jackie but had been stalling in case her answer wasn't the one he wanted to hear. His assignment with Jolly's had been for two weeks. Today that time was up and as Jackie hadn't told him otherwise he assumed Jolly's no longer needed him. He really enjoyed working here. Jackie was a very fair boss and also fun to work for. People were beginning to recognise him as part of the office staff and he was beginning to feel part of the Jolly family. As a temporary employee he knew he shouldn't have allowed himself to settle in but he couldn't help it: the place and its people had had that effect on him. He really didn't like the thought of moving around from job to job, always feeling like an interloper, possibly working with people who weren't as friendly or receptive as the staff were here.

He opened his mouth to ask Jackie if his contract had any chance of being renewed but was stopped by the telephone on her desk which began shrilling.

Jackie hoped that the caller wasn't someone wanting her for something time-consuming. After she had finished the day's typing she had other jobs to deal with before she went home, and didn't want to have to stay late and leave Keith waiting for her twice in one week. Moments later she put the telephone down, a puzzled expression on her face.

Al couldn't fail to notice and asked her, 'Everything all right, Jackie?'

She shrugged. 'Don't know. Mr Rose wants to speak to me in his office.' She wondered what it could possibly be about as not once in all the fortnight he'd been in charge had he enquired of her how she was managing to keep the general office running smoothly with just herself and a temp, or how the rest of the staff were faring either.

Skirting her desk, she went over to the boss's office door, tapped on it, and when she heard his summons went inside, shutting the door behind her.

Approaching the desk, she said to Harold Rose politely, 'You wanted to speak to me, Mr Rose?'

He looked up from his work. As usual he didn't look directly at her but over her shoulder. There was a tremor in his voice when he said, 'Ah, Miss Sims, I've just had a telephone call from Mrs Jolly.'

Before she could stop herself Jackie excitedly blurted, 'To tell you Rhonnie's much better and they're coming home?'

He said stolidly, 'Miss Sims, would you please let me finish? I have a lot of work to do and really must get on. Mrs Jolly didn't call to say they were on their way home, just the opposite in fact. Mrs Buckland isn't well enough to return yet and it isn't envisaged she will be for the foreseeable future. I assured Mrs Jolly that all was well here and that there was no reason for her to concern herself.'

As he said that, Jackie immediately wondered how he could assure Drina of that when he had no idea himself what was going on in the camp beyond the accounts department. She would not even know he was occupying the boss's office if she didn't see him arrive in the morning, take him in his morning and afternoon beverages, and see him leave at night.

He was saying to her, 'Mrs Jolly asked me to pass on her gratitude to you for all the hard work you're doing to keep the general office running smoothly in her absence. She asked for that gratitude to be extended to the rest of the staff too. I'd appreciate it if you'd see to that, Miss Sims.'

Harold then returned his attention to his work, signalling to her that the interview was over.

In all the time Drina had been heading up Jolly's, Jackie had never known her leave the business in another's hands during the season, except for the few odd occasions when she'd had functions to attend – and only then when Rhonnie and Dan were in charge. If she was doing so Jackie knew that Rhonnie's condition had to be very serious. She was greatly distressed to learn that her friend was still so badly affected. All Jackie could do was try to ensure there would be a business to return to, but that wasn't going to be plain sailing with the likes of Harold Rose at the helm.

Thinking that Harold Rose had summoned Jackie into his office to inform her that the temp's services were no longer required as the boss had recovered sufficiently to return back to work, Al was very pleased when Jackie returned and asked him if he would consider continuing with the assignment for the foreseeable future. He left her in no doubt how he felt about that, much to her relief. She liked Al, was very satisfied with his work, and didn't like the thought of having to interview and teach someone else the ropes considering the workload she already bore on her young shoulders. If only Drina and Rhonnie would return . . . but no, Jackie thought. She was just being selfish. They would come back in their own good time, and till then Jackie and her more than capable assistant would do their best to keep Jolly's running smoothly.

CHAPTER EIGHT

Al was feeling very chuffed with himself. Jackie, up to her eyes in work, had entrusted him with the daily checking of the camp to make sure everything was as it should be. He meant to be very vigilant and justify her trust in him.

As he arrived outside in the courtyard he spotted a couple over by the photograph kiosk, looking at snaps the photographer had taken of them during their time here, deciding which to buy and take home as reminders of their holiday. For no particular reason a vision of his parents rose up. Despite their strict ideas of what was expected from him, and the way they'd refused to take account of his wishes, he did love them and miss them very much, dearly hoping that one day they could reconcile their differences.

Satisfied that everything seemed to be in order around the fountain area he went into the Paradise building, then on into the theatre. After speaking to the staff and finding they had no problems to report, he crossed to the row of shops, nursery and surgery to do the same there. After that he was heading down to the outdoor swimming pool when he stopped short. In the distance, heading down the path towards the indoor swimming pool, he saw three men. They didn't look like holidaymakers to Al. They were very smartly dressed and one in particular seemed to be having a good look round as he walked. Al thought they might be inspectors making a check to ascertain that Jolly's was keeping to the standards set up by the relevant government bodies. Officials used to visit his father's engineering works at least once a year to check that safety standards were being maintained, so Al knew this happened. He wondered if he should tell Jackie about them, then realised she would already know of their inspection tour as they would have had to clear it with management beforehand. So he forgot about the men and went on his way.

He was approaching the sports field to speak to the on-duty Stripey there while a father and son three-legged race was in progress. The spectators were making a deafening din, cheering on their favourites. Sadness filled Al as he reflected that his own father would never have felt it fitting for a man in his position to participate in such an event. Al's reflective mood was swept away when he saw Ginger come hurrying up the path towards him.

Not hiding the fact that she was pleased to see him, she said jocularly, 'Skiving, are you, Al, or on official business?'

'Official,' he told her. 'I'm taking Jackie's place today, doing the daily walk around as she's busy.'

'Oh, well, you're just the man I need then. I was on the way up to the office to report that some of the campers down on the beach aren't happy. Donkey Sam hasn't shown up and the kids are bawling their eyes out after their mams and dads promised them a donkey ride only for no donkeys to be seen anywhere. I have to say that in all the four years I've worked at the camp, I've never known Sam to skive off once. Makes me think there's something not right.' Ginger had tried a few times to afford Al the opportunity to ask her out but without any success. Never one to miss another opportunity, she continued, 'Oh, while you're here, Al, there's a few of us going into Mablethorpe tonight after work, if you fancy meeting up with us?'

Al liked Ginger and was well aware how much she liked him. She might not be a beauty but there was something very infectious and endearing about her and he would very much have liked to accept her invitation. But he hadn't the money to spare as all his savings were being put towards his plans for the future. 'Thanks for asking but I've other plans for tonight,' he said.

She tried to hide her disappointment by giving a nonchalant shrug. 'Oh, well, I hope you have a good time. I'll let you get on with finding out about Donkey Sam. I fear there'll be a riot on the beach if he doesn't show soon.'

Frowning in thought, Al watched her as she hurried off up the path towards reception. He wasn't quite sure what to do. Should he go back to the office and pass on this information to Jackie for her to deal with the problem, or should he try and resolve it on her behalf? It was probably just a simple case of Sam being under the weather and not reporting the fact yet, which Al could deal with to save disturbing Jackie. He knew where the donkey man's shed was. Part of it he lived in, and in the other part he kept his donkeys. Jackie had pointed it out during Al's initial tour around the camp when he had first come to work there.

Arriving at the shed fifteen minutes later, Al could hear the donkeys braying inside the building. He went over to Sam's side and knocked on the door, calling out, 'Sam, it's Al. You don't know me but I work with Jackie in the office. You're not down at the beach today so we assume you aren't feeling well. Do you need the nurse fetched?' He received no reply so called again, 'Sam, can you hear me?'

When he once more received no response it occurred to Al that maybe Sam was unable to speak because he was unconscious. 'I'm coming in,' called Al.

He unlatched the door and went inside. To his surprise he found the room empty with no sign of Sam at all. In fact, his bed didn't look as if it had been slept in, it was so neatly made. Al frowned. Jackie had told him that Sam was never seen without his donkeys, they all went everywhere together. The camp joke was that no woman would put up with coming eleventh in line behind ten donkeys and that was why Sam had never had a relationship, let alone been married. So if the donkeys were all in the shed, where was Sam?

Then Al realised that while he was here, Sam might be on his way to the office to report why he wasn't down at the beach today or had maybe called in at the surgery for treatment, not taking his donkeys with him for once.

Al was about to return to the main camp and resume his tour of duty when the soft sound of crying reached his ears. He stood and listened. Someone was very upset by the sound of it, and whoever it was was in the donkeys' part of the shed.

He went to the other door, opened it and poked his head around. Several donkeys were bunched together in one corner. Another was lying lifeless on its side a few feet away. A man he assumed to be Sam was lying beside the fallen donkey. He had his arms around its neck, his head resting on it, and was quietly sobbing. So this was the reason Sam hadn't appeared on the beach today. One of his beloved donkeys had died.

Al had never had a pet as his parents wouldn't entertain the idea of an animal in any way fouling their home, so he found it difficult to understand why people became so attached to them. He eyed the other donkeys tentatively. If it was possible to read a donkey's expression he could swear blind they were all staring at him, warning him to leave their beloved owner to grieve in private for their dead friend. The next thing he knew they were all heading towards him. Panic reared up in him. He wasn't going to wait around to find out what their intentions were. Al spun round in his tracks. In his haste to put some distance between himself and the donkeys, he not only forgot to shut the shed door behind him but instead of turning left to head back down the rutted path and join the tarmac one that would take him by the staff chalets and maintenance buildings, he turned right and the next thing he knew he was fighting his way through dense undergrowth and trees behind the donkey shed. Despite the snags to his clothes and scratches to his face from sharp branches that assailed him as he forced his way past, he had no intention of going back the way he'd come.

It seemed to Al that he'd been pushing his way through this jungle for miles, though it was actually only a few yards, when to his relief he suddenly stepped out into the far end of an overgrown yard. Across the cobbles stood a dilapidated house. There were holes in its slate roof, weeds sprouting out of spaces in the crumbling mortar between the bricks, guttering hanging down in places, broken glass in all the upstairs windows. The outbuildings were equally as decrepit, as was the large barn to the rear. From where he stood all the buildings looked to be in such a sad state of neglect that it seemed as if they could come crashing down like a house of cards with one good push. It was apparent no one had lived here for many years, except maybe the odd tramp. Jackie had briefly mentioned on the commencement of Al's temporary assignment that originally the site the camp stood on used to be a farm. What he had stumbled across must be the old farmhouse.

He was about to cross over to the other side of the yard and see if he could find another way out when he stopped as an idea began to take form. As it took shape, excitement began to swirl within him. This place might just have the potential to provide him with the space and privacy he needed for his work . . . Dare he hope that at least part of the house was habitable?

He knew that what was on his mind amounted to trespass, but as long as he was extremely cautious when coming and going he shouldn't be caught. Besides, only Sam came anywhere near this isolated place while leaving and returning to his abode with the donkeys on the other side of the thicket. Al had managed to get here by pushing his way through the undergrowth, but surely there must still be the original way in through a farm gate. Hopefully that was out of sight of Sam's shed, relieving Al of the worry of Sam accidentally seeing him coming and going.

It was all very well his formulating these plans, but it would be a total waste of time if no part of the house was habitable. The fact that he was supposed to be carrying out the daily check of the camp temporarily forgotten, Al hurriedly picked his way across the uneven, thickly weeded cobbled yard and over to the farmhouse to look in through a filthy window.

Dust motes danced in the light shining into the room beyond. To Al's acute disappointment he saw that the ceiling had caved in and several beams, splintered wood and chunks of plaster were piled in the centre of the floor on top of what looked like a sofa. Above the debris, lying at a precarious angle, was an old iron bed-frame which had obviously fallen through the ceiling. As it had come crashing down, the remnants of the ticking mattress and bedding that had still been on it at the time, now rodent-shredded and moth-eaten, were tossed into a rumpled heap. Al looked up through the huge gaping hole and into the room above. He saw the ceiling in there had come down too, and could see straight through the attic and on via a large hole in the roof to the sky above. To his great disappointment this side of the house was completely uninhabitable.

Praying for better luck on the other side, he made his way past the front door in the middle of the house and over to the other window, again shielding his eyes to look through it. This time, to his delight, Al could see that the room beyond looked to be intact, its ceiling too. Ribbons of cobwebs hung down from the plaster. In the centre of the room stood an old pine table with chairs around it, a dresser at the back of the room, and an old-fashioned black-leaded range which dominated the wall to the left of him. Sitting on top of it were several battered, blackened pans and a kettle, all covered in a thick layer of dust like everything else he could see in the room. An old pot sink sat under the window Al was staring through. A huge brass tap protruded over it, turned green and mouldy with age. The wooden draining board to the side of it, judging from the lumpy shapes visible under layers of dust and cobwebs, still held crockery.

Al's excitement mounted. With some hard work to clear it up, this room would suit his needs perfectly. Then another thought struck him. What in fact was stopping him from using this space not just as a work room but as living accommodation too? From what he had observed there was enough furniture lying around to meet his needs. The rent he saved he could put towards obtaining materials much sooner than he would otherwise have done and bring his plan for his future to fruition all the quicker. He would just need to pay for a couple of blankets, a pillow, a primus stove to cook on, and some candles or a paraffin lamp to see by since it was obvious this house had never been connected to mains electricity. Now he just needed to find a way in.

He went across to the front door. It still looked fairly solid, but like the window frames the door frame was badly rotted. It wouldn't take much effort to get the door open; a crowbar would do the deed. He would buy one along with some cleaning materials tonight on his way home from work and bring them all with him tomorrow, finding somewhere to hide them away from

Jackie's inquisitive eyes so that he could begin on the clean up after work tomorrow night. Hopefully he would have the room habitable in a couple of evenings and then all that remained was for him to transfer his possessions and, as he accumulated the money, his working equipment and materials. He would do that at night under cover of darkness. Now he just needed to find a more suitable access point than the way he had arrived.

Though it was almost obliterated by couch grass and weeds and it was doubtful it would ever open again without falling to pieces, Al was delighted to find the farm gate. Leaning over it, he looked in the direction of Sam's shed. He was pleased to see a clump of trees at the bend in the overgrown path, which should prevent Sam from seeing down to the gate should he happen to look this way from his shed. To the front of Al the path weaved along for a short way then seemed to come to an end as far as he could tell. Overgrown grass and weeds filled the space, telling him no one had headed over this way for a season at least. As long as he was extremely vigilant when coming and going, no one need ever know he was here.

He felt like he had a dozen jumping beans in his stomach, so excited was he about this surprising turn of events. This could prove to be the chance he needed to turn his dreams for the future into reality. He began to make more plans in his mind for what he needed to do to get matters moving. Then it suddenly occurred to him that if he lost this assignment with Jolly's he could wave goodbye to the golden opportunity and so had better get back to what he really should be doing.

About an hour later Al burst breathlessly into the office just as Jackie was about to go and organise a search party for him, thinking that somehow he'd got himself lost despite the signposts all around the camp-site to guide holidaymakers around. She exclaimed, 'Thank goodness you're back! I was beginning to think you'd had enough of Jolly's and gone home. I was just about to call the agency to send another temp.'

Al wasn't sure whether she was joking or not. He vehemently hoped not, especially now, and quickly informed her of the reason he'd taken so long over the tour.

On hearing the news about Sam she clasped her hand to her mouth. 'Oh, poor Sam. He'll be inconsolable.' Normally Drina would have dealt with this situation, and by rights Harold Rose should now, but judging by recent situations that he should have taken charge of, she knew he would profess that the work he was dealing with was too important to drop. She might as well get on with it. 'I must go and see if I can do anything for Sam,' she said to Al. 'Please hold the fort. I'll try not to be too long.'

He was bemused. 'But what can you do? The donkey is dead.'

'Before I realised how much his donkeys meant to Sam, I would have been of that opinion too, Al. But those animals are Sam's family. Losing one is as painful to him as it would be to us to lose a relative. If any other staff member had a death in their family, we'd all rally around and do what we could for them. I know Mrs Jolly and Mrs Buckland would want me to treat Sam no differently.'

Sam was a big, lumbering man of fifty-five. Most people took it upon themselves to believe he was mentally subnormal, judging him this way because of his slow way of talking in a thick Somerset brogue, and the fact that he preferred the company of his donkeys. The truth was he was as intelligent as anyone else; but his donkeys didn't look down on him in the way most humans did.

Jackie found him in the same position as Al had left him, lying next to the dead animal, his head resting on its neck, arm around it, quietly sobbing. The other nine donkeys had returned to the shed after seeing off Al and were back huddled in the corner looking on. The thought of being in such close proximity to a dead animal was actually repellent to Jackie and normally she would have refused to do it, but Mrs Jolly had trusted her to manage the staff, so that was what she must do.

She went over to Sam and squatted down on her haunches beside him, putting her hand gently on his arm. 'Sam, it's Jackie. I'm so sorry for your loss. Why don't you come with me to your side of the shed and I'll make you a cup of tea? Then we can discuss what we need to do.'

It took a moment for him to respond, and when he did it was in a choking voice. 'I can't leave Ermintrude on her own. Since the day she wa' born forty-six year ago, we've never been apart. Same as all the other donkeys. But out of all of 'em, Ermintrude is most special to me. Her mam died when she was born so me dad gave me the responsibility of raising her. Hand-reared her, I did. I used to sleep with her in the barn where we lived then, so I could feed her through the night. She thought I wa' her mother. She used to follow me everywhere. When I wa' at school, come rain or shine, she'd be waiting for me outside our back door in the morning to walk me to the end of the lane, and be waiting for me there when I came home again.'

He lifted his head then. Tears running from his red-rimmed eyes, he said, 'I knew deep down Ermintrude's time had to be nearing an end . . . donkeys only live to about fifty . . . but you always think those you love will last for ever 'cos you can't imagine life without 'em. I had no warning at all. She was herding the others back from the beach yest'day evening, showing no sign of anything amiss. If she was feeling under the weather before she'd always let me know. Why didn't she this time, Jackie? I might have been able to do something for her. I hate the thought she was without me by her side when she died, that I never got to say me goodbyes to her.'

Jackie's heart was breaking for him. She felt so guilty for the times when, in her ignorance of people like Sam in the past, she had joined in with other staff members who were poking fun at him.

'Ermintrude wasn't on her own when she died, Sam. The other donkeys were with her. Maybe she knew her time was up . . . they say animals sense these things, don't they? Maybe she never tried to tell you because she knew how upset you'd be. After all, she loved you as much as you did her, Sam,' Jackie told him.

He sniffed deeply as he looked back at her. 'I never thought of it like that. Thank you, Jackie.'

She patted his arm tenderly. 'We need to make arrangements for her, Sam.'

He told her with utter conviction, 'I ain't having her made into dog food. Me dad never allowed that to happen to any of our donkeys when he was alive, and neither will I. They're all buried proper. Ermintrude is going to be next to her sister. When she died ten years ago, Mrs Jolly . . . well, she wasn't in charge then 'cos Mr Jolly still was . . . but she heard what had happened and came to see Dad and kindly told him that we could lay her to rest in a bit of scrubland at the back of the farmhouse, which ain't no use for anything else, and that she would square it with Mr Jolly. So I know Mrs Jolly won't mind if I put Ermintrude there too.'

Knowing Mrs Jolly as well as she did, Jackie too didn't think she would have any objection. Jackie had asked Mrs Jolly once why the old farmhouse and strip of land surrounding it was just being left to fall into ruin. Her response had been that she couldn't bring herself to do anything with it because of the importance to her of the person who had once lived there. Without their benevolence the holiday camp would not now exist and, until she could bring herself to change things, the farm would remain as it was.

'When are you planning to have Ermintrude's funeral?' Jackie asked.

Sam obviously hadn't thought that far ahead. He stared at her blankly for a moment before he said, 'Well, I've already let the little kiddies down so I'd best get the other donkeys to the beach and make a start digging her grave after . . .'

Jackie cut in, 'You can forget going down to the beach today, Sam. You've had a huge upset and need time to get over it. At least take the rest of the day off, and tomorrow too if you need to. I'll have a message put out over Radio Jolly that due to a family bereavement donkey rides have been suspended for the moment.'

'Thank you, Jackie. I'll get started on Ermintrude's grave then. It'll take me a few hours to dig it. I'll hold her funeral about seven this evening.'

Mrs Jolly, she knew, would be offering to be there for Sam, so as her representative at the moment, Harold Rose should take her place. Jackie couldn't attend as she needed to get home and be ready for when Keith came to collect her as they had arranged to meet friends tonight to celebrate one of their birthdays and she knew he was looking forward to it. She told Sam, 'I'm sorry I won't be able to attend, but Mr Rose will be here to support you.'

As soon as Jackie walked into reception Ginger called her over to the counter, enquiring after Sam. Karen Green, the head receptionist, and her other assistant, Rachael Mooney, came across to join them, both obviously concerned about Sam's absence from the beach today. When Jackie told them about Ermintrude they all looked suitably sorry for his loss.

'Poor chap,' mused Karen. 'I'll put a broadcast out on the radio to let the campers know rides have been suspended for the time being.'

Ginger offered, 'Well, I'm not doing anything special tonight, so I'll go to the funeral in your place, Jackie. Between me and Mr Rose, at least Sam will have some support.'

'You won't get me going,' said Rachael, giving a shudder. 'I hate funerals. They're so miserable . . . everyone crying and wailing, pretending they're devastated by the person's death, when in secret they couldn't stand them and can't wait for the will-reading to see what they've been left.'

The other three women made no comment as there was truth in what she had said.

Thanking Ginger for making her offer, Jackie went up to the office.

Harold Rose's reaction to her news when she went in to tell him made Jackie's blood boil. As soon as he realised she was expecting him to represent Drina Jolly at the funeral he was making excuses that unfortunately he had a very important engagement he could not break tonight and passing the task back to Jackie.

All her instincts told her that he had no such important engagement he needed to attend tonight, but had just used that as an excuse to get out of going. At yet another display of his negligence, Jackie's lack of respect for the man deepened.

She knew Drina Jolly would be very upset to learn that no one from management had gone along to support Sam, so Jackie had no choice but to go herself. This meant that she and Keith were going to be very late meeting up with his friends, and he wouldn't be very happy to miss most of the celebrations.

The funeral proved to be very distressing. They found Sam just finishing piling earth back over Ermintrude, the other nine donkeys grouped together as though they were all comforting each other. Sam himself was inconsolable so Jackie took it upon herself to say the Lord's Prayer over the grave. As soon as she said 'Amen' Sam threw himself over the mound, unashamedly sobbing. The women decided to leave him to grieve in peace for his loss.

Had she not been aware that Keith was back at home waiting for her, Jackie would gladly have accepted Ginger's suggestion that they go for a drink in Groovy's. They were both in need of a boost to their spirits after the very sad occasion they'd witnessed.

Jackie finally arrived home at a quarter to nine. She was thoroughly drained after the day she'd had with no enthusiasm whatsoever for getting herself ready and going out with Keith's friends, but nevertheless would make the effort out of consideration of him. She wouldn't have blamed him in the slightest for being annoyed with her for another night ruined because work had intervened. Much to her relief, he didn't seem annoyed at all; just the opposite in fact. She found him in the back room, laughing and joking with her mother as they folded sheets she had laundered earlier, ready for her to iron another time. He obviously noticed how tired Jackie was, and she was grateful to him for insisting they spend what was left of the evening curled up together on the sofa, watching television along with her mother. Again Jackie reminded herself what a lucky young woman she was to have found herself such a considerate man in Keith.

CHAPTER NINE

Eyes sparkling with excitement, Joyce Caldecott blurted out, 'So as soon as we've had dinner we can go down to the funfair. I want to go on everything . . . the waltzers, big wheel, dodgem cars, the house of fun, helter-skelter, shooting gallery, hook-a-duck . . .'

Grinning in amusement, Roger Daventry interjected, 'Slow down, love. Save something for another night. We're here for another ten days. And don't forget we've a big day ahead of us tomorrow so we need to get ourselves a good night's sleep.'

'As if I could forget what's happening tomorrow! But now we've got everything organised, we're allowed to have some fun, aren't we?'

'Yes, of course.' He went over to Joyce, kissing her affectionately on the cheek, then took her seventy-year-old hand tenderly in his seventy-three-year-old one. 'Come on then, but don't blame me if all those rides make you ill.'

That evening the old couple were having so much fun at the fair they were oblivious to the fact that their antics were proving far more entertaining to other fair-goers than the rides and stalls were. And the rides never made

Joyce sick, nor even queasy, just eager to go on them again and again.

Roger woke at seven the next morning to find her already up. Dressed in a baby blue candlewick dressing gown, with matching slippers on her feet, and carrying her toilet bag and towel ready for her shower, she had her hand on the doorknob when she was stopped from turning it by Roger saying, 'You're keen.'

She turned and grinned at him. 'Keen is putting it mildly. I'm champing at the bit!'

He chuckled, 'Me too,' and threw back the bedclothes. 'Wait for me to collect my things and I'll come with you.'

At just coming up for two o'clock that afternoon Jackie and Al were working together to produce the hundreds of pamphlets announcing the next two weeks' activities, which were to be handed to the new arrivals along with their chalet keys on Saturday. Al was feeding in the paper and then turning the handle on the printing machine while Jackie was folding each printed sheet into three to form a concertina booklet.

It was two weeks since Al had discovered the derelict farmhouse. Having spent a couple of hours there each evening over several nights, he had achieved what was necessary to make the downstairs room habitable, moved in his belongings, purchased his materials, and was now happily living and working there. He still smiled at the memory of the taxi driver's face the night he had moved in. It was apparent the man's curiosity had been aroused by being called out in the early hours of the morning to deliver Al and his worldly goods to Jolly's Holiday Camp. But he had been really bemused when, instead of delivering Al through the gates as he'd expected to do, he'd been asked to pull over by the employees' entrance, where Al proceeded to pile his belongings on the grass verge by the side of the gate. Then had begun several stealthy journeys back and forth between the employees' entrance and the farmhouse, transporting as much at one time as he could carry.

He was struggling under the weight of the last of his belongings when he heard a noise that stopped him in his tracks just as he was approaching the maintenance building across the expanse of ground between that building and the back of the office and entertainment block. It had him quaking in fear that he was about to be discovered. Through careful enquiries he had found out that the security guards did their nightly check of the staff-only area of the camp around eleven, and as it was now approaching three in the morning it wasn't one of them that had made the noise. Al prayed it hadn't been made by an insomniac camper who had taken a wander off the beaten track in the hope of tiring himself out. If they did happen to spot him they would no doubt hasten to report his suspicious behaviour to security, which would mean he'd not only be out of a job but his plans for the future would be back at square one again.

With nowhere to hide himself, Al did the only thing he could think of to lessen the chance of being spotted. He quietly slid his burden down on to the ground then lay flat out himself, hardly daring to breathe. He only just stopped himself from yelling out in shock and fright as out of the darkness he saw the glint of a pair of eyes looking at him. As his heart hammered inside his chest, it took him several long moments to realise the eyes belonged to a fox. Getting up and shooing the animal away, he continued over to the farmhouse. Since then he'd had no further close shaves as he'd been coming and going, and meant to make sure it stayed that way until his need for the farmhouse was over.

Jackie stopped folding pamphlets for a moment to rub her aching wrists. She calculated that there were only about a hundred more left to do out of a batch of three thousand. In two weeks' time they'd repeat the process. They'd have finished this task a long time ago had it not been for the steady stream of staff constantly interrupting them with one thing or another, mostly petty things but enough to threaten the smooth running of the camp. In the last two weeks demands on Jackie's time had meant she'd had to stay late after work several more times, leaving Keith waiting for her, but tonight she was determined that nothing was going to stand in her way and she'd be ready when he arrived to pick her up at a quarter to eight. They were going to his best friend's engagement party, and now that his friend was settling down Jackie was hoping Keith might follow his lead and ask her to marry him.

Thankfully they had no more interruptions and half an hour later the task was done. Al was busy typing envelopes to put cheques inside for payments that needed to go into the post tonight, and Jackie was just getting into a rhythm typing a dozen or so letters to individuals confirming future bookings and receipt of deposits, when a harassed-looking Ginger walked in.

Jackie inwardly groaned. Normally she was glad to see her friend, but she hoped that whatever Ginger needed this time it would take only a second or two to deal with so that Jackie could keep on schedule.

As soon as Ginger told her they had a problem downstairs they needed her help with, Jackie's heart sank. The receptionists only called upon the office staff to help them out when the situation they were facing was serious.

Ginger explained, 'We've a woman in reception saying it's imperative she speaks to one of our campers who's apparently here on holiday with a friend. She says it's a matter of life or death. I thought it was a bit odd, though, because the name she gave me for the woman she's after is Caldecott, and when I checked our list of who's in what chalet at the moment . . . thankfully we keep that list in alphabetical order or it would have taken me ages considering we've nearly ten thousand people staying with us at the moment . . . we haven't got one Caldecott. So she then told me to look under the name Daventry. As it turns out we've got thirty-two Daventrys. Thank God the name wasn't Smith! We've hundreds of them, and Jones, and Browns, and . . .'

Jackie cut in, 'I don't mean to be rude, Ginger, but can you get to the point? We're very busy, as you can see.'

'Oh, right, sorry. Well, I managed to narrow it down to fifteen Daventrys by checking whether the chalets they're in are for two people or four.'

Jackie looked impressed. 'You missed your calling, Ginger, you should have been a detective.'

The other girl said seriously, 'I did think it was clever of me.'

Jackie hid a smile and asked her, 'Have you put out an announcement over the radio, asking for people called Daventry to contact reception?'

'Well, I did tell the woman I would do that, but she was adamant I wasn't to as she wants to surprise Mrs

Daventry. She's given me a photo of her so we know what she looks like.' She handed over the photograph she was holding to Jackie.

'Seems like a very sweet old lady. Well, I suppose this at least saves you dragging all the Daventrys away from whatever they're doing and coming up to reception so this woman can check if they're the one she's after. That's providing any of them are in their chalet at this time of the day. If not you'll just have to leave a note on the door, asking them to come to reception when they return. Does this woman know she may have a long wait?'

'She's made it clear she's not budging until she speaks to Mrs Caldecott or Daventry or whoever she is.'

Jackie eyed Ginger in confusion. 'Well, you seem to have this situation under control, so I'm not sure why you're telling me about it?'

'Ah, well, it's like this you see, Jackie. It's Rachael's afternoon off and Karen is about to do the afternoon announcements on Radio Jolly and then she's got to visit maintenance and get some chalet keys cut to replace the spare ones we keep to give to campers who have lost theirs. If we don't keep some in, maintenance have to break in and replace the locks. It never ceases to amaze me how many campers either lose or mislay their keys, and some are found in the stupidest of places. Did I tell you about the set that was found . . .'

'Ginger, please, get on with it,' Jackie urged.

'Oh, yes. So anyway that just leaves me manning reception. All the Stripeys not on duty I could have asked to lend a hand, Terry Jones has commandeered to run through several new songs and routines for the show tonight. You know how hot Mrs Jolly is on us putting on good shows so as not to disappoint the campers. Their practice today, checking they're all kicking their legs in time and singing the right words, is very important.'

Jackie then twigged what assistance Ginger wanted from her. 'Oh, then you're after me to go and knock on all the doors looking for this woman, or pin notes on them if no one is in?'

'Oh, would you?' she cried in relief, thrusting the photograph of their quarry at Jackie along with a scribbled list of the chalet numbers occupied at the moment by campers called Daventry.

Jackie sighed heavily. It seemed she had no choice. The letters she was typing could wait to be finished off tomorrow. The cheques did need to be sent off tonight but Al had plenty of time to get those ready before the postman called into reception to collect the mail. There were other jobs that couldn't wait until tomorrow, but if she hurried and avoided getting into conversation with any campers she would have time to do them when she got back and still leave work on time this evening. She told Ginger, 'Yes, of course, I will. The sooner I go, the sooner I can get back.'

Ginger eyed her knowingly. 'Oh, of course, you're going to Keith's friend's engagement party tonight, aren't you, and hoping it's the night he's going to propose to you? Well, if he doesn't after seeing you in that new dress we went shopping for, then he wants his head examining. You look gorgeous in it.'

Jackie smiled. 'Thanks.'

Ginger then left her to it. After making sure Al was up to speed with what needed to be done and reminding him not to forget Harold Rose's afternoon drink at three if she herself wasn't back to see to it, collecting a notepad, pen and packet of drawing pins, Jackie left the office. As she headed through reception she caught a glimpse of the woman she was doing this on behalf of. She looked like a Victorian schoolmistress, grim-faced and very prim and proper. As she walked on Jackie wondered what was so important that she'd had to make the journey here and disturb someone's holiday.

Arriving at the first chalet on the list Ginger had given her, Jackie knocked on the door but no one answered. She learned from the neighbours who happened to be sunning themselves in front of their chalet, that the couple were both in their mid fifties, so too young for the white-haired lady in the photograph. She didn't bother leaving a note and carried on to her next port of call. The woman who answered Jackie's knock on the door was not pleased to have been disturbed from her afternoon snooze, and even less so when she learned that she had been woken for no good reason. Jackie immediately realised that the woman might be in the right age group but she looked nothing like the one in the photograph. After apologising profusely for disturbing her, Jackie made a hasty escape. This state of affairs continued for the next twelve chalets on the list, all with good distances between them, until a thankful Jackie finally knocked on the last door and the woman she was after opened it to her.

Joyce was no taller than five foot and still showing signs of having been a very pretty woman in her youth. Jackie had obviously caught her about to go out somewhere special as she looked extremely smart in a baby blue Crimplene two-piece costume, low-heeled cream court shoes on her feet, her snow-white hair tinged with a pink rinse and newly washed and set. On spotting Jackie's Jolly's staff badge, she smiled welcomingly at her. Assuming she knew what Jackie was calling about, she said, 'Oh, you are kind, dear, coming in person to tell us our taxi is here. It's half an hour early, though. Still I suppose it's better than not turning up at all.' She called behind her, 'Roger, put your shoes and jacket on. A very nice young lady is here to tell us our taxi is waiting.'

Jackie told her, 'But I haven't come to tell you your taxi is here, Mrs . . . er . . . just to confirm . . . you are Mrs Daventry, aren't you?'

'No, dear, I'm Mrs . . .' The woman suddenly stopped when she realised what she was about to say and quickly switched it to, 'Yes, of course I'm Mrs Daventry. If you've not come to tell us our taxi is here, what are you calling on us for?' She then asked worriedly, 'He hasn't called to say he isn't coming, has he?'

Jackie told her, 'I'm sorry, I know nothing about your taxi. I've called to tell you that you have a visitor . . . a lady . . . wishing to speak to you back in reception. I can't tell you her name either, I'm afraid, as she wouldn't give it. Said she wanted to surprise you. It is strange though as, at first, she asked to speak to Mrs Caldecott, then she changed it to Mrs Daventry. She doesn't seem to know what your name is.'

To Jackie's shock a look of abject horror crossed the old lady's face, which simultaneously drained of colour until it resembled parchment. Jackie had to leap forward to catch hold of her before she collapsed to the floor as her legs began to buckle beneath her.

On hearing the commotion, still in the process of pulling on his suit jacket, a bewildered Roger Daventry appeared in the doorway. Jackie was struggling to keep the old lady upright while she manoeuvred her inside so she could get her seated. With surprising strength, the wiry, elderly man threw aside his jacket then scooped Joyce up in his arms and carried her over to one of the beds, gently lowering her down on to it. Jackie followed him.

A moment later Roger was holding a glass of water to Joyce's lips, encouraging her to sip from it. Assuming he knew why she had almost fainted, he told Jackie, 'It's the excitement, it's proved too much for her. She'll be all right in a minute.' He then urged Joyce, 'Come on, love, take a sip, it'll make you feel better.' He turned to Jackie. 'Do you think you could go and ask the driver to wait for us? I'm sure Joyce will be as right as rain in a few minutes.'

Before she could respond, Joyce seemed to rally a little and uttered, 'Not here . . . taxi.'

Roger urged her, 'What was that, dear, I didn't understand you?'

Joyce was now trying to take small sips of water from the glass he was holding so Jackie answered for her. 'I haven't come about the taxi but to tell you . . .'

'She's here, Roger, she's found us!' Joyce blurted out.

He stared back at her, frozen-faced. 'But . . . but . . . she can't have! We were so careful. I never told any of my family or friends . . . never breathed a word to anyone of our plans. You didn't either did you, Joyce, like we decided, so we wouldn't risk jeopardising everything?' When he saw the guilty flash in her eyes he exclaimed, 'Oh, Joyce, who did you tell?'

Wringing her hands together, distraught, she uttered, 'Only Harriet. She's been our ally through it all. We would never have got this far without her. I knew she'd be worried if I just disappeared without a word. I swore her to secrecy and she promised me faithfully she wouldn't breathe a word.'

He heaved a deep sigh, running one hand through his tidily combed hair and dishevelling it. 'Well, she obviously did, and we know who to.'

Joyce urged, 'Harriet would never have told Clarice our whereabouts. Not unless she had absolutely no choice.'

'I know that, love. But once she realised you were gone, Clarice would not have let up on Harriet until she got the information out of her. Knowing you as Clarice does, she would have realised you would tell your best friend.' He looked at a puzzled Jackie whose brain was thrashing as she tried to work out just what was going on. 'I know it's not right to ask you to do this, my dear, but could you tell Clarice she's made a mistake and there is no one of Joyce's description staying here?'

Joyce interjected, 'We can't ask the young lady to do that, Roger, it's not fair to put her in such a position.'

He looked shame-faced. 'No, you're right. I'm sorry.'

Joyce then said to Jackie, 'You must be wondering what on earth you've walked into, dear. But of course you are, it's only natural. Please don't worry. We aren't murderers or bank robbers, but we are here in hiding.' As Jackie looked at her, intrigued, Joyce went on, 'The woman in reception is Clarice, my daughter. All Roger and I want to do is be allowed to spend what days we have left together, but she is determined that is not going to happen.'

Frowning, Jackie asked, 'But why would your daughter want to stop you from being happy?'

Joyce drank the remains of the water, passed the empty glass to Roger, then wrung her hands together in her lap as she told Jackie, 'Because she thinks it's disgusting a woman of my age getting married again. That's where the taxi is going to take us this afternoon, to the register office in Skegness, to get married at four-thirty.' Joyce heaved a forlorn sigh before she continued. 'My husband was a decent man. He was good to me, we were happy and had a lot of fun together. When he died ten years ago I missed him dreadfully. I was so lonely, rattling around the house by myself, having no one to share my life with. But I did my best to get on with it, like other widows have to. Then six months ago I met Roger and everything changed. He brought fun and happiness back into my life.'

She paused for a moment and gave him a tender look before she continued, 'Roger had been widowed himself three years before. Like me he'd a very happy marriage, and when his wife died he missed her dreadfully and was so terribly lonely with no one to share his life with on a day-to-day basis. He'd fallen off a ladder cleaning his windows and broken his leg. The WI committee got to hear about it and, as his late wife used to be a member, felt it right that we rally round to make sure he was fed and comfortable while he was unable to fend for himself. Another widow woman and I were asked if between us we'd oblige. Of course we both said we'd be happy to.

'During my visits Roger and I used to chat while I cleaned around for him and made him a meal. We discovered we had a lot in common in our likes and dislikes. I found myself really looking forward to it being my turn to visit, and he made no bones about the fact he looked forward to me coming. Six weeks later he had his cast off so didn't need our help any longer. As I prepared to leave for the last time, Roger asked me if I'd like to go old time dancing with him sometime. My husband and I used to dance regularly until his illness stopped us, which was a sad time for us as we really enjoyed it. I was thrilled to accept Roger's invitation. So we went out together a few times and before we knew it we were in a relationship. I asked Roger if he minded keeping the relationship under wraps as I knew if Clarice found out she wouldn't approve, and I didn't want her to make me feel guilty for having a bit of a social life. I did tell her that I had started going out with a friend, but led her to believe it was a female friend. I did, though, take my best friend Harriet into my confidence . . . we women tell our best friends everything, don't we? She's a widow woman herself, and I know she would like nothing more than to have a bit of romance in her life too. She was thrilled for me and very supportive.

'Nine weeks ago Roger and I finally admitted to each other that we'd fallen in love and just going out socially wasn't enough. We wanted to be together all the time. Roger asked me to marry him and I was delighted to accept. At our age it's silly waiting as time is not on our side. We decided to get married as soon as possible, and that he would give up the tenancy of his house and move in with me as I'd got all my friends nearby and he didn't want me to miss them. By pooling our pensions, and Roger's savings . . . he showed me his bank book to prove to me he wasn't flannelling . . . it seemed we'd live a good life together. Since my husband died money has been quite tight for me so I thought it would be a relief not to have to penny pinch so much in future. Roger told his family and they were happy for him and couldn't wait to meet me. Clarice's reaction, though, was completely the opposite.

'My hope that she'd be pleased for me and give me her blessing was a waste of time. Instead she held nothing back in letting me know how disgusting she thought me for taking another man into my bed at my age. She also accused me of being disloyal to her father's memory. She told me that in her opinion a man of Roger's age only took another wife to make sure he'd someone to care for him in his dotage. I would end up nothing more than a drudge, she said. If I thought she was going to stand by and watch me make a fool of myself then I could think again. She flatly refused to meet him.' Joyce paused and said to Jackie, 'Does Roger look to you like he needs someone to take care of his every need? Does he look incapable or as if he will be any time soon?'

Jackie looked at him. He must be over seventy, judging by Joyce's age, but Jackie would have put him in his early sixties. He was a trim, healthy-looking man, and had to be fit from the way he'd picked up Joyce and carried her to the bed with apparent ease. 'No, he doesn't,' Jackie responded truthfully. She had no doubt whatsoever how Roger felt about Joyce. Love for her radiated from him, and he was treating her as if she was his most treasured possession. It was such a pity that Joyce's daughter had not taken the trouble to get to know him before she made up her mind about him.

Joyce said with conviction, 'If Roger did ever become infirm then I would happily look after him. When you love someone enough to marry them, you take them for better or for worse.'

He took her hand and squeezed it affectionately. 'That goes for me too.'

Joyce took up the tale again. 'I pointed out to Clarice

how narrow-minded she was in believing that marriage was only for the young. Besides, I was entitled to do as I wished, and I wished to marry Roger and was determined to, whether or not I had her blessing. She was determined it wasn't going to happen. Said it was obvious to her I was losing my mind. She bundled up my personal belongings and forced me to go home with her, telling me it was for my own good and she wasn't going to allow me back until she was convinced I'd seen sense. My son-in-law and two grandchildren were all on my side but dared not cross Clarice on a matter she felt so strongly about or she would have made their life hell too.

'I was beside myself with worry that Roger would believe I'd just gone off without a word, and knew it would break his heart, but there was nothing I could do about it. Clarice was watching me like a hawk. But thankfully Harriet knew me well enough, and how I felt about Roger, to realise I loved and respected him far too much just to finish our relationship for no apparent reason, without even having the decency to tell him face to face. So she made the journey to see me, travelled on two buses all the way across town . . . she's a couple of years older than me and suffers badly from arthritis . . . to find out for herself what was really going on. In the few minutes Clarice left us on our own while she made tea, I managed to convey to Harriet what had happened.

'She did her best to make Clarice see that she was wrong to prevent me from being with Roger, but Clarice wouldn't listen. So behind her back Harriet became our go-between, passing messages between us. We made a plan that I would toe the line for a few weeks and then Harriet would inform me that she had heard Roger had met someone else and was pursuing them, and then I'd make out that if he'd got over me so quickly then Clarice was obviously right and I'd had a lucky escape. That way she would relax her vigilance over me. I did not at all like deceiving my daughter, but she'd given me no choice.

'So that's what we did. It was a long few weeks for both of us, not seeing each other, just surviving on the messages Harriet passed between us, but it paid off. With Clarice believing that Roger was out of my life, she had no reason to keep watch on me any longer and allowed me to go back home. As soon as she settled me back in and left, I wasted no time in letting Roger know and we made arrangements to go away somewhere and while we were there get married by special licence. Once we're married Clarice will just have to like it or lump it. We were going to a hotel in Skegness, but when we were looking in the paper for a suitable one to book we saw an advertisement for Jolly's. We thought the camp would be perfect for us as we could get married in Skegness and have fun here doing all sorts of things for our honeymoon.

'So Clarice wouldn't worry about me, I left a note for her on my kitchen table, telling her that after all that had happened I felt the need for some time on my own and had gone away for a few days. I underestimated her, didn't I? She obviously twigged I hadn't gone on my own and that I'd been duping her all those weeks, and immediately went to see the one person who would know where I was.' Joyce paused, gave a sad sigh and said to Jackie, 'I suppose I'd better come back to reception with you to face her. If I don't, once you tell her I'm here, she won't leave without me.'

Roger interjected desperately, 'And then she'll never let

you out of her sight again. I can't lose you, Joyce! I can't imagine my life without you in it. Let me go and try and reason with her. You never know, meeting me in the flesh she might see I'm not a philanderer or a doddering old fool who needs a nurse. Maybe she will change her mind then.'

Joyce wearily shook her head and said with conviction, 'She won't. Once Clarice has made up her mind about something, she never changes it.'

Jackie's thoughts meanwhile were racing. It didn't seem right to her that these two very dear elderly people were being denied a chance of a good life together through the bigotry of another. They had worked hard to get this far, and from what she'd been told, if they failed, it didn't seem likely they'd get another chance. Jackie's mind was made up. She was going to help them fulfil their ambition.

'Just a minute,' she urged. 'What time did you ask the taxi to come and pick you up?'

Roger answered, 'At a quarter to four, by the entrance gate. Why?'

She told them what she had in mind. 'I'll get you both outside the camp by a route that doesn't pass reception. You can go out of the employees' entrance. Then I'll go and tell the taxi where to pick you up. That way we won't risk your daughter spotting you out of the window if she happens to be looking. Once I've seen you safely off to Skegness in the taxi, I'll go back to reception and tell your daughter that I've spoken to all the Daventrys staying here and no one of your description is among them, so it must be another holiday camp you're staying at.'

Both Roger and Joyce were gawping at her. Joyce

uttered, 'But that means you'll be lying for us. I said before, we can't let you do that, it's not right.'

'But if I don't do this, I'll be breaking company rules. Mrs Jolly is emphatic that her staff should do everything they can to make sure the guests go home having had a time to remember. If you go home not married your memories of Jolly's won't be good ones, will they? And then I'll have failed in my duty towards you.'

Their expressions were a delight to behold.

Fifteen minutes later the three of them were hurrying around the back of the reception and entertainment blocks and over to the employees' entrance. They arrived through the gate just in time to see the back of a taxi heading off down the country road towards Mablethorpe.

'Oh, no!' Joyce cried in distress. 'The driver obviously thought we weren't coming. By the time we get another to fetch us, we'll have missed our appointment. We got the only slot available for the next three weeks, and we're due to go home in six days.'

'Is there a bus due?' Roger asked hopefully.

Jackie shook her head. 'Not until a quarter to six. Even if there was one due now, you'd still have to catch another bus from Mablethorpe to Skegness and wouldn't arrive in time for your appointment.' The disappointment and dejection on the faces of the old couple would have made the hardest man cry, and Jackie was having a tough job not to give in to tears on the spot. They had gone to such lengths to be together, she just couldn't let them fail now, not over a transport problem, not when she had the means to resolve that for them. She quickly calculated that she could get them to Skegness and be back here at Jolly's in time to go home and be ready in time for Keith to pick her up. It would mean abandoning work that really should be done by this evening, but this time she was going to put her personal life before that.

All she told them was, 'Don't give up hope of getting married just yet. I know where I can get transport to take you to Skegness. Stay here. I'll be back as quick as I can.'

With that she rushed off. Moments later, making it appear she had come from the direction of the chalets, she went into reception. She found Joyce's daughter anxiously pacing up and down while glancing out of the large window for signs of Jackie returning with her mother in tow. On seeing her enter on her own, Clarice stopped her pacing and demanded, 'Where's my . . . Mrs Daventry?'

Giving a performance worthy of an acting award, Jackie told her, 'I did manage to locate most of the Daventrys staying here with us, and those I didn't see face to face I got descriptions of from campers staying nearby. I'm afraid none of them match the woman you are here to see.'

Clarice stared at her for a moment as she digested this information before her face glowed purple with anger. She spat, 'That damned woman lied to me! I should have known she'd not divulge where they'd really gone and would send me on a wild goose chase instead.' She took a deep breath, her face set tight. 'Well, when I'm proved right, my mother needn't think she'll get any sympathy from me.'

Jackie pretended she hadn't a clue what Clarice was ranting on about. She said evenly, 'I'm sorry you've had a wasted journey. Can I get reception to order a taxi for you, to take you wherever you need to go?'

'Yes, to the station.'

Jackie left the furious woman, to cross over to the

reception desk where Ginger had been doing her best to eavesdrop on the conversation.

'I take it you never found the Mrs Daventry she's after?'

Jackie whispered back, 'Actually, I did. Don't ask me any questions, I haven't time to explain or we could be late.'

Ginger frowned in confusion. 'Late for what?'

'I'll explain later.' Then loudly, so Clarice could hear, she added, 'Would you please order a taxi to take this lady to the station? And make her a cup of tea while she's waiting.' Lowering her voice again to a whisper, she added, 'Tell them to come in half an hour, so we've time to get clear.'

Leaving Ginger champing at the bit to know what Jackie was up to, she turned and hurried over to the door leading upstairs to the office. While dashing to her desk to pick up what she had come in for, she told a bemused Al that she had to go out for about an hour but hopefully would be back before he left for the night. Then, giving him no chance to enquire where she was going, she dashed out again.

When Jackie rode up on her Lambretta to join Joyce and Roger their faces were a picture. She said to them both, 'It's the best I can do at such short notice, I'm afraid. It'll be a bit of a squash and I'm not sure if it's legal to have three riding on it at one time, but . . .'

She didn't get to finish as Roger blurted out to Joyce, 'You game, love?'

She nodded vigorously. 'I am if you are.'

Jackie grinned. 'Then let's go and get you two married!'

With Joyce at the back, arms clamped around Roger's waist, Jackie herself virtually sitting on his knee, she revved up the engine. Wobbling precariously due to the extra weight the scooter was unused to carrying, they set off.

The journey of twenty or so miles took longer than it would normally have done because not only was Jackie's second-hand vehicle struggling to cope with being overloaded, she was worried about encountering a constable cycling around on his beat or the possibility of Joyce's daughter passing them in her taxi on the way to Mablethorpe, so had decided it would be best to take a route off the beaten track. Perched precariously on Roger's bony knees as she was, Jackie was having difficulty steering the scooter around the winding, bumpy back lanes, many with deep fens full of water to either side. She was constantly mindful that time was rapidly ticking by towards four-thirty. Thankfully they finally arrived outside of the register office with three minutes to spare after no mishaps. As soon as he got off the scooter, Roger bent over to give his knees a vigorous rub and then stamped his feet several times hard on the pavement, saying. 'Thank goodness we arrived when we did. My legs have gone dead!'

'Oh, but that was fun, wasn't it?' Joyce enthused as she straightened her clothes and did her best to smoothe down her tousled hair. 'I enjoyed myself as much as I did at the funfair the other night, especially when we took that corner a little fast and I did worry for a moment we were going to land in the ditch. How about you, dear?' she asked Roger.

Diplomatically he replied, 'Well, let me just say I won't be forgetting that journey in a hurry.' Then he said to Jackie, 'We can't thank you enough for all you've done for us.'

She smiled at them both. 'Just doing my job. Now hurry up and get inside before the registrar thinks you've changed your mind. Best of luck.'

Joyce looked at her aghast. 'But you can't go! After what you've done for us, we'd both be very honoured if you'd be a witness, wouldn't we, Roger?'

He said with conviction, 'Oh, goodness, yes.'

Jackie felt privileged to be asked but she really hadn't time, not if she wanted to leave promptly tonight, but then she reasoned with herself that the ceremony would only last for fifteen minutes and she could just about spare that. Besides, she could tell by their expectant expressions that they would both be dreadfully disappointed if she declined, and hadn't the heart to do it to them.

With her as one witness it just remained to find another. The old man he approached wasn't at all interested until Roger offered him a couple of pounds for his trouble when he soon changed his mind. All four of them went inside.

It was forty minutes later when they returned, having had to wait twenty-five minutes as the appointments were running behind. Jackie had never seen such a radiant bride and groom, having finally achieved their dream of becoming man and wife. They were both aware they would have to face the inevitable backlash from Joyce's daughter when they returned home, but were determined she would not come between them. With the old man already on his way to the pub to spend his windfall, Jackie gave them both a hug and waved them on their way to a restaurant for a celebratory meal before they got a taxi back to Jolly's, then she climbed back on her scooter to speed her way back to the camp.

CHAPTER TEN

It was just gone a quarter-past six by the time Jackie arrived back in the office. Reception closed at six so she was spared having to answer Ginger's curiosity over what had transpired. Until she next saw her that was, when Jackie knew she would demand a blow-by-blow account. Harold Rose had gone home as usual on the dot of half-past five, but Al was waiting in case Jackie had need of him, keeping busy meantime by making a list of stationery supplies they were running low on for her to order.

She said to him apologetically, 'I'm so sorry for keeping you back late. I haven't got time now as I really need to get home but I'll tell you why tomorrow. Nothing that needs my attention tonight, I hope?'

He shook his head and told her, 'Chef Brown and Jim Smithers the photographer wanted to see you, but that can wait until tomorrow. I took a couple of calls from people hoping to make last-minute bookings and wrote down their details for you to contact them.'

She took the notes from him. 'Thank you, Al. Put the extra time on your agency time-sheet to make sure you get paid for it. Now get packed up and off home.' Then she realised he would have missed the bus and the next one wasn't due until half-past seven. She felt in the circumstances she really ought to offer him a lift at least partway home. 'I'm going out tonight, Al, and have to rush like mad to get ready in time for Keith picking me up at half-seven, but I can give you a lift to Mablethorpe?'

His thoughts whirled. He'd need to be careful how he responded, not give Jackie any inkling whatsoever that he was no longer residing in lodgings in Skegness but was installed in a dwelling right here on the site, without permission. 'Oh, er . . . I'm not going straight home tonight. I'm going . . .' Where was he going? Then he said the first thing that came into his mind. 'I'm . . . er . . . meeting Ginger and we're going for a drink in Paradise . . . er . . . at the carousel bar.'

Jackie thought it strange that Ginger had agreed to have a drink in that particular bar as it was the favourite haunt of the older campers. Still, she must have her reasons for arranging to meet Al there. Ginger had been after a date with him for a long time and Jackie was pleased that she had finally got her wish. She told Al, 'I hope you enjoy yourselves.'

He couldn't meet her eye when he responded, 'Thank you.'

Half an hour later Jackie wheeled her scooter down the entry behind the terraced house where she lived with her mother and younger brother, quickly secured it for the night, then hurried across the slabbed yard to the back door, letting herself inside. There was a steaming pan on the stove with a covered plate set on top. That would be her dinner. She'd have to gobble it down quickly if she was going to stand a chance of being ready in time for Keith to pick her up. She heard the sound of the television coming from the back room and presumed her mother was watching one of her favourite programmes, *Crossroads*. Jackie decided she would go and join her while she quickly ate her dinner. Since her father had died, Jackie's dearest wish was that her mother would find happiness again, but as she never went out socially, except to visit friends in their homes or for the occasional game of bingo at the local hall, seeing that wish fulfilled didn't seem likely. Still, her mother seemed happy with her life the way it was, and so as long as she was happy so was Jackie. Picking up a tea towel, she lifted the cover off the plate on the pan, then carefully carried it through to the back room.

Stepping in at the doorway she opened her mouth to greet her mother, but the sight of two people on the sofa, entwined together passionately kissing, shocked her rigid. Jackie dropped the plate, which smashed on the floor.

The unexpected noise set the couple on the sofa springing apart, eyes darting in the direction it had come from. When they saw who was standing in the doorway, they both froze, stupefied.

The three of them stared at each other for what seemed like an age. It was Gina Sims who was the first to gather her wits. 'Oh, there you are, love. Keith arrived early to pick you up so we were just watching the television. We were worried you were having to work late again and wouldn't be home in time to go to the party. Never mind the mess. I'll clean it up and make you something else . . .'

Jackie's mind had completely shut down. It was as if she didn't want to acknowledge what her eyes had just witnessed in an effort to stall the pain this was going to cause her. She blankly watched her mother get up and hurry towards her, automatically moving aside to let her pass by to go into the kitchen. Then she told Keith, 'I'll go and get ready.'

At Jackie's words his frozen face thawed. Smiling brightly at her, he responded, 'Take your time, it won't matter if we're a few minutes late.'

She responded matter-of-factly, 'But it does really. You're the best friend of the prospective bridegroom and he won't be picking you as his best man for the wedding if you're late for his engagement party.'

She walked across the room and placed her hand on the knob of the door leading upstairs. It was then that her brain suddenly whirred into life again. What she had seen and the repercussions of it exploded like a bomb inside her head. She spun back to face Keith and said, 'You were kissing my mother when I came in, weren't you.' It wasn't a question but a statement.

He had relaxed back on the sofa by now, his eyes fixed on the television screen, but her words set him jerking upright to stare at her. 'No . . . no, we weren't. Of course we . . .'

Jackie interjected, 'You had your arms around each other and your lips pressed together. I've always understood that when two people do that they're kissing, Keith.' Devastating pain shot through her then, like bolts of lightning searing through her entire body. She hurled at him, 'That was no friendly kiss you were having either. What I saw was two lovers kissing.'

He was vehemently shaking his head. 'No, you've got it . . .'

'Don't you dare take me for an idiot, Keith. I may be stupid – you and my mother between you have proved to me I am – but I'm not blind. I know what I saw. How long have you been carrying on together behind my back? HOW LONG, KEITH?'

Gina appeared by her daughter's side then, placing a hand on her arm, imploring, 'Please listen, love. It really wasn't what you think . . .'

But Jackie shook her arm free, jumping away from her mother as though the touch had seared her skin. 'It's not what I think! I repeat, I know what I saw. Lovers kissing. Why can't you both be honest and admit it?' Mystified she asked, 'How could you betray me like this, Mum? I'm your daughter, for God's sake. I always hoped you'd meet someone and be as happy with them as you were with Dad, but did you have to pick on *my* boyfriend?' Then she spun round to look at Keith, hurt oozing from her. 'As for you! I thought you were the most loyal, kind, caring man I could ever wish to meet. I really believed you loved me. I really thought we were together for life. I stupidly imagined you were going to propose to me soon . . . maybe even tonight. I was so pleased my mother and boyfriend got on well. I just didn't realise how well, did I? If I hadn't walked in when I did tonight, would we have gone to the party with you acting the part of being happy with me, when all the time it was my mother you wanted to be with? Would you have carried on deceiving me until you could both summon up the courage to tell me? Now, I asked you before, how long has this been going on?'

Gina implored, 'It hasn't, Jackie. It was just tonight . . . we got carried away . . . it was only that one kiss you saw when you walked in. It was a moment of madness . . .'

Keith interjected, 'No, I can't carry on like this, Gina. Jackie deserves to know the truth.' He looked at her steadily as he said, 'I care for you very much, Jackie, but I've fallen in love with your mother. We never meant this to happen. It just did. I've been spending a lot of time with her while you've been working late and . . .'

Incredulous, Jackie cut in, 'You're blaming *me* for this because I've had to work late?'

He gave a shrug. 'No . . . well, maybe I am. If you hadn't had to work late then maybe I wouldn't have got to see a side of Gina I hadn't before. Not Gina the mother but Gina the woman . . . the wonderful woman she is . . . and, well, I couldn't help myself. I fell for her.'

'But she's old enough to be your mother!'

'No, she isn't, Jackie. She's only eleven years older than me. Besides, age doesn't matter when you love someone.'

Jackie turned her pain-filled eyes on her mother and asked, 'And you love Keith?'

Gina looked at her for several long moments before she lowered her head and murmured, 'Yes, I do, Jackie. We were trying to work out the best way to break this to you so we could . . . well, I didn't want to lose you, Jackie. I still love you.'

She snapped, 'If you *loved* me then you would never have allowed yourself to become involved with my boyfriend in the first place!'

Gina said quietly, 'It's not as simple as that, love. You can't pick and choose who you fall for. Keith and I fought our feelings, neither of us wanting to hurt you, but eventually it became impossible. I was just hoping . . . we were both hoping . . .'

Her voice trailed off, so Jackie finished for her. 'That I'd be understanding, give you my blessing, be chief bridesmaid at your wedding?' The looks on both their faces gave her her answer. 'You both hoped for a lot, didn't you? I'm sorry I can't oblige. Does Robby know about this?'

Gina shook her head. 'No.'

'Well, when you do tell him, I hope he's more understanding than I am.'

Jackie felt an all-consuming need to get out of here, away from the two people who had brought her world crashing down around her. She kicked up her heels and fled upstairs where she rammed her clothes and personal belongings into a holdall. When she arrived back downstairs her mother was crumpled on the sofa, head in her hands, sobbing her heart out. Keith sat slumped in an armchair, staring transfixed at the television, though it was apparent he was neither seeing nor hearing the programme being transmitted. His face was stricken.

It was glaringly obvious that they had been telling the truth; they'd not wanted to hurt Jackie but their feelings for each other had proved to be too strong for them to deny. Now they were both suffering from dreadful remorse. At the moment Jackie could find no shred of compassion for either of them as her own pain was too great. They had each other to turn to for comfort. Rhonnie or Drina, or both together, would have come to her rescue, offering her a shoulder to cry on, words of wisdom, their unwavering support to see her through this trauma. Ginger would too, but there was no one available to her right now. Jackie was completely alone. She hurried across the room and into the kitchen, grabbing her coat from the hook on the back door. Without stopping to put it on, she left.

With her belongings wedged precariously on the back of the Lambretta, she drove down country lanes with not a clue where she was heading, so consumed was she by misery, until a pair of high iron gates seemed to materialise out of nowhere before her, the letters welded inside them sparkling in the last rays of the setting sun: JOLLY'S HOLIDAY CAMP. Jackie was not surprised that her subconscious had brought her here.

CHAPTER ELEVEN

Wearing a well-worn winceyette dressing gown, a towel wrapped around her wet hair, Ginger swung her toilet bag as she jauntily made her way back to her chalet from the staff shower block. For a change she'd had a long leisurely shower, with no one badgering her to get a move on as they'd got to get back to work or were meeting friends. There weren't many nights Ginger wasn't meeting friends herself for an evening out, but she was broke until payday so tonight she had no option but to stay in. Surprisingly, she was quite enjoying having the place to herself while her chalet mate was on duty in the Paradise bar. She had tackled some washing, had a tidy around, and after her shower she intended to snuggle down in bed and read magazines until she was tired enough to sleep.

She was almost at her front door when she suddenly stopped, turned and retraced her steps to stand before a chalet several down from the one she herself occupied. Ginger looked at it thoughtfully. The two girls who had shared this chalet had both resigned their posts and left only this morning, claiming they were too homesick to stay. As yet replacements for them hadn't been found and as far as she was aware the chalet hadn't been allocated to any other member of staff. She would know if it had, working on reception. Whoever was inside had to have broken in without a key. One of the staff must be using the place to entertain a friend privately. If security caught them then they could face the sack. She wouldn't like to see anyone lose their job through a lapse of common sense, most likely caused by a bit too much to drink, so for their own good she felt she should have a word with them.

Going up to the door, she rapped purposefully on it, calling out, 'Whoever you are in here, you know you shouldn't be! I'd get out now before security do their rounds . . .'

Before she could get any further, to Ginger's shock the door suddenly flew open and she nearly fell backwards as a body launched itself at her. A pair of arms held on tight to her and a familiar voice cried out: 'Oh, Ginger, I thought you were out tonight with Al. Oh, it's all so terrible! I can't bear it . . . I really can't.'

It was the last person Ginger had expected to see. It took her a moment to shake off her shock before she exclaimed, 'Jackie, what on earth has happened? You're supposed to be out with Keith, aren't you?' Then a dreadful thought struck her. For Jackie to be this distraught something terrible must have happened to him. 'Oh, God, he's not . . . he's not dead, is he?'

Jackie pulled away, giving her wet blotchy face a wipe with the sleeve of her cardigan before she faltered, 'No, but I wish I was. You have no idea how much I wish I was.'

Ginger was reeling from this turn of events, her mind

turning somersaults, trying to fathom why Jackie should be wishing she was dead when only a few hours ago she'd been so full of life, convinced that the man she adored was on the verge of asking her to marry him. Ginger grabbed hold of her friend's arm and pulled her back into the chalet, kicking the door shut behind them before sitting Jackie down on a bed and perching beside her. With real concern, Ginger asked, 'Tell me what's happened?'

Tears flooding down her cheeks, Jackie muttered, 'What would you do . . . how would you feel . . . if you found out your boyfriend and your mother were having an affair?'

Ginger snorted, 'I'd never find myself in that position! My dad managed to sour my mother for life against men, to the point where she'd have every last one of them thrown in a pot of boiling oil if it was up to her.' Then the reason for the question dawned on her. 'You mean . . . you've found out that Keith and your mother are?'

Jackie nodded miserably. 'I walked in on them after work tonight, so wrapped up in each other they never heard me come in.'

Ginger stared at her in amazement for several long moments before she blustered, 'Well . . . er . . . maybe one of them was upset about something and the other was comforting them?'

'You don't kiss your future mother-in-law or son-in-law like they were doing. Besides, they both admitted it when I confronted them.'

'Oh! Oh, I see.' Round-eyed, Ginger stared at her and murmured, 'I'm so sorry, Jackie, really I am.' She took a deep breath then slowly exhaled. 'Well, I suppose all hell broke loose when you gave them what for? Smashed plates and all that.'

Jackie surprised her by saying, 'No, nothing like that happened.' She eased herself back on the bed and sat with her back propped against the wall. She drew up her legs and rested her chin on her knees before she continued in a low voice, 'I was so shocked to start with that what I'd seen didn't really sink in. Then, when it did, I felt completely numb. I couldn't have ranted and raved even if I'd wanted to.'

Ginger said in bewilderment, 'Are you telling me you didn't put up a fight for Keith? Just walked out and left them to it?'

Jackie heaved a forlorn sigh. 'Oh, believe me, a couple of years ago I would have done just that. Got down on my knees, clung to his legs and begged him to stay with me. I've grown up since then. Rhonnie and Drina have taught me a lot about how to conduct myself, and screaming and shouting, pleading and begging, to get what you want is definitely not the way to go about things. Women who make men stay with them through blackmail or pity can never be truly happy, knowing that the other person doesn't really want to be with them but someone else.'

Ginger nodded in agreement. Then, her face grim, she said, 'It's bad enough finding out your boyfriend has been cheating on you, but I can't imagine how that would feel if the other woman was my own mother. Yours is so lovely, though, and Keith is such a smashing bloke. They're the last people I'd have said would do anything like this.'

Jackie sighed miserably. 'Well, like my mother said, you can't help who you fall in love with.'

'Love! You believe they love each other and it's not just a fling? Of course it's a fling. Why, your mum is old enough to be Keith's mother and . . .'

Jackie cut in, 'Actually, she's not. Mum had me at sixteen and Keith is five years older than me so there's only eleven years between them. That might seem like a lot to some people, and I've no doubt they won't have an easy ride of it thanks to certain narrow-minded individuals, but the age difference is no problem to them. This is no fling on their part. I only had to see the way they looked at each other, how they acted with each other, to have no doubt at all how they really feel. My mum is a beautiful woman and lovely-natured; Keith's a decent, sincere, good-looking man. So is it any wonder they fell for each other?'

Jackie heaved a regretful sigh. 'Maybe if I hadn't had to work late all those nights, which threw them together, this situation would never have come about . . . who knows? But who am I, Ginger, to stand in the way of two people being happy together?'

Ginger puffed out her cheeks, considering this. 'Well, when you put it like that . . . So are you telling me you'll give them both your blessing?'

Jackie gave a wan smile. 'I'm no saint. I'm hurting too much right now just to forgive and forget. I don't like to think how long they would have carried on behind my back, with me believing Keith was going to propose, if I hadn't found out like I did tonight. I need time to get over both their . . . their . . .'

'Betrayal, Jackie. When all's said and done, that's what they did to you.'

'Yes, but it wasn't intentional, Ginger. When they told

me they'd both fought against it, I believed them. That's why this is all so difficult for me.' She continued wistfully, 'I'll get over Keith in time, I've no choice, but my mum is a different kettle of fish. She's been a good mother to me, and not just my parent but my friend too. I love her. I couldn't bear the thought of never seeing her again. But then, I can't bear to face her at the moment either.'

Ginger told her, 'You need time to get over this shock before you make any plans for how you're going to handle the future.'

Jackie nodded. 'Yes, I do.'

Ginger chuckled. 'Look on the bright side, gel. You're free and single now, and there's no better way of getting over a bloke than dolling yourself up and hitting the town to have a good look round at what else is out there. I should know, I've had to get over enough of them in my time.'

Jackie shot her a wan smile 'Landing myself another man is the last thing on my mind at the moment. But, yes, you're right, Ginger. Moping around, feeling sorry for myself, isn't going to help me get over this in a hurry. Getting dressed up and hitting the town is the way to go. But not tonight, eh?'

'Well, no, 'course not. I meant when you're feeling like it, in a day or two . . . a week . . . whatever.'

Jackie sighed and nodded. Something suddenly struck her then and she asked Ginger, 'Did you not bother to go and meet Al tonight for some reason?'

Ginger looked confused. 'Eh! I wasn't supposed to meet him, was I? Considering how long I've been trying to get him to come out and ask me on a proper date, I wouldn't have forgotten that, Jackie.'

'Oh! I could have sworn he told me he was meeting you and some others for a drink tonight. I was in a hurry to get home at the time so I must have heard him wrong.'

Ginger pulled a thoughtful expression. 'I'm beginning to wonder about him, you know.'

'What do you mean?'

'Well, he's a good-looking lad, and not shy at all, but he doesn't seem to have a girlfriend . . . or if he has, he's keeping it very quiet. But he always makes excuses not to come out and have some fun . . . well, it's not natural, is it?'

'Just because you love going out and having fun, doesn't mean everyone does, Ginger. Maybe he's the stay-at-home type who likes to read or make model airplanes.'

'Mmm, maybe. Anyway, what are you going to do about work? I mean, after what's happened you won't feel like going in for a day or two. Would you like me to explain to Mr Rose . . .'

Jackie interjected, 'I'll be at work as usual tomorrow, Ginger. I need to keep my mind busy, and work is the best place to do that. This is going to sound so bad of me but Rhonnie's terrible situation is a blessing in disguise for me right now. Drina is relying on me to keep the office running smoothly while she helps Rhonnie heal. That's enough to get me out of bed tomorrow morning, and every morning after that until I've healed and work is no longer an excuse.'

Ginger leaned over and patted her hand. 'And I'm here to help you. Not just as a friend to go out with, but any time you want to bend my ear just let me know.'

'Thanks, Ginger.' Jackie felt her shoulders sag despite her resolution to stay strong. 'When I was at that wedding today, listening to the old couple saying their vows, I was just picturing myself in a wedding dress, Keith by my side, saying my vows to the vicar. I hadn't a clue then that my wedding was never going to happen.'

Her friend's misery finally proved too much for Ginger. A lump formed in her throat. With tears pricking in her own eyes, she took hold of Jackie's hand in hers, squeezed it tightly, and in an effort to lift her mood, said, 'You'll have a lovely wedding one day, just not to Keith.' She could have bitten her tongue out then at her own clumsiness. In an effort to counteract it she blustered, 'My mam would consider you'd had a lucky escape. She reckons that as soon as a man has a ring on a woman's finger, he thinks she's his property, to treat as he wishes, and all women end up as drudges to men.'

Jackie shot her a look which left Ginger in no doubt that her friend had been well aware what faced her after her wedding day, but looking after Keith, their home and the children she'd hoped to have with him would never have been perceived as drudgery but rather a labour of love. Ginger wished she had kept her mouth shut as her attempt to lighten Jackie's mood had only resulted in worsening it. Then something struck her. 'You couldn't have been at a wedding today, you were at work.'

'I'm not losing my marbles, Ginger, I *was* at a wedding today. The woman who came into reception looking for Joyce Daventry . . . only she wasn't actually Joyce Daventry then, though she is now . . . well, that was Joyce's daughter, and the friend she said Joyce was staying here with was her boyfriend. They'd come to Jolly's secretly with the express intention of getting married before the daughter found out and put a stop to it.'

With Jackie's dire situation taking precedence, Ginger had temporarily forgotten that she'd been desperate to discover just what the woman had wanted to tell one of their campers that was so urgent she had to disturb their holiday. Now she just had to know whether the daughter had got her way or not. Eagerly she blurted, 'Did she manage to scupper the wedding? And why did she want to stop her own mother getting married anyway?'

Glad to have her mind taken off her own problems, Jackie told her the whole story. When she had finished, Ginger was laughing. 'Oh, I'd have given anything to see your hair-raising drive to Skegness. Three of you on your scooter, and Joyce's hair looking like a bird's nest by the time you got there!'

'Well, luckily I managed to avoid ending up in a ditch a couple of times, and missed the herd of cows we came upon round a corner. But I won't be offering to do that again in a hurry, I can assure you. It was worth all the stupid risks I took, though, to see how happy they both were when we came out of the register office. They'll have a good life together, I've no doubt of that. I wouldn't want to be in their shoes, though, when they return home and have to face Joyce's daughter.'

Ginger snorted. 'Well, how selfish of her to try and stop her mother from having some happiness in her final years.' Then Ginger gave a wicked grin. 'I'm glad you helped the old dears and the daughter didn't get her own way. So I take it you'll be living in the camp for the foreseeable future?'

'Well, I hadn't thought that far ahead, just borrowed a roof over my head for tonight.' She took a glance around the small chalet before she added, 'Yes, I suppose this will be my home for the time being, at least until I've grown used to the idea I'm on my own now and can think more clearly about the future. Thank goodness I'm entitled to accommodation as a member of staff or I don't know what I'd have done. Before the season ends I'll have to make an effort to look out a bedsitter for myself, to live in over the winter months.'

'Or a flat if you found someone else to share with you?' Ginger said meaningfully.

Jackie looked at her for a moment before just as meaningfully she replied, 'Do you happen to know of someone who'd want to share a flat with me . . . someone I like and get on with?'

Ginger grinned. 'Happen I do. I know she wouldn't say no to sharing a chalet with you either, as the chalet mate she's got at the moment is nice enough but *so* pernickety. All she talks about is her wonderful boyfriend, who in fact is a twerp, so she's driving me mad!'

'Well, she'd better go and collect her stuff as I wouldn't say no to her moving in tonight. In fact, I'd be glad of her company.'

Ginger clapped her hands excitedly and jumped up off the bed. She was just about to make a dash for the door when a thought occurred to her. Hopefully she asked, 'Did you bring your record player and discs with you?'

Jackie shook her head. 'It's a scooter I have, Ginger, not a car.'

She tutted in disappointment. 'Oh, it's just that it

would have come in handy for any parties we have in future. We'll just have to make do with my transistor.'

With that she shot out to collect her belongings.

At that moment Jackie was very grateful for her busy job and the good friend she had in Ginger. With work occupying her mind during the day and Ginger hell-bent on getting her out and about socially in their free time, Jackie knew she wasn't going to have much time to mourn her loss.

CHAPTER TWELVE

'Kids should all be drowned at birth, in my opinion. I think the government should issue a health warning against having them. Why any woman feels the need to dedicate her life to such a soul-destroying task as raising a child . . . who except for the very isolated case will cause her nothing but trouble and heartache . . . is beyond me.'

Jackie stared in astonishment at Sister Beryl Pendle as she soaked water into the makeshift bandage, caked in dried blood, that she was in the process of unwrapping from around Jackie's injured knee. Beryl was a small, well-rounded, homely-looking woman in her early forties, appearing every inch the motherly sort, so Jackie had always assumed she had at least two children of her own. This admission from her had come as quite a shock. 'But you're a nurse!' Jackie exclaimed.

Beryl responded matter-of-factly, 'How observant of you, Jackie.'

'But . . . well . . . as a nurse, aren't you supposed to care for all humanity? And I've seen you when you've been treating children. You're so good with them.'

'Just doing my job. I derive a great sense of satisfaction

from making the sick well again, but that doesn't mean I want to take them all home and mother them. Some women are not naturally maternal. I'm one of them.' Beryl stopped what she was doing for a moment and, with a twinkle of amusement in her eyes, said, 'I bet you wished the mother of the young chap who mowed you down on his bicycle had drowned him at birth, and saved you from being scarred for life?'

Jackie couldn't deny that she had felt rather like that at first on finding herself unexpectedly sprawled on the hard tarmac while on her way back from having lunch in the restaurant. The pain emanating from her right knee was acute enough to bring tears to her eyes, and certainly too much for her to chase the young teen who had caused her fall.

Having been helped up by several campers, and finding Sister Stephens with a queue of people waiting to be attended to, Jackie had limped back to the office to wrap a makeshift bandage around her knee, to stem the flow of blood. She then took a couple of Aspirin to help ease the throbbing from her wound, and had not then found the time to visit the surgery until she'd finished work for the day at just after seven. By this time her annoyance against the lad who had injured her had faded somewhat. She preferred to believe his riding into her had been purely accidental and not on purpose.

She told Beryl, 'I'm sure it was just an accident.'

Beryl said dryly, 'Well, let's hope for the sake of other innocent campers that you're right. I'm married to a policeman. Like him, I believe all perpetrators of crime should be made to pay accordingly. Now, brace yourself . . . this might hurt,' she said, and immediately swiped off the remaining bandage that she had been unable to unstick using tepid water. A chunk of dried blood came off with it, exposing a large gouge in Jackie's knee.

'Ouch!' she yelped. 'That stings.'

Beryl said matter-of-factly, 'Well, I warned you it would.'

'Yes, but you didn't give me any time to brace myself.'

'Oh, I don't believe in prolonging the inevitable. It would have hurt just as much if I'd given you time to brace yourself. If you'd attended surgery sooner the scab wouldn't have formed, so you brought the extra pain on yourself. Now, you're going to suffer worse when I give your wound a clean with antiseptic, but it's either suffer that or risk gangrene setting in and having to have your leg amputated. Your choice?'

Jackie couldn't work out whether Beryl was joking or not, but regardless wasn't prepared to take the risk. Clenching her hands around the arms of the chair, she told the nurse, 'Just get on with it.' And vowed that should she ever sustain any similar injury in future she wouldn't leave it so long to seek treatment, and cause herself more suffering than she needed.

As she finally applied a liberal amount of Germolene ointment to the clean wound and began to dress it, Beryl asked, 'Apart from your knee, how are you?'

Jackie inwardly groaned. It had been barely twenty-four hours since she'd walked in on her mother and Keith, and her hope that she could keep her break-up secret so as to begin to get over it before every Tom, Dick and Harry began to quiz her about what had caused it had been futile. How on earth they'd all found out so soon she had no idea. Presumably the fact that she'd started sharing a chalet with Ginger had been noted and the right conclusion drawn. Ginger was the only one who knew for sure and she would never have blabbed, true friend that she was.

In an effort to convey to Beryl that she really wasn't ready to talk about it, Jackie said shortly, 'I'm fine, thanks for asking.'

The nurse flashed her a look of understanding. 'If you say so. My final words on the subject are: if you need anyone to talk to, or something to help you sleep, come and see me.'

Jackie gave her a wan smile and said gratefully, 'Thank you, Sister.'

Moments later Beryl went over to the sink to wash her hands, saying to Jackie, 'You'll live. Come back tomorrow and let us have another look to make sure there's no sign of infection. My medical advice is: in future avoid cyclists as much as possible.'

It was approaching one o'clock in the morning when Beryl Pendle settled herself back into the comfortable easy chair in the corner of the surgery after making herself a cup of tea to accompany the potted meat sandwiches and slice of fruit cake she had brought with her. It had been a very quiet night, only a couple of people consulting her when really they needn't have if they'd bothered to use their common sense. She would have preferred to be busy as that way the time would have gone by much more quickly than it had, albeit she had managed to pen a couple of letters to far-off friends and read from cover to cover several women's magazines, ripping out a pattern for a Fair Isle jumper which would suit her husband and several tasty-sounding recipes she intended to try out on him, so she'd managed to fill the time pleasantly enough.

As Beryl folded up the recipes, she knew her husband was going to really enjoy them when she cooked them for him, and the knitting pattern would be kept secret for the time being so the jumper would be a nice surprise. She smiled as a vision of Trevor rose in her mind's eye.

Trevor Pendle was tall at six foot three and heavily built, rather portly in fact, with a ruddy face, thinning hair and size thirteen feet. Beryl knew the locals on his beat affectionately called him PC Plod as he certainly did bear a marked resemblance to the character in Enid Blyton's Noddy books. Not every woman's ideal, but he was hers. Trevor was easy-going and good-natured, and treated Beryl like his most treasured possession. They had been happily married for twenty-three years, and apart from the odd little row over something trivial neither of them could remember five minutes afterwards, they lived together in perfect harmony. They shared so many traits, likes and dislikes, from their taste in food to what they preferred to listen to on the radio and watch on the television. Neither of them had felt any desire to upset the even tenor of their lives by introducing any offspring to disrupt it.

About this time, unless some inconsiderate criminal had decided to be active tonight on his patch, Trevor should be en route back to the station to take a break. Beryl had made up potted meat sandwiches and a slice of fruit cake for him too, but a larger amount. It was a standing joke between them that despite his age of forty-five, he was still a growing lad who needed plenty of nourishment. Their respective shift patterns meant that some weeks they hardly saw each other so time spent together was precious. Unusually they were both on nights this week, and during the long hours both of them looked forward to getting home in the morning and having a cuddle in bed before they slept the day away. Unusually, too, they both had this coming weekend off, something they were looking forward to greatly as they planned to take a trip in their Morris Minor to Lincoln for the day, have a browse around the shops and a good lunch in a pub before setting off back home. The weather looked as if it would be perfect.

Food finished and all still quiet in the surgery, Beryl laid her head back against the chair and allowed her eyes to droop. She wasn't worried about being caught napping on the job as she was a very light sleeper and would be awake and alert at the first squeak of the surgery door handle turning . . .

Then suddenly it did.

Beryl bustled out into the small reception area to be greeted by a young teenage girl, dressed in her nightclothes. She was bent over, clutching her stomach, obviously in a great deal of pain.

Stumbling over her words, the girl groaned, 'I've . . . a . . . belly ache. I think . . . me insides are dropping out.'

Beryl answered dryly, 'I doubt that. Is it that time of the month for you?'

The girl looked non-plussed. 'What time? Oh, you mean the curse? That's what me mam calls it. I ain't started them yet.'

That wasn't unusual as girls could start them any time between the age of twelve and sixteen, and at a guess this girl was fourteen at the most. Beryl asked her, 'When did you last eat?'

'I ain't today. Ain't felt hungry. I didn't eat much yesterday neither as I didn't feel too good.'

Beryl thought, Thank God that rules out possible food poisoning! Chef Brown had been furious enough when accused of giving it to campers at the start of the season, which had turned out to be false, so she dreaded to think how he'd react if he were accused again. She feared the girl could have appendicitis, though, and if that was the case Beryl needed to get her to hospital quick before the appendix burst and her life was put in danger.

'What's your name?' Beryl asked.

'Teresa.'

'Well, Teresa, have you ever had your appendix out?'

She looked blank. 'What's one of them?'

This girl wasn't the brightest spark, Beryl thought. 'I'll need to examine you. Go through to the medical room and get on the bed while I wash my hands.'

A minute or so later Beryl found the girl lying on her side on the bed, groaning softly. 'You'll need to turn on your back for me to check you.'

'I can't,' Teresa wailed. 'I hurt too much.'

Beryl went behind the girl and eased one arm under her shoulders. She lifted up her upper arm, tucking her own head underneath so the girl's arm was slung around her neck. 'I'm going to pull you on your back and I want you to help me as much as you can. I'll count to three . . .'

Teresa was well developed for her age, and not especially co-operative, so Beryl had quite a struggle to complete the manoeuvre. When it was done she stood at the side of the bed staring down at Teresa. The girl was not suffering from anything connected to her appendix. The size of her stomach told Beryl that she was pregnant, and her discomfort was caused by labour pains.

'Your baby is on its way. Hopefully we've time to call an ambulance and get you to hospital. I need to examine you internally to find out,' Beryl explained.

Teresa was gawping at her wild-eyed. She cried out hysterically, 'Baby? Waddya mean, me baby's on its way? I ain't having no baby. I'm only thirteen.'

So Beryl had been a year out, but even so there was no mistake in her diagnosis of Teresa's condition. 'I can assure you, you are. Now I need . . .'

The frenzied girl blurted out, 'But I ain't been with no man so I can't be having a baby.'

'Teresa, it's a myth that a woman can get pregnant after sitting on a toilet seat after a man has used it. There is no other way to get pregnant than to have sex with a man. Therefore you must have done.'

'But I ain't,' she insisted. 'Me mam's always warned me I must never let a man touch me where he shouldn't. I've only ever let the lad I met down the fair when it came to town last year touch me, and he was only fourteen, so that's all right, ain't it?'

Beryl inwardly groaned. 'Did you not know you were pregnant, Teresa? Did you not wonder why your tummy was getting bigger? Did you not feel the baby move? Did your parents not notice the changes in you?'

At that moment a strong labour pain hit Teresa. She grabbed hold of the nurse's hand, gripping it so tightly her knuckles shone white and Beryl feared bones would be broken.

'Take deep breaths and let them out slowly. Keep doing

that until the pain subsides. That's it . . . keep going,' Beryl ordered.

Several minutes later the pain had subsided enough for her to regain control of her hand and rub life back into it. It seemed the answers to her questions were going to have to wait. Beryl didn't need to examine her to know that Teresa was in the second stage of labour and the baby was going to make its entry into the world in a very short time. Her mother really ought to be fetched but Beryl feared there was no time for that either. She then silently prayed that the birth would be a straightforward one with no complications as the surgery was only equipped to cater for minor injuries.

Just under thirty minutes later, the wail of a newborn rent the air. Beryl gave a huge sigh of relief to note with her trained eye that the baby, a girl, was strong and healthy. Her prayer had been answered. The birth had been straightforward, although more of an ordeal than it should have been for Teresa, with no gas and air to help her through.

Having cut the cord, cleaned up the baby and wrapped it in a clean towel, Beryl went to hand her to her mother. 'Meet your daughter, Teresa.'

Terrified eyes looked back at her and the girl physically shrank away, as though the baby was contaminated with something deadly which she'd pass on. 'I don't want it,' she cried frenziedly. 'Take it away!'

Beryl spoke firmly. 'It's your baby, Teresa. You've had a great shock, I grant you, and you'll need time to get used to the fact you're a mother now. But the baby's going to need to be fed soon and you're the only one who can provide her with the milk she needs.'

The girl looked horrified. 'You mean, feed her like Mrs Withers next door feeds her new baby? No, no, I won't do that! It makes me feel sick.'

Beryl sighed heavily. 'I have to fetch your mother. She needs to be told about this and to take charge. You're a minor and she'll need to accompany you to hospital to have you and the baby checked over. Just a precaution. I've delivered enough babies in my time to know you're both fine, but I'd sooner be safe than sorry. When your mother gets here, I'll telephone for an ambulance.' Oh, dear, what a mess, thought Beryl. She didn't relish the idea of having to break this news to the girl's mother, but someone was going to have to. The family had big decisions to make as the new mother was only thirteen.

'Will you just hold the baby while I go into my office and telephone security to fetch your mother?' Beryl coaxed Teresa, hoping this would help her to bond with her child.

Eyes filled with terror, she vehemently shook her head. 'No! No, I won't. I don't want it. I don't want to be a mother. I want to be a shop assistant when I leave school, that's what I want.'

Beryl sighed again. She was getting nowhere with the girl. 'Your future is for you to sort out with your parents. At the moment my concern is the future of your baby. Tell me the number of the chalet you're staying in?'

Teresa stared at her wildly for several long moments before she blustered, 'Oh, but yer can't wake me mam up at this time. She hates being woken up . . .'

Beryl was fighting not to lose her patience. 'Teresa, your chalet number?'

She finally muttered, 'Four six five.'

Taking the baby with her, Beryl left the medical room

to go into the office. One-handed, she took off the receiver, laying it on the desk while she dialled the security extension then lifting the receiver to listen to the ring tone for a minute or so before it was answered. She quickly instructed Bert Simmons what she wished him to do, replaced the receiver and returned to the consulting room.

'While we wait for your mother, I think we need to try the baby with some . . .' Beryl's voice trailed off as she realised she was addressing an empty room. Her thoughts raced. Had Teresa decided to go and break the news to her mother herself or was she terrified of facing up to her and now in hiding?

She couldn't leave the baby on its own so there was nothing Beryl could do until Teresa's mother arrived or the girl herself came back. In the meantime she would take care of the new infant herself.

Still holding the baby in her arm, Beryl went and found an empty box and lined it with clean towels. She laid the child gently inside, then covered her up with another clean towel and put the box down in a draught-free corner of the room. While the baby slept she went off to the surgery store cupboard where thankfully they kept several tins of Cow and Gate formula, just in case of emergencies when mothers of young babies ran short, having miscalculated how many tins they'd need on holiday. Beryl made up a bottle ready for the baby should Teresa refuse to feed it herself.

That done and the baby still asleep, she returned to the medical room, stripped and cleaned the bed, and remade it with fresh covers ready for the next patient. She had just returned to the office to check on the baby when she heard a tap on the outside door. She arrived in reception to find that Bert Simmons had entered.

He looked perturbed. 'Ah, Sister, I just need to check that you gave me the right chalet number, only the ones in four six five haven't got a daughter called Teresa. Weren't happy about being knocked up at this time of night neither. Anyway, I must have taken the number down wrong. I am sorry, Sister. You did say to tell the woman she was needed urgently at the surgery . . . something to do with her daughter.'

Beryl silently scolded herself. How stupid not to suspect that Teresa would give her a false chalet number considering her state of mind after her traumatic experience and its life-changing aftermath. It seemed in the circumstances she had two choices. Either she should ask Bert Simmons to summon the police and let them deal with this situation or she could give Teresa an hour or so to return before she took drastic action which could have far-reaching consequences for the baby.

Beryl was aware that Bert was beginning to wonder why she hadn't responded to him, considering she had called him out to help her with an urgent matter. She hurriedly made her decision. No harm would come to the baby if she gave its mother time to come to terms with what had transpired. If Teresa or her mother hadn't returned by six in the morning then Beryl would have no choice but to take matters into her own hands.

Telling Bert that she was sorry she must have given him the wrong number, but it didn't matter now as the urgent situation had resolved itself in the meantime, Beryl went back to sit in the consulting room with the baby, waiting for its mother or grandmother to turn up and claim it.

CHAPTER THIRTEEN

Beryl woke with a start, nearly jumping out of her skin to find herself staring straight into a face so close to hers that it appeared grotesque through her unfocused eyes. 'What the . . .' she exclaimed.

The face withdrew and a relieved voice cut her short with, 'Oh, thank God. I thought you were dead, Beryl. All the time we've worked alongside each other, I can't ever remember arriving for a shift change and finding you asleep. Had a busy night?'

Beryl stared at April Stephens blankly for a moment until her sleep-fuddled brain cleared enough for the events of a few hours ago to come flooding back. Her face grim, she said, 'Oh, so she never came back then? Well, that leaves me with no choice but to alert the authorities and hand the problem over to them.'

April was looking at her in confusion. 'Beryl, what problem do you need to alert the authorities about?'

She pointed down to the box by the side of her. 'This problem, April.'

April looked inside the box, and when it registered with her just what was inside, she let out a gasp of shock. 'Where did you find it?'

'I didn't find it. I delivered it. And it's a "her". The mother was thirteen, can you believe, and thought it was all right to have sex with a lad she met at the fair because her mother had warned her not to let a man touch her, but he was only fourteen so a boy and not a man.'

She then told April all that had transpired and finished off with, 'Well, it's obvious no one is coming to claim the child so there's no alternative but to call in the authorities and let them take charge.'

April, the mother of three children herself, was shaking her head sadly. In contrast to Beryl whose head ruled her heart, April's heart very much ruled her head. 'Oh, dear. I don't know who I feel more sorry for . . . the child or its mother. The poor girl is going to feel guilty for the rest of her life for abandoning her baby, albeit she's hardly more than a child herself, and this baby is going to go through life knowing it wasn't wanted by its mother or her family, so it seems.'

'Well, we can't judge the girl's family too harshly as we don't actually know if Teresa has told them. I can't even be sure her name is actually Teresa.'

April's eyes settled on the baby sleeping peacefully in the box and she said wistfully, 'Oh, Beryl, she's such a sweet little thing. I'd take her myself if I hadn't got my hands full already with my three, and Roy's adamant there should be no more. I don't think they'll have any trouble finding a couple to adopt this little one. She's perfect, isn't she? Who could fail to fall in love with her? But what worries me is that it's the luck of the draw whether that couple can love her the same as they would if she was their own. People fall instantly in love with kittens and puppies, not seeming to consider that they don't stay small and adorable for long. It's the same with children, of course. What fills me with dread, though, is that this little mite is going to spend time in a children's home while they seek out a new family for her. Have you ever been inside a children's home, Beryl?'

She shook her head.

'I have. Horrible places. Before I took this job with Jolly's I applied for a job at one. It broke my heart to see how babies and children are treated there. The babies are left for most of the day lying in their cot, mostly in soiled nappies which as you can imagine causes terrible nappy rash. The staff just haven't time to spend with them except for feeding, and then as soon as they're burped they're returned to their cots until next feeding time – no cuddle or anything. It's not the staff's fault but the authorities' for not hiring enough people to provide proper care and attention.

April dragged her eyes away from the baby and fixed them on Beryl meaningfully. 'Whether we like it or not, we have this child's future in our hands. Before we take the drastic step of handing her over to the authorities, we really should give her mother more time to come back and fetch her . . . another day or so at least. Look, it's only hours since the birth, it's not like it's days. Maybe Teresa hasn't built up the courage to tell her parents yet. Maybe she has but the parents are still reeling themselves. This is going to be one hell of a shock for them, isn't it? If we've had no sign of them come Monday then we take action. That's the fair and just thing to do, for the sake of the baby, don't you agree?'

Beryl looked at her thoughtfully for a moment before

she nodded her agreement. 'And what do we do with the child meantime? We can't keep her here, can we?'

April looked thoughtful. 'Mmm . . . no, we can't. I'd take her myself if it was just for the weekend. Roy wouldn't have any objection so long as it was no longer, but it's your weekend off so I can't, can I?' She looked at Beryl meaningfully. 'That just leaves you.'

She exclaimed, 'Me!' The thought of having a baby to care for, even for a short time, filled Beryl with horror. Trevor would panic just as much.

April was well aware of Beryl's feelings about children, couldn't fail to see the panic in her eyes at the thought of having the care of one for even a short time. She knew her colleague was about to come out with all manner of excuses not to take the baby, but April herself was adamant that this child was not going to face an uncertain future unless there was no other choice. Smiling broadly she said, 'That's settled then. You'll take the baby for the weekend and I'll telephone you immediately Teresa or her family show up. And if they don't come by Monday morning then we hand her over to the authorities.' April got up. 'I'll go and sort out the things you'll need for her from the store cupboard. I'm sure there's a couple of old nightdresses and nappies in the box of stuff people have left behind.'

Beryl sighed heavily. She wasn't at all happy about having her much-looked-forward-to weekend scuppered, and wasn't relishing informing Trevor of it either.

He wasn't back home by the time Beryl arrived. This signalled to her that he must have had a busy night and still be at the station handing over to the day relief. Whoever got home first when they both happened to be on night shift would make a start on breakfast so they could eat together before they went to bed, but she had a baby to deal with first. She needed to find something better than a cardboard box for the child to sleep in during her stay with them, and any time now she would be waking for a feed so Beryl ought to have a bottle ready.

Putting the kettle on to boil she went in search of a makeshift cot.

She had just settled the baby down, after her feed and change, into a dressing-table drawer she had emptied of its contents and lined with a blanket, then she had gone into the kitchen to make a much-needed cup of tea and a start on the breakfast when the back door opened and her big husband lumbered in. He smiled lovingly at his beloved wife, saying as he took off his helmet and stripped off his uniform jacket, 'Sorry I'm late, love. Had a hell of a night. A drunk decided to take out the window of the pub because the landlord refused to serve him, and we had to stop a husband from trying to throttle his wife because he caught her in bed with their neighbour when he arrived home from his shift earlier than was expected.'

Pulling out a chair from under the kitchen table, Trevor eased his large bulk down on it and began to pull off his boots while he carried on talking. 'Thank God I've got a long weekend to look forward to with my darling wife. I thought we could go to the pub and have dinner, save you from cooking tonight.' He stopped talking to look pointedly at the stove when it struck him there was no sizzling pan on it and no smell of cooking sausages and bacon assailing his nostrils. 'I take it you've had a busy night and just come in yourself too, love? Let me finish taking my boots off then I'll help you with breakfast.'

She told him, 'Eating at the pub tonight sounds good but I'm afraid we won't be able to. You see, we have a visitor.'

'Eh!' His face fell, voice lowering to a whisper as he said, 'Don't tell me your mother has descended on us? I could cope with anyone else but not her.'

'Oh, that's fine then. You'll be able to cope with a baby.'

Trevor sat speechless for a moment. Then, his face paling, he ventured, 'You did say a baby?'

She nodded and proceeded to tell him just how they had ended up looking after one.

By the time she had finished, Trevor was looking perturbed. 'Oh, goodness me, what a turn up for the books. As hard work as she is, I'd sooner you had told me it was your mother we had stopping. I don't know about this, love. You ran a mile if your sisters so much as hinted about you holding one of their babies when they were little. All I know about them is that it's a continuous job, filling them up at one end and cleaning them up at the other.'

'Well, that's all you need to know because at this little one's age that's all that needs doing.'

'But what about our weekend? We were so looking forward to . . .'

Beryl snapped, 'Don't you think I'm as upset as you are about having our weekend disrupted? Whether we like it or not, we're lumbered with this baby for the next couple of days unless the mother or her family turn up to claim her meantime. We have no choice but to get on with it. In the meantime, I suggest we'd better get some sleep while the baby is. We're going to need it.'

Beryl woke with a start, eyes darting to the alarm clock on her bedside table. It was three-thirty. She made to turn over and go back to sleep. She'd be up in just over three hours to get ready for work. Then suddenly panic struck as she remembered the baby. She had been due a feed at two but hadn't woken for it. Beryl hoped that meant she had slept through, not that something was wrong with her and neither Beryl nor Trevor had heard her cries. Diving out of bed, she grabbed her robe, pulling it on as she hurried over to the spare bedroom where the baby was sleeping in the drawer on the bed.

A shaft of light beaming down from a crescent moon was bathing the makeshift cot in a soft glow, casting everything else around it into eerie darkness. Padding quietly over to the bed, Beryl leaned over and placed one hand gently on the baby's chest, mortally relieved to feel it rising and lowering. The child was fine, just peacefully sleeping. She made to return to bed when the hairs on the back of her neck stood up, all her senses telling her that she and the child were not the only ones in the room. 'Who's there?' she whispered.

It was Trevor who whispered back, 'It's only me, love.'

Peering hard, she just made out the outline of him, lying on the bed to the other side of the drawer, one arm bent, head resting in his hand. She tutted. 'Oh, you daft lummox, you gave me such a scare! I was so worried when I realised she hadn't woken for her feed at two, I didn't notice you weren't in bed beside me. Just what are you doing here?' Beryl quizzed.

'Actually, the baby did wake at just after two. I was on my way back from a visit to the toilet when I heard her. I was awake already and it seemed a shame to wake you, so I fed her myself.'

'*You* fed her!' exclaimed Beryl, astonished.

Trevor gave a small laugh. 'Don't sound so shocked. Men are as capable of feeding babies as women. I've watched you do it enough times over the weekend to know what to do. I made sure she was well winded and changed her nappy too. And before you ask, no, it didn't fall off when I picked her up. She went straight to sleep when I put her back down.' He looked tenderly into the cot and stroked one finger gently down the side of the baby's face. 'She really is a good little thing, isn't she? Hardly cried all weekend.'

Beryl was astounded by this turn of events. In all the time she had known Trevor he had broken out in a sweat if anyone asked him to hold their baby for so much as a couple of minutes while they saw to something. So for him voluntarily to feed one and change its nappy, and to speak about it so affectionately, was just incredible to her. All she could think of by way of response was, 'No, she hasn't been much trouble.' Then she asked, 'You must have finished dealing with her a while ago. Why haven't you come back to bed?'

There was silence for a moment before Trevor awkwardly responded, 'Well, I was just . . . er . . .'

His voice trailed off. Knowing her husband as well as she did, Beryl realised he was finding it difficult to tell her the reason, which was upsetting for her as they told each other everything. Perching on the side of the bed, she coaxed him, 'Tell me, Trevor. You were just what?'

He took a deep breath and slowly exhaled before answering, 'I was just watching the baby, love.'

'Why? Were you worried something wasn't right with her? You should have fetched me to check on her.'

'No, no, I wasn't worried.' He took another deep breath before he continued. 'I was just watching her, that's all. I can't explain it, love, but I've got used to having her here. I've found myself feeling very protective towards her, which is natural enough, but when I was holding her in my arms feeding her tonight that feeling . . . well, it overwhelmed me and I started worrying about what was going to happen to her when you hand her over to Social Services later today. We've had no telephone call from April so the family obviously have abandoned her, haven't they? I'm worried about what sort of people will adopt her. Will they love her like she was their own and take care of her properly?' He gave an embarrassed laugh. 'Tell me I'm an old fool, Beryl. I've never felt remotely like this about any kiddy before so I must be having a mid-life crisis or going doo-lally in my old age.'

Beryl was looking at him thoughtfully. The emotions he was describing were familiar to her as well. She had fought hard to shut them out, but there was something about this baby that had purely and simply captured her heart. Beryl desperately wanted to care for her and protect her. Now it seemed that Trevor felt the same.

He was looking back at her hopefully. 'You're not telling me I'm an old fool, Beryl?'

She sighed. 'No, love, I'm not. Because if you are, then so am I.'

He said in astonishment, 'You mean, you feel the same about the little mite as I do?'

'Yes, I do. I've tried not to . . . God, how I've tried . . . because I like my life the way it is, just you and me, doing what we want, when we want. But since this little girl arrived in our lives, I just can't picture our future without her being part of it. The thought of handing her over in a few hours, walking away from her, leaving her whole life in the lap of the gods . . . well, it fills me with dread. I don't think . . . no, I know . . . I'll never sleep soundly again, worrying what's become of her.'

'No, I don't think I will either.'

They looked at each other for several long moments more before Trevor took the lead. 'So . . . what are we going to do, love?'

Beryl sighed. 'If we both feel like this then there's only one thing we can do, isn't there.'

He nodded.

'Taking on this child is going to change our lives out of all recognition. I'm going to have to give up work so money will be tight. Holidays will be a thing of the past; so will lying in bed on Sunday mornings reading the papers until we feel like rising. We can expect to be mercilessly ribbed by families and friends over this turn of events, considering we've always been adamant children are not for us. So are you sure about this, Trevor, because once we set the ball rolling there'll be no going back?'

He replied without any hesitation, 'I don't think I've ever been surer about anything . . . oh, except about marrying you, of course.'

Beryl chucked. 'Well, that settles it then. We're going to become parents. I never thought I'd ever hear myself say that.'

Trevor was frowning. 'But it's not just a case of us deciding we're going to keep the baby, is it? What if Social Services won't let us keep her, for some reason? I mean, we're no spring chickens. They might say we're too old.'

Beryl said matter-of-factly, 'There's no reason for them to become involved. The mother and family aside, there's only you, me and April who actually know of the baby's existence. April will keep our secret if it means the baby is going to have a good home and future. So, as far as anyone else is concerned, the baby is our natural child.'

'But I'm a copper, Beryl. If I get caught out in such a whopper of a lie, my time in the force will be over and my reputation as a pillar of the community will be in tatters.'

'The only way anyone will find out is if you tell them. I know some people would see this as telling lies, but I prefer to think of us as being a little sparing with the truth. Surely we can be forgiven that if it's for the sake of a baby?'

'Mmm, when you put it like that, it's the right thing we're doing.' Trevor paused for a moment then asked, 'Think me a bit thick, love, but won't people ask questions when you suddenly produce a baby . . . like, how can you have one without being pregnant?'

'During my time as a nurse I've delivered at least fifty babies, and five of them were to mothers who had no idea they were pregnant. I'll say I didn't have any idea whatsoever I was pregnant until the baby suddenly arrived, not long after I'd got home from work on Saturday morning, and you helped to deliver her. The reason we haven't told our families or anyone yet is because we have both been in too much shock at suddenly having an addition to our family.'

'Well, it seems you've thought of everything, love, apart from one thing. What if the mother changes her mind?'

Beryl looked thoughtful. 'Well, from what I know of her, I feel that's a very remote possibility. She's probably pushed all this to the back of her mind and is getting on with her life. There's no worry about the father as he was just a lad she met at the fair. I doubt she even knew his name. As I told you, she's what my mother would've termed "tuppence short of a shilling". And if she does turn up in the future . . . well, for the sake of the little one, we'd stick to our story. It would be her word against ours and she'd have no proof that the child is hers. Don't think I won't feel bad for her because I will and I know you will too but, surely, putting the child's well-being first justifies our behaviour.'

Trevor said with conviction, 'Yes, it does. All that remains is for us to think of a nice name for her.' He thought for a moment and offered, 'What about Rosie? It's a very pretty name and she looks like a little rosebud, doesn't she?'

Beryl smiled. 'Yes, I like that. Rosie it is then.'

Trevor looked down at the sleeping child and said tenderly, 'Well, little Rosie, I hope you like your new mum and dad because it seems you're stuck with us.'

CHAPTER FOURTEEN

Later that morning Jackie was staring at April Stephens in utter astonishment. 'Sister Pendle has had a baby, a little girl, and she had no idea she was pregnant? My goodness, I'm in shock myself just hearing this, so I can't imagine how she and Mr Pendle are feeling. She was only telling me on Thursday evening that she wasn't the motherly type.'

April smiled. 'Well, she's going to have to be now, isn't she? You can appreciate, though, why she can't serve any notice.'

'Yes, of course. We'll have to see about another nurse to work alongside you, Sister, and to start as soon as possible.' Jackie thought about it. Harold Rose wasn't going to be able to push this on her like he'd done all the other matters he should have dealt with as temporary boss. Hiring a chalet maid Jackie could handle, but a qualified nurse was an entirely different matter.

'I appreciate that,' April was saying. 'I've spoken to Sister Blundell who comes in when we need cover like she did this weekend, and she's willing to do Sister Pendle's shifts meantime.'

'Oh, that's good of her. I'll organise a collection around

the staff for a leaving present for Sister Pendle. We'd best get her something for the baby as she'll have nothing for it, will she? I'm sure the staff will give as much as they can afford. Nurse Pendle was well liked.'

April got up to leave and Jackie was about to inform Harold Rose of this new development when the outer door to the office swung open and Pamela Randall, a junior Stripey, charged in and immediately approached Jackie. 'There's a problem at one of the shower blocks. Terry Jones wants you to come over urgently.'

April signalled she was taking her leave. Jackie responded jocularly, 'I can turn my hand to lots of things, Pam, but plumber I'm not. I'll get someone from maintenance to pop over. Which shower block is it?'

Picking up the switchboard handset, Al piped up, 'I'll put a call through to maintenance now.'

Pam said, 'It's not that kind of problem. I don't know the ins and outs but a woman has locked herself in, she won't talk to none of the Stripeys, so Terry was hoping you could persuade her to come out. There's going to be a mutiny soon if she doesn't as there's a queue building of people wanting to use the toilets and showers, and they're not too happy about not being able to.'

Jackie sighed. She really hadn't time to deal with this. She was behind with holiday enquiries for later this season; she'd several urgent orders to place with suppliers; and she must speak to Harold Rose about several matters she needed his approval on, including a replacement nurse for Sister Pendle. It looked like another late night for her tonight. Asking Al to hold the fort, something he was getting used to doing, she told Pam, 'Lead the way.'

Arriving at the shower block in question, Jackie made her way through a dozen or more disgruntled holiday-makers, apologising to them all for the difficulty they were experiencing and reassuring them that normal service would be resumed imminently. Finally she reached the door to the shower block where Terry Jones was waiting for her.

Terry was the head Stripey. Although he was extremely good at his job and well liked by the holidaymakers, Jackie found his overwhelming self-confidence and belief that he was God's gift to women insufferable. Always careful how she approached him, so as not to give him the slightest reason to think she was coming on to him, Jackie asked stiltedly, 'What's going on, Terry?'

He shrugged. 'I'm not sure exactly. All I know is that a woman attacked Helen Green, gave her a left hook a boxer would have been proud of, then shot into the shower block and barricaded herself in. Now she's sobbing her socks off.'

Worriedly, Jackie asked, 'Is Helen badly hurt?'

'She's going to have a right shiner, that's for certain, but as for anything else we'll have to wait until Sister Stephens has taken a look at her. Helen did manage to tell me that she has no idea why the attack took place. The woman won't talk to me so I was hoping you might fare better.'

Jackie felt doubtful. 'Well, I'll have a go. Do you know her name?'

He shook his head. 'I tried to find out so I could fetch her husband or whoever she's staying here with, but as soon as I told her who I was she screamed at me to bugger off, saying she refused to talk to a Stripey.'

Jackie frowned. 'She seems to have a beef against Stripeys for some reason, doesn't she?'

Terry shrugged again. 'I can't imagine why. None of us Stripeys would have treated her any differently from the way we treat the other campers. All the Stripeys are well aware that the camper is always right, no matter what.'

Jackie rapped loudly on the door and called out, 'Hello, my name is Jackie, I'm from the office. You're obviously upset about something Stripey Helen has done. She's no idea what it is. Will you tell me so I can try and sort it out?'

The harsh response came back, 'That bitch is lying! She knows exactly what she's done. Just keep her away from me or it'll be more than a punch in the eye she gets. Now I don't want to talk about it so go away and leave me alone.'

Jackie coaxed her, 'But other holidaymakers need to use the facilities . . .'

The woman screamed. 'I said, go away and leave me alone!'

Jackie sighed and spoke to Terry again, over her shoulder. 'Helen is positive she has no idea why the woman attacked her?' When she received no response she turned round to look at him and saw his attention was completely centred on a pretty young woman who had come to join the growing crowd of spectators, intrigued to know what was going on along with the rest of the queue of people wanting to use the shower block. Tutting disdainfully, Jackie snapped, 'Terry?'

He spun back to face her, grinning, explaining away his distraction with: 'Just doing my job, keeping the campers happy, Jackie.'

She hissed back, 'Pity you don't pay as much attention to all the other campers as you do to the young pretty ones. There's a camper behind this door who is definitely *not* happy and we need to find out why. That's what you should be giving all your attention.' Jackie was about to repeat her question to him when she realised she was only wasting her time as Helen would have said when first asked if she knew why the woman had attacked her. What Jackie really needed to do was get in and talk to the woman herself. The door was barricaded from the inside, she suspected by the wooden wedge that was used to keep it propped open in hot weather to help keep the building cool, so the only way in was via one of the frosted windows at the back of the building. She had to hope that one of them was on the latch. 'Come with me,' she ordered Terry.

Around the back of the building Jackie was relieved to see that one of the windows was open. The narrow space, several feet above them, was just about wide enough for her to squeeze through. Standing underneath it, she said to Terry, 'Give me a leg up, please.'

He looked at the window then at her. 'You're going to climb through?'

Jackie shot him a withering look. 'You have any other suggestion as to how I can get inside? The door is jammed and I'm not a bird so I can't fly in.'

Terry had always had a strong fancy for Jackie and never missed an opportunity to let her know how willing he was to act on it. The fact she had been courting for the past eighteen months hadn't deterred him one bit. Now that relationship had broken up, he felt it was only a matter of time before she succumbed to his charms. The only reason she hadn't yet was because she was playing hard to get. He eyed her seductively. 'Just bothered you could end up hurting yourself, doll, that's all. That's the kind of man I am, see, naturally considerate.'

She eyed him darkly. 'If you were that considerate you'd have offered to climb through the window yourself. And how many times have I told you not to call me "doll"? Now give me a leg up, and just hope I don't happen to kick you in the face by accident.'

He moved closer to the wall then cupped his hands together and bent over, hiding a smirk, as usual misinterpreting her behaviour towards him as tacit encouragement.

As she put her hands on his shoulders and her right foot into his cupped hands, something struck Jackie. She looked Terry in the eye and spoke warningly. 'If I catch you looking up my skirt, Helen won't be the only Stripey needing Sister Stephens' medical assistance.'

With a strenuous heave from Terry, Jackie was able to grab the metal frame of the window. He kept pushing her up and she managed to slide the top half of her body through the open window. She was glad to see a sink below her, one of a row of twelve fixed to the wall. Hopefully it would stand her weight when she manoeuvred her legs down and stood on it before lowering herself to the ground.

Jackie then scanned her eyes around the interior of the shower block. She could hear the woman crying but couldn't at first see her. Finally she spotted her by the door, sitting hunched on the floor with her back to it, forehead resting on her knees, so consumed by her own misery she didn't know she was being watched.

Easing one leg through the window, Jackie twisted herself around to bring the other through with it, then slowly began to lower herself down. The first she knew that her skirt had caught on the window catch was when she heard a loud tearing noise as her feet reached the sink. She fumed inwardly, annoyed with herself for not having the foresight to check that her clothing wasn't caught on the protruding metal catch. The blue, green and yellow plaid mini-skirt she was wearing was one of her favourites and hadn't been cheap. Hopefully the rip was on a seam and could be repaired. She was relieved, though, that the sink showed no sign of giving way beneath her. Climbing down on to the white-tiled floor, she made her way over to the crying woman and squatted down before her. In a soft voice Jackie said, 'Hello . . .'

She got no further as the woman gave out a terrified yelp, screaming, 'Who the hell are you? Where did you come from?'

In her own shock at this unexpected outburst Jackie toppled backwards, landing on her back, legs flying into the air. She lay dazed for a moment before gathering her wits and scrambling back up on her knees, thankful no men were present and getting an eyeful of her knickers.

'I'm sorry I surprised you like this, but as you won't let anyone through the door, I had to climb through the window. My name is Jackie, I work for management in the office. You're obviously upset, think one of our Stripeys has done something . . .'

The other woman hysterically interjected, 'I don't think – I know. She stole my husband. I know I shouldn't put all the blame on her. It takes two to tango, doesn't it? They're planning to run off together, I know they are.'

'But why would you think that?'

'I saw them together, and the way they were acting it was obvious they were plotting something. We women know when our husbands are up to something, and soon after we got here last Saturday mine kept disappearing: telling me he was popping to the shop for cigarettes when he'd a full packet in his pocket; going to the toilet again when he'd not long been; off to check the entertainment board to see what's on when we've a pamphlet in the chalet. Each time I offered to go with him he'd make an excuse for me not to. What woman wouldn't get suspicious when her husband was acting like that?

'When he made an excuse to go out without me this morning, I decided to follow him. He met up with that woman behind the shops. She was waiting for him when he arrived. I watched them talk for a bit and she was showing Clive something, I couldn't see what it was but he studied it for a moment then pointed at something and she nodded. It must have been a bus timetable – they were probably agreeing what time to meet at the stop to go off together. As he left her Clive looked really happy with himself. She looked pleased too. I shot back to the chalet. When he came in he was empty-handed so I asked him where he'd been as he hadn't got his cigarettes, and he made some lame excuse about there being a queue at the shop. Said he didn't want to wait so would go again later.'

She heaved a miserable sigh and wiped the back of her hand under her running nose. 'I'm not usually the violent sort, but you see Clive and me haven't been getting on that well for some time now. We're both desperate for a family. Been trying for a baby for the past five years. Nothing has happened and it's caused a strain between us. It doesn't help that both our families are constantly nagging at us to give them grandchildren. I've been really down just lately because the doctor told me that the reason I wasn't conceiving could be due to the fact I'm overweight and I should try losing some. I have tried really hard but the weight won't come off.

'It was Clive's idea for us to come here on holiday. He said away from it all, having ourselves some fun, it just might happen. It's happened for him all right, hasn't it? He's met someone else who's more than likely able to give him the family he wants when I obviously can't. So that's why this morning, when he came back from having supposedly gone to the shop and lied about it when questioned, I just saw red. What made it worse is that it's my birthday today and Clive hasn't even mentioned it. No card, nothing.

'I've never punched anyone before but I gave him a smacker in the face then went off in search of his floozy and did the same to her. Trouble is, I feel so ashamed of myself now for lashing out like a fishwife . . . I know people saw me, and they must be thinking all sorts about me and now I daren't show myself. That's why I locked myself in here, because I'm too embarrassed to go out and face them all. I just want to get away from here . . . as far away from Clive as I can. I wish I could hate him for what he's done to me. He's not just broken my heart, he's smashed my life to smithereens. He's the only man I've ever loved, or could ever see myself loving.'

She wrung her hands in distress. 'I can't blame him for falling for that other woman. She's pretty and slim whereas I'm plain and plump.' Through red-rimmed, swollen eyes, she looked pleadingly at Jackie. 'I can't bear to hear Clive tell me he doesn't love me any more so I can't go back to the chalet in case he's there. Could you arrange for someone to pack my stuff up for me, and for me to get to the station so I can catch a train home? Tell Clive that I'll have all his stuff packed up and he can collect it from his mother's so he can start his new life with . . .'

A fresh flood of tears stopped her from saying any more.

Jackie's heart went out to her. She knew at first hand just how wretched and betrayed this woman was feeling, having suffered the very same fate herself. The difference was, though, that her mother and Keith had fallen for each other over time but fought their feelings, conscious of the pain it was going to cause Jackie when it came out. Whereas this woman's husband appeared willing to devastate his wife and throw away his marriage for a woman he'd known barely more than five minutes. He should be ashamed of himself.

Jackie was surprised though that the other woman was Helen. She didn't know the young woman well, but Helen had always come across as a straightforward sort of person. She didn't seem the type to run after a married man, and fraternising with holidaymakers was a sackable offence. This incident would mean she would not receive a favourable reference so it was going to prove very hard for her to secure another job in the holiday industry. And more puzzling still was the fact that Jackie was sure a miffed Ginger had told her only the other week that the barman she had fancied for a while was off her list of possible boyfriends now as she'd found out he was courting strong with a Stripey called Helen, and there was a rumour of a possible engagement. It seemed that this woman's heart was not the only one that would be broken today, but Helen's boyfriend's too when he found out about her and Clive.

'Come with me to the office and I'll make the arrangements for you,' Jackie suggested.

The woman looked horrified. 'Oh, but that would mean going outside and facing all those people, and I just can't. Please don't make me! You came through the window. Can't we leave that way?'

Jackie's mind raced. She'd only just managed to squeeze through the narrow gap. This woman had already been made very upset by a thoughtless doctor telling her she was too fat to conceive. Mentioning her size was not an option. Jackie just couldn't bring herself to do it, so made an excuse by telling her, 'I don't advise we leave that way. There's a long drop from the window to the ground, and we'd more than likely both end up in hospital with broken bones. I could ask Terry Jones for his jacket to put over your head and that way you won't have to face anyone?'

The woman thought about this for a moment before she said, 'Yeah, that sounds okay.'

Getting her to move away from the door so she could remove the wedge to open it, after telling her she wouldn't be a moment, Jackie went outside.

Terry immediately pounced on her. 'Where is she then? Couldn't you talk her out? Only there really is going to be trouble if this shower block remains out of use for much longer.'

Jackie glanced at the snaking queue of disgruntled

people waiting to use the facilities. She was about to tell Terry what had transpired and get him to hand over his jacket when she was stopped by a worried-looking man who barged his way towards them through the crowd. He was sporting a black eye and a bloodied, cut lip.

'I've heard a woman has locked herself in the shower block and is really upset. I can't find my wife Colleen anywhere and I'm worried it's her. Is it?'

Clive appeared to be a decent man, and genuinely concerned for his wife, but knowing what she did Jackie couldn't stop herself from hissing at him, 'It's a bit late to be worried about your wife, isn't it? After what you've done to her. She doesn't want to see you and I can't say as I blame her. I hope breaking up your marriage for a woman you hardly know is worth it. And I shan't hold back from letting Helen know what I think of her when I sack her, which will be immediately after I've sorted out your devastated wife. Now, if you've got any compassion for her at all, you'll make yourself scarce while I get her out of here and make the arrangements for her to return home. I'd go and pack if I were you because as soon as Helen has been spoken to, I want you both off the camp.' Jackie hadn't the authority to order him off the camp or to sack Helen, but she soon would if Harold Rose ran true to form and handed her over responsibility. For once Jackie would willingly accept it.

Clive was looking utterly bewildered. 'Look, I really don't know what you're talking about. What's this about breaking up my marriage for some woman I hardly know. And what's Helen . . . I presume you mean Helen the Stripey . . . got to do with this?'

Jackie tutted disdainfully. 'Please don't try and act the innocent with me, Mr . . . Your wife told me that you've been constantly disappearing, telling her you're going to the shops and all other manner of excuse to avoid taking her with you, just so you can meet Helen and make plans to run away together. Don't try and deny it because she followed you this morning and saw you both looking at a bus or rail timetable.'

He exclaimed, 'What!' Then he eyed Jackie imploringly. 'Look, I admit I have been sneaking out to meet Helen, but not for the reason my wife thinks. Colleen's been so down lately. We've been trying for a baby for the last five years and nothing has happened. She feels it's all her fault, thanks to her thoughtless doctor telling her the reason could be that she's overweight. She's not overweight, she's cuddly. After what the doctor said, though, she got it into her head she wasn't attractive to me any more and that I'd want to find myself someone else who was and wouldn't have any problems giving me children. Whatever Colleen was, fat or thin, I would still love her with all my heart. She means everything to me. If we never have children, we just don't, because I wouldn't want them with anyone else but her.'

Clive heaved a sigh. 'I thought bringing her away, 'specially somewhere like this with loads to do, would cheer her up, help take her mind off things. I was aware that while we were away it would be her birthday and wanted to do something special for her. As soon as we arrived I made an excuse to go to the shop for some cigarettes while Colleen was unpacking, but what I was really doing was looking for a Stripey who would give me some ideas for a nice surprise for my wife and help me arrange it. Helen was the first Stripey I came across and I couldn't have wished to find a more helpful person . . . she's been marvellous. She's booked a meal for us tonight at a top-notch restaurant in Skegness, and they're going to bring a birthday cake out to Colleen when we've finished our main course. Helen's arranged for a taxi to take us there and back, and what Colleen saw us looking at today was a list from the local florist for me to choose a bouquet to be delivered later this afternoon. That's the truth, honest. I thought I was being clever, covering my tracks. I never thought for a minute Colleen would become suspicious, follow me and reach the conclusion she has.'

Jackie was feeling mortified. Clive had left her in no doubt whatsoever that he was telling the truth. When she had first started to work with Rhonnie and Drina, a young and naive girl, she'd often made snap judgments, mostly to find she'd been totally wrong. They had both told her that there were always two sides to a story, and it was dangerous to jump to conclusions until she had heard both of them. Pity she hadn't remembered their words of wisdom today and taken the trouble to ask Clive for his version before she had judged him a philandering husband, and Helen a harlot. Jackie promised herself not to make that mistake ever again.

Shame-faced, she said to him, 'I apologise for speaking to you like I did. I shouldn't have judged you before I'd heard your side of the story. It's a shame after all the trouble you've obviously gone to, but in the circumstances you've no alternative but to tell your wife what you've been up to: that you're not planning to leave her but organising a special surprise for her. I'm sure it'll still be a wonderful evening even if it's not exactly a surprise any longer.'

He gave her a wan smile. 'I hope so. It's costing a fortune. But as long as it shows Colleen how much she means to me then it'll be worth every penny. I won't be planning any more surprises in a hurry, that's for sure.' He glanced at the queue of disgruntled people waiting to use the facilities before adding, 'I'll get Colleen out as quickly as I can.'

Jackie smiled. 'We'd appreciate that.'

As he disappeared inside the shower block, she said to Terry, 'Well, thankfully that's turned out all right. I need to get back to the office. Will you tell the crowd the show's over, and the people waiting to use the showers that they shouldn't have to wait much longer.'

As she started to walk away, Terry called after her, 'Nice choice in knickers, Jackie. Does your bra match?'

Her temper rose. So he had looked up her skirt when she was climbing through the window, despite her warning him not to. That man was beneath contempt. She wouldn't give him the satisfaction of telling him exactly what she thought of him, though. Instead she pretended she hadn't heard him and marched purposefully back to the office, ignoring the fact that people were staring after her open-mouthed once she had passed them by.

She arrived back to be handed a wad of telephone messages, several needing her immediate attention. Still feeling mortified for the way she had ticked off Clive before she had heard the explanation for his behaviour and embarrassed by Terry's remark, Jackie uncharacteristically snapped at Al. 'These will have to wait until I've spoken to Mr Rose about hiring another nurse to replace Sister Pendle.'

Al told her, 'He's gone out for the rest of the day.'

'Oh, where?'

He shrugged. 'He didn't say.'

Jackie inwardly fumed. Neither Drina nor Rhonnie would ever go off during office hours without saying where they could be reached in case of emergency. What was the man playing at, going off without a word, leaving her in sole charge of the camp – something she was neither fully equipped nor remunerated well enough to do. She sincerely hoped nothing else came up today. She'd had enough crisis-solving. She spun on her heel and began striding over to her desk to get stuck into her work, but was stopped by Al calling out, 'Er . . . Jackie?'

She spun back and snapped at him, 'What now, Al? You do know how busy I am so I hope this is important?' She immediately felt remorseful for taking her mood out on him, but that was quickly dispelled when he muttered, 'Er . . . it was nothing.' She shot him a withering look before she went back to her work.

Later that evening Jackie sat hunched on her bed, confessing everything to Ginger who was lounging on the bed opposite. Her tone remorseful she said, 'I feel awful for tearing a strip off that poor chap like I did, when all he was guilty of was trying to organise a nice surprise for his wife.'

Ginger gave a yawn and stretched her arms. 'Don't be too hard on yourself, gel. It's understandable you'd react like you did, considering what you're going through yourself.'

Jackie heaved a sigh. 'It's not right to let my private life affect my work. I did apologise to him. Anyway, hopefully they're both in Skeggy now, enjoying a nice meal together. Helen suffered no more than a black eye and I told her to take a couple of days off until the swelling goes down. The bruising can be disguised with make-up. Terry isn't happy about having to do without her, but he can lump it.'

'Did you tell Helen you branded her a marriage-breaker?'

'No. I've made enough people think badly of me today without adding her to the list.'

'Apart from the woman's husband, who else have you upset then?'

'I snapped at Al, took my mood out on him when he was only trying to tell me something. Then he decided not to, which only made me more cross with him, and I was curt for the rest of the afternoon. I know he was glad when home time came and he could make his escape. I'll apologise to him first thing in the morning. That's if he decides to come in. After all he's only a temp'

Ginger assured her, 'Al's not going to give up a job he enjoys just because you were off with him this afternoon.' She secretly hoped he didn't ask the agency to reassign him as she was still hopeful that he would ask her out one day. 'You didn't join us in the restaurant for dinner this evening so I take it you haven't eaten?'

'I had to work late today again doing some jobs that couldn't wait. Most of the work was what Harold Rose should have been dealing with. He went home early today without even affording me the courtesy of telling me. Anyway, I'm not hungry.'

Ginger looked at her knowingly. 'And your lack of appetite has nothing to do with your day today. It's to do with your mother and Keith, isn't it?'

Tears of misery glinted in Jackie's eyes. 'I feel so mixed up, Ginger. I miss my mother dreadfully. Normally she would have been the one I would have turned to, to help me through something like this. But I can't, can I? Because she's the problem, isn't she? I can't seem to accept the fact that she's chosen Keith above me. I hate her yet at the same time I love her. I miss him so much too. I was going to write a letter to my mother, but I can't tell her that she deserves happiness at my expense . . . even though I do want her to be happy. Oh, I'm hurting so much.' Jackie rubbed her hands wearily over her face. 'God, this is just unbearable. If Harold Rose did the job he was supposed to then I wouldn't have walked in on them like I did.'

Ginger had to stop herself from giving the stock response all women told their friends at times like these: that there were plenty more fish in the sea. At this moment all the other fish were of no interest to Jackie, just the one who was now lost to her. So Ginger made the other stock response instead: 'Time's a great healer, Jackie.'

'So they say. Pity someone hasn't invented a forgetting pill you could take to wipe certain memories out. They'd make a fortune, wouldn't they?'

Ginger chuckled. 'I'd be a good customer, that's for sure.' Then she looked at Jackie enquiringly. 'Look, I know you're going to say you're not ready, but it would do you the world of good to go out and have a drink and a dance in Groovy's for a couple of hours. Take your mind off things. You haven't seen the new resident group yet, have you? They started last week and I've seen them three times now and they're ever so good, as good as some of the groups in the charts to my mind. They played "I Can See for Miles" and "Little Red Rooster" the other night, and if I hadn't known better I'd have sworn it was the Who and the Stones.' There was a twinkle in Ginger's eyes when she added, 'The rhythm guitarist is worth writing home about, believe me.'

Jackie sighed. 'Maybe tomorrow night, Ginger, but tonight I haven't even got the energy to get myself dressed and walk across to Groovy's, let alone have a dance. Just 'cos I'm a misery guts doesn't mean you have to stay in, though.'

Ginger, as always, was in the mood for having some fun but wouldn't at the expense of leaving her friend on her own at a time when she needed support. 'I'm not really in the mood either. We'll have a girly night in then. I've a Miner's face pack I've been meaning to try so we'll put that on and make ourselves beautiful, then we'll set the world to rights. And I've a bottle of cider in my bag. How does that sound to you?'

All Jackie wanted to do was crawl into bed and hope sleep would release her for a while from her heartache. But Ginger was trying to cheer her up and Jackie hadn't the heart to deny her that. 'It sounds great, Ginger. I'll go and have a shower first.' She inched herself off the bed, then collected her shower bag and dressing gown.

As Jackie made for the door, Ginger received a view of her back. Her eyes widened, jaw dropped in shock, then she burst into hysterical laughter.

Confused as to what she could possibly have found so funny, Jackie spun round to face her.

Through her fit of mirth Ginger managed to splutter, 'It wasn't only Terry you gave an eyeful of your knickers to today, Jackie. Al and the rest of the campers you passed on your way back from the shower block must have seen them too.'

She gawped in confusion. 'What are you going on about?'

'Your skirt. You've a rip in the back big enough to drive a bus through.'

'What!' Jackie exclaimed, mortified, trying to swivel the top half of her body around. She couldn't so she felt for the hole with her hand. She found a large L-shaped tear, the torn material flapping. She didn't need to see it to know that the hole was exposing part of her bottom and the top of her legs. 'How did that . . . Oh!' she mouthed as memory returned. 'I caught my skirt on the window frame as I climbed through and then I just forgot about it.' Her face glowing red with embarrassment, she exclaimed in horror, 'Oh, God, that was what Al was going to tell me before I snapped at him. He obviously decided my mood was bad enough without telling me about it. And I wrongly accused Terry of looking up my skirt . . . thankfully not to his face, but I still thought the worst of him when he made his comment. And after that all those campers saw me too . . .' She gave a loud groan. 'My life's going from bad to worse. I don't know how I'm going to face everyone tomorrow.'

Ginger was laughing so hard tears were spurting from her eyes. 'Oh, it could have been much worse, gel. You just be thankful you never ripped your knickers too, or you'd have been showing off your bare bum to the world!'

Jackie supposed Ginger was right and she should be grateful for small mercies. Ginger's laughter then began to become too infectious for Jackie to ignore and, despite her low spirits and the acute embarrassment she was feeling, she started to laugh along with her friend.

The good laugh did wonders to lift Jackie's mood. After they had both managed to control themselves, the rest of the evening passed very pleasantly and Jackie snuggled down into bed that night grateful that she had such a good friend in Ginger, who was helping her through a difficult time.

CHAPTER FIFTEEN

The next morning just after eight-thirty Jackie was updating Mr Rose on matters that he needed to deal with, though whether he would accept the responsibilities he was supposed to remained to be seen. The interview hadn't got off to a good start as far as Jackie was concerned as Harold Rose had not attempted to explain to her why he'd left early yesterday.

As usual he was looking mortally uncomfortable and everywhere but at Jackie as, in a stuttering voice, he said to her, 'Well . . . er . . . in respect of the charity organisation asking for us to donate however many chalets we can spare for a week in August to give orphans a holiday . . . I do know that Mrs Jolly is in favour of that sort of thing if we're in the position to help. Since you know what availability we have in August you'll be the best person to confer with the charity and sort it out. As to the dinner and dance at the Skegness Town Hall for the Mayor's fund-raiser, you say I need to attend as Mrs Jolly's representative . . . well, you see, I can't, I'm afraid. I already have an important occasion myself for that date which I can't get out of so why . . . er . . . don't you attend instead, take your boyfriend? You'll have a very good time, I'm sure. Regarding the hiring of a nurse – I suggest you place an advertisement in the local newspapers. Between yourself and Sister Stephens you'll find a suitable replacement for Sister Pendle. Now, if that's all, Miss Sims, I must get on.'

Jackie inwardly fumed. As usual Harold Rose had managed to offload all the work on to others, mainly herself. She appreciated that he'd a busy job handling the large amounts of money that came into the camp weekly via fees and till receipts from the bars and shops, plus sums going out again to pay suppliers and other bills, but they were experiencing a time of crisis when all the staff needed to pull together. Everyone else was doing their bit, some more so than others, particularly Jackie herself, yet for whatever reason Harold Rose didn't seem to understand that his role involved him doing more than swapping one desk for another. It really wasn't fair of him to pretend to Drina he was doing an exemplary job of covering for her when he updated her via her telephone calls.

Jackie made to leave the office when something struck her. Mr Rose had just told her he was already engaged on the date of the dinner and dance, but how could he know that when she hadn't actually told him which date it was being held on?

Suddenly her weeks of being unfairly put upon by this man became too much for Jackie. Before she could stop herself she blurted out, 'No, Mr Rose, that is not all. Mrs Jolly put *you* in charge, not *me*. You walked out early yesterday without affording me the courtesy of telling me you were leaving for the day, and left me alone to deal with everything. I'm sick and tired of doing work that *you* should be taking on. I certainly don't have the authority or the knowhow to hire a nurse or deal with a charity organisation. I'm already trying to cover two people's work, my own and Rhonnie's, and most nights I have to work late. By the time I do finish I'm too tired to go out so I've no social life. And it's *your* fault I lost my boyfriend. While I was having to work late, he found someone else.'

At the memory of that, her anger turned to misery and she burst into tears.

Harold Rose was staring at her blankly.

Through her sobs it suddenly struck Jackie that no matter what she felt about this man, he was after all her boss and had every right to sack her for her outburst. That would leave her with no job and nowhere to live either. Oh, why hadn't she checked herself before she had opened her mouth? She started to talk again but this time there was no anger in her voice, only remorse. 'Mr Rose, I'm so sorry. I shouldn't have spoken to you like I did. Please don't sack . . .'

To her utter surprise he shot out of his chair and dashed over to her. He gently took her arm and led her to the chair before the desk, pressing her to sit down. Once she was seated he took a clean, neatly folded handkerchief from out of his jacket pocket and handed it to her, saying, 'It's I who should be apologising to you, Miss Sims. I can't very well sack you for speaking the truth, can I?'

Opening the handkerchief, she wiped her wet eyes then looked up at him in bewilderment as he returned behind the desk, sank down in the leather chair, took off his horn-rimmed glasses and rubbed his hands over his face. His eyes were fixed on his desk when he spoke. 'I should have told you I was leaving yesterday,' he said remorsefully. 'Well, left a message with Mr Stanhope to give you when you returned. I do apologise, but in my defence I'd forgotten I had a dental appointment until the last minute and rushed out without telling anyone as I was too concerned about being late and annoying the dentist.' He heaved a deep sigh then before going on. 'I . . . I . . . can't imagine what you think of me, Miss Sims. Just what most people do, I should think, rude . . . obnoxious . . .'

That was what she thought of him but Jackie only said, 'I can't understand why you accepted the job if you'd no intention of doing it, Mr Rose?'

He heaved a heavy sigh. 'It wasn't that I had no intention of doing the job, Miss Sims. I'm . . . I'm . . . well, you see, I'm just not capable of doing it.' He paused for a moment, seeming to have difficulty finding the right words before he went on. 'Much of it involves dealing with people and that's where the trouble lies, you see, Miss Sims. I find it very difficult to be around others. Whenever I have to converse with anyone, I break out in a cold sweat and never know what to say. I'm so frightened of making an utter fool of myself. The only company I feel comfortable in is my own. I do envy people like you, Miss Sims, who don't seem to find it difficult at all dealing with anything life throws at them.'

He paused for a moment, and from the expression that crossed his face then Jackie got the impression he was experiencing pangs of deep regret that he'd been born with such a debilitating character trait. And after what he'd just told her, she also realised that it wasn't at all easy for him to open up to her about his problems. Taking a breath, he continued, 'When Mrs Jolly asked me to step into her shoes while she was away, I was terrified. I didn't sleep at all that night from worry. But it would only be for a couple of weeks at the most, Mrs Jolly told me, so I had no choice but to get on with it. She did assure me that you, Miss Sims, were very capable . . . there was nothing you didn't know about how the company was run . . . so I thought in that case I could leave you to get on with it. You seemed to be coping very well, which came as such a relief to me. It meant I wouldn't have to get involved. I never really gave a thought to what it was doing to you.'

Jackie felt guilty now for thinking Mr Rose a snob and a shirker when in fact he was neither, just painfully shy and very insecure. As the outgoing person she was, who'd never had any trouble expressing herself, she was finding it difficult to imagine what life was like for him. Very solitary, she had no doubt. Her curiosity about the man got the better of her then and she asked, 'Have you always been so shy or did something happen to make you like you are?'

He was still addressing the desk when he responded, 'Always have been. As a baby, I would only let my mother care for me. If she disappeared from my sight, I would scream blue murder until I had her back again. No one could hold me, do anything for me, except my mother. My father died just after I was born and my mother was very protective of me as her only child. Knowing how I was, she never exposed me to situations she knew I'd find uncomfortable.'

His face clouded over with hurt. 'She couldn't protect

me at school though. Those years were terrible for me. I was always the butt of the other kids' fun. They used to steal my tuck money, lock me in cupboards, leg me over, call me four eyes because I wore glasses . . . just continuously torment me, because they knew I was too cowardly to stand up to them The teachers knew I was being bullied, yet did nothing to stop it. In fact, to me they seemed to encourage it. They would purposely put me in situations that they knew terrified me witless, making me stand in front of the class and read out a long poem, that sort of thing, and I would stammer and stutter and on one occasion I was so anxious I wet myself. They said nothing to help when the rest of the class jeered and laughed at me. I couldn't tell my mother what was going on, because I knew how upset she'd be, and if she'd gone to the school to complain it would just have been worse for me. Mother was my only friend. She died last year and I miss her terribly.'

Of course he would; she'd have been the only person he felt truly comfortable with, Jackie realised. She did wonder if the teachers at school had in fact been trying to coax him out of his shell by putting him into situations that he found uncomfortable so as to accustom him to them. Maybe they did reprimand the class for their reaction, it was just that Harold didn't see it as he was so walled up in his own nervous world. Obviously his mother thought she was acting in her son's best interests, shielding him from situations she knew were torture to him, but to Jackie's mind she hadn't done him any favours by not encouraging him to face up to things, and help build his confidence. Had she done so he might not be quite so reserved as he was now.

A man for whom she'd felt nothing but contempt, she now felt mortally sorry for. If he wasn't helped to overcome his anxieties and build his confidence in himself just a little, Harold Rose was going to end up very lonely, as if he wasn't already. He obviously wasn't happy about this state of affairs or he wouldn't have told Jackie he envied outgoing people like herself. Her thoughts began to whirl. All Harold needed was a helping hand to encourage him to overcome his difficulties – and maybe she was just the person to do that. She would have to tread carefully, so she needed to put some thought into how she could help without worsening his difficulties and making him into a complete recluse. She felt the best way to proceed was by taking small steps. She had an idea how to make a start. Her need to help Harold overcome his shyness and build some self-confidence meant she had no choice but to break his confidence and let those she needed to recruit to aid her plan know why he was the unsociable, aloof individual he was, so that they would agree to help her make life better for him.

She realised he was talking to her again.

'You . . . er . . . said that I was responsible for you losing your boyfriend because of the way I am. If that's true, then all I can say is that I'm very sorry and I do hope you can still patch things up.'

His remorse was so genuine, she knew it wasn't fair of her to let him continue believing he was entirely responsible for her break-up with Keith, when he wasn't.

Meanwhile it had suddenly hit Harold that he had opened up to a stranger, something he had never done before. Although it had proved a relief finally to explain to someone that he couldn't help the way he was, at the same time he was squirming with embarrassment, worrying that if the young woman had had any morsel of respect for him before she had entered the office, she would have absolutely none left for him now.

So before Jackie could put him right about his contribution to her break-up, addressing a spot on the wall over her shoulder he brusquely said, 'I really am busy, and I expect you are too, Miss Sims.'

She was, and also desperate to make a start on putting her plan into action to help this man to lead a better life.

It was an exhausted Jackie who made her way back to her chalet at just after six that evening, intending to freshen herself up and once Ginger had done likewise they could walk across to the restaurant together to join the other girls for the evening meal. Jackie's appetite was still very poor but she was aware, from Ginger constantly telling her, that if she didn't eat she'd be ill. Personally she couldn't care less, feeling as low as she did, but if she was incapacitated for any length of time, there wasn't anyone else who could take over her responsibilities, and that would in turn affect the running of the camp and mean letting Mrs Jolly down, so regardless Jackie would have to try and force some food down her.

Arriving at her chalet, she opened the door and got the shock of her life to find not Ginger waiting for her but her own mother, sitting on Jackie's bed looking anxiously over at her.

Through her turmoil – a mixture of delight to see Gina again conflicting with feelings of hurt and anger at her betrayal – it struck Jackie forcefully just how dreadful her usually well-groomed mother looked. Her clothes were rumpled, hair unbrushed, eyes red-rimmed and puffy from crying.

At the sight of her, Gina said tentatively, 'Hello, love. You've a good friend in Ginger, she's very loyal to you. She didn't want to let me in to wait for you, but I managed to persuade her so please don't be cross with her. She's gone over to the restaurant to give us some privacy.'

Jackie responded sharply, 'Yes, Ginger does know the meaning of loyalty. Unlike you, Mother. I don't know how I'd be getting through this if it wasn't for her. Your journey here has been wasted, I'm not ready to talk . . .'

Gina jumped up and pleaded with her, 'Jackie, please don't throw me out! I know I deserve it but please listen to what I have to say. Please, love, please?'

She vehemently shook her head and harshly cried, 'You surely can't expect me just to accept that you and Keith are now together, and play a daughterly part in your happy little family? I love you, Mum, I miss you so much and want to forgive you, believe me I do, but you have to understand how hurt and betrayed I feel. I'll need time to get over this. At this moment I can't promise you I ever will. Now please just go and get on with your life with Keith, and leave me to try and get on with mine.'

'But that's what I've come to tell you, love. Keith and I are not together. It's over between us.'

Fury filled Jackie. 'It's over? You mean, this was all just a fling and you broke my heart for nothing!'

'Oh, Jackie, you're my daughter and the thought of

losing you . . . well, I can't bear it. If it's you or Keith, for me there is no contest. I've come to tell you that I've sent him away. If you could just visit me, or maybe even one day come home . . . Your brother misses you too. If you can't bear to see me just yet, please consider coming to see him. I told him the truth about why you've gone away and understandably he hates me at the moment, won't even talk to me. It's all so awful and I've only myself to blame. Anyway, that's all I wanted to say.'

In the midst of her own heartache, it was causing Jackie intolerable distress to witness her mother in so much pain, having to choose between two people she obviously cared for deeply. She asked, 'Do you and Keith really love each other, Mum, enough to tolerate the gossip and backlash about how you got together and the age difference between you both?'

Gina responded with conviction, 'That doesn't matter, love. All that matters is trying to repair the damage my stupidity has caused.'

'It does matter to me, Mum. Please answer my question?'

Gina hung her head, gave a deep sigh and said softly, 'Yes. You know how much I loved your father. I never believed I could meet another man who made me feel like he did, but Keith does. I'm not a stupid woman, blinded by a man's attention after not having any for so long. Keith has left me in no doubt that he loves me. He did care for you very deeply and was devastated . . .' She paused as tears filled her eyes. 'Please don't make me go on, love. Hearing this is only adding salt to your wounds.'

Jackie told her with conviction then, 'I want you to go on, Mum.'

She looked at her daughter for a moment, fiddling with the button on her crumpled cardigan, before she gave a resigned sigh and continued, 'Well, as I was saying, Keith was devastated by the way you found out about us. I don't suppose any way would have been less painful for you, but at least if we'd sat you down and explained properly, it might have prevented you from judging us so harshly. Anyway, when I ended it between us, he . . . well, I can't explain it any better than to say he was a broken man. He said he can't bear staying around here, possibly seeing you and knowing how much hurt he's caused you, and possibly seeing me and knowing what he's lost, so he's going away. He might have already gone for all I know.'

Silently Jackie turned and stepped over to the window, pulling aside the floral curtains to look outside at the comings and goings of the staff. A few minutes went by before she turned back to face her mother, saying, 'Hopefully Keith hasn't gone yet and you can stop him. If he has, find out where he's gone and get him back.'

Gina's face was screwed up in bewilderment. 'Pardon?'

'If you love each other that much, Mum, then I'm not going to stand in your way.'

Astonished at this unexpected development, Gina sank back down on the bed. 'You're giving our relationship your blessing?'

Jackie went over and sat down beside her. 'I suppose I am. There are three desperately unhappy people at the moment, when two needn't be. Despite what's happened, I do love you, Mum, and just want you to be happy.

That's all I've ever wanted for you. If that can only be with Keith, then so be it.'

Gina stared at her, stunned, for several long moments before she uttered, 'You really mean that?'

She nodded.

'But what about me and you?'

Jackie sighed. 'You'll have to give me time, Mum. I can't see you and Keith together, not right now, not for a long time, I just can't. You'll understand that I won't ever come back home to live in these circumstances, but maybe in the future I'll be able to come and visit. I'm thinking of getting a flat with Ginger so I'll be fine. I'm nearly twenty-two, it's about time I learned to stand on my own two feet. I need to get over this and start to rebuild my life.'

Gina's eyes filled with tears. 'Oh, love, I . . .'

'Don't say any more, Mum. Just go and get Keith back and be happy together. I'll meet Robby out of work one night and talk to him, tell him I'm okay with all this, and hopefully things will get better between you.'

This was far more than Gina had hoped for. Mother and daughter had always been very demonstrative towards each other. She desperately wanted to hug Jackie now in an effort to take some of her pain away, but knew that wouldn't be the right thing to do at this moment. Instead she patted her daughter's hand, fully expecting it to be pulled away and mortally grateful when it wasn't.

Before she departed, Gina asked, 'Can I at least write to you, love? And if you feel like it you could write to me . . . just a few lines, to let me know how you are.'

Jackie nodded.

Ginger arrived back at the chalet a while later, carrying

a covered plate of food, to find Jackie sitting on her bed looking very pensive. She had obviously been crying.

Ginger jumped to the conclusion that the meeting between mother and daughter had not gone well. Putting the food down on the small chest by the door, she dashed over to the bed and sat down by her friend. 'Oh, Jackie, I'm so sorry I agreed to let your mum wait for you in the chalet. I thought I was doing the right thing as she was desperate to talk to you and . . .'

Jackie quickly assured her, 'It's fine, Ginger, really. It was just very emotional.' She then told her friend what had transpired.

When she had finished Ginger was staring at her in amazement. 'All I can say is that you must love your mum very much to do what you have. I suppose I'm envious as I've not got such a close relationship with mine. Now . . .'

Jackie cut in, 'I hope you're not going to suggest us going out on the razz tonight?'

'Well, actually, I was going to say you need to get some food down you as you weren't in the restaurant at dinner-time, and you only picked at your food at breakfast so I know you've not eaten anything substantial today. I got one of the waitresses to make you up a plate.'

Despite her low spirits Jackie smiled. Though she had no appetite she said to appease Ginger, 'Give me the plate and I'll eat what I can. Thank you for getting it for me.'

The piece of battered fish, chips and peas was by now only lukewarm and didn't look very inviting when Jackie took the cover off and saw it, but the smell wafting up seemed to trigger hunger pangs and before she knew it she had cleared the plate.

Having succeeded in her mission to get her friend to eat, Ginger decided she'd nothing to lose by having another try at getting Jackie to go out. As she took the empty plate from Jackie she said casually, 'I was thinking of going to Groovy's for an hour. It's one of the chalet maids' birthday and I said I might pop in for a drink. It's only the DJ on tonight but it'll still be good down there. I suppose the last thing you feel like is a night out, but I'm sure it would do you more good than moping around here, so give it some thought.'

Jackie did. It *was* the last thing she felt like doing, but Ginger had made a good point. When this had first happened to her, she had vowed she wouldn't mope – and that's exactly what she had done. She surprised her friend by telling her, 'Well, if you're just going for an hour, I think I could manage that.'

Ginger grinned. 'Well, we'd best get ready then.'

As it was, Jackie's intended hour out turned into four. At first it seemed strange to her, going out socially without Keith by her side, but she soon became caught up in the company of her friends and the music the chatty, long-haired, flamboyantly dressed DJ was choosing. He played the latest hits by the Beatles, Stones, Yardbirds, Cream, and plenty of Tamla Motown, which was her favourite sort of music at the moment, in particular the Four Tops, Smokey Robinson and the Miracles, and the Temptations. To her own surprise she even agreed to join the girls dancing on the packed floor, although she did decline several offers of dances from male holidaymakers she'd caught the eye of, far from ready to take that leap yet.

Her determination to enjoy herself faded only once when she had to slip off to the cloakroom to shed a quiet tear while the DJ played Elton John's 'Your Song', which had been the last record she had danced to with Keith, on their last evening out together, before she had found out it wasn't actually her he wanted to hold in his arms. To her credit, she then quickly managed to control herself and rejoin her friends before anyone noticed her absence.

Jackie snuggled down into bed that night feeling proud of herself for making a start on rebuilding her future.

CHAPTER SIXTEEN

Mid-afternoon, two days later, beads of nervous sweat were forming on Harold Rose's brow as he stuttered, 'Er . . . well, er . . . can't it wait until Miss Sims returns? I'm very busy.'

Al responded, 'Chef Brown was very insistent he needed Jackie . . . er, Miss Sims . . .' he quickly corrected himself, feeling that he ought to refer to staff by their titles when in Mr Rose's company, the same as he was in the habit of doing '. . . to go across immediately, so I assume whatever he needs her for is urgent. I'd put the telephone down before I remembered that Miss Sims had only just left on the tour of the camp and won't be back for at least an hour.'

'And you can't oblige Chef Brown?' Harold hopefully asked.

'I can't leave the switchboard or the office unattended, Mr Rose.'

'Er . . . no, no, of course not.' It seemed to Harold he had no choice but to put himself into a situation that was repellent to him. Hopefully the matter was something trivial and he could manage to solve it without making an idiot of himself in front of Chef. Reluctantly he told Al, 'I'd best go and see what he wants that is so urgent.'

As Al returned to the general office, the beads of anxious sweat on Harold's brow turned into a stream. Taking a handkerchief out of his pocket he wiped them away, only for them to be replaced by a fresh stream. He took several deep breaths to quell a fit of shaking that had engulfed him at the prospect of what he was about to face.

How Harold loathed the way he was. Being painfully shy and so easily intimidated had robbed him of having any proper life for himself, doing everyday things that the majority of other people took for granted; in particular marriage and having a family of his own, something he would give his eye teeth for, though as matters stood it seemed as unobtainable to him as walking on the moon. He despaired of ever having the confidence to say hello to a woman he liked the look of, let alone ask her out. How he wished he could find a way to overcome this disability, but as there was no magic pill to cure him it seemed he was destined to spend the rest of his life living as a virtual hermit.

As he always did when he was out and about in public, Harold hurried along with his head bent so he didn't catch the eye of anyone and risk them stopping him for any reason and drawing him into conversation. It wasn't likely as the campers wouldn't have a clue who he was. Most of the staff didn't either.

Thankfully the kitchen staff and waitresses were all on their rest period before the evening session began so Harold had no one to contend with as he made his way into the kitchen in search of Chef Brown. He found the huge man, dressed in stained whites, taking a tray of cooked items out of a huge oven and putting it on a spotlessly clean metal table.

Spotting Harold's arrival Eric Brown boomed out, 'Ah, there you are, Mr Rose. You couldn't have timed it better.'

On learning of Harold Rose's situation when Jackie had approached him to help her execute the plan she had formed, Eric Brown had been very willing. His brother had suffered from shyness as a child until Eric and his other siblings had encouraged him out of it, so Chef knew at first hand what a terrible effect it could have on people's lives.

Harold was taken aback for a moment as Chef seemed to be expecting him not Jackie, then reasoned that Al must have telephoned to explain that he was coming.

As he busied himself taking dishes off the tray, Eric Brown was saying, 'I can't believe we've both worked here for years and never crossed paths before. Well, I suppose that's because we're both busy men. Now we have met, if you ever find yourself at a loose end, I'm here most afternoons taking advantage of an empty kitchen to try out new recipes or listing orders I need the office to put in for me, but I'll always find time for a cuppa and a natter.' With a cloth he picked up two of the dishes from the tray and placed them before Harold, who had now joined him by the work surface. Chef handed him a spoon telling him, 'Tuck in, and tell me which out of these two cottage pies you prefer?'

Harold fixed his gaze on the dishes Eric had put before him, hoping he was hiding the redness he knew was creeping up his neck and the anxiety that was gnawing away in his stomach. Nervously he blabbered, 'Well, Chef Brown . . .'

'Oh, Eric, please, we're not on duty now.'

'Well . . . er . . . Eric, I'm not really qualified, I'm no expert on food at all. You'd be better getting someone else.'

Eric cut in, 'You know what food you like to eat and what you don't, don't you?'

'Well . . . yes, of course.'

'Then you're qualified, so tuck in.'

Seeing he had no choice, and thinking the sooner he got this over with the sooner he'd make his escape, Harold tentatively put the spoon into the first dish.

'Well?' Eric urged him.

'Oh, er . . . well, it's delicious,' Harold ventured.

Chef looked pleased. 'Glad you think so. Now, what about the other?'

Hoping that Eric would not notice his hand shaking, Harold dipped his spoon into the other pie and tasted it. Then he told Eric, 'That was very nice too. Now if that's all . . .'

As he made to rush off, Eric grabbed his arm. 'Hang on, you haven't told me which one of the pies you prefer?'

Terrified he would insult Chef by getting it wrong, he stuttered, 'Oh, er . . . well they were both delicious but to my mind the first dish had an extra tastiness to it, which I liked better.'

Eric smiled, pleased with his comment. 'Good. That's my new improved version. So glad you liked it. Hopefully now the campers will.'

'Right, well, I'll leave you to it then.'

'Not so fast, Harold. I've five other dishes for you to give me your verdict on yet.'

Half an hour later, having given his opinion on the rest of Chef's dishes, Harold really was desperate to make his escape. 'If that's all, I'd best be off.'

'But I was just about to make a cuppa . . .'

By now Harold's anxiety was reaching fever pitch, his heart hammering so erratically he was worried he was about to have a seizure. 'No, I really must get back to the office,' he insisted.

Eric looked disappointed. 'Oh, right. Well, thanks, Harold. I really value your opinion. Don't forget to drop . . .' His voice trailed off as his reluctant visitor was already halfway across the kitchen on his way out.

Back in the office, with the door firmly shut, Harold sat down in the chair behind the desk and took several deep breaths in an effort to calm his racing heart, mortally relieved that particular uncomfortable situation was over for him and vehemently hoping that Mrs Jolly's return was imminent. Tomorrow wouldn't be soon enough for Harold. With Drina back at the helm, he could return to his solitary job as accounts manager without further risk of ever again facing situations like this.

Then there was a tap on the door and his heart began to race again. Sweat poured down the sides of his face and from under his arms as terror took over. Thankfully, it was just Jackie with his afternoon tea.

As she put it down on the desk, she said to him, 'Your tea and biscuits, Mr Rose.'

It was as if their intimate conversation of a couple of days ago had never happened. Without looking at her, he responded dismissively, 'Thank you, Miss Sims.'

As she turned to go out of the office, Jackie smiled to herself. She should be feeling very ashamed for purposefully instigating a situation that had apparently caused Harold Rose a great deal of torment. She wasn't at all, though, just pleased that her mission to force him to face his fears and lead a more rewarding life was off to a flying start.

Harold wasn't going to be the only one to face a situation today that was difficult to deal with. Jackie was meeting her brother after work, which she was actually looking forward to as she missed Robby so much, but she didn't enjoy thinking about the lies she was going to have to tell him in order that his relationship with their mother could begin to mend.

At five-thirty she began tidying her desk and said to Al, 'I'm finishing on time tonight. What's not done will have to wait until tomorrow as I've an appointment in Mablethorpe. I can give you a lift there, if you like, so you've only one bus to catch to Skegness and not two?'

Al momentarily froze, seeking a plausible excuse. He didn't need to go to Mablethorpe as he didn't live there any longer. In his desperation not to be discovered it seemed he was going to have to accept the ride and just not get all the work he'd planned for tonight done. Just as he was about to, another idea came to him – one that wouldn't encroach on his time.

'Oh, thanks, Jackie, much appreciated, but I was thinking of going to Groovy's tonight. One of the staff I've arranged to go with has offered me a bed for the night, only a sleeping bag on his chalet floor but it means I'm not going home.' To avoid her quizzing him any further, he excused himself by telling her, 'Just nipping to the loo.'

* * *

At just after seven-thirty Jackie flopped down on her bed, letting out a deep sigh before she told Ginger, 'Well, my brother seemed to buy my story so hopefully he and mum will get on better from now on.'

Ginger closed the magazine she was thumbing through and asked, 'What did you tell him?'

'Oh, that it was I who broke off with Keith because he wasn't really for me. That I told Mum and Keith to get together as I thought they liked each other and were better suited than me and Keith, despite the few years' difference between them. And that I'd left home because it made sense while I was putting in all the extra work while Drina and Rhonnie were away.'

'Did you ask him how your mum and Keith were getting on?'

Jackie shook her head. 'No. I still find it difficult to think of them together at the moment, so I don't think of them at all, if you understand me.'

'You will, though, one day, and it won't be painful then,' Ginger reassured her.

Jackie wanted to get off this still very hurtful subject and told her, 'Oh, I've some news for you.'

Her friend said dryly, 'Good, I hope?'

Jackie smiled. 'I know you'll think it is. Al is going to Groovy's tonight.'

Ginger's eyes lit up. 'He is?'

Jackie nodded.

Then her friend's face fell. 'Not with a girl?'

'Well, whoever he's going with, he's kipping on their floor tonight so I assume not.'

Ginger jumped off the bed. 'What are you waiting for? Get ready! We're going out tonight and no excuses from you. I'm not missing this opportunity to try and get a date with Al.'

As she joined Ginger to get ready, Jackie sincerely hoped her friend would get her wish. Ginger was not lucky in love. Any man who took her fancy either didn't seem to notice her or only dated her for a very short while before he was off with someone else. Jackie suspected that that was because Ginger wasn't conventionally pretty, with her mass of unruly corkscrew-curly hair, pale skin covered in freckles and gawky frame. It annoyed Jackie that these men didn't seem to have the brains to look past these unconventional looks and see what a funny, kind, caring and fiercely loyal person Ginger was. They'd be lucky to have her. Jackie had no doubt, though, that there was a man out there who would see Ginger for her true worth one day. It was just that he hadn't arrived in her friend's life yet. Whether Al was that man, as Ginger seemed to be hoping he was, Jackie wasn't sure. Good-looking though he was, Al hadn't seemed to show any interest in the girls around the camp as far as Jackie was aware, despite quite a few making it very plain they had a fancy for him. Maybe he wasn't interested because he had a girlfriend back in Skegness, although he'd never mentioned the fact. Well, hopefully tonight would show whether Al did return Ginger's feelings. If not, then at least her friend would be put out of her misery.

Groovy's was heaving as usual. The heat and noise hit them as soon as they entered by the door at the top of the stairs and began to make their way down to the basement club. Although Ginger had told her they were very good, Jackie had not yet heard the new resident group who called themselves the Upbeats. But from what she was hearing now of their interpretation of the Foundation's top ten hit 'Baby, Now That I've Found You', they were more than good, they were great.

Her eyes always on the look out for Al, Ginger led the way over to the bar. Joining the queue of others waiting to be served, she said, 'I can't see him, Jackie. He definitely told you he was coming here tonight? Only you thought that a few weeks ago and he never showed.'

'Well, this time I am positive. Al definitely did tell me he was coming here. It's like looking for a needle in a haystack through this lot. Just because you haven't spied him yet doesn't mean to say he isn't here. Once we've got our drinks we'll have a walk around to see if we can spot him.'

Armed with glasses of cider the girls did two circuits of the huge room. Back where they began, a very disappointed Ginger said, 'Well, unless he's in the gents, he's not here, is he?'

'Don't give up yet, it's only just after nine. Maybe he and the mate he's coming with have gone for a drink in one of the bars upstairs first before they come down here.'

Ginger's disappointment lifted. 'Oh, they might have, mightn't they?' The band then began to play the Equals hit 'Baby Come Back' and she exclaimed, 'Oh, I love this one, let's go and dance.'

Knocking back the remains of their drinks, they weaved their way through the gyrating dancers in search of a space on the crowded floor. It was Jackie who heard their names being called and turned and saw a couple of girls they knew, waving them over. Grabbing Ginger's arm, she pulled her along. They were both greeted enthusiastically. Putting their handbags on the pile of others in the middle of their circle, they began to dance.

It was apparent by their behaviour that the rest of the girls had already spotted a potential conquest and were each doing their best to attract attention with their seductive dancing. Ginger hadn't yet spotted who she was hoping to see. As she danced she continued to look around furtively in search of Al. Jackie was not interested in anything other than letting the music and lively atmosphere of the place take her mind off her recent trauma.

They had all danced non-stop for over an hour. By now two of the girls had managed to catch the eye of the men they had a fancy for and were dancing with them. Still not having spotted Al yet, Ginger had slipped off to patrol the room again in search of him. Jackie was not only beginning to flag but also feeling very hot and sticky. She decided she would slip outside for a few minutes to cool down. As she made her way through the tightly packed throng of other dancers she couldn't help but feel slightly inadequate. Some of them were still dancing energetically with no sign of flagging at all and they had been on the floor when she and Ginger first arrived. Jackie was only twenty-one but already age seemed to be having its effect on her.

Outside in the open air she took several deep breaths as she fanned her hot face with her hand. She made her way through crowds of milling holidaymakers to the fountain and perched her backside on the edge of it to watch them going about their evening's entertainment while she cooled down. Several holidaymakers recognised her and she returned their friendly waves and called out to them that she hoped they were enjoying themselves. A young couple perched nearby on the edge of the fountain were closely entwined, passionately kissing. Jackie chose to ignore them and all the other couples acting in any way affectionately towards each other as that was too upsetting to her. Instead she concentrated her attention on two young boys of around ten, darting around between the pedestrians, squirting water from pistols at each other, thinking they wouldn't be laughing if they misfired and hit one of the adult holidaymakers instead.

She didn't realise anyone had joined her until a voice cut into her thoughts, saying, 'Well, we can't have this, can we?'

Jackie turned her head to see a man of about her own age standing next to her, one of his long legs planted on the side of the fountain. He was looking down at her, leaving her in no doubt he liked what he was seeing. He was ruggedly good-looking with a wide square jaw. Fashionably dressed too in tight black trousers, black-and-white striped crew-necked jumper and a black waistcoat, with a black Bob Dylan-style hat covering the top of his long mop of wavy brown hair.

He seemed familiar to her and for a moment she studied him while she tried to place him. Then it came to her. 'Oh, you're one of the Upbeats. Bass guitarist, aren't you?'

He looked miffed. 'You don't seem very impressed. Usually girls are honoured to have me single them out.'

His egotistical response made Jackie's hackles rise and

she answered sharply, 'Well, I'm not your usual type of girl.'

He eyed her keenly. 'Oh, very intriguing. So what kind of girl are you, then?'

'One who's not easily impressed.'

He swung down his leg and perched next to her, saying, 'Even more intriguing. My name is Hats.'

She eyed him, taken aback. 'What on earth made your parents call you that?'

He smiled, showing his slightly crooked teeth. 'They didn't. It's Barry actually. But it's hardly cool to be in a band and called Barry. We've all got nicknames. Mine is Hats because I'm never seen out in public without one on. Gary's is Strings because he's always breaking his guitar strings and having to replace them. Vic's is Sticks as he's the drummer, and Steve the singer is Chips as he's always stuffing his face with them. So what's your name then?'

Jackie inwardly sighed. She didn't want this man's company, and in an effort to make him leave her in peace she answered shortly, 'Just plain old Jackie.'

Her manner seemed to have no effect on him. He asked, 'So, Jax, how long are you here on holiday?'

She didn't appreciate him taking it upon himself to shorten her name and her response was abrupt once more. 'I'm not, I work here.' She decided to put him straight before he wasted any more of the time he could be spending chatting up another girl, one who'd jump at the chance of being singled out by him. 'Look, I really am flattered you've decided to honour me with you presence, but I'm not interested.' Jackie felt she was being a bit harsh with him so added, 'It's nothing to do with you, Hats. You could be Clint Eastwood or Steve McQueen and I still wouldn't be interested. I'm off all men at the moment.'

He eyed her knowingly. 'Oh, just been dumped, eh? The best cure for that is to find yourself someone else and stick two fingers up at the jerk who did it to you. I've got to get back as we're due on again in five minutes but we finish our stint at eleven when the DJ takes back over, so meet me then for a drink at the bar?'

She shook her head. 'I don't think so, but thanks all the same.'

He pleaded, 'Ah, come on. I fancy you, Jax. I'm not asking you to marry me, just have a bit of fun that's all. Come on, wadda you say?'

After her rejection by Keith it was doing her deflated ego good to know that a man wanted her company when there were a few hundred other girls back inside the night club who would have been flattered by the offer. She relented. 'Okay, just one drink.'

He jumped up. 'Fab! See you at eleven then.'

She watched him dash off through the throng of holidaymakers and disappear inside the foyer of the Paradise building.

Back inside Groovy's herself a few minutes later, she bumped into a fed up-looking Ginger as she was making her way back to the spot on the dance floor where she had left the other girls a while earlier.

'You haven't found Al then, I take it?' Jackie asked her.

Ginger shook her head. 'He must have changed his mind about coming.' She heaved a forlorn sigh. 'I really thought my luck might be in tonight. I've had enough now. Shall we go and get a bag of chips and go home?'

Jackie shuffled her feet awkwardly. She felt guilty for having made herself a date when they'd come here with the sole purpose of getting Ginger one. 'Er . . . well, why don't we stay a bit longer? I mean, there are plenty more lads here who might take your fancy, only you haven't given them a look in because you've only had Al on your mind.'

A look of suspicion flashed into Ginger's eyes. 'Considering you really didn't want to come out tonight until I gave you no choice, it seems odd you want to stay. Oh, I get it, you've met someone, haven't you? Well, good for you. Best cure for getting over Keith. Who is he? What's his name? Hang on, I never saw you dancing with anyone at all. The ones who asked you, you turned down. So how did you meet him?'

'Just now when I went out for some fresh air. I've agreed to meet him for a drink at eleven, that's all.'

'Why eleven?'

'Because that's when he finishes his stint on-stage.'

Ginger gawped. 'You've got a date with one of the band! You jammy bugger. Which one?'

'The bass guitarist. Hats.'

'Hats! Well, don't tell Mina. She's been after him since they first started here and he hasn't so much as batted an eyelid at her.' Ginger wagged a warning finger at Jackie. 'Now you listen here, I want a blow-by-blow account when you get back to the chalet.'

Jackie laughed. 'There'll be nothing to tell. I've agreed to have one drink with him, that's all. I can tell you now that I'm not going to prolong the agony. When I met him just now he was certainly full of himself . . . expected me to be grateful he'd singled me out to chat up. I bet he spends all the time we're together telling me how great he is and how the group are going to be the "next big sensation".'

Ginger chuckled. 'The Upbeats are good but definitely not in the same league as the Bee Gees or the Beach Boys. Knowing you as I do, if he goes on too much you'll put him straight. I'll stay with you until eleven then I'll leave you to it.'

By the time eleven came and Ginger had taken her leave with a warning to Jackie not to do anything she wouldn't, Jackie herself was regretting agreeing to meet Hats because, as stupid as she knew it was, she felt she was being disloyal to Keith. It wouldn't be fair of her to stand him up, though. She would have the promised drink with him, then take her leave.

She was waiting by the bar for him when the group took their final bow on the stage over at the other end of the big room to loud cheers and clapping from the audience, they left the stage as the DJ immediately took over, keeping the atmosphere lively by playing Steppenwolf's 'Born to be Wild'.

As Hats made a beeline for Jackie and made it apparent she was with him by draping one arm around her shoulders and pulling her close into his side, she could not help but notice other girls giving her jealous glares.

Jackie told him she would like a cider and they had only just got their drinks when two of the other band members joined them, both accompanied by girls clinging to them and hanging on their every word. Then, to Jackie's embarrassment, all three band members started larking about, pushing and shoving each other, which the other girls thought hysterical. Considering they'd all been prancing about energetically onstage for the last four hours, with only a couple of short breaks in between, they seemed to be full of life still. But then, Jackie supposed they'd have been either sleeping or lounging around all day, unlike her who'd done nine hours' work before she'd come out tonight. When she was younger she would have been just like these other girls, lapping up the juvenile antics of the young men, but now she was just extremely uncomfortable and did not want to be associated with their puerile behaviour.

She decided to find somewhere to put down her drink and slip away while Hats' attention was elsewhere. But then, to her surprise, a hand grabbed her arm and the next thing she knew she was being pulled through the crowds towards the exit.

It wasn't until she was seated in a comfortable chair in the quiet lounge upstairs that she was able to assess just who her abductor was. Sitting in the chair next to her, drinking from a mug of beer, was a man of twenty-five or so, about five foot ten, slim-built, with a mop of long dark wavy hair framing a face that some would deem as unattractive. It was long and thin with a prominent chin, large hooked nose and narrow hazel eyes set close together. He was dressed in flared blue jeans and a shirt and tie under a navy blue crew-necked jumper. The man was looking back at Jackie with amusement in his bright eyes.

He said to her, 'I could see you needed rescuing. They're a good bunch of lads but they do all act like silly schoolboys.' He extended a hand towards her. 'I'm Vic . . . or Sticks as the rest called me.'

'Oh, you're the group's drummer. I'm sorry I didn't recognise you,' she told him apologetically.

He chuckled. 'Hardly anyone does, I'm stuck right at the back behind the other three. It suits me. I'm not one for the limelight. Anyway, I'm not a pretty boy like the other three so the girls don't chase after me like they do them.' He took a packet of Peter Stuyvesant cigarettes out of the pocket of his waistcoat and lit one with a match from a box of Bluebells. Then he offered the packet to Jackie but she waved it away, telling him she didn't smoke. 'I'm the quiet one,' said Vic. 'They'll all be partying for the rest of the night, come back to their chalets at the crack of dawn, fall on their beds still fully dressed and spend the day sleeping it off. I don't mind going to a party and letting my hair down now and again, but after a gig I prefer to wind down with a drink somewhere quiet.' He looked at her for a moment before adding, 'I'll understand if you've better things to do and need to get off.'

After he'd rescued her from what threatened to be a boring interlude Jackie thought it would be extremely rude of her to slide off. 'I'll finish my drink, if that's all right with you?'

He smiled at her, showing his uneven teeth. 'So how long are you here for on holiday?'

She told him she worked here, and before she knew it was also telling him about her happy childhood in Mablethorpe, how she'd joined Jolly's on leaving school, and briefly mentioned her recent breakup with her boyfriend without going into details on how it had come about as she was still far from ready to open up to anyone else about that.

In his turn Vic then told her about his own background. He too had had a happy childhood, growing up in a close family, the youngest of two brothers and a sister. His father worked as a machine operator in a local factory, his mother was a housewife. Money was tight but there was always food on the table and shoes on their feet. As a young child he'd driven his mother mad with his favourite game of bashing her saucepans with a wooden spoon. When his father had noticed that he was actually making rhythmical sounds, he had scraped together the money to buy an old drum kit from the local pawn shop, cleared a space in the outhouse, and set the kit up in there.

On leaving school, he'd joined his father in the local factory as an apprentice tool-maker and in the evenings formed a skiffle group with his friends. They spent every night after work practising and became good enough to get some gigs in local pubs and working men's clubs. Saving up his share of the small amount of money they were paid, along with any spare from his wages, Vic made a down payment on his first proper drum kit and paid the rest off weekly.

Then two of the members of the group started courting strongly and wanted to be with their girlfriends, not practising or spending their nights playing for peanuts, so the group broke up. But news that Vic was free got around those in the business and he was asked to join another group who played regularly in night clubs in the town. The money was a lot better than he had been getting. Eventually the group started to get gigs further afield, which meant not getting back home until it was virtually time for him to get up again. His work started to suffer, thus giving him a difficult choice to make. Did he leave the group for the sake of his job, or give up his job to stay with the group? His family were against him giving up a good job to pursue such a precarious living, but they also appreciated it was his decision to make. Since he had his training to fall back on if it all fell foul, they gave him their blessing.

He'd been in several groups since, each with better musicians and singers than the last. He'd been with the Upbeats for five months. The others were fully convinced that it was only a matter of time before they were spotted by a talent scout, got a record deal and were heralded as the next pop sensation, but Vic was far from being so optimistic. The Upbeats were good enough to play at the likes of Jolly's but their guitar player was no Jimi Hendrix or Jeff Beck, and the singer no Mick Jagger. Vic was realistic enough to know that as a drummer he did not possess the magic of Keith Moon. He doubted the Upbeats would ever achieve the success the other three were adamant was just around the corner. Unlike the other three, who spent every penny they earned on enjoying themselves, Vic saved his up, determined that he wasn't going to live the same hand-to-mouth existence his parents did. When his drumming days were over, he'd have his own business selling records and musical instruments, living in his own decently furnished house and taking a proper holiday once a year.

From what he had told her, Jackie thought him very wise to have the attitude he did. The conversation then turned to music they liked and disliked, until it came as a shock to her to realise that the staff were starting to close the bar. It was almost one o'clock and she really needed to get to bed or her work would be suffering tomorrow.

She needn't have crept back into the chalet because as soon as she inched open the door and stepped inside, Ginger switched on the shared bedside light and sat bolt upright. 'That was a long drink,' she said.

Shutting the door behind her, Jackie replied, 'Actually, I had three.'

'Well, you've been with him for hours so you obviously had a better time than you thought you were going to. So what did you get up to? Where did he take you? What's Hats' kissing like?'

Jackie did not respond until she had stripped off her clothes, put on her pink baby dolls and clambered into bed. With her legs drawn up and the bedclothes under her chin, she told Ginger, 'Well, actually I have no idea what Hats' kisses are like as I didn't spend the evening with him! I was with the group's drummer, Vic.' Jackie laughed at the expression on Ginger's face and proceeded to tell her how Vic had come to rescue her and they'd spent the rest of the evening chatting in the quiet lounge.

Ginger wasn't looking at all impressed. 'I was imagining you being whisked off by Hats to a wild party or something equally as exciting. Sounds as though after I left you your evening was no more exciting than mine, sitting in here reading my magazines. This Vic sounds a bit boring to me. I have to say, I've never really taken much notice of him myself. He's not very good-looking, is he?'

Jackie admitted, 'No, he's not a handsome man, I admit, but he's got a lovely personality. He made me feel perfectly at ease with him. And what was great for me was that, for all the time I was talking to him, I wasn't thinking about Keith and my mother together.'

Ginger leaned across the divide and patted her friend's knee. 'Anyone who takes your mind off those two is okay in my book, boring or not. Are you seeing him again?'

'No, of course not. I'm nowhere near ready to start dating again. We just said our goodbyes and went our separate ways.' The truth was he hadn't asked her. It came as a shock to Jackie to realise how disappointed she now felt. She really had liked him. Maybe it was because she wasn't his type. She preferred to believe that it was because he knew she had only just ended a long-term relationship and didn't want to be the rebound date on her part.

She told Ginger that they'd both better get to sleep or they'd be struggling to get through the day tomorrow when, as always at Jolly's, you never knew what was going to be thrown at you.

CHAPTER SEVENTEEN

The next morning Jackie was bemused as to why Al was looking back at her like she'd just caught him red-handed stealing money out of the till, when all she'd done was mention the fact that she didn't see him at Groovy's last night. 'Al, what you do with your free time is your business, this isn't the Spanish Inquisition.'

'Oh, I know, I know,' he blustered. 'The chap I was going with changed his mind and I didn't want to go on my own, so I went home after all.'

'You must have missed the quarter to six bus by that time so you had a long wait for the next at nine?'

'Oh, I er . . . I didn't wait for the next bus, I walked to Mablethorpe to catch the bus to Skegness.'

'What, nearly six miles? I wouldn't have fancied that trek after a day's work.' Jackie looked at him thoughtfully. She hadn't seen him on her journey back from visiting her brother in Mablethorpe, and she would have done surely if he'd done as he said. 'I rode back from Mablethorpe at just after six and I never saw you or I'd have given you a lift.'

'Oh, er . . . that's because I cut across the fields. It's much quicker that way. Do you want me to ring through the orders for supplies the cleaning supervisor brought up yesterday afternoon?'

'Oh, yes, please.' His abrupt change of subject did not go unnoticed by Jackie and for an instant she had the overwhelming feeling he was lying to her. People who lied had something to hide. She wondered what it was that Al didn't want her to know about. But she had a mountain of work that was waiting to be dealt with so hadn't time to be wasting on speculating further.

Later that morning Terry Jones, the Head Stripey, flicked the stub end of his cigarette into the bushes and said to Jackie, 'If I agree to help you, what's in it for me?'

She inwardly groaned. She might have known Terry would want something in return. She was not stupid. She knew what he was angling after, and he could angle as much as he liked but he would never get what he was after from her. She'd sooner die first. Still, he obviously wasn't going to agree to help her unless she did tempt him with an inducement. 'I'll buy you a drink the next time I see you in Groovy's,' she offered.

'One drink! That's hardly fair exchange for what you want me to do. Go on a date with me and we might have a deal.'

Jackie inwardly shuddered at the thought of spending any longer than necessary with this ferret of a man who really believed he was God's gift to women. How he always seemed to have a string of girls clamouring after him she had no idea. She could only assume that it was his position as Head Stripey that attracted them. It seemed if she wanted Terry's help she would have to agree to his terms, but she didn't have to go ahead with it when it came to it, did she? She responded sweetly, 'We've a deal. But trouble is, Terry, as much as I'd love to go on a date with you, I can't make any firm arrangements at the moment as I'm working all the hours God sends covering for Rhonnie and Mrs Jolly. But when they come back we'll sort something out.'

He eyed her knowingly. 'Think I'm stupid, eh, Jackie? You found time for a date with the drummer from the Upbeats last night, so you can't be working all hours.'

Jackie inwardly groaned. Nothing any of the staff did was secret at Jolly's, thanks to the camp grapevine. She told him, 'For your information that wasn't a date I had with Vic last night, he just happened . . .' She then inwardly scolded herself, realising what she was doing, and snapped at him, 'I don't need to explain myself to you. Are you going to do what I ask?'

'Only if you agree to have a date with me and we make the arrangements now.' Terry leered at her. 'You know you're desperate to. It's only 'cos you were courting that you didn't before. Well, now you're free and single. For God's sake, just admit you've got the hots for me, Jackie! And if flashing your knickers at me the other day wasn't a come on, then I don't know what is.'

She scoffed, 'Do you seriously believe that I purposely ripped a good skirt to give you a flash of my underwear? You really are something else, Terry Jones.'

He completely misconstrued her comment and said proudly, 'About time you admitted that. So do you want my help or not?'

He wasn't going to budge so she either agreed to his demand or she'd have to forget this particular way of helping Harold Rose to overcome his shyness and think of something else, getting people to help her who wouldn't demand such a high price from her in return. But it was such a good idea, and if it worked as well as she hoped then it would go a long way towards achieving Jackie's goal. With great reluctance she told Terry, 'Okay, one date.'

He grinned smugly. 'It's my night off on Monday. I'll meet you in Groovy's at eight.'

Before she could make any protest he had shot off inside the Paradise where his small office was located in the foyer, to resume his task of sorting out the Stripeys' staff roster.

Jackie was already beginning to regret agreeing to his demands. There could be any number of staff members in Groovy's on Monday night, and if she was seen with Terry . . . well, the gossips would have a field day with it. Knowing Terry as she did, he was not going to allow anyone to think he had blackmailed Jackie into a date with him, but would lead them to believe she was mad for him and it was she who had asked him out.

When she whispered to Ginger at dinnertime in the restaurant the situation she had got herself into, her friend's immediate reaction was to convulse with laughter. Jackie had hoped Ginger would come up with a get out, but she gleefully said there wasn't one she could think of. So, having made her deal with Terry all Jackie could do was grin and bear it and live with the consequences.

At three o'clock that afternoon, Harold Rose lifted his head from his work when there was a tap on the door.

Calling out for whoever it was to enter, he expected it to be Al or Jackie with his afternoon cup of tea and biscuits. It was Al but he wasn't carrying anything.

'Sorry to bother you, Mr Rose,' he began. 'But there's an urgent situation over in the Paradise ballroom and Jackie is out on her daily tour of the camp. I can't leave the office unattended to deal with it.'

Harold felt himself go hot under the collar. Dealing one to one with Chef Brown the previous day had been purgatory enough for him, a situation he was still not quite recovered from, but the Paradise ballroom at this time in the afternoon would be full of people attending the afternoon tea dance. To enter a vast room full of people was to him as fearsome as entering a ravenous lion's cage. His legs began quaking under his desk, his palms running with sweat as his thoughts raced to find a plausible excuse.

Before anything came to him, though, Al, as Jackie had instructed, said, 'I'll tell the Stripey on the telephone that you're on your way.'

With that he did an about turn, leaving a highly anxious Harold Rose staring blindly after him, knowing he had no choice but to take himself over to the Paradise to find out what the problem was and hope he didn't make a complete idiot of himself in front of all the people there.

Nervously approaching the large wooden double doors leading into the ballroom, Harold Rose almost jumped out of his skin when he heard his name being called and spun around to see a skinny young Stripey with a mop of long fair hair come out of one of the double doors leading into the Paradise, letting out a blast of 'The Tennessee Waltz' which the band were playing as he did so. It faded to a distant strain as the door shut behind him and he hurried over to Harold.

Terry Jones said with a confident air, 'Hi, I'm Terry Jones, Head Stripey.' He then looked thoughtfully at Harold's stout brogues. 'Not really dancing shoes, but they'll have to do.'

Harold took off his horn-rimmed glasses which had steamed up in the heat coming off his face, took a handkerchief from out of his pocket and gave them a swipe, then another quick pass over his sweating brow before he put his spectacles back on. 'Er . . . my shoes will have to do for what, Mr . . . er . . . Jones?'

'Dancing.'

'I'm sorry! Oh, I . . . er . . . think you're confusing me with someone else. I'm Mr Rose, Temporary Manager. I was told you have an urgent situation, and as no one else is available I've come to see how I can help.'

'That is our urgent situation, Mr Rose. Les Hunter, he's one of my senior Stripeys . . . cracking dancer, the old dears love him . . . we'll, he's gone and sprained his ankle. One of the old chaps got carried away doing a tango and tripped him up. Anyway, Sister Stephens has strapped Les up and told him he's to rest it for a couple of days. Well, I can sort something by tomorrow to cover for him if he's still off, but it's too short notice for today. So that means I'm short a dancer.'

Harold's face turned ashen. 'Am I to understand that you wish me to take his place?' His heart began to thump painfully, his legs threatening to collapse beneath him.

Harold stuttered, 'Oh, but you will have to get someone else, I'm afraid. I'm far too busy with work.

Anyway I . . . I . . . I don't dance so I'd be no good to you at all.' That wasn't quite true as Harold was in fact a good dancer, having been taught by his mother to her collection of dance-band records. She'd loved to dance and there'd been no one else to partner her. But dancing with her in privacy was one thing; in a ballroom full of people it was very much another. It seemed Terry didn't hear him, though, as he was already holding open one of the double doors for Harold to follow him through.

Inside the ballroom the band were now loudly playing a military two step. Harold was still protesting, 'Look, Mr Jones, you don't seem to have understood me . . .'

He was cut short by the arrival of two old ladies. One was small and fat with a head of tightly permed white hair tinted pink. She was very fussily dressed in a bright pink frilly dress with matching dance shoes. The other lady was tall and thin, her grey hair scraped back in a tight bun at the nape of her scrawny neck. She was wearing a calf-length black dress, its high neck and full sleeves edged with white lace. A cameo brooch was pinned to one shoulder. They had their arms hooked together.

The short, fat lady spoke first, in a high-pitched squeaky voice. 'Oh, Terry, is this the young man you've brought in to replace Leslie?' She smiled at Harold coyly, showing a set of badly fitting false teeth, then said to her thin friend, 'I saw him first, Agnes, so it's only fair I get first dance with him.' Before Harold could stop her she had slid her arm through his and was propelling him to the middle of the dance floor.

Next thing he knew they were surrounded by dozens of other dancing couples, their ages ranging from the mid-forties to the advanced years of the old lady who had commandeered him. She had by now clamped herself tightly to him, obviously expecting him to take the lead. All he could think of was that the sooner he got this dance over with, the sooner he could make his escape from this nightmare situation. But that wasn't to be. When the music stopped his partner was elbowed aside to be replaced by her thin friend, who was demanding he partner her for the next dance.

This situation carried on. It was over an hour and a half before a chance to escape came, and that was only because the afternoon tea-dance session had come to an end with the band's final chords of 'The Anniversary Waltz'.

Excusing himself from his last partner, Harold hurried over to the exit but was waylaid by Terry Jones. 'Well, you certainly proved a hit with the ladies, Mr Rose. They're all saying what a wonderful partner you made.'

Harold eyed the other man, astonished. Terry was making that up, surely? Harold had been a nervous wreck, had several times tripped over his own feet and many times lost the beat; several times he forgot steps to a dance his mother had painstakingly taught him. Those comments must just have been made to be kind. 'You will excuse me? I have to get back to work,' he murmured, and with that he shot off.

Back in the general office he scurried through without even acknowledging Jackie or Al. In his own office he shut the door firmly behind him, desperate for the sanctuary it afforded him. He had barely sunk gratefully into his chair when there was a tap at the door and he almost leaped to his feet again. Terrified this could be another summons to appear somewhere in the camp when he'd had no time as yet to recover from his last ordeal, he anxiously called out, 'Enter.'

Harold stared wildly over Jackie's shoulder, as she came in and walked over to his desk. He was mortally relieved when she said to him, 'I understand there was a problem in the Paradise while I was out, Mr Rose. I'm sorry I wasn't here to deal with it myself, now I know how hard it is for you to deal with strangers.'

He appreciated her thoughtfulness. 'Well, er . . . it couldn't be helped, I suppose.'

As though Jackie didn't know, she asked him, 'Did you manage to sort out the problem or do I need to go over there?'

'Er . . . well, yes, I did resolve it. Mr Jones was short of someone to partner the campers at this afternoon's tea dance as one of the Stripeys had sprained an ankle and been ordered to rest. I . . . er . . . obliged.'

She looked at him admiringly. 'Then after what you told me, Mr Rose, I think you should congratulate yourself. That situation couldn't have been easy for you. It's funny how scared we can feel when we're faced with doing something that we don't want to, and then afterwards realise it wasn't half as frightening as we thought it would be. Maybe, in fact, quite enjoyable?' The look on Harold's face told her that for him the situation had proved to be just as frightening as he had thought it would, and he had definitely *not* enjoyed it. This made Jackie realise that if she had ever thought her task was going to be an easy one then she'd been badly mistaken. She was going to have to come up with a few more situations such as the one she had just engineered before he even started to build up his confidence. She felt a bit sorry for what she was purposely putting Harold through, but wasn't going to let that stop her from finishing what she had started, however long it took.

She said to him, 'You look like you could do with a cup of tea. I'll see to it for you. Oh, and to keep you informed, we've had several replies for the replacement nurse and Sister Stephens is going to whittle them down to the ones she feels are worth interviewing.' She omitted to tell Harold then that she intended him to be sitting in on those interviews, too, whether he liked it or not.

That evening Jackie and Ginger decided to spend the night catching up on washing, and on cleaning their chalet. Some of the other female off-duty staff had other ideas, though, and in a steady stream they descended on the two girls until there were eight of them crowded into their cramped accommodation, sharing bottles of cider and wine, the cleaning and washing forgotten about. At just after twelve Jackie and Ginger managed to get the others to leave and started clearing up the mess left behind so they could go to bed.

Jackie collected the empty bottles for disposal and the glasses for washing while Ginger gathered together discarded chip wrappers. She spread out a sheet of newspaper, meaning to wrap up the rest of the paper inside it. An article on the open page caught her eye and she began reading it with great interest.

Just wanting to get the place straightened up enough to go to bed, Jackie was annoyed to see that Ginger seemed not to be helping but was instead reading an article in the newspaper. She snapped at her, 'Ginger, are you helping clear up or what?' When she made no response, Jackie stepped over to look at the newspaper, asking, 'What's so interesting?'

'This!' Ginger stabbed a finger on the part of the paper she was reading.

Jackie's eyes settled on the lead article and she quickly read it. It was a follow-up report about a bank robbery that had taken place in London the week before. The thieves had got away with nearly half a million pounds. Through their sources, the police were certain they knew the four vicious villains responsible, but they and their haul seemed to have vanished into thin air. Accompanying the article were mug shots of the four suspects along with a request from the police for the public to report to them any sightings, but certainly not to approach the men as they were highly dangerous individuals. One mug shot in particular grabbed Jackie's attention and she had to force her eyes away from it so as to look at Ginger and quizzically ask, 'What's so interesting about a London robbery?'

Ginger tutted. 'That's not the article I'm interested in. It's the one below. A clothes warehouse in Lincoln was robbed last week of designer clothes that were ready to be delivered to shops.'

Jackie shrugged. 'So?'

'Well, let's hope the police do as bad a job there as they are with the London bank robbers and don't find the culprits. Then we can bag ourselves some bargains we'd never otherwise be able to afford, because you can bet your bottom dollar some of the stuff will end up on Skeggy Market. We need to get ourselves down there before others beat us to it.'

Jackie's eyes lit up. 'Yes, we do. Let's see if we can wangle a couple of hours off on Friday morning.'

Ginger pulled a face. 'That's easy for you as you're practically your own boss at the moment, but I'll have to see if one of the other receptionists will swap our half-days off. Looks like I've a bit of sucking up to do.'

'Well, I'm sure you'll manage it if a designer dress at a cut-price rate is at stake,' Jackie said dryly. Giving a loud, tired yawn, she gathered together the newspaper chip wrappings, screwed them up into a ball and threw them at the bin by the small chest of drawers, only she missed her target and the ball of newspaper rolled under her bed. She said to Ginger, 'Oh, let's leave this tidying up until tomorrow. I need my sleep.'

She was just dozing off when, much to her annoyance, Ginger's voice jolted her awake.

'Oh, by the way, Jackie, did you find out from Al why he changed his mind about going to Groovy's last night? It wasn't because he found a girl and took her out instead, was it?'

Testily Jackie responded, 'He told me that the mate he was going with changed his mind and so he went home.'

'Oh, that's all right then. At least I'm still in with a chance.'

Jackie herself was wondering if Ginger was reading the signs from Al all wrong; that his smiles were just polite and certainly not come ons. He'd been working at the camp for weeks now and had had plenty of opportunities to ask Ginger out, but so far had not. Jackie felt as Ginger's friend she should maybe point this out to her, but then she could be wrong. Maybe, like Harold Rose, Al was just lacking in confidence when it came to approaching girls.

Maybe, just as she was trying to tackle Harold's shyness and lack of self-confidence, the time had come for her to give Al a nudge and find out once and for all how the land lay as far as her friend was concerned. If she got the opportunity she would do just that.

Jackie said to her now, 'If you don't go to sleep you won't be in with a chance with anyone . . . I'll have battered you to death!'

Ginger giggled.

CHAPTER EIGHTEEN

Ginger's prophecy was correct. To both girls' delight they returned from their trip to Skegness Market with two top designer dresses each along with a crocheted top for Ginger and a skirt for Jackie, at only a pound or so each garment more than they would have paid for off-the-peg items from their usual stores. It was quite apparent to them that the stallholders they bought the clothes from were well aware where the merchandise originated as during the sales process they continually kept an eye out for any signs of the law approaching. Tongue-in-cheek, Ginger asked Jackie if she was going to wear one of her new dresses on the date with Terry next Monday. A look from her left Ginger in no doubt that none of the treasured new clothes were going to be wasted on the likes of him.

All the staff at Jolly's awoke the next Saturday morning to open their chalet curtains at just after the crack of dawn, and all of them heaved groans of despair. The hot sunny weather, it seemed, had temporarily departed, to be replaced by dark clouds and torrential rain. It meant they were not only going to have to cope with the already busy changeover day, but also be running around like headless chickens organising an assortment of indoor activities to entertain the campers until the weather improved enough for outside programmes to commence again.

Jackie's personal opinion of Terry Jones might be that he was a conceited weasel of a man but she could not deny that he was excellent at his job. This morning he had rallied his staff, firing off instructions to them on which events to organise and in which different facilities, so that none of them clashed.

Terry might be good at his job but, regardless, he was no miracle worker. That day he was also having to cope with a seriously depleted complement of staff as over a dozen of them had woken that morning with terrible sore throats and raging headaches and were unfit to work. Terry was finding himself without a bingo caller in the hastily organised event in the Paradise hall as all the rest of his staff were otherwise occupied.

Usually in situations like this he would have called on a receptionist to help out or one of the general office staff, but as they were already up to their eyes as it was transfer day, poaching one of them to help out was not an option. It seemed there was no alternative but to do it himself. He didn't want to, though, preferring to go around acting the part of the boss, not undertaking a job that one of his minions should be doing. Then an idea struck him. Yesterday he had purposely helped set up a situation to aid Jackie in her aim to prod Harold Rose into tackling his shyness – though why the likes of the vivacious Jackie felt the need to waste her time on a middle-aged man she couldn't possibly have any romantic interest in was beyond Terry when he himself was on offer to her. But then, it had won him a date with her, something he'd been trying for a long time by now. Now he saw another chance to make her grateful to him. Hopefully she would show the proper level of gratitude to him on their date on Monday night.

Terry sprinted through the belting rain over to reception. He pushed his way through the soaked crowd outside forming a disorderly queue, there being no spare Stripeys to keep them in order, then through the door leading up to the offices. Without pausing to tap on the manager's door and wait for a response, Terry barged straight inside and announced, 'Mr Rose, we're in a right pickle and need your help urgently.'

Shocked at having his sanctuary invaded, Harold Rose looked up stupefied.

He finally found his voice. 'Well . . . er . . . as you can see, I am very busy. Jackie will assist you, I'm sure.'

Terry stared at him blankly. He'd understood from what Jackie had told him that their temporary boss was reclusive, but did Harold not realise it was changeover day? Had he not also observed the adverse weather conditions, which always caused them added problems? Surely this was a time when personal issues must be shoved aside, for the sake of the camp's good name. Terry announced, 'You obviously don't remember that Jackie and Al are already up to their eyes helping on reception as it's changeover day. Due to the weather I have had to organise some extra inside events to keep the campers happy, but as several of my staff are ill and so unable to work today I've been left short of a bingo caller. The ballroom is full of women waiting for the session to start and I fear if I don't find a caller soon I'll have a riot on my hands. I can't do it myself as I'm already judging a hastily organised kids' talent show in one of the Paradise lounges. I'll walk you across to the ballroom now and introduce you to Kim, who will be your assistant.'

Harold gulped as sheer panic swamped him. He couldn't just walk out on-stage to face a ballroom full of women all looking back at him, expecting him to take charge of the proceedings and keep his nerves in check for at least a couple of hours. What he had faced yesterday seemed like nothing in comparison. But Terry Jones was giving him no choice, waiting at Harold's open office door to escort him. Taking several deep breaths in an effort to force down a surge of panic and stop his legs from quaking, he rose from behind his desk and followed Terry over to the ballroom, wishing that a miracle would happen and the ground would open and swallow him up.

It wasn't until later that afternoon that Jackie found out about Harold's courageous efforts. Terry made sure to let her know what he had done to aid her cause. He collared her as she was on her rounds of the camp much later on. Through pressure of work Jackie had not eaten since breakfast that morning. Feeling hungry and tired, she was not very receptive when Terry approached her and neither was she at all happy with what he had done.

Sheltering under an umbrella to help ward off the still battering rain, she snapped, 'Oh, for God's sake, Terry, did you not listen to me yesterday when I took you into my confidence over Mr Rose? That man has been scared of his own shadow all his life. He needs to be helped to build up his confidence slowly and surely, one step at a time . . . not be plunged straight into situations that would scare the living daylights out of me, let alone him. Oh, you really are the limit! Anyway, I haven't time to stand here arguing with you now. I have a tour of the camp to make and then I must head back to the office and see for myself that Mr Rose has not suffered a heart attack or worse after what you just thoughtlessly put him through.'

Terry responded defensively, 'Well, I thought you'd be pleased. I saw the opportunity to help you and . . .'

She cut in, '. . . and hoped I'd show you my gratitude on Monday night? Go to bed with you, is that what you were after?' She saw by his expression that it was exactly how grateful he'd hoped she would be. Jackie shot him a look of contempt and, as she hurried off, called over her shoulder, 'I appreciate that you tried to help my cause with Mr Rose, but I would think a lot more of you if you'd done it to help Mr Rose himself and not thought about what *you* could get out of it.'

Her round of the camp would go down in the record books as the quickest Jackie had ever done. Due to the rain most of the outdoor areas were deserted so it was only the indoor sites she needed to visit The staff were doing an exemplary job of keeping all the campers entertained during the atrocious weather and she was gratified not to uncover any pressing problems that needed dealing with, for a change. Back under cover in the office, after quickly confirming with Al that nothing he couldn't handle had transpired while she was out, Jackie went to check on Harold to see what state he was in after what she knew would have been a terrifying ordeal for him.

In her need to find out she forgot to wait courteously for him to call out that she could enter after she'd tapped on his door and went straight in.

Harold himself had only returned a few minutes before. Jackie found him seated behind his desk with his head cradled in his hands, his whole body shaking.

Her heart went out to him. Her first instinct was to rush over and offer him comfort; tell him how sorry she was that he'd been given no choice but to put himself in such a nerve-wracking situation, and promise to do her utmost to make sure it never happened again. But she managed to stop herself, because otherwise she would be doing exactly what his mother had done: not helping him to face his fears and overcome them, but sheltering him from ever making the effort. Jackie needed to do the opposite.

She went over to the desk and sat in the visitor's chair. The noise she made set him starting nervously as he had not heard her come in. Before Harold could say anything Jackie told him, 'Mr Rose, I've just been told by Terry Jones how you came to his rescue today. I bet you're very proud of yourself? If not, then you should be.'

He wiped the sweat from his face with a handkerchief and blustered, 'Proud! I hardly think so, Miss Sims. I daren't think what all those women must think of me. I only went on-stage in the first place because the young girl who was checking the numbers and handing out prizes gave me a push. But as I did they all stamped their feet . . . it sounded like thunder, believe me . . . then they all jeered and that made me trip over my own feet and crash into the ball machine which toppled over, broke open, and the balls scattered all over the ballroom. The whole room erupted into laughter. They were still laughing while everyone helped pick up the balls. If I hadn't been so terrified they'd form a lynch mob and do goodness knows what to me, I'd have made a run for it then and there.

'Then later on I thought I was doing okay until I was calling out some of the numbers and they all started heckling me . . . they were yelling things like "Kelly's eye", "two little ducks", "all the fives", and so I'd become flustered and call out the next number wrongly and then have to put it right. As soon as I'd called out the very last one, I couldn't get out of there fast . . .' He stopped talking for a moment to look at her with a hurt expression. 'See, even you're laughing at me now! I'm so useless.'

Jackie wiped away tears of mirth from her eyes with the back of her hands. 'Oh, Mr Rose, I'm laughing because I have no doubt you gave them the best entertainment they've ever had at a bingo game.'

He eyed her, bemused. 'How do you come to that conclusion after what I just told you?'

'Well, for a start, those women had been waiting quite a while for a caller to turn up. Stamping their feet and cheering was their way of showing you they were pleased to see you. Then, when you tripped and crashed into the ball machine, they would have assumed it was part of your act. They weren't heckling when you called out some of the numbers – what they were calling out was bingo slang. "Kelly's eye" is number one. "All the fives" is fifty-five. "Key of the door" is twenty-one. Most of the numbers have a nickname but I don't know them all. I have no doubt that if you'd stayed just a little longer at the end, instead of high-tailing it out of there, those women would have given you a standing ovation and be demanding to be told when you were going to be the caller again, because they'd enjoyed themselves so much.'

Harold shook his head in disbelief. 'I know you're just saying that to be kind and I appreciate it but . . .'

His self-pitying attitude got the better of Jackie then. It was apparent to her that she was wasting her time trying to help him to a better life as you couldn't help a person who obviously had no intention of helping themself. Her patience suddenly snapped. 'You're accusing me of lying to you and that's not right, Mr Rose, when I'm not. I've worked at Jolly's for a long time and I know that those women in the ballroom today came here on holiday expecting to have a good time. From what you told me, albeit unintentionally on your part, you certainly entertained them today.

'You know, you really have to start showing some belief in yourself. See yourself as the smart, intelligent man you are . . . someone whose company people would enjoy if you'd give them the chance, instead of making yourself look like a bumbling idiot by always scuttling away from them.' She was on a tangent now and just couldn't stop. 'Your mother might have thought she was doing her best for you by protecting you from difficult situations, but what she should have been doing was encouraging you to face up to them. Then, more than likely, you wouldn't be anywhere near as lacking in self-confidence as you are today. But obviously you're happy with having no friends and being a lonely man, or you'd want to do something about it.'

Jackie realised then she'd gone too far – been so rude Harold could quite justifiably sack her.

Jumping up from her chair she fled from the room.

Back in the office, as she made her way around her desk and slumped down in her chair, Al asked in concern, 'Is everything all right, Jackie. Only I heard you . . . well, not exactly shouting, but your voice was raised and you sounded annoyed to me?'

She gave a despairing groan. 'No, everything is not all right. I couldn't stop myself from losing my temper with Mr Rose and I've more than likely managed to get myself the sack.'

He looked aghast.

'What did you say to him?'

She heaved a forlorn sigh. 'A lot of things I never should have done to a man in his position.'

The switchboard buzzed and Al picked up the receiver to answer the caller. A moment later he replaced it and looked across at her gravely. 'That was Mr Rose, Jackie. He wants to see you in his office.'

Feeling like she was about to place her head on the executioner's block, she obeyed the summons. Standing before Harold's desk she felt she was only wasting time. She knew he was going to tell her to pack up her belongings and leave the camp. But Harold did not utter any word of reproof.

Looking down at his desk, he murmured, 'I've got a nerve asking this, Miss Sims, but would you be willing to help me?'

She eyed him, taken aback. 'Er . . . well . . . yes, of course I will, if I can. What with?'

He shocked her further by lifting his head and looking directly at her. 'That pathetic buffoon of a man you just described . . . I don't want to be him any more. I'm so desperately lonely, I'm terrified that one day I will die on my own at home and my body will lie there rotting for years before anyone notices. I don't think I could ever become the life and soul of the party type . . . I've left it far too late ever to hope I could meet a woman willing to take me on and start a family . . . but if I could just get myself to the stage where I could have a conversation with someone and feel comfortable, not desperate to run away and hide, and maybe a friend to spend some time with, then I'd be happy with that.'

If he'd only realised it she was already trying to help him. 'I'd be more than willing to, Mr Rose,' Jackie said enthusiastically. She then heaved a huge sigh of relief and blurted out, 'I really thought you'd called me in here to sack me. I wouldn't have blamed you if you had. I should never have spoken to you the way I just did, and especially what I said about your mother. I am sorry.'

He gave a wan smile. 'My mother was a lovely woman, Miss Sims. She was very soft and gentle . . . my whole world. But you were right. Instead of shielding me from situations that terrified me, she should have encouraged me to face them. Had she done so I might not be the bumbling idiot I am today. It took you pointing that out to make me see more clearly. In truth, I've been hiding behind your skirts, haven't I, and in turn making your life hell? It is I who should be apologising to you, in fact. I don't know how you can ever forgive me for making you lose your boyfriend through the extra hours you did while covering the work that I should have been doing.'

She enlightened him. 'Well, you did me a favour in a way because if I hadn't worked late I might not have found out that my boyfriend wanted to be with someone else other than me. They're together now and, as far as I know, very happy together.'

'And you?' he asked.

'Oh, I'll be fine in time. I've got good friends helping me through. And that's what we're going to get you . . . some good friends for you to enjoy being with, who'll be there for you when you need them. We need to build up your confidence one step at a time. We could start tomorrow with you coming with me on the daily tour of the camp. It's actually Al's turn to do it but I know he won't mind swapping with me. If you find it too much, we'll cut the tour short and come straight back. What do you say?'

Harold studied his desk top thoughtfully for a moment. Such a simple thing, to accompany her on a tour around the camp, but one that filled him with dread. He was very aware, though, that should he refuse, Jackie more than likely wouldn't offer to help him again. If he wanted a better life then he needed to help himself get it. Before he could change his mind he said, 'Yes, I'll do it.'

Jackie grinned at him. 'Good.' Then she added with conviction, 'Before you know it, you'll be doing the tour on your own.'

CHAPTER NINETEEN

'You look nice.'

Jackie spun around and stared at Ginger, who was coming into the chalet after having a shower.

'I don't, do I! I don't *want* to look nice. My intention is to look as awful as I can.'

Ginger kicked shut the door behind her and flung herself down on her bed, telling Jackie, 'I was being sarcastic. You look like a relic from the nineteen forties. Where on earth did you get that skirt and blouse from?'

'I raided the Stripeys' dressing-up box. It was a toss up between this skirt and blouse or a hideous Crimplene dress.'

'Oh, of course, it's your big date tonight with Terry.'

'Don't remind me! I want to look so embarrassing he won't want to be seen with me and will make an excuse to cut things short.'

Ginger snorted, 'Jackie, that man is besotted with you! You could turn up in a sack tied in the middle with rope, and he'd still think he'd won the pools, being out with you. I'm surprised you've not heard already – he's so cock-a-hoop he's taking you out tonight that he's told everyone who will listen. The way he's making it out is that *you* asked him, of course.'

Jackie's face darkened thunderously. 'The slimy toad!' She then heaved a miserable sigh. 'Tonight is going to be the longest of my life.'

'Well, my advice is to think twice next time before you rope someone in to help you with your hare-brained schemes. How is the Mr Rose Project coming on, by the way?'

Jackie smiled. 'So far so good. He's been on two tours with me now around the camp, and today he actually summoned up the courage to ask a camper how they were enjoying their holiday. He was so proud of himself afterwards you'd have thought he was the first man to reach the top of Everest. He has no idea yet but tomorrow I'm going to suggest to him he sits in on the interviews for the new nurse.'

She turned back to assess her reflection in the small mirror she had taken off the wall and propped up on the chest of drawers so as to get the best view of herself. She shook her head. 'I can't go out like this, can I? The only one I'll be embarrassing is myself.'

It was coming up for eleven o'clock, Jackie had now been with Terry for three hours, and for her it had proved to be three hours of hell. When she had arrived at their rendezvous he had already been waiting for her, and from that moment on had made sure they were seen together, particularly by the staff, especially the males, gloating over his 'conquest' of her. The female staff were all looking at her askance, as if to ask why on earth she was out with Terry when she could be with anyone she wanted. Only the immature female holidaymakers were looking jealous, Terry being the object of their misguided juvenile desires. His arrogant behaviour was actually making Jackie feel nauseous. If this was his attempt at trying to show her what a great catch he was, then he was failing miserably. If only Harold Rose possessed one-tenth of Terry's misguided self-confidence!

For the last hour she had been subjected first to Terry's dance moves – he'd thrown himself about in the firm belief others were admiring his Mick Jagger technique – and then to his constant insidious efforts to get close to her.

Standing by the bar, with his arm draped around her shoulders, Jackie was doing her best to resist being pulled any closer to Terry as she drank the cider he'd just bought her. To her dismay he was just telling her that when Groovy's closed a group of Stripeys were off down to the beach to have themselves a party, obviously believing she would be thrilled by the idea. It was all too apparent his intention was to end up alone with her in the sand dunes. Jackie was racking her brains for a plausible means of escape, and failing miserably, when she felt a hand grip her arm and heard someone say: 'Sorry to disturb you, Jackie, but I really need to speak to you privately for a minute.'

She turned her head to find Vic by her side.

Smiling apologetically at Terry, he then said, 'You don't mind if I borrow Jackie for a minute, do you.' It wasn't a question but a statement.

Judging by Terry's expression he obviously did. He snapped, 'Jackie isn't on duty, she's out with me, so whatever you want her for will have to wait until tomorrow.'

Vic responded politely, 'If it wasn't urgent, I wouldn't have dreamed of disturbing her.' He dragged Jackie free and steered her off towards the stairs, calling over to Terry, 'I'll have her back with you before you know it.'

Upstairs in the much quieter Paradise foyer, Vic let go of Jackie's arm, giving her an opportunity to ask him in concern, 'What is so urgent that you need to see me now, Vic?'

He gave a shrug. 'Nothing.'

She frowned. 'So why did you say what you did and drag me away?'

He grinned at her. 'Are you going to tell me you're not glad I did?'

Then she twigged what he had done. 'Was it that obvious?'

'I've been watching you all night, and Terry Jones must be both thick and blind not to realise you weren't exactly enjoying yourself.'

Jackie smiled. 'That's an understatement!' Then she eyed Vic gratefully. 'It seems you're turning into my knight in shining armour. Thank you. Now I just have to think of a good excuse to give him for not going back.'

Vic smiled. 'I'm sure you will.' He looked at her for a moment before saying, 'You gave me the impression the other night that you were just out of a long-term relationship and not interested in going out with anyone else yet?'

She vehemently insisted, 'Oh, being with Terry tonight wasn't a date, although he thinks it was, but not as far as I'm concerned. He did me a favour and let it be known I owed him a date in return.'

'Oh, I see. Only I was hoping you were ready to start dating again. I'd really like to take you out, Jackie. When you are, if you fancy going somewhere with me, will you let me know?'

She was very surprised to find that she would like to do that. She had certainly enjoyed Vic's company the other night, had found him very interesting and liked the way that he respected her situation and hadn't been pushing her for an immediate date. He had come to her rescue twice now and the least she could do by way of a thank you was buy him a drink.

'Yes, I'd like that. Whenever you like,' she said.

Vic looked delighted. 'You would? That's great. Well, it's still early so what about we go somewhere now?'

Jackie looked aghast. 'But I can't go back into Groovy's with you. Terry will still be there.'

'I should have explained myself better – I meant, off the camp. We could go to Skeggy. Meet me by the fountain in a couple of minutes,' Vic told her, and before she could ask why he'd shot off towards the camp entrance.

Assuming he'd gone to use the public telephone to ring for a taxi she made her way to the fountain, hoping Terry didn't come looking for her in the meantime.

Looking for a sign of Vic returning through intermittent groups of holidaymakers coming out of the Paradise and cinema to make their way back to their chalets, Jackie was surprised when a dirty old transit van pulled up beside her. The driver's window was wound down and a grinning Vic poked out his head, saying, 'Your carriage awaits, Ma'dam.'

She chuckled to herself as she hurried around the other side and climbed in through the passenger door he'd leaned over and opened for her, settling herself on the bench seat beside him. Her so far disastrous evening was suddenly turning into a much better one.

The front well of the van was full of old food wrappers, empty bottles and discarded items of clothing, which Vic had obviously swept off the seat before she had got in. He said to her apologetically, 'Sorry about the state of the van. If I'd have had more time I'd have given it a clean out in your honour.'

Jackie was no snob. Keith hadn't had a car so they'd used her scooter to get around when the bus wasn't an option, and before him any lad she had been out with had had no transport either, so to be with a man who did was a novelty to her.

When Vic parked the van on Skegness sea front half an hour later, despite the hour the promenade was still teeming with holidaymakers buying souvenirs and rock from the parade of canvas-topped stalls and enjoying themselves in the arcades, in the funfair or strolling down the pier. The pubs were shut by now but there was still food to be had in fish and chip shops and a couple of restaurants, and dancing at several night clubs which didn't shut until one.

'So what do you fancy doing?' Vic asked her.

Jackie really didn't mind and told him so. Vic suggested they should try their luck on the slot machines in the arcades. Having both changed silver coins into pennies and halfpennies they tried their luck on several, emerging a while later having lost their stake. They then went to a shop and bought a bag of chips each, liberally sprinkled with salt and vinegar. They walked down to the beach and sat on wooden benches looking out across a wide expanse of golden sand illuminated by a full moon in a starry sky. While they ate they chatted amicably together.

Many times in the past Jackie had visited Skegness with Keith and done exactly what she was doing now with Vic. At this realisation she couldn't stop the memories crowding in, and feelings of sadness and loss engulfed her.

Vic obviously noticed she had suddenly gone very quiet. Guessing the cause, he said to her, 'Best be getting you back to the camp or you'll be accusing me tomorrow of making you too tired for work.'

She realised that he'd guessed the reason for her sudden change of mood. What a thoughtful man he was, wanting to get her away from a situation that was obviously causing her grief. The more she got to know Vic the more she liked him.

She was just about to stand up when a couple walking barefoot across the sand about thirty feet away from her, their hands clasped tightly together, heads bent towards each other deep in conversation, arrested her attention. It wasn't their obvious closeness or apparent contentment at being in each other's company that drew her eye so much as who the couple were. It was her mother and Keith. And if ever Jackie had witnessed a couple in love, it was these two.

Suddenly something changed within her. Witnessing them together, the two people she cared for the most in the world, their total devotion towards each other made her feel proud that she was responsible for bringing it about. The emotional pain she had suffered as a result felt worthwhile suddenly. She knew fate had brought her here tonight to make her understand that Keith had come into her life not to be her own life-long partner, but to bring her mother the happiness Jackie had so vehemently wished Gina would find. All the hurt and anger she'd felt towards them was gone, to be replaced by an inner peace. She could let the past go now and move forward, allow another man into her life who was meant to bring her the same sort of happiness that Keith and her mother shared. It was still too soon for her to rekindle her relationship with them both but seeing them together tonight had brought that time closer.

Vic broke into her thoughts by asking, 'Ready to go?'

Jackie turned to look at him, smiled and nodded. 'Thank you so much for bringing me here tonight.'

He was bemused by her gratitude. As far as he was aware he'd brought her here to help make up for the miserable time she had suffered with that awful Terry Jones, albeit Vic was secretly grateful to the little weasel for giving him the opportunity to spend more time with Jackie. He responded, 'Well, if you enjoyed yourself that much maybe you'd like to go out with me again? A proper date next time. Wednesday night is the band's night off.'

Certain that she was ready now to start dating again, Jackie readily agreed.

She entered the chalet a while later to find Ginger sitting up in bed reading a Mills and Boon romance which she immediately slapped shut, desperate to hear the gory details of how her friend's dreaded evening out with Terry Jones had gone.

'Well?' Ginger demanded.

Throwing herself on the bed, head propped on one

hand, with a dreamy look in her eyes, Jackie said, 'It was a wonderful evening, Ginger. He's such a lovely man. Very thoughtful. I think I could get to like him very much.'

Ginger was gawping back at her astounded. 'Have you lost your mind, gel? That man is a lecherous cretin! What happened with your mam and Keith must have affected you more badly than you realised. First thing in the morning I'm going to make sure you go and see Sister Stephens. I'll drag you there myself if I have to!'

Jackie snapped, 'There's nothing wrong with me, Ginger. I thought you'd be happy that I'd met someone who made me want to start dating again?'

'Yes, I am, of course I am, but not the likes of Terry Jones, for God's sake!'

Jackie burst into laughter. 'I'd sooner die than go out with him again. It's Vic, the drummer with the Upbeats, I'm talking about.'

Ginger exclaimed, 'Oh, thank God for that! Bloody hell, you had me worried you'd lost your marbles for a minute there, Jackie.' Then she asked, bemused, 'So how did you end up with him tonight then when it was Terry you had the date with?'

Jackie told her all the events of the evening.

Ginger sat listening, entranced. When her friend had finished, she said, 'Well, it seems to me, whether you like it or not, you have a lot to thank Terry Jones for.'

'Not that I'll ever tell him so and make his head any bigger than it is already, but yes, it seems I do, in a roundabout way. If he wasn't so full of himself, Vic wouldn't have needed to come to my rescue. And if we hadn't been on Skeggy front tonight, I wouldn't have seen my mother and Keith together and realised what I did.'

Ginger nodded. 'God moves in mysterious ways, so it's said.' Then she looked excited. 'You being back to normal is a good excuse for us to throw a party. Leave it to me, I'll organise it for Friday night.'

As Jackie scrambled off the bed to put on her night clothes, she replied matter-of-factly, 'Since when have you ever needed an excuse?'

CHAPTER TWENTY

Harold Rose was looking curiously at Jackie as she stood closely watching the employee manning the helter-skelter ride. They were positioned a discreet distance away, just by the dodgem cars.

'Miss Sims, may I ask why you're watching that young man? He simply appears to be doing his job to me, so why are you so interested in him?'

'Yes, he does seem to be doing an exemplary job, chatting and laughing with the campers, getting them to have a go on the ride, but as we were passing I saw him slip a fare into his own pocket instead of his money pouch. Just to make sure, I'm watching to see if he does it again. Of course, he might have spotted us going by so if he is up to something he won't risk it again until he knows we've left. I've a pile of work to do back at the office so I'll give it another couple of minutes then go and find the funfair manager. Tip him off to keep an eye out.'

Harold took a glance around at the rides and side stalls in his line of vision, and asked, 'How do you know all the ride operators and stall assistants aren't up to the same thing?'

'We don't, Mr Rose. There is no way the funfair

manager can be sure what any of the rides' or stalls' takings will be on any particular day. We just have to trust that those running them are being honest with the takings they hand over each night. They're warned at the start of their employment that should they be caught doing anything they shouldn't, then they will be instantly dismissed and face prosecution. Most of the employees are as straight as a die, but you do get the odd cocky one who thinks they're too clever to be caught.'

Thoughtfully, Harold stared across at the employee in question. As Jolly's accountant he'd felt no need to educate himself in the day-to-day management of the business, but since this young girl had taken it upon herself to help him overcome his shyness, over the last month he'd been having his eyes well and truly opened. It had never before occurred to him just how much work was involved in the daily running of Jolly's, as well as the time-consuming ad-hoc situations that cropped up. He felt guilt-ridden for having left her to cope with it virtually alone all these weeks. But if this young girl could find the strength within herself to do all she had, then surely he could find it within himself to control his nerves and lift some of the burden off her young shoulders.

He shocked Jackie now by suggesting, 'If you need to get back, I'll find the manager and have a word with him.' As soon as the words were out of Harold's mouth, he could have kicked himself. Now he'd have to deal with someone he'd never met before and present an authoritative manner towards him, warn the man that one of his staff had been observed lining his own pockets – something the manager should have noticed himself. He might not like the implied criticism, and choose to retaliate!

Jackie tried to hide her shock at Harold's offer, knowing what it was going to take for him to see it through and also wondering what had suddenly given him the impetus to make this momentous leap forward. But not wanting to say anything that would give him any cause for self-doubt, she responded, 'I'd appreciate that, Mr Rose. Can I leave you to it then?'

Harold fought the urge to tell her that he'd changed his mind, that he wasn't up to doing this and had said it in a moment of bravado, then reminded himself he had promised to start pulling his weight. He managed a firm, 'Yes, of course. I'll see you back at the office shortly.'

Jackie immediately hurried off.

En route she was just passing the sports field and tennis courts at a fork in the path when she spotted a middle-aged woman hurrying out of the chalet complex, heading towards her to join the path leading to the front of the camp. The woman looked extremely upset and distracted. Jackie automatically changed direction to meet her and enquire what the matter was and if she could help.

'It's . . . it's my Fred,' she burst out, panic-stricken. 'I woke him up from his afternoon nap. He got up, clutched his chest and collapsed on the floor. I can't wake him up. I'm on my way to fetch the nurse.'

Jackie's thoughts raced. 'Carry on to the surgery and tell Sister Stephens what has happened. Meanwhile I'll go to your chalet and see what I can do for your husband.' Not that she would have a clue about the medical procedures necessary but the woman wasn't in any state to be sent back to wait with a sick man until help arrived. 'What's the number of your chalet?' Jackie enquired.

In her deeply distressed state the woman was obviously

still trying to take in Jackie's instructions. 'Er . . . three two one. Oh, no, that's the number of the chalet we stayed in last year . . . or is it? Oh, dear, I can't remember. Four five two . . . or is it four two five? Yes, that's the one.'

'Four two five,' Jackie repeated.

The woman looked doubtful but responded, 'Yes, that's it.'

Sending the distraught woman on her way, Jackie was about to hare off to the chalet and what awaited her inside when out of the corner of her eye she saw Harold Rose heading up the path towards her, on his way back from the funfair. The fact that he looked extremely upset and seemed to be in a desperate hurry to get back to the office did not register with her – or that he seemed to have dealt with the problem there very quickly. Jackie just saw someone to accompany her into the unknown territory she was about to enter.

Grabbing his arm as he hurried past, not seeming to see her, she blurted out, 'We have an emergency, Mr Rose.' She quickly told him what had transpired and ended, 'Will you come with me? I'm terrified the man is dead. I've never seen a dead body before.'

Having been worried himself about how he was going to face Jackie and tell her that, at first sight of the fiercesome-looking, barrel-chested funfair manager, he had completely lost his nerve and made a bolt for it, Harold brightened up unexpectedly. For once he could be of some use because of the simple fact that during the long lonely nights after his mother had died, books and the radio had been his only friends, and one of the books he'd studied from cover to cover had been on first aid.

He confounded Jackie for the second time that day by telling her, 'Lead the way.'

Being almost half his age, she was much quicker on her feet and was a good distance in front of Harold, reaching chalet 425 well ahead of him. Outside, she hesitated just enough to take a deep breath and steel herself, then she opened the door and hurried inside.

To her shock it wasn't a body she encountered but two very much alive men, one middle-aged and the other maybe in his early thirties. They were lounging on the two single beds, reading newspapers. Despite its being broad daylight outside, the curtains were tightly drawn and the light was on. The room stank of stale body odour, cigarette smoke, beer and food. In one corner was a stack of old newspapers, empty beer bottles, fish and chip and hamburger wrappers. At the end of a bed was a large case with a jumble of clothes inside and a couple of wigs lying on top. In the gap between the beds was the small chest of drawers on top of which lay a pack of cards. These men couldn't have left their chalet since they'd arrived.

At Jackie's unexpected entry both men sat staring at her in shock.

It was the older one who was the first to gather his wits. Sitting bolt upright he demanded, 'Who the hell are you, barging in here like this? Get out!'

Obviously she had been given the wrong chalet number by the confused woman. But what caught Jackie's attention was the nose of the man who had rudely addressed her. It was badly misshapen, obviously having been broken not once but several times and never re-set properly. Unable to take her eyes off it, Jackie blurted out,

'I'm so sorry, really I am. I was told a man had collapsed in this chalet. I must have been given the wrong number.'

'Yes, you must. Now get out!'

Apologising profusely, she backed out, shutting the door behind her.

Panting heavily, Harold reached her then. She told him, 'The lady gave me the wrong number. I've just barged in on two men who weren't at all happy about my intrusion.' Then something struck her and she added, 'I wonder what they would need wigs for?'

Harold eyed her in confusion. 'Wigs! What wigs?'

The urgent need to get to the sick man and see what, if anything, they could do for him until proper help arrived occurred to Jackie then. 'Oh, it doesn't matter.' She frowned in thought. 'Now, what were the other numbers she mentioned? Oh, yes, three two one. No, she said that was the number of the chalet they stayed in last year . . .' Then she realised it must be the other number the woman had mentioned: 452. She told Harold, adding, 'Let's hope it's that one or I haven't a clue where the man is.'

Jackie raced off, with Harold trailing in her wake. Arriving at chalet 452, conscious of her last reception Jackie first knocked on the door and, receiving no reply, cautiously turned the door knob and went inside. A middle-aged man lay crumpled on the floor. Dashing over, she knelt down beside him. His skin was the colour of parchment, his lips blue. She looked up as Harold arrived.

'I think he's dead!'

Without a word Harold pushed her out of the way, heedless of the fact that he had been a bit too rough and she tumbled sideways. Harold meanwhile picked up the man's limp wrist and felt for a pulse.

'He's alive . . . barely, but still alive.'

He then turned the man over so he was lying on his back and placed both hands over his heart. Harold began to pump up and down, counting as he did so, taking a rest after so many compressions, ready to begin again. He then squeezed open the man's mouth, placed his own over it and blew into it several times. Then went back to pumping the man's chest. Harold was still continuing with this procedure when the ambulance men arrived twenty minutes later. Jackie anxiously watched, willing the unconscious man to show signs of life.

A while later, after shutting the doors of the ambulance, a crewman said to Harold, 'Mrs Blenkinsop has asked me to thank you for what you tried to do for her husband and she'll thank you herself when she's feeling better but she's too upset to at the moment. I am sure you can appreciate that.'

Looking down at the ground, Harold was nervously shuffling his feet. 'But I failed, didn't I? So she's nothing to thank me for, has she?'

The man patted his arm. 'You tried your best to save her husband's life, Mr Rose, kept going when others would have stopped long before. In my book that deserves a pat on the back. After all, we can't win them all, can we.'

A steady crowd of campers had gathered around the chalet when the ambulance had first arrived and they all watched solemnly as it drove away. Desperate to get himself out of the glare of public attention, believing he knew what was being said by others about him, Harold began to scuttle off back to the office, Jackie trotting after him. The only way to go was via the crowd. As

Harold passed through they started clapping and patting him on the back by way of showing their appreciation. Jackie could see that the attention he was receiving was at first making Harold very uncomfortable. Then she noticed a remarkable change come over him. His drooping shoulders began to straighten, his bent head to rise, his scurrying walk to become more of a confident stride.

She caught his arm and asked, 'Mr Rose, are you all right?'

He looked her straight in the eye for the first time since she had known him. 'Yes, Miss Sims, I think I am. It's hard for me to explain but it's like a fog has cleared and I can register things clearly now. You see, I've always felt that if I make a single mistake in front of anyone they'll see me as a blithering idiot and reject me as not being worthy of their attention, so I've purposely avoided mixing with people to prevent that from happening. I realise, though, that it isn't a question of success or failure. Just now, when I saw that poor man lying there, for once I didn't think about my own worries for a second, I just got on with what I needed to do. You're right, Jackie. I have to believe in myself more, and the rest will follow.'

She heaved a deep sigh of relief. 'Yes, that's exactly what you need to do, Mr Rose. It won't happen overnight and, like you said, you may never become the life and soul of the party, but at least you won't be cowering in the corner any longer and should begin to make some friends for yourself. Like everyone else, sometimes you'll be faced with doing things that fill you with dread, but each time you face your fears, it will become easier for you.'

He looked at her searchingly. 'You're very wise for such a young woman. I owe you a huge debt of gratitude, because if you hadn't taken the trouble to try and help me change myself then I would have ended up an old man, dying alone, with no one to attend my funeral. Not now, though. I'm determined that won't happen.'

'You don't know how happy I am to hear it.'

He then looked at her shamefaced. 'There is something I need to tell you, though. You see, I bottled out of facing the funfair manager. I took one look at him and did an about turn.'

Jackie chuckled. 'I did exactly the same thing the first time I came across him. Mr Davis does look rather frightening, but in his case looks are deceiving. He's really a pussy cat, but believe me he can turn into a raging tiger if he finds any of his staff are making a fool of him behind his back. I wouldn't like to be in that thief's shoes, I can tell you, when Mr Davis finds out what he's been up to. At the time you suggested going to see him yourself, I did think you were being a bit over-ambitious. Would you like me to come with you now and we'll tell Mr Davis together?'

'Yes, please.' Harold then added optimistically, 'And hopefully very soon you won't need to babysit me like you have been doing.'

If he kept up this attitude, she felt she certainly would not.

A while later, back at the office, Harold informed Jackie that the hospital had telephoned to let him know that Mrs Blenkinsop wanted her husband to be buried back at home and arrangements were being made to organise that. In turn, Harold had stressed that Jolly's would do anything they could to help Mrs Blenkinsop through her difficult time.

* * *

It was just gone half-past five that evening and Jackie was finishing making alterations to the accommodation log book when Al called across to her, 'All right with you if I put the switchboard on night service, Jackie?'

Thinking it was only about four o'clock and wondering why he would be suggesting getting ready to go home already, she automatically looked up at the large clock on the wall above his desk and exclaimed, 'Good gracious, is it that time already? Yes, of course, Al, or you'll risk missing the bus.' She needed to get a move on herself and finish for the night as she had a date with Vic and wanted time in advance to make herself look nice.

As he tidied his desk Al said to her, 'I can't believe the change in Mr Rose. He even agreed to take that tricky phone call with the coach-hire company. Your plan to help him get out of his shell seems to be working.'

Jackie smiled. 'Yes, I'm pleased to say it is. I never thought I'd hear myself say this but, as much as I'm looking forward to Mrs Jolly and Mrs Buckland coming back and us becoming The Three Musketeers again, I hope they don't until Mr Rose has built up his confidence even more.' She suddenly realised what Drina and Rhonnie's return would mean for Al and hurriedly added, 'Oh, not that I'm wanting to see the back of you, Al, not at all. You've settled in well here and are doing a great job. I couldn't have managed without you.'

He was secretly hoping that the two women didn't come back just yet either as he hadn't quite finished what he needed to accomplish. Another two or three weeks should do it, the way he was progressing, then they could return whenever they wanted. 'I know what you mean, it's all right,' he laughed. 'I'll be sad when my time here ends – I do enjoy working with you, Jackie – but I'm only a temp after all, and I've always been aware I'd be moving on at some time. Anyway, I'm off now. I'll see you in the morning.'

'Have a good night, Al.'

He had just closed the door at the top of the stairs when Harold appeared out of the boss's office. He was looking very pleased with himself.

He said to Jackie, 'Well, I think that went well. I was quite firm and told the manager of the coach company that we went to a great deal of trouble to sort out the slots to avoid congestion, and it's up to them to inform their passengers that the departure time they gave out was wrong and to give them the correct one. He got very stroppy, and I will be honest and tell you that my nerves began to get the better of me at one stage, but like you advised I excused myself, took several deep breaths, then went back to the phone and stood my ground with him.'

'This really is a red letter day for you, isn't it, Mr Rose? You carry on like this and soon you won't be able to recognise yourself. Is it all right with you if I finish up now? There's nothing that can't wait until tomorrow. I have a date tonight and don't want to keep him waiting.'

He wondered why Jackie was asking his permission when before she had always just informed him she was going, which had only been on the very rare occasion he had still been in the office after her. Then it struck him that this was her way of reminding him he was in fact the boss and she was showing respect for his position.

Maybe one night it would be him telling her he was rushing off for a date, he thought wistfully. This young girl before him had made him believe that could happen if he kept up his determination to work on his confidence, which he fully intended to. 'Yes, of course, you get off, Miss Sims. I'm just going to ready myself.'

He returned to the boss's office, to tidy his desk and collect his belongings. As she always did before she left, Jackie did a check around to make sure all the drawers were locked and, not doubting Al at all, double checking that the switchboard had been put over to night service. Gratified to see it had, she was just rounding his desk when she noticed something sticking out from under the call log book and saw it was Al's wallet, which he'd obviously forgotten to take with him. He wouldn't be able to pay his bus fare without his money and the conductor would throw him off. If she rushed she might just catch him at the stop.

Quickly telling Harold why she was dashing off and asking him if he minded locking up, which he assured her he absolutely didn't, Jackie shot out.

Outside the camp gates, from a position affording her a good view of the bus stop, she surveyed the queue. Chatting and laughing together were several chalet maids who lived locally and the two women who worked in the accounts office. There was also a handful of campers obviously going into Mablethorpe for the evening or on to Skegness. Al wasn't amongst them. She frowned in confusion. Where was he? Then she saw the bus in the distance. She looked back towards the staff entrance gates. Still no sign of Al. The bus drew up at the stop and the queue got on. The bus pulled away again. If Al wasn't on the bus then the only way he was getting home tonight was by walking. Giving a shrug, she put his wallet in her handbag and made her way over to the chalet to wait for

Ginger to return. They would eat at the restaurant together before Jackie returned to get ready for her night out with Vic.

An hour later she was sitting on a chair before the small chest of drawers in the chalet, peering into the propped-up mirror, putting on her make-up.

Ginger was sitting on her bed unwinding huge rollers from her hair in an effort to straighten it a little, which it would do but only for a short while before it sprang back into its usual mass of spring-like curls. She was meeting the girls who worked with her on reception and they were going to watch the weekly talent show held in the Paradise ballroom. 'So where is Vic taking you tonight?' she asked Jackie.

'I don't know. Damn, I've smudged my mascara! Have you got a tissue or cotton-wool ball handy?'

Ginger threw her a cotton-wool ball which landed beside Jackie on the floor. Bending to pick it up, she dabbed at the offending smudge under her lower lashes until it was gone, then spat on her block of black mascara, ran the little brush over it, and when it was fully loaded began blackening her lashes again with a thick layer. 'I'm determined that I'm going to pay for at least one round tonight. I feel so guilty that every other time we've been out Vic hasn't let me put my hand in my pocket. I know he's saving hard to be able to buy himself a business when he's ready to leave the band.'

Ginger sighed wistfully. 'Yes, he is the generous sort. I wish I could find a bloke who wants to buy me a drink, let alone pay for a night out. And I'd certainly love to be on the receiving end of that silver bracelet and necklace he bought you.'

Jackie looked down at the bracelet adorning her wrist and then fingered the delicate heart-shaped locket around her neck. Vic had given her them as a present on two separate occasions and she'd been overwhelmed. He was spending money on her like there was plenty more where that came from when he was meant to be saving for his future.

'There's a man out there who will treat you just like that, Ginger,' Jackie reassured her. 'It's just that you haven't met him yet.'

Ginger eyed her strangely. 'Didn't you pinch that line from me?'

'Yes, and it seems it was true in my case, so it will be in yours.'

Ginger sighed. 'Well, let's hope he's just around the corner and not well down the road so I haven't long to wait until I meet him.' Then she looked over at Jackie meaningfully. 'You've been seeing Vic for a few weeks now. Seems to me you're really getting to like him.'

Jackie studied her reflection in the mirror for a moment, seeing if she could make any improvements to her make-up. Happy with what she saw, she swivelled around to look at Ginger. 'Yes, I do really like him. I'm not in love with him but I'd be very upset if Vic decided he didn't want to see me any more. He's helped me get over Keith, made me see there's life after him, so to speak, and I'm grateful for that.'

'And for the presents,' Ginger commented flippantly.

Jackie scolded her, 'Ginger, you know me well enough by now to know that my feelings for Vic have nothing at all to do with him buying me presents. I'm not like that.' Then, for no apparent reason, a vision of the man who'd responded angrily to her when she'd mistakenly barged into his chalet earlier occurred to her and she said absently, 'I recognised that man from somewhere but I can't put my finger on . . .'

'What man?' Ginger asked.

'That one I told you about, who went for me this afternoon when I barged into his chalet by mistake.'

'Well, it's obvious where you've seen him, you daft clot. Around the camp.'

'No, no, that's not it. Anyway, from the state of the chalet I don't think he's left it since he arrived so I couldn't have done.' Jackie stood up then and smoothed down the short red tent dress she was wearing. 'Will I do?' she asked her friend.

'You'll have him champing at the bit.' Ginger then stood up and gave a twirl in the narrow space between the beds. 'What about me?'

She was currently going through a hippy phase and was wearing a long colourful psychedelic-patterned skirt together with a cream halterneck top.

'You'll knock 'em dead,' Jackie assured her.

Both having assured each other that they looked great, they set off on their respective evenings out.

Tonight Vic had taken Jackie for a meal and drinks in a pub in the small market town of Louth and she had thoroughly enjoyed herself and not hesitated to agree when he asked her to meet him in two days' time after he'd finished his session with the band at Groovy's. They'd have a drink in the Paradise and then go for a walk down to the beach. Jackie knew he liked her a lot and did wonder when he would make a move on her, to take their relationship further. She wasn't quite ready to just yet, but felt she soon would be. It was also beginning to cross her mind that if she did fall for Vic, it wasn't going to be easy for her to say goodbye to him when the season ended and he and the band went on their way. She'd just got over one painful break up and didn't like the thought of another.

On arriving back in the camp Vic dropped her off outside the Paradise while he went to park the van. Jackie waited for him to return so they could walk together over to the staff chalets. Arriving back, he took her hand and they were just about to set off when Jackie stopped short, surprised to see two teenage girls and two boys scaling the large concrete sculptures of the dolphins in the middle of the water. As her eyes travelled upwards, Jackie's surprise turned to sheer panic to see a girl at the top trying to stand on the mermaid's head, seemingly oblivious to the danger she was in and also to the crowd gathering below. They like Jackie were horrified and were shouting to the girl to come down before something serious happened to her.

Vic had seen her by now. 'What on earth does she think she's doing?' he exclaimed.

'We have to try and get her down before she . . . Oh, my God, now she's standing with her arms out, looking like she's going to jump off. Is she so drunk she thinks she can fly? Oh, no, she's going to jump . . . Oh, hell, she has!' Jackie exclaimed.

The whole crowd watched dumbstruck as the girl came crashing down to earth, to land with a sickening thud on the hard tarmac between some spectators. Unaware of what had happened to their friend, giggling hysterically at their own antics, the other four teenagers were still trying to clamber up the fountain.

Gathering her wits, Jackie ordered Vic, 'Get those others off the fountain before anyone else is hurt, while I fetch the nurse and call an ambulance.'

A while later Jackie and Vic were both sitting in the nurse's office in the surgery, sipping cups of hot sweet tea.

A shaken and upset Jackie murmured, 'I've had one too many a few times in my life but all I get is giggly. And I've done a couple of stupid things I had to apologise for the next day, like being sick in the taxi home, but I've never got it into my head that I could fly.'

Sister Kitty Popple had been working for Jolly's for a couple of weeks now and had quickly become liked by staff and campers. She was fifty-two years of age, of medium height, with a body that resembled a beachball. When she laughed, which was often, her whole body would wobble from side to side. Tonight, though, she was looking solemn as she responded to Jackie's comment. 'Well, that girl was very lucky to get away with two broken legs and one fractured arm, but it's my medical opinion that she had consumed something else besides alcohol. So had her friends, but thankfully they were stopped from doing anything so stupid themselves. Now their parents are dealing with them.'

Jackie frowned at her. 'What had she taken?'

'That's for the hospital to confirm, and as soon as they do I will pass the information on to you, but some sort of hallucinogen.'

Jackie looked bemused. 'Halluci-what?'

Vic told her, 'Sister means drugs, Jackie.'

She exclaimed, 'Drugs?'

Kitty nodded. 'I'm almost positive she took Lysergic acid diethylamide, or LSD as it's known for short.'

Jackie shook her head, refusing to believe it. 'But Groovy's is no London nightclub, we don't get that sort of thing here.'

Kitty folded her arms under her enormous bosom. 'Taking recreational drugs isn't just confined to London, dear. You can buy them in any town in the country as well as at a holiday camp, if you know the right people to ask.'

Jackie snapped, 'Not any longer at Jolly's. It stops right here and now. I'll call the police in.'

Vic spoke up. 'I wouldn't advise that, Jackie. The last thing you want is them making an investigation and maybe closing Groovy's down. Think what that would do to the reputation of the camp when the nationals got hold of it, and they would be bound to with a story like this.'

She looked horrified. 'That could finish us. No, no, we can't get the police involved, can we? So we'll have to think of some other way to stop this person selling drugs to our campers.'

'Well, we don't know for certain yet that the girl had taken drugs,' Vic reminded her.

'No, we don't, but if it turns out she has and got them off someone here in the camp then we can't just turn a blind eye. Someone might end up dead if we do.'

'Well, yes, I suppose,' mused Vic. He then eyed her meaningfully. 'Look, Jackie, I speak from experience, having played in clubs and pubs up and down the country. I'm no stranger to certain members of the audience getting high on drugs . . . not that I condone it myself, most certainly I don't, and wouldn't touch them personally. I value my sanity and life too much . . . but say you catch this person selling drugs here, there'd soon be someone else taking their place.'

She eyed him closely. 'So you are saying we should turn a blind eye to this, are you?'

'All I'm trying to point out, Jackie, is that unless you strip-search everyone who comes into the camp, I don't see how you will be able to stop drugs being taken by those who want to take them.'

She could see his point and sighed heavily. 'Well, Vic, maybe we won't be able to but until Mrs Jolly comes back and decides what measures she wants to put in place to prevent this kind of thing going on, then it's down to Mr Rose and me to do our best to put a stop to it.'

Kitty put in, 'As a member of the medical profession with a good idea of the dangers of drug-taking, I agree with you, Jackie. It is your duty as part of management to do your best to stop these youngsters putting their lives in danger.'

Jackie suddenly froze as a memory struck her. She pondered it for a moment before worriedly asking Kitty, 'If someone had taken some sort of drug, would they have glazed eyes and be dancing like . . . well, demented chickens? That sort of thing?'

Kitty nodded. 'Amphetamines would cause them to act like that.'

Jackie looked even more worried as something occurred to her. 'A few weeks ago, me and Ginger were in Groovy's and there were some girls dancing crazily. We just thought they were drunk . . . and I've seen both girls and lads acting like that since . . . but now I wonder if it wasn't drink that was the cause but drugs. If that's the case then this has been going on for a while and it can't be one of the campers they're getting the drugs from but a member of staff.' She issued another despairing groan, scraping her hand through her hair. 'Oh, God, it was bad enough thinking a camper was dealing the drugs, but a member of staff . . .

'The drugs must be changing hands somehow in Groovy's. I'll speak to the staff, ask them to keep a special eye out for anything they see they think is suspicious, and report it back to management.' Then another thought occurred to her. 'Oh, but then, what if it's one of the Groovy's staff who's the culprit and I'm warning them we're on to them? They could make a bolt for it before we can get them arrested by the police, and be free to carry on their business at another camp or town.' She looked at the others imploringly. 'I shall have to tell Mr Rose, of course, but apart from telling him we have to keep this to ourselves, so whoever it is doesn't get wind and scarper before we can bring him to the attention of the police.'

Having received their assurances they would not breathe a word, Jackie's thoughts returned to coming up with a plausible plan to catch the dealer red-handed. Another memory returned. A couple of years ago they'd discovered they had a thief amongst the staff and Jackie spent long evenings with Drina, Rhonnie, Dan and the receptionists, hiding for hours in cramped conditions, until the guilty people were observed, caught and prosecuted for their illicit activities. It seemed to her that the only way to catch the drug dealer was to use the same plan, spending every evening in Groovy's looking out for any suspicious goings on. Jackie enjoyed going to Groovy's once or twice a week, but the idea of spending all her evenings there for the foreseeable future did not appeal at all. But if that was what it took to catch the guilty party and keep the good name of the camp intact, then so be it.

She outlined her plan to Vic and Kitty, concluding with, 'We can't ask Mr Rose to help patrol Groovy's as he'll stick out like a sore thumb.' And without thinking she added, 'As would you, Kitty.'

The nurse's eyebrows rose in indignation. 'Thank you for reminding me that I've one foot in my grave, dear.'

Jackie gasped and exclaimed, 'Oh, I'm so sorry, Kitty, I didn't mean . . . look, what I meant was . . . er . . .'

The nurse chuckled. 'Stop panicking! I'm having fun with you, dear. I know you wouldn't say anything deliberately to hurt me. I'm well aware my days of throwing myself around a dance floor are gone. In my day the jive was all the rage and to me that's what you call dancing, not all this jiggling around you youngsters do now. Anyway, my long shifts here and my home life don't allow me much, if any, free time, so as much as I'd have liked to, I'm not able to offer you any help, I'm afraid.'

Jackie smiled at her. 'I appreciate the fact that you would have helped if you could.' She then turned to look at Vic. 'You can't help either, as you'll be on stage playing with the band except for Wednesdays. Next Wednesday, if you've nothing better on, your help would be appreciated. But let's hope by then we've caught whoever it is and life's back to normal. I realise that it will look odd if I'm in Groovy's by myself playing detective so I will have to recruit someone else, but the person I have in mind is perfectly trustworthy.'

When she told them that person was Ginger they had no argument with her choice.

As Vic walked her back to her chalet later, Jackie noticed that he was unusually quiet. 'Penny for them?' she asked.

'Eh! Oh, it's just that I look forward to the time we spend together, but with you on this mission to catch the person selling drugs it means I won't get to be with you until they're safely behind bars. I'll miss you, that's all.'

It surprised Jackie to realise how much she would miss him too. Again she reminded herself that she was on the road to heartache if she carried on allowing her feelings for Vic to deepen as come the end of the season they would have to part. Trouble was, she couldn't seem to make herself act on her own advice

Back at the chalet, Jackie took Ginger into her confidence and requested her help in uncovering who it was dealing drugs, which would involve them going to Groovy's every night. Ginger was so excited at being involved in what she saw as an undercover operation, especially when it meant having an excuse to go to her favourite venue every night, that she bubbled over to the point where eventually Jackie had to tell her to shut up about it so they could get some sleep or they'd be fit for nothing the next day.

CHAPTER TWENTY-ONE

Arriving early in the office the next morning so she could speak to Harold Rose about the previous evening's developments, Jackie had taken the switchboard off night service and was about to go over to her desk when the internal line from the surgery lit up. It was Sister Stephens informing her that Sister Popple had asked her to pass on a message to Jackie as soon as she came in. It appeared that the girl from last night had admitted taking a couple of pills and so had her friends. They had no idea what they were though, had just believed what they were told by another friend who'd bought them that they would make them feel good. The doctor Sister Popple spoke to had added that the girl was extremely lucky that the amount of amphetamine she had taken hadn't actually killed her. But there was no hope of finding out where they'd come from; the kids claimed they couldn't remember.

Harold was dumbstruck when Jackie explained to him the events of the previous evening. In his closeted world he knew nothing of such things except for the news items he had read in the newspapers about the growing drug culture in London. Since it was a world away from the corner of Britain he lived in, he hadn't taken much notice. His immediate response was that they must inform Drina Jolly of this development and get her instructions on how to deal with it, but Jackie managed to persuade him that she had enough on dealing with Rhonnie.

Not having been in a situation like this before, Harold openly admitted to Jackie he hadn't a clue how they went about catching a dealer, and didn't hide his relief when she said she had a plan. Ginger and she were going to pretend that they were normal clubgoers at Groovy's while secretly keeping their eyes open for any suspicious carryings on. For his part Harold offered to hang around the Paradise foyer, inconspicuously on the lookout for anything suspicious.

With this problem on her mind, Jackie completely forgot about finding Al's wallet the previous evening. She saw him rummaging around in his desk when she came out of Harold's office and automatically asked him what he was looking for.

Worried, he told her, 'My wallet. I took it out of my pocket yesterday afternoon so I could buy a bar of chocolate from the shop and I didn't realise I'd not put it back until I went to check last night. I couldn't find it. But it's not here so . . .'

Jackie interjected as she grabbed her handbag and fished out the wallet, 'Stop worrying, I've got it. I spotted it on your desk after you'd left last night as I was checking all was secure before I left myself.'

She walked across to hand it to him.

As he took it from her Al said, 'Thank goodness I've not lost it as I'd not have managed until payday without what's in here.' It then struck him that Jackie might wonder how he'd managed to pay his fare home and back to work today on the bus without his wallet and told her, 'Thankfully I had enough coins in my pocket to pay my bus fares but this will teach me to check I've got everything before I leave at night.'

Jackie looked taken aback. 'You caught the bus home last night? But I chased after you with your wallet and was just nearby when it arrived. I never saw you get on it.'

Of course she hadn't, because at the time he'd been stealing his way around the perimeters of the camp to his temporary home in the derelict farmhouse. He stared back at her frozen-faced, panic tightening his stomach. Unwittingly, Jackie had just caught him out in a lie and he had no idea how to get himself out of it without arousing her suspicions. He knew she was the inquisitive sort; where he was living and what he was doing must not be uncovered by her. She might not be understanding, as his family had not been, and then he'd be turned out immediately, which was the last thing he wanted when he was so very near to reaching his goal. The only option Al could see open to him was to brazen it out and hope she'd accept she'd made a mistake.

As matter-of-factly as he could, he responded, 'It's a mystery to me why you didn't see me. I did catch that bus.' He added jocularly, 'Maybe it's time for a visit to the optician.' It was obvious to Jackie that for him this conversation had ended as Al collected a pile of filing out of the tray and began to sort it into alphabetical order.

It was a mystery to Jackie too. There was nothing

wrong with her eyes. She knew what she'd seen, or hadn't seen in this case, which was Al at the bus stop or getting on the bus. He was obviously lying to her, but why would he need to about such a petty thing as whether he'd caught the bus home or not?

She wasn't given chance to ponder any longer as the door opened then and Maureen Watson, the elder of Harold's two assistants, arrived carrying two huge ledgers with a pile of paperwork on top.

Jackie smiled a greeting at the pleasant middle-aged woman. 'Morning, Maureen.'

As she met up with Jackie she responded accordingly before launching into, 'Well, that was a bit of a rum do yesterday, wasn't it? The behaviour of some people never ceases to amaze me.'

Instantly the words were out of her mouth panic reared up in Jackie that, despite all their precautions, gossip had leaked out that they had a drug dealer amongst them. Then her fears subsided as Maureen continued.

'That girl jumping off the fountain like she did and ending up almost breaking every bone in her body! I expect that'll teach her not to drink so much in future.'

Jackie said shortly, 'Well, hopefully it will. Mr Rose is in his office, so I'll just call through and let him know you're here to see him.'

'Thanks, Jackie. I'll be glad to put this lot down. These books weigh a ton.' Maureen then leaned closer, lowered her voice and said, 'Mr Rose hasn't received a thump on the head, has he?'

Jackie looked at her strangely. 'Not that I'm aware of. Why are you asking that?'

'Well, something must have happened to bring about

such a drastic change in him. When I went into his office to update him yesterday, he actually looked me in the eye, smiled, and asked me how I was. Could have knocked me down with a feather. I could see he was a bit uncomfortable about it, but he did it all the same. He's not what you'd call a handsome man, is he? But he's got a lovely smile, which certainly improves his looks no end. After all this time working with him, it was a pleasure finally to see it. I was beginning to wonder if he didn't smile because he hadn't any teeth.'

Maureen paused to chuckle at her own joke before she continued, 'Anyway, whatever has brought about this miraculous change in him, I hope it lasts. This new version of Mr Rose is a great improvement on the off-hand, po-faced one we had before. To be honest, me and Sally have enjoyed our jobs so much more since he's been doing his stint as boss in here, being free to laugh and chat, make tea when we want, and not having to whisper to each other and mind our Ps and Qs, because that's how he made us feel we had to behave. Because of the more relaxed atmosphere we've got more done and the time has passed so much quicker. We were dreading him coming back and us having to go back to working in a mausoleum again, but now . . . well, maybe we needn't dread his return. I live in hope at any rate. Anyway, give him the nod I'm here then, love, before my arms drop off.'

Just over two weeks later Ginger heaved a fed-up sigh and moaned to Jackie, 'Just think, I used to get so excited about dressing up and coming to this place, wondering if this would be my lucky night and I'd meet Mr Wonderful.

I didn't think I'd hear myself say this but if I never came here again, it would be too soon for me. If I hear Hats singing "I'm a Believer" one more time, I think I'll scream.'

Ginger was voicing exactly what Jackie was thinking. She felt she knew the Upbeats' repertoire better than they did, and the DJ's too.

The two young women, doing their best to act just like the rest of the Groovy's revellers, had kept their eyes peeled for any suspicious activity going on from the moment it opened until it closed. Harold Rose had done his bit in the Paradise foyer and intermittently had a nose around the other recreation rooms. None of them had witnessed anything going on between a member of Jolly's staff and the campers, or even camper and camper, that looked like money being exchanged for drugs.

Ginger was griping again. 'Look, Jackie, we've kept a watch on all the bar staff over the last two weeks or so and seen none of them acting at all strangely, and we've approached at least a dozen people we think have taken drugs, pretending we're after buying some for ourselves, and apart from the couple it was obvious didn't know what the hell we were talking about, from the rest we've had the same answer . . . "from the shop". Did they think we're so bloody daft we'd believe you can just go into a shop and buy illegal drugs!

'But this same stupid answer has got me to wondering if we've been sussed out by the dealer, and he or she has given those that buy from them our descriptions and threatened them they're not to blab to us or else they'll live to regret it. If that's the case, I don't know how we're ever going to catch them red-handed as they're not going to do any deals while they know we're hanging around nearby, so all we're doing here is wasting our time.'

Jackie heaved a sigh. 'You could be right, Ginger, but unless you've got any other bright idea how we can catch the dealer . . .?' Her friend gave a shrug by way of telling Jackie she hadn't. 'Well then, we have no choice but to stick with what we're doing because at least it's better than doing nothing. No matter how clever this person is, or how well they believe they've covered their tracks, everyone makes mistakes. They will sometime and we'll be there to nab them when they do.' She then looked at her friend meaningfully. 'Look, when I roped you in, to be honest I never thought we'd still be here over two weeks later and no further forward than when we first started. I'll understand if you don't want to do this any more.'

Ginger sighed. 'Well, if I'm being honest, I don't, but you're my friend and I will see this through with you until the bitter end. At least we have each other, unlike poor Harold who's patrolling upstairs on his own.'

Jackie chuckled. 'He did tell me the other day that he was worried some people who have seen him there night after night might think it's him that's up to no good in some way and report him to us. Fancy another drink?'

'Oh, go on then.'

They began to make their way towards the bar when suddenly Jackie pulled Ginger to a halt as her attention was caught by a barman leaning over the bar towards a female customer. She watched them exchange a few words, then the woman opened her handbag to take something out while he took a look around, it appeared to Jackie, to see if anyone was watching him before he put his hand in his pocket. Jackie held her breath, her heart thumping in anticipation. Just what was he going to bring out? Had they at long last caught the dealer red-handed? If this was the case then just who he was came as a big shock to her. Rodney Miller was a very personable young man, the last one she would have thought would be involved in anything like this. Then her heart-rate returned to normal and her anticipation faded when she saw what came out of Rodney's pocket. It was a lighter, and what the girl had taken out of her handbag was a packet of cigarettes.

Ginger meanwhile had noticed her distraction and was demanding, 'You've seen something? What is it? Have you just seen a deal taking place? Have we caught the bastard at last?'

Jackie shook her head and said in disappointment, 'No. I thought Rodney was our man for a minute as he was acting suspiciously with that female the other side of the bar, but it turns out she was asking him for a light for her cigarette. When I thought he was checking around to make sure he wasn't being watched, he must have been checking the counter at the back for a pack of matches first. Seeing none, he offered her his lighter instead.'

Ginger scoffed, 'You actually suspected Rodney Miller! He's that naive he wouldn't know the difference between LSD and a saccharin tablet.'

Jackie said dryly, 'Just like us then.'

Ginger chuckled, 'Yeah, just like us. Shall we get that drink?'

It was the Upbeats' night off tonight and the DJ was

playing his last up tempo record of the night, The Turtles' 'Happy Together'. The dance floor was jammed with gyrating dancers giving it their all before the tempo slowed down for the last hour with the 'smooches', so that meant it was just before eleven. Every Wednesday on the band's day off, while the other members were sleeping off their previous night's revelry, Vic would take himself off in the van to visit his parents and friends in his home town of Leeds, but would be back no later than seven in order to take Jackie out for the evening.

Since her quest to uncover the drug dealer had begun, feeling that the best place to do that was Groovy's, Vic would still turn up at seven after his trip to Leeds then aid Jackie and Ginger in their search, which she thought was very good of him considering he spent every other night of the week in Groovy's as it was. As Vic hadn't arrived to meet her yet she assumed he had stayed later in Leeds and that she wasn't going to see him tonight. It looked as if she was out of luck there as well. So, completely taking Ginger by surprise, she replied, 'No, let's not. Let's have an early night instead. I just want to go back to the chalet and get to bed. We'll check in with Mr Rose on the way out and update him that once again we've drawn a blank, as I suspect he has too. I expect he'll be glad to call it a night too and get himself off home. By now he must be getting as fed up with our vigilance as we are.'

Ginger was more than happy to go along with that but, to their surprise, although Harold had had no more luck than they had, he didn't appear to want to go home but was quite happy to stay on until the place shut down for the night.

Leaving him to it, the two women made their way out of the Paradise building. Immediately the tantalising smell of fish and chips assailed their nostrils. Unable to resist, they walked across to the parade of shops to join the queue of other holidaymakers at the fish and chip kiosk, wanting a snack after their night of entertainment before they went to bed. There were at least ten people in front of them and as they slowly moved up the queue the person in front of them arrested Jackie's attention. She thought it was odd that on such a warm night the man was wearing a heavy winter overcoat, with a cap pulled well down over his head. He was hunching himself over like he was shielding himself from the cold. Beneath his cap grey hair sprouted, telling Jackie he was elderly. Old people suffered lots of illnesses and obviously this old gent had something that affected his ability to keep warm. Presently it was the man's turn to be served. Armed with his parcels of food he turned to go. As he did so Jackie caught a glimpse of the lower part of his face and she watched thoughtfully as he shuffled off in the direction of the holidaymakers' chalets.

The man had caught Ginger's attention too. She exclaimed in a hushed whisper, 'Did you see the conk on that old man? It looks like he's had a fight with a sledgehammer!'

'I did see, and I've seen that nose before but I just can't remember where.'

Ginger said matter-of-factly, 'Well, you must have seen him while going round the camp.'

Jackie shook her head. 'In the camp, yes, but not going around it and not recently either, which doesn't make sense as the longest campers come here for is a fortnight, isn't it? And it's really strange but I get a feeling there are chips and a bed associated with it . . . and another man too.' Ginger eyed her strangely but before she could make any comment they both realised they were at the front of the queue and, all thoughts of the man with the misshapen nose forgotten, they ordered two bags of chips with plenty of salt and vinegar and hungrily tucked into them as they made their way back to their chalet.

CHAPTER TWENTY-TWO

The next day the furious activity of changeover day was for once going relatively smoothly. Only a small number of people had caused the reception staff and their drafted-in helpers, including Jackie, time-consuming problems, such as having mislaid their chalet keys or personal belongings, so that the staff had to ferret through the Lost Property box to see if they had been handed in. Sometimes even family members were mislaid and Stripeys had to go and hunt them down before their coaches left without them. It usually turned out they were having one last go in the arcades or else buying last-minute souvenirs.

It was after two in the afternoon and Jackie had long since lost count of the number of campers she had personally checked in. She was looking after a young family when a man being dealt with by the receptionist working next to her caught her attention. He looked the rough and ready sort, with ginger hair and a matching droopy Mexican moustache. There was nothing about him that she found attractive in a man or would explain why her interest had been piqued by him. But although he had just arrived to start his holiday so she wouldn't have encountered him before, Jackie knew she had – and here in the camp. And somehow he was connected to the man with the disfigured nose and, most peculiar of all, a bed and something to do with chips . . . Not being able to fathom how these things were connected was beginning to madden her. Her sixth sense, though, was screaming at her that it was important she did.

The man having been dealt with, Jackie momentarily forgot the campers she was dealing with and thoughtfully watched the redhead as he turned to leave and disappeared in the crowd awaiting their turn. Then, for no reason other than that she felt compelled to, Jackie quickly excused herself for a moment and pulled the receptionist who had dealt with the man aside before she tackled the next in line.

'Jill, that man you just checked in . . . did he mention if he'd been here before?'

She shook her head. 'No. Why?'

'Oh, er . . . I just thought I knew him, that's all.' Jackie made to go back to her station when, having no idea why it was important, she asked, 'What number chalet is he in?'

'Eh! Oh, come on, Jackie, I can't recall that after the hundreds of campers I've dealt with today.'

'Nor could I, but just do me a favour and check his name on the booking confirmation he handed you against the alphabetical sheets in the office. It won't take you a second.'

'As if I haven't enough to do! Okay, being's it's you.' Jill stepped back to her station, did what Jackie requested, then came back and told her, 'Eight two four. His name is Samuel Green and he's here with his father, Albert

Green. Now are you going to explain to me what this is all about?'

Jackie shrugged and flummoxed her by saying, 'I wish I could, but I've no idea.'

That evening she arrived back at the chalet to drop off her work bag. She would meet up with Ginger for their evening meal then it was back to the chalet to ready themselves for their vigil at Groovy's.

She heard Ginger's shrieks coming from inside the chalet while she was a hundred yards away. Thinking her friend was being murdered, Jackie dashed the rest of the way. Holding her handbag aloft like a weapon, she barged inside. She then stopped short, confused not to see what she was expecting. Ginger was alone in the room, standing on her bed, frenziedly flailing her arms and screaming hysterically.

Jackie shouted, 'Ginger, for goodness' sake, what's got into you?'

The screaming stopped abruptly as her friend spun round to face her, looking hugely relieved. Wildly she retorted, 'Oh, I've never been so glad to see you in all my life. It's huge, Jackie, enormous. It's . . . it's got great big teeth! You won't let it get me, will you? You'll get rid of it? Please, Jackie, please. I saw it run under your bed when I came in and I've not seen it come out again, so it's still there.'

Jackie's panic-stricken eyes darted over to the bed. Her imagination ran riot. Just what monstrous creature was crouching under there waiting its moment to pounce and make a meal of them both? A lion or tiger that had escaped from a zoo? There was a rumour going around that a black panther had escaped from somewhere down south, and had been roaming wild for weeks avoiding its would-be captors. Had it made its way up to Lincolnshire and into their chalet? She stuttered, 'You . . . you stay there, Ginger. Don't move a muscle. Don't do anything to alarm the . . . the . . . beast while I go and get . . .'

Ginger frantically cried out, 'Don't you dare leave me with it! Don't you dare, Jackie.'

Afraid that the noise they were making would spur the animal into action, she urgently hissed back, 'You expect me to save us from it! I'm not Tarzan, Ginger, strong enough to break its jaws just as it's about to bite my head off. And keep your voice down in case you upset the thing.'

'Oh, yes. Sorry, Jackie. But we'll miss our dinner if you don't do something quick to get rid of it. Just make it come out then flatten it with a good wallop from your handbag. That should do the trick.'

Jackie gawped at her. Apart from the fact that she couldn't believe that Ginger's priority in this dire situation was filling her stomach, did she really think a bash over the head with her handbag was going to be enough to stop a vicious animal from making a meal of them both? Then it suddenly struck her that the space underneath her bed was very narrow. Considering what she had stored under there the creature couldn't be bigger than a small puppy, let alone anything larger. She demanded, 'Ginger, just what did you see running under my bed?'

'A mouse. It was huge, Jackie, honest!'

She exclaimed, 'A mouse? A bloody mouse! God, the way you've been carrying on, I thought it was a Yeti at least.'

'I'm terrified of mice, Jackie. I hate them, I really do. I'd sooner be faced with a hungry lion than a mouse. Get it out of here, please,' begged Ginger.

Jackie sighed heavily. She was no lover of mice either but it was obvious Ginger wasn't going to be any help in evicting it so it was going to have to be her. Putting down her handbag, she looked around for a makeshift weapon, spotted a pile of magazines and grabbed one of them, rolling it up. The chalet door was still open and what Jackie was hoping was that if she could frighten the mouse into coming out from its hiding place it would make a dash for freedom, then she would shut the door quickly after it and that would be the end of their lodger.

Not at all looking forward to her task, she went over to her bed and got down on her hands and knees to look tentatively into the dim recess. Beneath the top of the bed was her empty suitcase, a layer of fine dust building up on its lid. She gave it a thump on the side with the rolled-up magazine but nothing stirred so she then gingerly pulled it out from under the bed to look into the space behind. Still no sign of a lurking rodent. She then cautiously gave her pile of dirty laundry a bash with the magazine in case the mouse was hiding amongst it. But still nothing.

'Can you see it yet?' Ginger wailed.

Jackie snapped back, 'You'd have heard me scream louder than you if I had.'

Inching herself further down on the floor, she used the rolled magazine to scatter her shoes in case the mouse was hiding in one of them, then knocked over a pile of paperbacks and poked the end of the magazine at her vanity case in case it was hiding behind it. Still no sign of a mouse. All that remained now, she saw to her shame, was a collection of debris: a couple of empty wine and cider bottles, empty sweet and crisp packets, and scrunched-up newspaper chip wrapping that had somehow found its way under the bed during the time she had lived here.

With one hefty sweep of the rolled-up magazine Jackie swept all the rubbish out from under the bed, hoping the mouse would be with it. The empty bottles rolled across the floor and under Ginger's bed, the rest of the rubbish flying out over the floor. Scrambling up, holding the magazine aloft ready to strike the offending creature, she studied the debris which was now scattered around the open door. There appeared to be no mouse amongst it. It must have made its way under Ginger's bed without either of them seeing it, so this meant Jackie now had to repeat the whole process. Then she spotted it: the side of its grey furry body protruding from under an empty Lux soap wrapper. She leaned down and gave the furry object a little poke with the end of the rolled-up magazine. It didn't move. So she poked it again. It still didn't move. Was it dead? She took a closer look. Then a closer one still. Then, giving out an annoyed tut, she picked up the furry object between two fingers, turned and held it out towards Ginger, saying, 'I found your mouse. Only it's not a mouse . . .'

Before she could say another word, Ginger screeched, 'It's a rat! Oh, God, it's a rat. Get it out, Jackie, quick before it . . .'

She cut in, 'It's not a rat either, Ginger. It's a ball of fluff. You caused all this commotion over a ball of fluff!'

Ginger immediately ceased her frenzied display, her face filled with shame. She mouthed, 'Oh.' Then justified herself with, 'Well . . . it looked like a mouse to me.' She clambered down off the bed, shame-faced, saying, 'I'm starving. Are we going to go and have our tea?'

Jackie couldn't help but say, 'Don't you want to give your mouse a decent burial first?'

Ginger snorted, 'Very funny. You coming or not?'

'As soon as we've cleared up this rubbish or we are risking a real invasion of vermin. The least you can do is help. While we're at it, we'd best check under your bed too.'

Ginger knew by Jackie's tone that she wasn't going to be allowed to go for her meal until she had. While she cleared out the rubbish from under her own bed, Jackie found an empty brown carrier bag and started to put things into it. She came to the scrunched-up sheet of greasy newspaper chip wrapper which she picked up with two fingers, and was just about to add that to the bag when memories began to flash through her mind of the man with the misshapen nose and the other one who had caught her attention today, both lying on a bed. Then those disappeared, to be replaced with one of herself and Ginger eating chips. This piece of dirty newspaper had triggered these memory flashes. Could it possibly hold the key to her putting all these pieces of puzzle together and remembering where she had first seen the man with the disfigured nose?

Stepping over to her bed, she sat down on it and carefully unscrewed the newspaper, wrinkling her nose in disgust at the rancid smell that emanated from it. Before she had fully spread it out, the mug shots of four men were glaring back at her, stained with chip fat but still identifiable. Two of the men she didn't recognise but the other two she certainly did. Jackie issued a triumphant 'Yes!' as all the pieces of the maddening puzzle slotted together.

On hearing her, Ginger jerked her head up from rubbish-collecting to look over at her fearfully, demanding, 'You've found a real mouse this time?'

'There never was a real mouse in here, Ginger. What I have found, though, is the whereabouts of two bank robbers the police have been trying to find.'

Ginger screwed up her face in bewilderment. 'What?' She scrambled up and came across to join Jackie, peering over her shoulder to look at the article on the grubby sheet of newspaper.

'Recognise him?' Jackie urged her, stabbing a finger at one of the photographs.

Ginger shook her head. 'No.'

'Look closely at his nose. Do you recognise that?'

She looked hard at it for a moment before exclaiming, 'Oh, yes. It's similar to the one we saw on that old man in the chip shop queue.'

'Not similar. It's the same one.'

'It can't be. That man in the queue was old and the man in the paper is . . . well, it's hard to tell due to that greasy stain but he's a lot younger. From that photograph he doesn't look like a nice man nor do the other three either. Definitely not the sort I'd like to come across on a dark night.'

Jackie told her, 'Well, I did come across him when I went into his chalet by accident a few weeks back, and he's not a nice man. Nasty he was to me. There was another man in the chalet at the time and it was that man there,' she said, stabbing her finger at another mug shot. 'He was in reception today, booking in for another stay for himself and his father under the name of Green. He had red hair and a moustache but all the same I just know it was him. Ginger, I reckon . . . no, I'm positive . . . those bank robbers are hiding themselves here at Jolly's . . . well, at least two of them are, and have been since they did the robbery . . . until the heat dies down and they stand a better chance of making their escape with the money they stole, abroad is my guess.'

Ginger looked sceptical. 'Don't you think you're letting your imagination run away with you? Villains hide from the law in some isolated farmhouse or something like that . . . well, they always do in the detective programmes I've watched on the telly . . . so why choose a holiday camp where they stand the chance of thousands of people recognising them?'

'Don't you see, that's where they thought they were being clever when they planned their getaway? Not hiding themselves in some isolated place but amongst a huge crowd of people, the last place the police would think to look for them. They obviously booked several chalets under different names to cover a certain period of time. After their fortnight's stay in one, they pretended to leave with the rest of the campers, then must have hidden somewhere until the coaches arrived bringing the new campers, then one of them would turn up in reception to book in under the name they booked the next holiday in.

'While I was in the chalet, apart from the fact that it stank and it was obvious from the state of the place they hardly went out, I noticed an open suitcase at the foot of one of the beds. It had several wigs on top of a pile of clothes. Each time they went out to re-book into their next chalet or fetch food, shower or whatever, they used different disguises. They were obviously shocked when I turned up unexpectedly as they weren't in disguise. Had the man with the nose not been so nasty to me, I might not have taken any notice of him . . . after all, we get all sorts of people coming here with disfigurements, don't we? A broken nose isn't so out of the ordinary even if his is the worst I've ever seen. But he was aggressive with me and now I can recognise him from the newspaper photograph.'

Ginger was looking shell-shocked. Scraping her fingers through her thick corkscrew locks she issued a long, 'Phew! If it turns out these men are part of the bank robber's gang, then we'll be heroines, won't we?' Her eyes lit up with excitement. 'I can just see the headlines in the nationals. "*Bank Robbers' Hideout Uncovered by Eagle-eyed Anita Williams and Jacqueline Sims Doing the Job the Police Couldn't*". We'll be asked to open fêtes and all sorts.'

Jackie did a double take. Ginger's only contribution to all this was her fear of mice bringing to light a discarded chip wrapper carrying the report of the bank robbery and the photographs of the suspects. Jackie cared for Ginger too much, though, to deny her her moment of fame, albeit she would make sure the newspapers printed her own name first! She said sardonically, 'Before you start planning what dress you're going to wear when you're honoured by the Queen, let's see what the police make of all this.'

* * *

An hour later, inside Harold's office, Inspector Clayburn, a portly, ruddy-faced man with a mop of grizzled grey hair, sat in a chair before the desk, deep in thought.

Harold sat behind the desk, hands clasped tightly, looking expectantly at the inspector as did Jackie, both of them anxiously awaiting his verdict on her story. Ginger, sitting by Jackie, had temporarily forgotten the reason for them being in the office at all as her attention was focused on the fresh-faced, gangly PC sitting next to Inspector Clayburn, his helmet in his lap, notepad and pencil poised ready to add to the notes he had already taken of proceedings so far. She was thinking what a gorgeous specimen of manhood he was, and just her type. Had he a girlfriend? Hopefully not. But was she the type of girl he found attractive enough to ask out . . . she dearly hoped so. She saw that the young man, who had been introduced to them by Inspector Clayburn as Constable Paul Nuttall, kept glancing at her now and again and going red in the face when he saw she was looking back at him. Ginger hoped this was a good sign.

The waiting finally proved too much for Jackie. Deciding that he doubted her story she broke in, 'I'm not wasting your time, Inspector. I'll stake my life on the fact that the two men I pointed out to you in that newspaper article are staying here at Jolly's and have been for weeks. If you . . .'

Inspector Clayburn then seemed to rally himself out of his trance-like state and cut in. 'Oh, I don't think for a moment you're wasting our time, Miss Sims. We police rely very much on observations by the public. Many of our most dangerous criminals would never have been brought to justice without tip offs we received from people like you. What you've told me most definitely warrants investigation. It's just that . . .' He suddenly stopped his flow and turned to address PC Nuttall. 'You don't need to note this down, lad. It's off the record.'

He turned his attention back to Harold and Jackie. 'Well, Scotland Yard is heading up this case and it's my duty to inform them of this new lead. We'll be ordered to observe the situation in the meantime and they'll take charge when they arrive up here, which will probably be in about four hours. The lads in Scotland Yard consider us all to be country bumpkins north of Watford Gap. Admittedly we don't get the level of crime in these parts that they do in the smoke – we've mostly petty thieving, stolen tractors, that sort of thing. So this is a great opportunity for us to show them that we're as good at law-enforcing as they are. One in the eye for us, so to speak.'

He shifted position in his chair. 'I retire at the end of December after thirty years in the service, and what a way to end my career – by arresting the Dolan Gang, or at least two of them. The man with the broken nose is Finbar Dolan. He got it years ago when he was a bare-knuckle fighter, and a nastier character you couldn't wish to meet. The man you saw shacked up with him is Roddy Jenks, who was just a petty crook until Dolan saw his potential and took him under his wing. Dolan is suspected of being responsible for a number of murders, including those of the two security men shot during the bank raid, along with a list of crimes longer than your arm. Scotland Yard has been after him for years but he's always managed to slip through their net so far.' The inspector scowled and said with conviction, 'But not on my watch. It's just how I go about it without blotting my copy book with the chief and putting my men or anyone else in danger . . .'

Ginger, in an attempt to impress PC Nuttall, offered, 'Those chalet doors aren't strong so why don't you just charge in the place and catch them by surprise?'

He shook his head gravely. 'You don't surprise men like Finbar Dolan. Even though he's been holed up here for weeks and thinking that by now he's got away with it, his guard won't have dropped. His hand won't ever be far away from one of his sawn-off shotguns, and as soon as we burst through the door he'll have it aimed at whoever's first in and blast them to Kingdom Come. A shoot out is the last thing we want.' As the seasoned copper he was, it hadn't escaped his notice that Ginger had taken a shine to his young PC and her suggestion was made purely to impress him. As the kindly man he also was, to save her any embarrassment, he added, 'Good suggestion, though, and thanks for volunteering it.' He heaved a deep sigh. 'We need somehow to entice Dolan and Jenks out of the chalet, away from their firearms, so that we can arrest them without fear of a repetition of the Gunfight at the OK Corral. And another thing. We'll need to get the people in the surrounding chalets out of danger without alerting Dolan and Jenks that something is going on. Far easier said than done. Anyone got any suggestions?' he asked them all hopefully.

Harold did have one, but although his confidence had built up significantly recently it wasn't yet strong enough for him to risk making an idiot of himself in front of a police inspector so he remained silent.

Ginger had no more to offer than she had already and neither had PC Nuttall. An idea was forming in Jackie's mind, though, but she needed to explore it a little more before she volunteered it.

Not coming up with anything either, Inspector Clayburn saw his opportunity to show up Scotland Yard fizzle out. He asked Harold, 'All right to use your telephone, Mr Rose, to call London and alert them to this development? Get their instruction on how they wish us to proceed.'

Harold was just about to respond when Jackie piped up. 'Inspector, er . . . I might have a plan that will get those men out of their chalet without their guns.' She then told a very receptive inspector what it was.

They spent a while pulling the plan apart to uncover any pitfalls. Having resolved all they thought of, Inspector Clayburn eyed her, impressed. 'Could just work, Miss Sims. Yes, it's definitely worth a try. We just have to hope that they fall for it.' He then eyed her in concern. 'The success of this will rest on you. Do you understand the danger you'll be putting yourself in?'

Harold was inwardly fighting with himself to undertake the part in the plan that Jackie had offered herself up for, but knew that should his nerves get the better of him he might give the criminals a hint that something was afoot and be responsible for a possible bloodbath.

Jackie was terrified of what could happen to her, but something had to be done to apprehend those dangerous men and get them off the camp before innocent holidaymakers and staff could come to any harm. She nodded her head.

Inspector Clayburn rubbed his hands together. 'Let's get this show on the road then.'

At just before nine that night, having received the go ahead from Inspector Clayburn, reminding herself that the success of this operation now depended on her, Jackie, dressed in a Stripey's uniform, pushed the heavily laden trolley down the dimly lit path to park it at the entrance to chalet 824. Thankfully, most of the occupants of the surrounding chalets were out enjoying the evening's entertainment and those that had stayed in had been moved to a safe place without alerting the occupants of the chalet in question. Taking another deep breath, Jackie stepped the short distance to the door and rapped on it. She heard movement through the thin walls of the chalet and saw the curtain inch slightly aside at the window to the right of her.

Pretending she hadn't noticed, she rapped on the door again, calling out loudly, 'Mr Green, I'm here to tell you that you have won the chalet raffle, and to give you your prize.'

She had already heard Finbar Dolan's voice and the one that responded wasn't his. It had to be Roddy Jenks'. His tone was suspicious. 'We ain't entered no competition, we can't have won anything.'

This had already been anticipated and Jackie had an answer ready. 'You were entered automatically when you checked in earlier. At the Paradise, during the band interval, all the chalet numbers of new arrivals are put in the bingo drum, given a good few turns, and the Head Stripey pulls one out. Tonight your chalet number was the winner. As you obviously weren't at the Paradise, I was asked to bring it to you.'

She could hear voices inside, though not loud enough for her to make out what was being said. Obviously Roddy Jenks was relaying to Finbar Dolan what was transpiring. Shortly his response came back. 'We ain't got any use for no cheap knick-knacks. Let someone else have the prize.'

It was a good job they had all agreed the prize had to be something irresistible to the villains, in order to lure them out of the chalet to claim it. 'Oh, I can assure you, at Jolly's our prizes are far better than cheap trinkets. You've won three bottles of spirits and three boxes of chocolates. I've brought along a selection for you to choose from.' Surely these were enough to lure them out of the chalet? Her plan had centred around the men wanting something for nothing, then she worried that neither of them drank spirits or ate chocolates. She quickly added, 'The spirits can be exchanged for a crate of beer. Newcastle Brown, Pale Ale, Guinness . . . whatever your preference.' Afraid she was being overzealous in her efforts to get them out and praying they did not take her literally, she said, 'If tonight isn't convenient, you can always come and collect your prize from reception tomorrow.'

She saw the curtain move aside slightly again. She was being checked out. Thankfully she had managed to park the cart where lamplight shone on it so it could be seen from through the window. The curtain fell back into place. Nothing happened again for several long moments although meanwhile Jackie could hear movement inside. She heard a key turn in the lock . . . they'd obviously taken to keeping the door locked since she'd unexpectedly burst in on them a few weeks back . . . and the door started to swing open.

And that was when it hit her like a bolt of lightning just what serious danger she had voluntarily put herself in. What if the men inside had not fallen for the ruse to get them to come out and these breaths she was taking were her last? Just as she was leaving on her mission, Ginger had grabbed her arm, warning her that she'd better come back in one piece as she was impossible to replace. As she had tightly hugged her back, Jackie had promised that she would. She was worried now she should never have made that promise.

To her the door seemed to be opening in slow motion. All her mind's eye could envisage was the barrel of a gun appearing around it and the loud bang as it was fired. She felt her legs begin to buckle, a scream of terror threatening to escape. But, no. She could not be responsible for that. She had volunteered to do this and must keep her nerve and see it through.

Forcing a smile to her face, a light tone to her voice, she greeted the opening door with, 'Oh, thank goodness you've decided to take your prize now. I didn't fancy hauling this heavy trolley all the way back to the Paradise again. Come and have a look to see what you want.'

It was Roddy Jenks' head that appeared round the door. He had a quick scan around, presumably confirming she was on her own, before the door opened wide enough for him to step out. He was wearing the same disguise that he had worn earlier: a ginger wig and matching droopy moustache. She was grateful to note that he wasn't carrying anything in his hand. Obviously, though, their offer had not been enticing enough to get Dolan out to make his choice of the goodies and he'd sent Jenks out to make it for him. For all Jackie knew Dolan was inside with a gun trained on her as a precaution.

Jenks stepped over to her and began looking at the bottles of drink and boxes of confectionery on the trolley. Jackie was desperately hoping he did not sense that beneath her calm exterior was a mass of jangled nerves and a heart beating so thunderously she feared he would hear it.

His selection made of a bottle of Bell's whisky, Bacardi and Captain Morgan rum, a box of Rowntree's Today chocolates, Cadbury's Milk Tray and Terry's Peppermint Creams, without a please or thank you Jenks made to walk back into the chalet. Jackie's mind was screaming to her that if she didn't do something to stall him and get Dolan out then the plan had failed. How the police from Scotland Yard, whose arrival was imminent, would apprehend these violent criminals did not bear thinking about.

Jenks was just about to re-enter the chalet when an idea for stalling him and getting Dolan out as well struck Jackie. It was a lame attempt but she just hoped they fell for it. She called out, 'Oh, just a minute. I need you to sign for the prize. It's so I can show my boss that you've had the stuff and I haven't pocketed it.' She gave a chuckle before continuing, 'He doesn't trust any of his staff and that's a joke as we all know he's got his hand in the till. I need your father's signature too as you both won the prize.' He turned and looked suspiciously at her. She quickly told him, 'I know, daft rule, but that's how it is. I'll have to take the prizes back else.'

Now in possession of his booty, Jenks didn't like the thought of parting with it. He poked his head into the chalet and she heard him say, 'Can you just come out here for a sec and sign with me that we've had this stuff, else we don't get it?'

Inside Dolan had obviously been looking forward to his unexpected treat of alcohol and chocolates. Greed would not allow him to have it snatched away. Wearing a wig and glasses as a disguise, he appeared behind Jenks and stared to follow him over to join Jackie.

That was when she realised that she had nothing with her for them to sign. She had no idea how she was going to explain that to them, without raising their suspicions that this had all been a ruse. With the fear of God on her, she shut her eyes and prepared for the worst. Next thing she knew all hell broke loose. She had been knocked flying and was tumbling across the tarmac path to land a short distance away, sprawled flat on it, an agonising pain shooting from her right knee, ears ringing with cries of, 'You effing bastards!'

She heard metal clanging, glass breaking, and the command, 'Get them cuffed.'

Struggling to sit up, she saw several police officers hauling a handcuffed Dolan and Jenks to their feet, both of them screaming out death threats to their captors. The trolley that had been holding the bottles of drink and chocolates now lay on its side several feet from where it had been, its contents smashed and scattered around. As he was dragged away, Jenks turned and looked over at Jackie. She gave a shudder at the murderous glare she received from him.

It was getting on for midnight. Jackie, Ginger and Harold were seated in his office waiting for the return of Inspector Clayburn and PC Nuttall, who were seeing off the police from Scotland Yard along with their prisoners.

Of course news that there had been a police raid and two people arrested had gone around the camp like wildfire and so a very brief announcement had been made by Terry Jones on-stage in the Paradise ballroom, informing the campers that it had been discovered that two wanted criminals were hiding in a chalet and the police had carried out a raid to arrest them. It had been successful and the campers had nothing to worry about. Jackie had had the deep gash on her knee cleaned and dressed by Kitty Popple, and was ordered to drink lots of sweet tea and to watch out for delayed shock. Despite the serious danger she had been in, she was feeling far too euphoric over the part she had played in the capture of the two vicious criminals for any trauma to manifest itself. For the umpteenth time since they'd been sitting in the office waiting for Inspector Clayburn to return and officially tell them he had no further need of them tonight, she was very vocally reliving the events of earlier, making it sound like it had all been an exciting adventure. Ginger and Harold, out of respect and admiration for what she had done, hadn't told her to shut up, but no one was more grateful than them finally to see Inspector Clayburn walk in, followed closely by PC Nuttall.

With a Cheshire Cat grin on his face, Clayburn strode

in purposefully to say, 'Well, that's them safely off back to London. Boy, were those Scotland Yard lads one unhappy bunch, us country bumpkins having stolen their thunder! Joy to behold, it really was. Can't say Dolan and Jenks were very happy either, especially not sitting in the car so close to the suitcase containing their share of the robbery.

'Scotland Yard have now turned their attention to other holiday camps, hoping that the remaining two members of the gang could be hiding out in one of them. No mean feat considering how many are dotted along the coastline the length and breadth of the British Isles, so I don't fancy their chances. As soon as those other two thugs get wind of what's happened to Dolan and Jenks, they'll be long gone. Still, at least the head of the gang and his main henchman have been caught, and half the money recovered. Better than nothing.' Arriving by the side of Jackie, he patted her shoulder. 'It's you that's responsible for us bringing these men in. We need people like you in the force, so if you ever fancy a career change?'

She grinned up at him. 'I'll bear that in mind.'

'Right, well, you good people must be desperate to get to bed, I know I am.' Clayburn shot a grin at PC Nuttall before continuing, 'And it's well past your bedtime so we'll be on our way. We've got your statement Miss Sims, but if we need anything else we'll be in touch. Just remember what I've said about the press. Until the court case is over you have nothing to say. After then you can sell your story to whoever you like. Be good publicity for Jolly's, people reading how observant and brave their staff are.'

When the policemen had departed Ginger said disappointedly, 'That means I've got to wait for God knows how long until I get my name in print and become a celebrity.' Then her good humour returned and her eyes lit up with excitement. 'Still at least we got saved from trawling Groovy's tonight. And I managed to get myself a date with PC Nuttall! I'd begun to think he wasn't interested, but he collared me when they got back to the office to wait for the police from Scotland Yard to arrive. He's going to call me on reception to make arrangements for us to go out on his next night off.'

Jackie wasn't listening. Her thoughts were of Vic. He would be wondering why she hadn't been at Groovy's tonight. She hoped he didn't think she had stood him up. She should really pay a visit to his chalet and tell him what had gone on – well, as much as she was allowed to – but then he might have gone to bed by now, and she wouldn't want to wake him so it would have to wait until tomorrow.

Having locked up the offices and the door to reception, Harold said his goodnights to Jackie and Ginger and went off to his car to drive back to Mablethorpe while the girls headed off to their chalet.

CHAPTER TWENTY-THREE

Both girls should have been dead on their feet considering the night's events, but both, for their own separate reasons, were still far too keyed up for sleep.

Jackie said to Ginger, 'If I go to bed now I'm not going to sleep. I think I'll go for a walk, see if that will tire me out. I won't make a noise when I come in.'

'I'm not going to sleep either. I'll come with you. Shall we head for the beach?' Ginger looked up at the sky. A half moon shone down from the darkness, affording some light. A slight breeze was blowing. 'Just the sort of night to have a snogging session in the dunes with a boyfriend. If things go the way I hope with Paul then maybe that's just what I'll be doing with him soon. But I'll settle for a paddle now.'

Jackie smiled at her. She hoped things worked out well. Paul had come across as a pleasant man and she hoped he would appreciate Ginger for the many good qualities she possessed. Jackie agreed with her that it was a lovely night, cool enough to need a cardigan but not a coat. Since it was nearing the end of August it was doubtful whether they would get another such night this year, it being so close to autumn, so they should take advantage. But she saw a problem.

'Sounds just the ticket, Ginger, but we might not be the only ones down there on a night like this. I don't know about you but I can't face being pestered for details of more information than they were all given earlier tonight.'

Ginger pulled a face. 'Mm, that never crossed my mind. I suppose wherever we go we risk meeting campers. Maybe we'll just give the walk a miss.' Then a thought struck her. 'We could just take a stroll around the back of the staff chalets, and creep past Donkey Sam's hut so we don't wake him or the donkeys and cause mayhem. There's not much risk of coming across anyone else there at this time of night, except the security guards doing their rounds.'

Jackie shook her head. 'As conscientious as our security guards are, I doubt they venture around the boundaries of the camp very often unless they hear about a tramp camping in the undergrowth and need to chase him away. A walk over there sounds good to me.'

They set off. Unusually for the two women they walked in silence, just enjoying the peace and quiet which was only broken by the occasional hoot of an owl. As they tiptoed past Donkey Sam's hut, they both had to fight to stem an outburst of hysteria as the sounds of loud snoring filtered through the walls. They remained undecided as to who was actually making the terrible noise . . . Sam himself or one of his donkeys.

A few yards past the shed the path wound its way around a thick section of neglected trees and undergrowth, and was difficult to negotiate. The walk though had done for the women what they'd hoped. They were both tired enough, they felt, for sleep to work its magic on them. But to turn back now would take them twice as long to reach their chalet than it would to keep going forward, so that was what they opted to do. Before long they arrived at the old rotting farm gate, the bottom half of it covered by thick weeds. They stopped for a moment to rest their arms on top of it, gazing into the deserted overgrown yard beyond at the derelict farmhouse which looked eerie in the light cast by the moon.

Ginger whispered to Jackie, 'Those dark attic windows look like eyes glaring down at us, don't they?'

She nodded. 'They do. And the front door looks like a mouth ready to open and gobble us up.'

They both chuckled at that.

Jackie then mused, 'I'd forgotten this place was here. The one and only time I've seen it was when I first came to work for Jolly's, got the tour around and was warned the place was out of bounds because of the terrible state it's in.'

'Yeah, me too,' said Ginger. 'I wonder why Mrs Jolly hasn't had it knocked down and used the land to build something else.'

'From what I was told, I think it holds too many memories for her of the old gent who used to own the original farm. Maybe she'll get around to it one day, though.'

'Well, the place is giving me the willies. I keep imagining some ghost from the long-distant past is going to come out of the door any minute, so shall we go?' urged Ginger.

Jackie took one step away, and as she did so a flash of

light coming from a downstairs window caught her eye. Wondering where it had come from, she stopped to stare over at the house again. She could not see anything that would have caused the light. She then stepped back to the place she'd been standing in previously, and as she did so the flash came again.

Ginger, by now a few feet ahead of her down the path, realised that Jackie wasn't with her. She turned back and saw her staring at the house. 'What are you looking at, Jackie? You haven't seen a ghost, have you?' She said it jokingly. The last thing she wanted Jackie to tell her was that she had.

'If I had seen a ghost, Ginger, I would have been tearing past you, screaming blue murder. No, I saw a flash of light coming from behind a chink in the curtains.'

'Well, it's probably just the moonlight reflecting off the glass.'

'No, it's not. The light is definitely coming from inside the house. Come and see for yourself.'

When Ginger rejoined her Jackie explained that she needed to stand in the precise spot where she had been while they had been chatting over the gate then take a step to the left, just as Jackie had done. Ginger did and saw the flash of light too.

'Oh, you're right, Jackie. What do you think is causing it?'

'I don't know.' She meant to find out though. She repeated her actions and came to the conclusion, 'I think it's a candle.'

'A candle!' Ginger repeated. 'That means there is someone there then. It'll be a tramp,' she said with conviction.

Jackie looked bothered. 'Well, that side of the farmhouse isn't as derelict as the other, but all the same the tramp could be risking his life taking shelter inside.'

'Tell the security guards and let them deal with it. I'm knackered now and just want my bed,' grumbled Ginger.

'Yes, so do I, but I won't be able to sleep, worrying about that tramp. I need to go and warn him of the risk he's taking. I won't be long. See you back at the chalet.'

Ginger looked horrified. 'I can't let you go and face him alone. What if he turns nasty, seeing as you're trying to evict him from his shelter for the night?'

'Ginger, I've just risked life and limb with two violent thugs. Dealing with an old tramp pales into insignificance.'

She heaved a fed-up sigh. 'As if I haven't had enough excitement for one night. Come on, let's get this over with or we'll never see our beds tonight.'

After clambering over the old gate they stole their way over the uneven weed-strewn yard to the farmhouse door, deciding that would be the first place to try. They were expecting it to be as unyielding as the gate due to decades of disuse and they'd have to fight their way around the house to find the same way as the tramp had got in, via a broken window or the back door maybe. They were therefore both surprised when, on trying the knob of the front door, it turned easily and opened noiselessly. They both looked at each other, both thinking the same thing. The hinges had been well oiled, meaning that whoever was inside was no overnight visitor but had been living here for a while.

Ginger tried to urge Jackie to reconsider and leave this situation for the security guards to deal with, but she was already making her way inside and down the dark, dilapidated corridor.

Jackie pushed open the door to the room where they'd seen the light. Ginger was following close behind. They had both expected to find the room in a state of severe neglect, but were stunned to find this to be far from the case. Whoever was living here wasn't present at the moment but they had certainly made it homely.

The room was lit by several intermittently placed candles. The once cream walls were now dingy yellow, the plaster missing in parts. There were water stains on the ceiling, but otherwise the room had been swept clean and the wooden floor washed. A faded old rug covered part of it. Across the floor, set against one wall, was a narrow rusting iron bed, neatly made with an odd assortment of shabby but clean bedclothes. By it was an open suitcase holding folded clothes. Basic household equipment and food items sat on the table. A thick pair of curtains hung at the window. The bottom corner of one was caught up, revealing the flicker of light that Jackie had observed from the burning candle sitting on the draining board under the window.

There were other items visible but they went unnoticed as both women had their eyes riveted on what was hanging from the room's picture rail.

It was Ginger who found her voice first. 'My God, Jackie, look at those clothes.'

'I am looking,' she responded. 'They're just stunning. What I wouldn't give to have a dress like that!' she uttered, pointing to an ankle-length evening dress in canary yellow satin and chiffon. 'It looks to be my size too.'

'I want that one,' said Ginger with longing, pointing to a red wool mini-dress with a long white pointed collar and white cuffs, a double-buckled wide white leather belt around the waist.

Drawn like a magnet they both went over to look at the dresses more closely and at the dozen or so other garments hanging alongside them.

Jackie was imagining what she would look like wearing the yellow dress.

Ginger's thoughts had travelled past how stunning she would look in the red dress, and how PC Nuttall's knees would buckle at the sight of her, to wondering where all these clothes had come from. Her conclusion had her exclaiming, 'Jackie, these have got to be part of that warehouse robbery a few weeks back. This stuff hanging up must be what's left of the haul.'

Jackie was at a dance now in a posh hotel, all the other women in their cheap shop-bought dresses looking on enviously as she was spun around by a stunningly handsome man dressed impeccably in a black dinner suit. 'Eh?' she murmured. Then her vision vanished as just what Ginger had said registered with her. 'Oh, don't be daft. I mean, what are the odds of discovering two sets of criminals hiding out here in one . . .' She stopped talking as it struck her what other explanation could there be for expensive clothing to be hanging up in a place such as this?

She clamped a hand to her forehead and let out a despairing groan. 'What is it with criminals at the moment, thinking they can use Jolly's as a hideout?' Her eyes darkened thunderously. 'Well, like those bank robbers tonight, this one is going to find out that he picked the wrong holiday camp to hide out in. We'd best get Inspector Clayburn back here quick sharp. He wants to end his career with a bang. Well, with this on top he'll be ending his police career with an explosion!'

All that was in Ginger's mind was the danger they must be in. She frantically urged, 'Let's just get out of here, Jackie. The warehouse robber could have a gun too for all we know and we're about to be blasted to hell.'

Fear swamped Jackie then. What were the odds of escaping two life-threatening situations in one day? She wasn't prepared to wait around and find out. 'Yeah, come on, let's get out of here quick.'

They were just about to leave when Ginger caught Jackie's arm and stunned her by announcing, 'I'm having that red dress. It's not like the robber can report me to the police for stealing it, can he?'

Before Ginger could make a move to take it, though, they both froze as they heard the muted sound of the outer door opening and shutting and slow steady footsteps heading their way. Their eyes then darted to the door as they saw it starting to open. As terror of the unknown consumed them, they huddled together and clung to each other, shaking.

A man came in. He was wearing a long khaki Parka jacket, the hood pulled up to cover his head and obscure his features. He was lumbering under the weight of a bucket of water. Putting it down by the range, he pulled back the hood of his jacket and took it off. As he turned to hang it on the back of a chair, light from the candles illuminated his face and Jackie and Ginger gave a gasp of recognition. At this sound the man jumped, letting out a yell of shock as he spun round to face the intruders.

For a moment the three of them stared at each other dumbstruck.

It was Al who spoke first. 'How did you find out I was here?'

Jackie responded, 'It was just your bad luck me and Ginger decided to have a walk around here tonight. You hadn't shut the curtain properly so we were able to see light from a candle.'

After months of sneaking around, every moment fearing he would be discovered, Al realised all his hard work and dreams for his future had come to an abrupt stop now. He had almost reached the point of being ready to try his luck at getting himself into the world he so longed to be in and now there was no telling whether he would have the opportunity to finish his task, so he desperately blurted, 'Look, Jackie, I know I . . .'

She held up a warning hand. 'It's the police you need to be pleading your case to.'

He paled, eyes filling with alarm. 'Oh, Jackie, you wouldn't report me to the police for this, would you? I know what I've done is wrong, but I could end up in jail!'

She incredulously snapped, 'And you don't think that's what you deserve for robbing that warehouse?'

Ginger piped up sardonically, 'If we'd known it was you behind it, we could have come direct to you for the dresses and saved ourselves a trip to the market.' Then a thought occurred to her. 'How much will you let me have that red dress for? And Jackie has a fancy for the yellow one.'

'Ginger!' Jackie scolded her. 'Those dresses are evidence. Do you want to be done as being an accomplice if we're caught with them? We need to get rid of those we bought off the market too just in case the police decide to search our wardrobes, being's we know Al.'

Ginger snapped, 'I bloody well paid good money for those clothes, so 'til Al is safely locked away I shall hide them where the police can't find them.'

'Be it on your own head then and don't expect me to visit you in prison if the police find your hiding place,' Jackie warned her. She then addressed Al, her tone a mixture of hurt and anger. 'I can't believe that I was so wrong about you. I never would have had you down as a common thief. Well, I hope you think it was worth it when you're locked up in your little cell.'

Al's mouth was opening and closing, fish-like. He blabbered, 'I don't know anything about a warehouse robbery. Honest I don't.'

'So where did you get those clothes from if you didn't steal them then?' Ginger demanded.

He heaved a deep sigh and said quietly, 'I . . . I made them.'

They both looked at him, astounded.

Jackie laughed harshly. 'Do you think we were born yesterday! Well, if you won't tell us the truth, we'll leave it to the police to get it out of you.'

He cried, 'I did make them, Jackie. It's the truth I'm telling you. There's my sewing machine over there.'

They both looked over to the corner of the room where sat an old Singer treadle sewing machine, beside it a table piled with material offcuts and other sewing paraphernalia. There was an ironing board with an old-fashioned iron and a dressmaker's dummy with an unfinished blouse on it, none of which they had noticed before since their attention had been riveted on the hanging clothes.

They looked back at him questioningly.

Ginger accused him, 'You're one of them transwhatsits that likes dressing in women's clothes? God, to think I've been fancying you since you first came here, praying for you to ask me out, and all the time you were a pansy!'

'I'm neither transvestite nor gay,' he told her with conviction.

'So what are you then?' Jackie asked him.

He heaved a sigh. 'According to my family and friends, I need locking up in a mental institution and receiving treatment for what they see as my disorder. You'll more than likely think the same when I tell you about it. But is someone mentally ill or perverse just because they have a dream for themself and are determined to follow it?'

While Jackie and Ginger watched bemused, he walked over to the bed and sank down miserably on it. 'I was a normal kid who enjoyed playing football and scavenging on bombsites with my mates, but ever since I can remember I've also had a passion for designing women's clothes. I always knew that was what I wanted to do when I left school, and used to sit for hours in my bedroom drawing sketches of my designs when my parents thought I was reading my books. My parents were very strict and had set ideas about the world. A man's job was providing for the family, and seeing to the heavy jobs around the home. A woman's was cooking and cleaning, sewing and knitting. I knew they would not be at all understanding of my choice of hobby.

'The mother of one of my friends used to do dressmaking and alterations, and my mother used to send me down to her with the clothes she needed work doing on. I used to make excuses to stay and watch her cutting out clothes and sewing them up. She was an astute woman and soon cottoned on that my interest in what she was doing was far more than mere politeness. One day as I was watching her attach a collar to a dress, she asked me outright why I preferred to stay in and watch her work instead of playing out with my mates.

'Being put on the spot like that, I hadn't time to come up with a plausible excuse so I told her the truth. I thought she'd react the same way I feared my parents would, but in fact it was the opposite. She told me she would teach me how to sew properly if I wanted her to, which of course I jumped at. She also asked me to show her my designs. When I did she told me she thought I had talent and that I should pursue my dream and not let anything stand in my way. So while my parents thought I was out playing with my friends, I was with Mrs Maybury learning all I could off her. Eventually I got to the stage of helping her alter clothes and make new ones for her clients.

'When it was time for me to leave school I had no choice but to tell my parents that I didn't want to join my father in the family engineering business but instead go to college and do a fashion degree, with the hope that would get me into a couture house in London as a designer. My father hit the roof, telling me I was unnatural to want to do a woman's job. He wouldn't listen when I said that it was a man, Norman Hartnell, who designed clothes for the Queen and it's men who mostly head up all the big fashion houses. He wouldn't budge. To him, dressmaking was women's work and that was that. He flatly refused to fund me through college and demanded I join him in the family firm. If I insisted on pursuing a career as a dress designer, then I was dead as far as he was concerned.

'I thought my mother was having a seizure, she took the news so badly. She collapsed on the sofa, clutching her heart, and we had to have the doctor fetched to sedate her. She then tried to get him to have me sectioned in a mental hospital, to receive treatment for my "disorder", and ordered the doctor out of the house when he tried to tell her that there was nothing wrong with me mentally. She was terrified that all her friends would believe her son was a homosexual, although she knew I wasn't, and she wouldn't ever be able to go out of the house again for the shame of it. She sided with my father, saying unless I stopped this nonsense then she had no son.

'I was devastated by their reaction. Without their backing I couldn't go to college, and without a degree no reputable fashion house was going to consider me as an apprentice, so my dream was at an end. I joined my father in the business. When I told Mrs Maybury she was devastated for me too as she was really convinced that I had what it took to make a name for myself in the world of fashion. I resigned myself to my lot in life and tried to make the best of it. I quite enjoyed office work but my father is not easy to work for. As I said before, he's very set in his ways. It's his way or no way. And he didn't pay me very well as he was of the mind that it would all be mine one day when I was running the show, so until then I could make do. I did the normal things lads of my age did. I hung around with my mates, went to football matches, dances, had several girlfriends . . . but deep down I resented what I was doing and was miserable.

'I'd been working for Father for four years when I read an article in a newspaper. It was about a woman who wanted to train to be a carpenter when she left school, but because that was considered to be a man's job no firm would consider her seriously. She still wasn't prepared to give up her dream of working with wood. She got a job in a factory to earn some money so that she was able to buy herself some tools and decent cuts of wood, and set about making pieces of furniture to show potential employers the abilities she had. It was a hard slog for her but finally her persistence paid off as the boss of one firm she went to see took a chance on her. Now she owns that business and is doing very well for herself, with people paying good money to own furniture designed by her and made in her factory.

'Her story really inspired me. It got me to thinking I should take a leaf out of her book. If I could design and make up a collection of clothes myself, I could take them down to London and tout them around the fashion houses. Hopefully one of them would think I had enough talent to take a chance on me. I was so excited about resurrecting my dream of becoming a designer again. I knew this would mean I would have to leave my job and home as there was no way my parents were going to allow me to turn my bedroom into a workshop and make women's dresses in there. They have always been strict with me and very dictatorial but I do love them and the thought of being cut off by them was very painful to me. I hoped that if I could make a success of myself then they would see that they were wrong to stop me from following my own path and I would be reconciled with them again.

'I signed on with an employment agency and got myself temporary lodgings. Cowardly as it was, I left my parents a letter telling them what I was doing, asking for their forgiveness but saying this was something I had to do as I couldn't face another row with them and to see looks of disappointment on their faces again.

'I had a little money saved, which was enough to buy what I needed to make a start, but living at home you don't realise how much things cost. By the time I'd paid out for my lodgings and bought food, then put money aside for bills, there wasn't enough left to rent a room to use as a workshop. I was beginning to despair that I would ever get my dream off the ground when my luck changed and I came here to Jolly's. At the start it was just another normal couple of weeks' cover, but then it turned out to be longer, which I was so pleased about as I like working here. Then the day Sam's donkey died I came across this place . . . well, it was the answer to all my prayers.

'When I investigated I was excited to find that this side of the house hadn't deteriorated as badly as the other. With a bit of work I could make this room habitable, and after having a scavenge around I found enough furniture to do me. I could get water from the stream nearby. I had to hope that while I was living here the ceiling didn't come crashing down on me. I knew I was trespassing but it was either risk being caught and paying the consequences or else turn my back on ever trying my luck at becoming a designer, as I knew I was not going to find something like this again in a hurry. Not having to pay any rent or electric or gas bills meant more money from my wage to buy equipment and materials.

'Once I'd cleaned out the room, I set about getting my stuff up here. I did it all late at night, got a taxi to drop me off a few yards from the staff gate. It took me a few trips to get everything up here. I had to dismantle the treadle sewing machine and bring that up bit by bit then put it all together again. Since I've been living here being spotted by either Donkey Sam or the security guards has been my main worry, but the guards hardly ever venture up this end of the camp, and I always crept by Sam's hut so as not to alert him or his donkeys. Up to tonight I've been lucky.'

He then eyed Jackie contritely. 'I feel very guilty for deceiving you, Jackie, especially that night when I lied about being at the bus stop after you chased me with my wallet, and the other lies I've told you to cover up for being here. I'm very close to finishing my collection. I've just two garments to finish hemming and a pant suit to make, then I'll have enough to show what I'm capable of to potential employers. If you evict me from here, I can't afford to rent lodgings and a workshop, and that means I won't be able to finish my collection. I need you to know that once I had finished, I wasn't planning just to up and leave you in the lurch but to stay until you didn't need me any longer. You have my word on that.'

Al paused long enough to look at the women, particularly

at Jackie who had the authority to make or break him, and then his tone turned to one of pleading. 'Please let me finish, I beg you, Jackie. Can't you turn a blind eye and pretend you weren't here tonight? Please?'

She heaved a deep sigh. The usually vocal Ginger was keeping her thoughts on this matter to herself. It was a difficult position Al had put Jackie in. She might well be in trouble herself for knowing he was trespassing and not doing anything about it, so this was her decision and she appreciated the way Ginger was allowing her to make it.

Jackie looked over at the garments hanging on the wall. She could sew on a button or stitch a hem, but as for designing her own dress, cutting it out and making it up, she doubted her efforts would be good enough to be seen outside the house – that's if they didn't fall apart on the first trying on. But to her layman's eyes Al's efforts were of a quality that would not look out of place in any exclusive dress shop, with a price tag on them that only the wealthy could afford. These were clothes she herself could only dream of owning. Mrs Maybury was not just being kind to Al when she'd said he had talent. Whether he was deemed as good enough by those in the fashion world remained to be seen, but to be the one to deny him the chance to find out . . . could she live with that?

She fought with her conscience, her loyalty to Drina Jolly against the guilt she knew she would suffer for ending Al's ambitions. If Drina were in her shoes what would she do? Jackie felt she knew what the answer to that was. After the young Drina had found out first-hand what it felt like to have ambitions but not to be allowed to fulfil them until later in life, she never failed to encourage and support any of her staff when it came to bettering themselves. Jackie was still concerned about leaving Al to live in an unsafe building, but hopefully it wouldn't deteriorate any further over the next couple of weeks or so until he had left.

All she said to him was, 'Get your collection finished, and by the time you have hopefully Mrs Jolly and Mrs Buckland will be back. If not the agency will find us another temp to take your place. I will miss you though, Al. You've fitted in just great and I can't fault your work.'

He stared blankly at her for a moment, wondering whether he had misheard her, then his face lit up as he cried, 'Oh, Jackie, do you mean it? You're going to let me stay to finish off my collection? Oh, I don't know how to thank you.'

She smiled at him. 'You can do that by getting yourself a job doing what you dream of, and making a success of yourself.'

Ginger was just happy to know that the reason Al had not asked her out wasn't because he didn't fancy her but because taking girls out hadn't figured in his plans while he was following his dream. Whether that was in fact the case didn't figure with her, she just preferred to think it was. She piped up, 'And when you're this big fashion designer, don't forget me and Jackie when you no longer have any use for the sample clothes you've made for models to parade in on the catwalk.'

Jackie grabbed her arm. 'For goodness' sake, let Al get a job first before you're hounding him for free clothes. Now come on, we've our beds to get to.' As she dragged her friend out, she said to Al, 'See you in the morning.'

He winked at Ginger by way of telling her that, should he achieve his wish, clothes would certainly be coming her way.

CHAPTER TWENTY-FOUR

Three weeks later Jackie was sitting in the quiet lounge of the Paradise with Vic, having a drink with him after his session at Groovy's had ended for the night.

Heaving a sigh, she said to him, 'Sorry. I'm not good company tonight.'

'I hope that's nothing to do with me?'

She quickly reassured him, 'You know it's not. It's just that we've been trying to catch the drug dealer and we're no nearer now than we were when we started looking weeks ago. It really infuriates and disgusts me that this . . . this mindless cretin is lining his own pockets, not giving a damn what damage he could be doing to others. I'm determined to catch him at it and make him pay. Trouble is, I've got to the stage that I dread another night spent trawling Groovy's, and I know Ginger is ready to slit her throat sooner than go again. As for Harold . . .

'Well, actually, no. I think his undercover role in the Paradise is helping build his confidence no end, because friendly people of his age have thought he's a camper here on his own and have asked him to join them, and of course that's meant he's had to talk to them and he's not going back to spend his evenings alone in an empty house, so at least some good is coming out of this. The only saving grace for me is that, except for when you go off to see your family and friends on your day off and sometimes don't get back until late, I get to see you every night while you're playing and spend some time with you when your session finishes, so at least I have that to look forward to.'

Vic smiled at her. 'I'm glad to hear that. But not catching this drug dealer yet isn't the only reason you're not yourself today, is it? You'll miss him, won't you?'

She lifted her head and smiled at him. 'Al? Yes, I will. It was very sad seeing him off today. It took me all my self-control not to cry. I just pray he's got what it takes for a fashion house to take him on. I think any of them would be stupid not to myself. Those clothes he designed and made were exquisite in my eyes. He has promised to keep us informed of his progress. I have told him that if it doesn't work out then we'll always find him a job here at Jolly's, although it might not be in the office as surely Mrs Jolly and Mrs Buckland will be back soon. It's months now since Dan died.' Her face was wreathed in sadness. 'I suppose, though, grief is a difficult thing. There's no time limit to it after the death of a loved one.'

'I'd never get over you if you died, Jackie.'

She eyed him, taken aback. She knew Vic liked her very much but was this his way of telling her his feelings for her were more than liking? Although she'd always felt they had an unspoken agreement between them that their relationship would never become permanent because of the nature of Vic's job, it hadn't stopped her developing feelings for him which wouldn't take much now to turn into love, despite her being well aware of the pain this would cause when it was time to say goodbye in a few short weeks' time.

Jackie didn't quite know how to respond in case she was reading too much into his words so just said, 'Hopefully I've got a few more years left in me yet.'

He looked at her for a moment as he drank from his pint of lager, then put the glass down on the table before he asked, 'Will you miss me when I leave at the end of the season?'

She didn't hesitate with her answer. 'Yes, I will, very much.'

'And me you.' Again he looked at her searchingly for a moment before he next spoke. 'But we don't have to miss each other, Jackie.'

She frowned at him, bemused. 'What do you mean?'

He leaned forward and reached for her hand, tenderly stroking it as he looked deep into her eyes. His voice was husky when he told her, 'I never thought about settling down and having kids before. All I wanted in life was to have my shop and a place of my own to live. Sharing it with anyone didn't figure. But after meeting you, getting to know you . . . well, you're feisty, funny, loyal. I could go on. Bottom line is, I've fallen in love with you, Jackie.

'I've had a bit of luck moneywise and it couldn't have come at a better time because it means that when the season ends I can finish with the band. I've grown to like this area of Lincolnshire and think Skegness would be a great place for me to set up my music shop. Will you help me find suitable premises for it and somewhere to live . . . Oh, damn it, Jackie, I'm asking you to marry me.'

This turn of events was so unexpected she blabbered,

'But . . . but . . . we've barely known each other more than three months.'

He gave a shrug. 'Is there a time limit on how long you should take to know you love someone and want to share your life with them? If so, no one told me. Some people claim they fell in love the moment they clapped eyes on their better half.' Vic's eyes twinkled with humour. 'It did take me a little longer than that to fall in love with you, Jackie. It was the second time I clapped eyes on you it happened. So am I going to be buying a bottle of champagne to celebrate, or walking away with my tail between my legs and crying myself to sleep?'

She needed no more convincing. He'd won her over enough to persuade her that he'd prove to be a good husband, give her a good future. Jackie suddenly felt light-headed, giddy with the knowledge that she was loved by Vic; the fine line between caring deeply for someone and loving them snapped inside her, and love for him completely overwhelmed her. Smiling happily she told him, 'I will marry you. Yes, please.'

He jumped up from his seat, yanking her up with him, to pull her into his arms and hug her fiercely, telling her, 'You've made me the happiest man in the world, Jackie.'

At that moment she doubted there was a happier woman in the world.

They decided to keep the news just to themselves for the moment, only telling those closest to them both as Vic wanted to do it the old-fashioned way and buy her a ring to announce their happy news to the world via a celebration party.

* * *

The next morning it was an exhausted Jackie trying to carry out her duties in the office, while down in reception a worn-out Ginger was fighting to concentrate her sleep-deprived brain on the job her boss was asking her to do, both girls having spent most of the night after Jackie had got back to the chalet talking excitedly about her forthcoming marriage to Vic. It would have been an exaggeration to say they got more than three hours' sleep between them before the alarm shrilled out that it was time for them to get up again.

Harold had shown great pleasure at being one of only two people Jackie was taking into her confidence for the time being. He gave her a wide smile and a hearty handshake of congratulation at her news when she told him first thing. This development did much to ease the guilt he'd felt at the part he had played in the break-up with her previous boyfriend, despite Jackie having told him many times since then that there were other factors involved.

At the moment, for the third time that morning, she was explaining to Olive Pilkington, Al's replacement, how their simple filing system operated. Olive just couldn't seem to get the hang of it. Eighteen years of age, Olive was an extremely tall girl, towering a good six inches above Jackie's five foot four, and very thin. Ginger's description of her was that she was a long streak of piss. Her dress sense was questionable, a mixture of fashionable and pre-war which didn't work and made her look ridiculous most of the time. Today she was wearing a brown and white peasant skirt which should have been ankle-length but on her was mid-calf-length, teamed with a Peter Pan-collared blue sprig blouse and short red cardigan with embroidered flowers down the front. She wore flat Roman-style brown plastic sandals on her size eight feet, and her straight long mousy brown hair was tied up childishly in two pigtails at the sides of her head.

A sense of humour seemed to have passed her by. She came across as quite gormless, plodding and slow. She did, though, possess two redeeming qualities, which were the reason why Jackie suffered her other shortcomings and had not asked the agency to replace her. She could type at eighty words a minute, her long fingers mesmerising to watch as they seemed to dance across the keys, and very rarely did she make a mistake, so the previous pile of typing waiting to be dealt with in the tray was now virtually non-existent. Also her manner on the telephone was exemplary. With the handset to her ear she seemed to change into a different person, becoming animated, and had a way with callers which instantly put them at their ease. Her message-taking was word perfect, but as soon as the call ended she reverted to her usual lacklustre self.

Jackie was losing hope that Olive would ever master the filing system, and it would be far less frustrating and quicker for Jackie to do it herself. She said, 'Look, leave the filing to me and you get on with the typing. First, though, will you make a drink for us all?'

As she got up Olive mumbled, 'Okay, Miss Sims.' Which was how she insisted on addressing her boss, despite having been told numerous times that Jackie would suffice.

As Olive went off, Harold came out of his office. He had taken to leaving his door open now. His need to lock himself protectively behind closed doors had substantially lessened as his confidence built. He was shaking his head. 'I understand now what people mean by "it's like pulling teeth" when they're dealing with something that is proving impossible for them. I couldn't help but overhear you trying to explain the filing system to that young girl for the umpteenth time. I would have given up long since. Anyway, I'm not so blind I can't see you didn't get much sleep last night, Jackie. I suspect you and Miss Williams had much to discuss about your forthcoming nuptials.' An old-fashioned expression that Jackie had to hide a smile over, but coming from Harold she felt it was very endearing. 'So I'm offering to do your turn of the camp this morning. Unless, of course, you feel the fresh air might prove of benefit to you? Blow the cobwebs away, so to speak.'

She was touched by his thoughtfulness and torn as to whether to accept or not. The fresh air and exercise could do wonders in revitalising her, but she didn't know whether she had the energy to begin her walk in the first place. Eventually she decided she was too tired to go. 'I appreciate your offer, Mr Rose, and I'd like to accept.'

Olive then returned with the drinks. Afterwards, Harold set off on his camp tour and Jackie sent Olive over to the Paradise bar to collect their stock order for next week, which the head barman had not yet brought over. Having already received the other departments' lists for the coming few days, Jackie had just picked up the receiver to begin making calls to suppliers when she heard the noise of the door leading to the stairs. Someone was on the way in. She inwardly groaned, praying it wasn't a Stripey coming to inform her that she was needed to deal with a crisis in the camp.

Despite what she was feeling, ever the professional, Jackie prepared herself to welcome the visitor and do her best to accommodate them.

When the newcomer stepped through the door, the smile of welcome on Jackie's face vanished to be replaced by a look of shock. It took her brain several long seconds to register that she really wasn't seeing things but the person smiling back at her was Drina Jolly.

There was no sign of Jackie's lack of sleep the previous night when she issued a whoop of delight, pushed back her chair, and dashed over to throw her arms around her beloved friend and boss. 'Oh, Drina, you're back. Oh, it's so wonderful to see you!'

Chuckling, she responded, 'It's good to see you too, dear.'

Untangling herself, Jackie blasted her with, 'How is Rhonnie? Is she better? Oh, can I get you some tea? And how is Artie? When are you and Rhonnie coming back . . .'

Still chuckling, Drina interjected, 'Whoa, slow down, Jackie. First let me thank you from the bottom of my heart for doing such a good job of keeping this place running in our absence. I know it was a big undertaking for a young woman of your age. Mr Rose has been keeping me updated when I managed to call him from a telephone box in the village. I'm glad to hear that apart from the normal day-to-day problems we take for granted, and the odd matter he needed my say-so on, everything has gone smoothly, thanks to you, Mr Rose and the rest of the staff. Of course, the news about the bank robbers came as a shock. How dare they use Jolly's as a hideaway? But all credit to you, Jackie, for uncovering them and drawing the matter to the attention of the police without bringing any discredit on the camp.'

She patted Jackie's shoulder. 'I'm so proud of you, dear. Now, to answer your questions. Artie is fine. He's just popped over to maintenance to let them know he's back. Thank you for the offer of tea but I'll say no this time. We've had a long journey . . . we broke it, stayed in a hotel last night and set off again early this morning. We've just dropped in to say hello for now before we go home and settle back in. As for Rhonnie, well, why don't you ask her how she is yourself?'

Her attention fully on Drina, Jackie hadn't seen Rhonnie come into the office behind her.

Jackie ran over to her, intending to hug her too. 'Oh, Rhonnie, Rhonnie, I'm so glad to see you. I've missed you and Drina so mu—' Her voice suddenly trailed off, her outstretched arms fell to her sides, and she stared in astonishment at what Rhonnie was holding in her arms. 'That's a baby!'

Rhonnie smiled. 'As observant as ever, I'm glad to see.' With eyes filled with adoration and love, she looked down at her son then back at Jackie. 'Let me introduce you to Daniel Arthur Buckland. We call him Danny.'

She gasped. 'Dan's son! But . . . but . . .'

Rhonnie told her, 'I was nearly five months pregnant when Dan died, Jackie. He knew, of course, from the moment I did myself. He was so excited about becoming a father, couldn't wait . . . Anyway, we didn't tell anyone else as I didn't want to be treated with kid gloves, being fussed over and Drina and my father insisting I eased back on work. I was lucky. I didn't suffer from morning sickness, swollen ankles, or any of those tell-tale signs a woman is pregnant. It had got to the stage where I couldn't hide my bump any longer so we had planned to tell you all just when Dan had his accident. As you know, I fell apart then. That's when Drina and my father decided to take drastic action.

'When I woke up in their car to find we were well on our way to Devon, I was furious, I told them that they'd wasted their time as I didn't care where I was. I'd still lost Dan, and the quicker I died myself the better for me. Dad and Drina would not be budged and told me they wouldn't take me back until I was well on the mend. I'd lost a lot of weight by that time and my stamina was very low. One night I started to have terrible pains in my stomach and began to bleed. It was apparent that something was wrong with the baby. Dad and Drina still didn't know I was pregnant so this was a terrible shock for them. They whisked me into hospital. It wasn't until the doctors told me they were concerned I was losing the child that something inside me seemed to snap and I realised I loved this baby . . . my baby and Dan's. I had someone to live for, and through our baby Dan would always be with me.

'I was in hospital for six weeks, only allowed home because Drina and Dad promised to make sure I didn't lift a finger. Travel was out of the question too, so that's why we didn't come back.' She smiled down at Danny again. 'To think how close I was to losing this precious bundle, and at the time I didn't care. It doesn't bear thinking about. Danny was born two weeks ago. He weighed six pounds three ounces, and he's perfect.'

'He sure is,' Jackie whispered emotionally, still reeling in shock at Rhonnie's tale. 'Can I hold him?'

'Of course,' she happily responded, carefully placing the sleeping infant in her arms.

While Jackie cooed over him, Drina told her, 'We didn't like keeping you in the dark about the baby, my dear, but we knew how worried you'd be. And you hardly needed that on top of the pressure of running the camp in our absence, so that's why we kept it to ourselves.'

Dan started to whimper. Rhonnie took him back and said to Drina, 'He's due a feed soon.'

'Right, we'd best be off. Artie will be back by now from checking with Sid Harper that everything is all right over in maintenance. I'll just pop into the office and tell Mr Rose we're back.'

Jackie told her, 'He's not in. He's out on the camp tour. Won't be back for another hour or so.'

Both Drina and Rhonnie flashed a look at each other, eyebrows raised in surprise. It was Drina who spoke. 'Really! Well, my dear, you've achieved something I've been trying to do for a long time: getting him to come out of his shell. When we first decided to take Rhonnie away to recuperate, I was concerned about leaving Mr Rose in charge. He's a first-class accountant, totally loyal and trustworthy, so I knew I was leaving the company finances in good hands, but I was well aware of his lack of confidence, how shy he was with people. I worried there were elements of being a boss that he wouldn't cope with. At the time, though, I thought it was just a figurehead I needed since I only expected to be away a few weeks.

'To be honest, though, when it became apparent just how ill Rhonnie was and that the baby's life was in danger, the camp was the last thing on my mind. Poor Artie fell apart then, desperately worried he could lose his daughter as well as his grandchild, so I had him to look after too. When I used to telephone Mr Rose for updates as regularly as I could as there was no telephone in the cottage, he always told me everything was fine and running smoothly, and I was very relieved to hear it as it meant I didn't need to worry and could concentrate on Rhonnie and Artie.'

She paused and eyed Jackie knowingly. 'You'll be eager to know when we're returning to work. Well, as you can appreciate, Rhonnie won't be back while Danny is so young. She wants to concentrate on being a mother but will still be playing a backseat role. As for me . . .' Drina paused and looked thoughtful for a moment before she went on. 'Jackie, I need to ask you if you'll continue working with Mr Rose for the time being, dear? Well, you've done a fantastic job for the last five months, and it's only just over three weeks to the end of the season. You see, I have plans to expand the camp and my time will be taken up with formulating them, having meetings with the bank and other bodies to see if what I have in mind is feasible, et cetera.'

She saw that Jackie was going to ask what the plans entailed and quickly told her, 'I will fully explain them once I'm at liberty to. And be assured, the plans include you.' She then looked at Jackie closely, her face clouded with worry as she declared remorsefully, 'How terrible of me! I've been so full of our news that I never noticed how tired you are. Doing what you have for as long as you have has obviously taken its toll on you and it's very wrong of me to ask you to carry on. I will . . .'

Jackie interjected, 'No, it's not that at all. I'm honoured you want me to continue and very happy to. I'd be lying if I said I haven't spent some sleepless nights worrying whether I'm up to the job or not, sometimes I know I haven't handled situations in exactly the way you would have, but they turned out all right in the end. I'm tired because I was up late talking with Ginger last night . . .' She was about to announce that she was getting married but then thought better of it, not wanting to eclipse Rhonnie's wonderful news. So instead she said, 'Boyfriend talk. We lost track of time and only had a couple of hours' sleep.'

Rhonnie smiled. Well, hope you managed to set the world to rights. You and Keith are okay, though?'

Now was not the time to explain to them what had happened with Keith and her mother so Jackie just said, 'Well, actually, we have split up. It was for the best. I've a new boyfriend now, but I'll tell you all about it another time.'

Both Drina and Rhonnie looked shocked. It was Drina who said, 'Oh! I thought you were rather fond of Keith and saw him as the one for you? We'll look forward to meeting your new boyfriend.' The baby began to whimper again. 'We really must get off now before Danny lets you hear just how powerful his lungs are. Please tell Mr Rose I'm sorry to have missed him and will telephone him later from the house to explain matters further. Once again, Jackie, thank you for all you are doing and I think you'll be pleased with the way I intend to repay you. Hopefully Mr Rose will too.'

After giving her a hug, Drina and Rhonnie left Jackie to it.

Harold was taken aback by the news that Drina and Rhonnie had returned. Of course he was gratified to hear that Rhonnie was well and about the baby, but this meant his time as temporary boss was coming to an end. The old Harold would have been delighted at the thought of returning to the solitude of his office in accounts, rarely having to interact with anyone; but the new Harold, although far from confident enough yet to ask a lady out for drinks or dinner, didn't want to return to that isolation. His sinking spirits lifted when Jackie proceeded to inform him that Drina Jolly wanted them to carry on for the time being in their respective roles and would telephone him later to explain.

'I'm desperate to know what Mrs Jolly's plans are for this place,' Jackie said to him.

He nodded. 'Yes, it is all rather intriguing, I must say. But until Mrs Jolly is ready to tell us then we must have patience.'

'Yes, I suppose,' she grumbled, patience not being one of her virtues. A look of remorse filled her face. 'I feel so guilty, Mr Rose, for the fact that Mrs Jolly is under the impression all is well in the camp when we know it's not.'

Gravely he responded, 'You're referring to the drug dealer in our midst?'

She nodded. 'Mrs Jolly put her trust in us to run this place as she would do. I'd really prefer that we get this dealt with before she takes back the reins. I worry that she might not think so highly of us when she finds out that we've known we've a criminal on the staff for weeks and not been able to catch them in the act. I don't want to risk going back to being just the office girl with no real responsibilities. We need to find this person, fast. Stop them from laughing at us behind our backs, thinking they are so much cleverer than us for evading us for so long. I want to prove to them they've underestimated us and wipe that smile off their face.'

Harold gave a helpless shrug. 'You don't know how much I wish I could come up with a way to catch this criminal, but apart from what we are doing I can't think of anything else.'

She responded dispiritedly, 'Join the club. But what we are doing is better than nothing. We could still have a stroke of luck.'

Harold nodded. As matters stood that was the only thing they could hope for.

By the time Jackie left the office that evening, the girls in reception had already closed up for the night so she was surprised not to find Ginger waiting for her. Back in the chalet, while she waited for her friend to arrive, Jackie read a letter from her mother that she had received in the post that morning. Gina wrote regularly to her twice a week, whether or not Jackie had replied to her last missive. The letters were always very diplomatic. Never once did her mother mention Keith in any way, just chatted on about daily life for herself and Robby. Jackie appreciated the fact that not once, in the dozen or so letters Gina had written by now, did she suggest they meet up, waiting for Jackie herself to make that decision when she was ready. At the moment, as much as she missed her mother, however much she loved her, she just wasn't ready to face her, though some time soon she must introduce Vic and tell Gina their happy news. When they met up for the first time all together, Jackie wanted to be sure she wasn't harbouring any lingering ill feeling towards her mother and Keith. In the meantime, letters would keep them in touch.

She had just replaced the letter in its envelope and was beginning to wonder where Ginger had got to when the woman herself barged in. She didn't look happy.

Before Jackie could say a word her friend exclaimed, 'Can you bloody believe it? My wonderful boss volunteered me to take over the running of the cigarette kiosk tonight so it'll be ten before I can meet you at Groovy's.'

Jackie wasn't happy to hear this because she didn't like the thought of being on her own there until her friend arrived to join her. She asked, 'What's wrong with Mandy Fisher that she can't do it then?'

'According to my boss, she gashed her leg on the corner of one of the shelves in the kiosk stockroom while she was putting new supplies away earlier. Pouring with blood it was, and deep enough to need stitches. Kitty Popple is seeing to her now and when she's finished Mandy is to take the rest of the night off. Apparently she was kicking up a real stink, insisting Kitty just bandage up her leg so she could get back to work. Kitty put her foot down and told Mandy that she was to do as she was told as in medical matters the nurse's word is law.'

'Mandy should be praised for being so conscientious, I suppose. She's a nice girl from what I know of her. I'm sorry to hear what's happened.'

'But it means I'm going to have to get straight over to

the kiosk as soon as I've finished my tea. It opens promptly at seven. A minute later and the queue of people in a hurry to buy their fags and matches and get over to the ballroom to bag a good seat for the show tonight will be forming a lynch mob. So come on, get your skates on or I won't have time to eat my meal – and I'm famished enough to eat a scabby dog.'

CHAPTER TWENTY-FIVE

At just coming up to a quarter to eight that evening Ginger was serving her umpteenth customer, a young man of around nineteen, his face barely visible beneath a mop of thick long hair. He was dressed in flared trousers and a bright pink satin shirt worn with Cuban-heeled boots. He had a girl with him of around the same age, wearing a red tight-fitting halter top and a skirt so short it hardly covered her knickers. She was hanging on his arm with one hand and in the other clutched a packet of Kensitas cigarettes and a box of Bluebell matches. Having concluded their dealings, Ginger was taken aback when, instead of walking away to make room for the next customer, the lad looked furtively around, obviously wanting to make sure no others in the queue behind were close enough to hear what he was about to say. He leaned over the counter, slid two half crowns towards her and whispered, 'I'll have one weed and two purples.'

She eyed him back like a village idiot, having no idea what he was asking for. She turned around to scan the shelves of various packets of cigarettes in tens and twenties, the selection of cigars, cigarillos and other smoking paraphernalia. Seeing nothing that might lend itself to the description he had given her, she turned back and said to him, 'You'll have to help me out as I haven't a clue what you're after?'

He eyed her warily. 'You are Mandy, right? I've got the right kiosk?'

'There's only one cigarette kiosk on the camp so you have got the right one, but I'm not Mandy. She's had an accident and I'm covering her shift for her. But . . .'

Before she could say anything else the young man had reclaimed his money and dragged the girl away.

Ginger had no time to think further about the incident as another customer was demanding her attention.

Several customers later she was serving a group of six teenage girls, who were getting on her nerves as they all kept changing their minds about the brand of cigarettes they wanted. Ginger wouldn't have been so irritated had she been selling them a packet each, but it was one packet of ten between them! Finally they made their choice, then made her wait while, giggling childishly, they divided out the cost between them before handing her the correct amount in pennies and halfpennies. Now money and goods had changed hands, Ginger bent forward to ask the next customer in line what she could get for him when one of the girls in the group whispered in her ear, 'Not so quick, we ain't finished yet.'

Ginger heaved a fed-up sigh. Forgetting all her customer service training, she hissed, 'Well, make it quick. There's a queue of other customers behind you waiting to be served.'

The girl shot her a nasty glare and hissed, 'Gimme six hearts.'

Assuming they were a brand of cigarettes, she sardonically told the girl, 'Cigarettes come in packets of ten or twenty, not sixes.'

The girl snarled, 'Yer daft cow, I ain't meaning fags. I mean . . . yer know?'

Ginger gave a shrug. 'No, I don't.'

The girl was getting impatient now, as were her friends who wanted to be dancing in Groovy's, and so were several people still waiting to be served who were all telling the girl to hurry up, some in language that would make an old navvy blush. She hissed again, 'Look, so I was rude, but that's no reason not to sell me what I want. Okay, if it's an apology you want, I'm sorry,' she said grudgingly. 'Now, gimme the hearts. Didn't have this trouble with the other girl who works behind this counter.'

Thinking by now that 'hearts' must be some sort of confectionery product, Ginger told her in no uncertain terms: 'This is a cigarette kiosk, not a sweetshop. Now stop wasting my time and clear off or I'll call the security guards to deal with you. Yes, sir?' she asked the irritated man behind.

As the fuming girl and her friends moved off, she heard the leader grumble, 'We'll have to make do with just booze tonight and hope that other gel is back behind the counter tomorrow . . . not that snooty bitch.'

Before nine o'clock struck, there were several more occasions when Ginger was asked for items she hadn't a clue about and had to send the none-too-happy would-be purchasers, all of them aged between mid teens and early twenties, away empty-handed. Something though was telling her that things weren't right here but she had no idea what.

Ginger was just pulling the shutters down when Terry Jones rushed up and off-handedly demanded, 'Twenty Number Six and a box of Swans.'

She knew why he was acting short with her. He still hadn't forgiven Jackie for walking out on him during the date he'd blackmailed her into going on. As Ginger was Jackie's best friend then Terry's wrath extended to her too. Well, two could play at that game.

She looked at him and said cockily, 'Say please and I might sell them to you.'

His eyes darkened menacingly. 'Don't mess me about, Ginger. I'm in a rush. I need to get back to the Paradise.'

'You're not the only one in a rush. I'm in a rush to lock up as I've got a hot date tonight,' she lied, and smiled sweetly at him. 'You had any hot dates recently that lasted more than two hours before the poor girl couldn't stand you any longer and made an excuse to escape?'

He glared at her darkly. 'Just give me my fags and matches.'

'Say please and I will, else these shutters are coming down and you'll have to wait until tomorrow for your smokes. Your choice.'

He knew she meant it. Shooting her another murderous glare, he said through clenched teeth, 'Please.'

Ginger said sardonically, 'Now that wasn't hard, was it?' She collected his purchases, made to hand them to him in exchange for his money when a thought struck her and she withdrew her hand, waving his cigarettes tantalisingly before him but out of reach.

'If someone asked you for weed or purples or some hearts or other funny-named stuff, what would they be after?' she asked.

He looked stunned at first then suspiciously asked, 'Why do you want to know that?'

Ginger didn't want to admit to him that it was because she felt stupid not knowing what people were asking for. 'Do you know the answer or not?' she challenged Terry.

'Might do,' he said cagily, then eyed her meaningfully. 'If I tell you, what's in it for me?'

She might have known he'd want something in return, the same as he had with Jackie when she asked for his help. Ginger leaned on the counter, gazing at him seductively, leaving him in no doubt what was in it for him if he told her.

Terry almost choked on his own spittle in anticipation of what was to come. 'Well, it's slang for drugs,' he blurted out. 'So now I've told you, when do I get what you've promised me?'

Ginger wasn't listening to him. Her thoughts were racing at the significance of this snippet of information. Those people in Groovy's that Jackie and she had surreptitiously approached, pretending they were in search of drugs, had been telling the literal truth when they'd mentioned that the shop sold them, not as they had thought taking the mickey.

She felt euphoric, elated, that she was the one to make this important discovery. Now she needed to update Jackie and Harold Rose on this turn of events. But she knew Jackie would tell her you can't accuse people of committing a crime without concrete proof – not unless you want to risk being accused of slander and possibly being charged yourself. She prayed that she could find that proof and bring their long vigil to an end.

Without further ado, she snatched Terry's money out of his hand and replaced it with his cigarettes and matches, telling him, 'And just what exactly did I promise you, Terry? Oh, I see, that look I gave you . . . you thought it was a come on, did you? Well, you were wrong. It was a look of disgust. Now clear off, you slimebag!'

Before he could respond, she made a grab for the bottom of the metal shutter above her head and yanked it down, afterwards locking it securely. She laughed as she heard him mutter a crude response from the other side. Ginger, though, was very conscious that the supervisor of the retail outlets on the camp would be along any minute to cash up so she needed to find what she was after before then or run the risk of being caught rummaging around, which would take some explaining. Or worse, the supervisor herself could be in league with Mandy and it wouldn't do to alert them that their game was up before it was brought to the attention of the police.

Ginger flashed a look around, not sure where to start her search, under the kiosk counter or in the well-stocked store-room behind. She tried to put herself in Mandy's position. She would want to make sure her illegal substances were to hand when a buyer approached her so that the sale could be made quickly and present the least risk to her and the purchaser. To Ginger's mind, under the counter was the logical place. She squatted down to take a look for a container of some kind that would hold a quantity of pills. A wide shelf, about ten inches deep, ran beneath. It was filled with all sorts of items: a box of paper clips, several blunt pencils, Bics and Biros, paper and a pad of order forms for replacement stock. There were also personal items belonging to Mandy herself: a comb and hairbrush, make-up bag, half-empty packet of biscuits and some packets of Smith's crisps. At the far right of the shelf, directly under the till on the counter above, was an old Crawford's biscuit tin with a pile of white paper sweet bags beside it. This looked promising.

Her heart hammering in anticipation, Ginger pulled out the tin and prised open the lid, gaping at what she saw inside. Her nose wrinkled involuntarily at the strange pungent smell that wafted out of it. There were numerous small plastic packets of green-looking stuff and several larger plastic bags, each holding a quantity of different-coloured pills. Also in the tin was a bag containing a sum of money in various denominations of silver coins, ten-shilling and pound notes. As innocent as she was in such matters, Ginger knew without doubt that this was the evidence that confirmed Mandy was the drug dealer.

In her haste to get it to Jackie and Harold, and to bring Mandy to task for her crimes, she forgot that she should wait for the supervisor to arrive and check the contents of the till tallied with the roll.

The precious tin clutched tightly in her hands, Ginger was dashing across the courtyard en route from the kiosk to the Paradise, to round up Harold in the foyer and Jackie down in Groovy's, when she literally bumped into Harriet Bailey, the retail supervisor, on her way to see her. Harriet was a pretty woman in her mid-twenties who had started as a chalet maid with Jolly's on leaving school and had worked her way up over the years to the position she now held. She was engaged to one of the maintenance crew, a veteran of three seasons, and this was to be their last year here as they were getting married in November and would then be living with her parents while they found new jobs for themselves and somewhere to live.

As Ginger ran by, the other woman called out: 'Where are you going? You're not supposed to leave the kiosk until I've checked the takings are correct and given you permission.'

Without stopping, Ginger called back, 'Sorry, Miss Bailey, can't stop. I'm . . . er . . . desperate for the toilet . . . got the runs . . . blame Chef's stew. And any shortages in the till, blame Mandy. I never make mistakes handling money, ask my boss.' With that she disappeared from Harriet Bailey's view, leaving her staring in amazement.

A while later, Harold, Jackie and Ginger, all grave-faced, were in Mandy's chalet, standing side by side at the bottom of her bed. None of them could believe that such a pleasant, quiet young woman of nineteen, who had never had to be reprimanded in any way for the slightest misconduct throughout her three years of employment with Jolly's, had turned out to be a drug dealer. It seemed she had fooled them all.

Mandy herself was propped up on her bed, her thickly bandaged leg raised on a pillow, the magazine she'd been reading when her visitors surprised her lying open in her lap. She was staring frozen-faced at the biscuit tin that Harold, as the most senior staff member, was holding. He, not having been in a situation like this before, was grateful to let Jackie take the lead in speaking to the girl.

She said to Mandy now, 'So what have you to say for yourself?'

Mandy continued staring blankly at her for another few moments before she frenziedly cried out, 'That's not mine! I've never seen it before.'

Ginger snapped, 'Stop lying, Mandy, of course it's yours. I found it hidden away under the counter in the kiosk where only you work. Admit it, you've been selling drugs. We've got the evidence here. People were mentioning you by name when they were asking me for stuff while I was covering your shift.'

'This tin was the real reason you made such a fuss, insisting you were well enough to return to work after your accident. It wasn't because you were a conscientious employee. You were scared to death that whoever covered the rest of your shift might discover what you were up to. And, bad luck for you, that's just what we did,' Jackie shot at her.

Harold spoke up soberly. 'Miss Fisher, you are aware of the seriousness of the situation you're in, aren't you? I hope you feel the money you made from your despicable trade was worth the loss of years of liberty. While you're sitting alone in your tiny cell, maybe you might spare a thought for the young people whose lives you have damaged by selling them your pills – such as the girl who will walk with a limp after the pill she bought off you made her believe she could fly.'

Jackie flashed a proud look at Harold. For the first time since she had known him he had actually volunteered to speak his mind openly instead of keeping his thoughts to himself for fear of looking a fool.

At being reminded of the seriousness of her situation Mandy was visibly shaking, her face a ghostly white, eyes filled with fear. She cried out, 'I didn't want to do this. I didn't! You have to believe me. He made me . . .'

'Who made you?' Jackie demanded.

Her expression turned to one of sheer terror then. 'I can't tell you. He told me what he would do to me if I ever told anyone. And I know he will after what he did to me to make me sell stuff for him.'

'This man . . . just what did he do to you, Mandy?' Jackie asked in a gentler tone.

The terrified girl look wildly back at her. It was apparent that memories of whatever he had done were still fresh, frightening and painful. Then Mandy's rigid shoulders sagged as she issued a deep sigh. It seemed she was actually relieved to be able to unburden herself after such a long time spent keeping the ordeal to herself. In a voice barely above a whisper she uttered, 'He raped me.' While the three of them gawped at her in shock, she continued her story.

'I had just finished my shift. It was early in the season, still dark at night, and I was heading back to my chalet. It was a Wednesday, I remember. Anyway, I was walking past the staff shower block when a man appeared out of nowhere it seemed to me, grabbed my arm and punched me hard in the stomach, warning me that for my own good I'd better not make a sound. He really hurt me and I could hardly breathe for the pain. I couldn't stop him from dragging me over to the woods by the old farmhouse. Next thing I knew I was on the ground and he was on top of me . . .'

She abruptly stopped talking to wipe away the flood of tears now pouring down her face, using the sleeve of her cardigan. Then she resumed speaking. 'When he'd finished he was still lying on top of me. He was heavy and I could hardly breathe. He grabbed my face, squeezing it hard, and held a knife to my cheek, telling me that if I didn't do what he wanted me to then there'd be worse things ahead of me. Much worse. And he'd get me if I ever dared breathe a word to anyone about what he'd done.' Mandy gave a violent shudder. 'His eyes . . . it was like the devil himself was looking at me. I knew he meant what he said. I was so scared I had to do what he wanted.

'He would give me a supply of stuff to sell for him. Then he would come to the kiosk every few nights. On the nights I knew he was coming, I had to leave the stockroom door open, which I wasn't supposed to, so he could slip inside. I was to listen out for him. If I had customers, I had to make an excuse that I needed something from the stockroom and sneak the tin in there with me. He would check what I'd sold and that the money I was giving him was correct, replace anything I was getting low on, then give me a pat on the face, telling me what a good girl I was, before he went out.'

She fixed her attention on Jackie then. 'You've always been so nice to me, I was desperate to warn you about him, what you could be getting yourself into, but then I worried you wouldn't believe me – or worse still that you were his partner in business too. It seemed safer just to keep quiet.'

Face screwed up in bewilderment, Jackie quizzed her, 'But why would you want to warn me about this man or think I might be his partner? Are you telling me I know him?'

The shock of Mandy's reply almost knocked Jackie off her feet then. 'He's your boyfriend.'

Both Harold and Ginger were rendered speechless by this shocking revelation.

Jackie's mind was screaming: This can't be true! Vic was a good, kind, honest man. She had never once witnessed him lose his temper, let alone attack a woman like Mandy had described.

Jackie shouted at her, 'You're lying, using him as a scapegoat to cover up the real identity of the person behind this! How could you do this to a good man like Vic? Now you tell us the truth or I'll wring it out of you myself.'

Now that she had divulged her abuser's identity, terror of the possible repercussions filled Mandy. She frenziedly cried, 'Jackie, please don't tell him I told you! Please, please, I beg you.'

Every fibre of her being told Jackie that this girl was not putting on an act, she was in terror for her life, but at the same time Jackie just couldn't believe that Vic was a sadistic violent thug who could use an innocent girl so callously.

'I don't doubt you have been badly treated, Mandy, but I'm having trouble believing that Vic is the man you say he is. I need proof. Can you give me that?'

The girl miserably shook her head.

Ginger was praying that this shocking story about Vic wasn't true, for Jackie's sake. Her friend had only just got over the devastation of losing Keith to her mother. And now this . . . what would it do to her?

Ginger was also finding it so difficult to believe that the man she knew could be the monster Mandy had described. Yes, they needed proof before they went any further with this. A thought struck her as to how they could obtain it.

'If he is supplying you with drugs to sell then he'll have a stash somewhere handy to replace supplies, won't he?' she asked Mandy. 'Have you any idea where Vic keeps it?'

Another shake of the girl's head.

Harold spoke up then. 'Close to hand in his chalet, do you think? In a suitcase under his bed perhaps?' Then old insecurities crept back and he added quickly, 'Or is that too obvious, do you think, and he will keep his supplies somewhere no one would ever think of?'

Ginger grinned and slapped his arm. 'You're a genius, Mr Rose. Why would he need to hide something he doesn't believe anyone is looking for? If they're not in his chalet, let's try the band's van.'

Desperate to settle this matter one way or another, Jackie dug out the set of master keys she always kept on hand in case of emergency. 'Yes, that's where we need to look. He'll be on-stage right now so this is the ideal opportunity. If Vic is innocent then I will explain to him why we invaded his privacy like this and the man I know will totally understand. But if he's guilty . . . well, then it won't matter what he thinks, will it?'

Mandy wasn't in a fit state to go anywhere so the other three hurried off to Vic's chalet, taking the biscuit tin with them. Unlike the other seasonal staff, the outside entertainers were deemed important enough to warrant chalets to themselves. Jackie had spent time in Vic's chalet before, occasions she had enjoyed, and as she entered it now ahead of the others she had to block these memories from her mind and concentrate on the search.

The chalet was clean and neat, with no clothes lying about but hanging on the rail against the wall between the beds or else folded in the bottom three drawers of the small chest. The bed was made. On the floor beside it stood a transistor radio. Jackie knew Vic constantly had it turned on when he was in, tuned to either BBC Radio One or Radio Luxemburg. His toiletries were all inside a large blue washbag. She momentarily wondered if he'd had a quick tidy round before he left for his session down at Groovy's tonight, in case she should come back with him later.

While Jackie and Ginger looked on, Harold squatted down in the space between the twin beds and looked under the one Vic used. Amongst a few other things, like shoes, some dirty clothes, and a pile of music industry publications such as *Melody Maker* and *NME*, were two suitcases. To Harold's mind, the smaller case was the most likely to be holding what they were seeking, and he pulled that out first. The women stood watching while he tried to open it, but it was locked. Harold picked it up. From its weight he could tell it had something in it. He shook it. A lot of small items from the sound of it. For Jackie's sake, Harold had been hoping that Mandy was using Vic as cover for the real culprit, but that hope was rapidly fading.

He got up and put the small case on the bed, saying, 'I think we have just cause to pry this open.'

Jackie knew that Vic kept a metal bottle opener, the type that had a hook at the end of it, along with other bits and pieces that were useful to him in the top drawer of the small chest. She fetched it and handed it to Harold.

He hooked the end of the bottle opener inside one of the two T-shaped locks on the case and gave it a sharp yank. The lock sprang open. He then proceeded to do the same to the other lock. He opened the lid.

It took Jackie just one glance at the contents to have her doubts about Mandy's claims quashed.

Spinning on her heel, she fled from the chalet.

Leaving Harold to take charge of the case and its contents, Ginger dashed after her. She found Jackie huddled on her bed in their chalet, miserably sobbing. Having trouble keeping her own emotions in check at seeing her friend in such a state, Ginger went over to her, sat down on the bed next to her and slipped one arm comfortingly around her shoulders.

For a while they sat in silence together, Jackie sobbing, Ginger feeling helpless to ease her suffering. Finally Jackie was cried out enough to lift her head, look at Ginger through tear-blurred eyes and say, 'You're going to offer up your usual cure for getting over a broken relationship, I suppose?'

'Wrong, Jackie, I'm not.' She then said flippantly, 'Only 'cos I'm sick of going out dancing at the moment, though. After a couple of nights in, there's a good chance I will be suggesting it again. Now I'm just here to let you know I'm sorry.'

Jackie managed a wan smile. 'Thanks, Ginger.' Silence reigned for several minutes as Jackie sat gently sobbing.

'I bet it's already around the staff that my boyfriend was dealing drugs,' she said finally. 'Thank God I'd kept the fact that we were going to get married quiet or the gossips would really have had a field day out of that! Terry Jones is going to love it, me walking out on a date with him in favour of a vicious drug dealer.'

'You won't stop the gossips, Jackie, so you might as well just grin and bear it. The talk won't last long. There will always be something else more juicy for the gossips to chew over in a place like this. You know that as well as I do.'

'Yes, I suppose.' Jackie heaved a shuddering sigh. 'I'm wondering now if Vic ever really loved me, Ginger, or just saw me as useful to him in some way. I mean, it was obvious that he was making good money through Jolly's, which would have ended with the band's contract at the end of the season, but with a wife working in the camp he would have had an excuse to come and go as he pleased and be able to keep operating his business from the kiosk, terrorising poor girls like Mandy into working for him.'

Ginger heaved a sigh. 'With a man like that, I don't think you'll ever be sure. Look, if it helps, I know you thought you loved him, but it was the act he put on to cover up what he was really like that you fell for. There's only so long people can keep up an act before their true colours start to show. With your nose for sniffing out things that aren't quite right, it wouldn't have been long before you sussed that Vic was up to something. And once he'd found out you were on to him, you would have ended up married to a man you were terrified of. There's no telling what he would have done to make you keep silent. I think you've had one lucky escape myself and should be celebrating the fact, not crying over a man who isn't worth your tears.'

Ginger's words set Jackie thinking. 'Ginger, you're

right, I have had a lucky escape, haven't I? God, one hell of a lucky escape!' She threw her arms around her friend and hugged her fiercely. 'Thank you. You've just saved me from wasting goodness knows how long pining over that man, when he's not worth one second.'

Ginger told her with conviction, 'I know there's a good bloke waiting out there for you, Jackie, the right man, one you'll love and who will love only you, with no hidden agenda.'

Jackie looked at her thoughtfully for a moment then made a sudden grab for her candlewick dressing gown that was lying on the bed beside her, using it to dry her wet face. She then got off the bed and stood up. 'Well, are you coming?' she asked.

'Where?'

'I like the sound of this man you've just described to me, and I'm not going to find him in here, am I?'

The police investigation revealed that Vic was not only plying his despicable trade in Jolly's through his blackmail of Mandy, but had other terrorised victims dotted about in towns in the Lincolnshire area, selling his wares for him. The other three members of the Upbeats were not spending their share of the earnings from Jolly's on enjoying themselves, as Vic had told Jackie, but handing most of the money back to Vic to pay for the addictions he was responsible for their developing. Vic's Wednesday off hadn't been used to visit family and friends, but to do his rounds of the dealers he supplied in the likes of Lincoln, Scunthorpe and Grimsby, and also visit his own supplier to replenish his stocks. His sideline had made him a great deal of money according to the amounts recorded in several bank books found under the drugs in the small suitcase. But Vic wasn't going to be spending any for many long years, not where he was going.

With the loss of their drummer, and unable to find a replacement for him at such short notice, the rest of the band had no choice but to pack up and go home, their future thrown into doubt. A decision was made not to find a replacement but to make do with just the DJ providing entertainment for the remainder of the season.

Drina was struck speechless when she was updated the next morning on the news that a drug dealer had been operating from her camp. Nevertheless she appreciated the efforts of her devoted staff in clearing up the matter conclusively. Hopefully Jolly's good name had been preserved.

CHAPTER TWENTY-SIX

Considering all the personal tragedies and catastrophes the management staff of Jolly's had had to deal with this season on top of their labours to ensure the campers enjoyed a holiday to remember, they were of the opinion that nothing else would happen to throw them into turmoil, for this season at least.

But they were bargaining without the vengeful man who'd been waiting in the wings for his moment to arrive. He had a devious plan laid to claim what he saw was rightfully his. The time had now come for Michael Jolly to act.

It was almost the end of the season, when the last of the campers would be waved off and Jolly's large iron gates closed for the winter. The camp would once again turn into a ghost town, the only signs of life inside being the handful of permanent staff working away to ensure the success of the new season ahead.

Artie had returned to his job of managing the maintenance crew, while Drina was working hard, aided by Rhonnie, to bring her plans for the development of the business to fruition. After many meetings with official bodies and sleepless nights spent worrying, Drina had one more important meeting to attend. If that proved to be successful she would be in a position to go ahead and put Jackie and Harold out of their misery, announcing to them what their future roles would be in the new venture.

Harold was still making good progress in overcoming his personal insecurities. Through his own hard work, and with the continued support of Jackie, he had at last acquired some new friends and the beginnings of a social life.

To her credit, Jackie had managed to keep the fact that she'd had a lucky escape from Vic's vile clutches firmly locked away in the recesses of her mind. The wonderful man Ginger had prophesied for her had not yet shown up but she was having fun looking for him meanwhile. What brought her much joy was the fact that finally her dear friend seemed to have found the right man for herself in PC Paul Nuttall. Over the last few weeks, his shifts allowing, the pair saw each other as much as they could and romance had blossomed between them.

The early October morning was a cold one, the sky covered by thick grey cloud, and a sharp wind was blowing off a choppy sea. At this time of year the camp was only half-full, the campers hardy types who did not care what the weather was like; all they were concerned about was the cheaper off-season rates Jolly's offered. At the moment the campers were enjoying their breakfast in the restaurant, but the majority of them would soon be dressed in thick anoraks and warm woollies, braving the cold to enjoy the outside facilities Jolly's offered, much to the disdain of the Stripeys overseeing these events, who would have preferred to be doing their job inside in the warmth.

Jackie had just arrived in the office. Olive was already behind her desk, getting herself ready to begin work. Having come out of his office to greet the two women, Harold was back behind his desk going over the accounts books to ensure they were all up-to-date before handing them to Drina later this morning as she needed to take them to the important business meeting scheduled for eleven.

Jackie looked over at the door leading to the stairs when it opened and saw Ginger coming in carrying a large box and some letters, which she brought across and put on Jackie's desk. Ginger had stayed out of camp last night in the spare bedroom at Paul's parents' house in Sutton-on-Sea, after they had been to the twenty-first birthday party of a friend of his. She had caught the bus to work that morning while Paul set off on his bike. Jackie herself had been out on a date the night before so the two friends had some catching up to do.

'How did the party go?' asked Jackie.

A big smile spread across Ginger's face. 'It was great! Paul's friends are really nice.'

'And his parents?' Ginger had met them for the first time yesterday.

'Oh, they're lovely, Jackie. Made me ever so welcome. I think they liked me.'

'And why wouldn't they?' Jackie responded with conviction. 'You'd make a smashing daughter-in-law.'

Ginger blushed. 'It's a bit early days for that yet, though I am hoping so. But don't mention it to Paul as I don't want to scare him off! Anyway, what I want to know is how you got on?'

Jackie pulled a face. 'He was nice enough, but too full of himself for my liking.'

'Oh! So no chance of a double date then?'

She shook her head. 'Not with him, no.'

'Oh, well, never mind. It was worth setting you up with him. He could have turned out to be the one. Anyway, there was another couple of Paul's single police colleagues at the party last night, good-looking ones too, so I'll see what I can do.'

Jackie was actually quite happy to remain single at the moment. She was enjoying doing exactly what she liked without the necessity to consider anyone else, but Ginger was hell-bent on helping her find this perfect man she knew was out there for her friend. Jackie knew she would be wasting her time making any protest. Looking at the box Ginger had brought in with her, she asked, 'Are you sure this is for the general office? We're not waiting for anything to be delivered, so far as I remember.'

Ginger's face lit up. 'It's not for the general office, Jackie. It's addressed to both of us.'

'Me and you! Who'd be sending us anything?'

'I suppose we could open it and find out.'

Jackie eyed her knowingly. 'I'm surprised you haven't already, knowing how little patience you have.' She scooped up a pair of scissors and held them out to Ginger. 'Go on then, you do the honours.'

She opened the box to find it lined with tissue. After she'd peeled this back they both gasped in shock to see two folded dresses side by side. One was of red wool with a thick white leather double-buckled belt, the other in canary yellow satin and chiffon. They both knew instantly who had sent them. Both far too overwhelmed by the gifts to speak, Ginger took out the red dress and held it against her, Jackie doing the same with the yellow one. Out of nosiness Olive, who today had dressed in a shapeless baggy brown calf-length pinafore dress with a thick hand-knitted petrol blue jumper underneath and clumpy red shoes on her feet, plodded over to take a look, pulled a face, then returned to her desk, saying, 'Not my style.' Jackie and Ginger shot quick glances at each other in bemusement, knowing her fashion sense.

Jackie then noticed a folded piece of paper lying in the box. She took it out and quickly read the message it contained. 'Oh, Ginger, Al's been taken on as a trainee designer with a fashion house in London! These dresses are his thanks to us for our help towards him landing the job. He didn't forget us then. He says he's sharing a flat with four other employees of the firm in a place called Soho . . . Anyway, he hopes we're both okay and he'll write soon. He's included his address so we can both write to him.'

Ginger was delighted to hear this but not as much as she was to receive her beautiful dress. 'Wait until Paul sees me in this . . . well, if he isn't in love with me now, he will be then – 'cos I'll be knocking his socks off!'

The door to the stairs opened and Ginger's boss poked her head into the room. 'Have you forgotten where you work?' she called. 'Come on, we've a queue of people waiting for our help and you're due to do the radio announcement in five minutes. Get your skates on!'

Ginger chuckled. 'That's me in trouble again. I'd best get back. Oh, take care of this for me,' she said, handing

Jackie her dress. 'Make sure you pack it up carefully. Oh, and . . .'

'Ginger, go back to work,' Jackie ordered her.

Not long after that Jackie's head jerked back up as she heard muted sounds coming from downstairs in reception. 'Sounds like there's a bit of a rumpus going on,' she said to Olive.

The girl didn't seem to hear, lost in her own little world as she folded letters and put them into envelopes ready to go in the evening post.

Jackie had just resumed work when the door opened and two men strode in, dressed in suits and overcoats and both carrying briefcases. They had an official air about them and Jackie wondered just what business had brought them here. She smiled over at them. 'Good morning. How may I help you?'

There was no answering smile or trace of warmth in the man who responded, 'We're from Her Majesty's Tax Inspectorate. We want to see your boss.'

All Jackie's instincts warned her that this was serious. She politely responded, 'I'll let Mr Rose know you're here.'

She picked up the receiver of her telephone and spoke briefly into it.

A moment later Harold appeared, looking quizzical. He first asked to see the men's identification and, when satisfied they were who they said they were, introduced himself. 'I'm Harold Rose, Company Accountant. I'm temporarily in charge while the owner, Mrs Drina Jolly, is otherwise engaged. I wasn't expecting a visit from your office. What can I do for you?'

The man who had spoken to Jackie was the one who

responded. His tone of voice was brusque. 'We're here to do an audit. We've reason to believe that major fraud is being committed. Leave everything where it is, and you and your staff . . .'

Harold looked completely shocked. 'Major fraud! May I ask on what grounds . . .'

The visitor sternly interjected, 'Mr Rose, round up all the staff in these offices and join the others from downstairs in the ballroom next door. We'll send for you if we need you.'

A worried Harold turned to Jackie. 'Would you please go and ask the staff in accounts to join us, Miss Sims? Tell them to leave everything on their desks just as it is.'

Jackie went off, returning a couple of minutes later with Maureen Watson and Sally Moulds in tow, both of them looking deeply concerned.

Then she went across to Olive. 'Can you put the switchboard on night service? We need to go.'

The young girl looked back at her in amazement. She had obviously been so lost in her own thoughts she had not been aware of what was going on until now. 'But I've not long got here, Miss Sims. Are you sacking me?'

Jackie snapped impatiently, 'Olive, just do as I asked and then come with us.'

As soon as she had, led by Harold, they all trooped out, leaving the two tax inspectors behind.

A short while later they had joined the reception staff and were all seated together in a corner of the quiet lounge in the Paradise building.

It was the head receptionist who spoke first. 'For government employees they had no manners, had they? Ordered everyone out of reception, including us, like we were a herd of cows, with not even the courtesy of an explanation. I can't imagine what the campers there at the time will be thinking.' She looked at Harold. 'Are you going to tell us what's going on, Mr Rose?'

He wasn't listening. Instead he said to Jackie, 'Mrs Jolly needs to be informed of what's going on. That's the first thing I should have done when those men turned up. I was so shocked by what they told me, I wasn't thinking straight. I can't recall her home telephone number, can you?'

Jackie shook her head. 'I've got it written down in the office but I've not had any cause to telephone her there for the last few months so I don't remember it off-hand. Oh, but isn't she coming over anyway, to collect the accounts to take with her to her business meeting? That's why you were behind closed doors this morning giving them a check over to make sure everything was present and correct.'

'Oh, yes, of course.' Harold looked at his watch. 'She'll be on her way now. Her meeting is at eleven in Lincoln, I understand. Oh, dear, I don't know whether this means she will have to postpone it. The inspectors won't let her take the books anywhere until they've given us the all clear. I'd best go and wait outside for her to arrive, and tell her what is going on.'

He made to get up but was stopped by the sight of Drina herself hurrying across the lounge towards them, looking very smart in a blue woollen two-piece and matching coat, low-heeled black court shoes on her feet and a matching handbag over her arm. She was looking extremely puzzled. Harold shot out of his chair and went to greet her.

'What is going on, Mr Rose? I've just tried to get into reception and it's locked. Why is that, and what are you all doing in here?'

As he explained, her face fell. 'Major fraud! What on earth makes the tax inspectors suspect us of that?'

Harold gulped. The accounts were purely his domain so to him this situation was his worst nightmare. It was resurrecting old insecurities he had worked hard to conquer. 'I've . . . I've no idea, Mrs Jolly. Someone has obviously given them a tip off that they have taken seriously enough to do an audit.' He began to wring his hands nervously. 'But, Mrs Jolly, please let me assure you . . .'

Drina cut in with conviction, 'You have no need to assure me of anything, Mr Rose. I know they won't find a penny out of place. Someone is obviously playing a mean-minded joke on us. What they hope to gain by this I can't work out, except for wasting all our time.' She then fumed, 'Oh, damn and blast. I shall have no choice but to postpone my meeting as without the accounts there's no point in having it.'

A thought struck Harold then. 'Mrs Jolly, it couldn't be that someone doesn't want your plans to go ahead, could it?'

She thought about this for a moment before she responded, 'No one else is privy to my plans except Rhonnie, Artie and my bank manager. The other parties involved wouldn't want to stop this going ahead as they would stand to lose valuable commission.' She noticed Harold was still looking bothered about something. 'What's on your mind?'

'Oh! It's just that I found it odd the inspectors didn't want me near at hand to answer any queries that might arise, that's all.'

'Mmm, yes, I would have expected that too.'

'And I'm surprised they didn't ask me to dig out the Fiscal Reports for last year before they sent us off. I would have thought they'd need those to aid their investigation and I keep a set locked in the safe.'

Before Drina could make any comment she heard her name being called and turned around to see Rhonnie heading over to them pushing a pram. On joining Drina and Harold, she said with a bemused frown on her face, 'I thought you would have collected the books by now and be on your way to your meeting in Lincoln. What's going on? After you left this morning, I was going to take Danny for a walk down the lane but then I thought why not come over here, pop in to see Jackie and accompany her on her walk around the camp today? The door to reception is locked though so I couldn't get in and it was the driver of your taxi who told me the same thing had happened to you and he'd seen you heading off into here.'

She looked extremely concerned when Drina enlightened her. 'It's got to be some disgruntled camper behind this whose holiday didn't match up to expectations and they've stirred up the Revenue to get their own back. They won't find anything.'

This explanation seemed to hold weight with Drina. 'Yes, of course, it's got to be.'

Harold sighed in relief.

Drina said, 'Well, all we can do is wait until the inspectors have finished their audit and are on their way. I'll just go and make a call to cancel my appointment, then I'd better wait here with you all just in case the Revenue have any questions for me as the owner.' She asked

Harold, 'Would you be kind enough to go and tell the driver I won't be needing him today after all?'

Rhonnie suggested Jackie order tea and coffee for them all. Drina returned, having made her telephone call, and sat down next to Rhonnie.

Harold returned looking very preoccupied. Drina asked why.

'Oh, it's maybe nothing, Mrs Jolly, but I was just heading back here after giving the taxi driver your message when I saw a Rolls-Royce coming through the gates. It drove down to reception and then a chauffeur got out to open the passenger door.'

Frowning quizzically, Drina asked, 'Did you see who got out?'

Harold shook his head. 'No, a crowd of campers were walking past on their way into the Paradise and blocked my view.'

Sitting next to Drina, rocking her sleeping son in her arms, Rhonnie piped up, 'Who would be visiting Jolly's in a chauffeur-driven Rolls-Royce?'

Jackie, who was sitting next to her, had a think and said to Drina, 'Mr Butlin has a Rolls-Royce, doesn't he? Maybe he's heard you're back and has brought Mrs Butlin over to congratulate you on the arrival of Danny. He's very thoughtful like that, isn't he?'

Drina smiled. 'Yes, he is. I'm sorry to have missed him. They will have gone off by now, finding reception locked . . . can't imagine what he'll be thinking about that . . . but I'll telephone Billy later and ask them both over for dinner the next time they're up visiting their camp in Skegness.'

Ginger, who had already had one reprimand that

morning so really didn't want to risk getting another so soon, had until then managed to keep quiet. By now mortally fed up with sitting around doing nothing, however, she didn't realise she was speaking her thoughts aloud.

'Them inspectors are taking their time, aren't they? How long does it take to look through a set of accounts anyway? I know they've locked us out but I've a good mind to climb up the fire escape and let myself in through the door on the second floor, ask them how much longer they're going to be.'

Harold shot her a stony glance. 'You'll do no such thing! I know from working for the tax office before I came to Jolly's that we could be in serious trouble for interrupting an audit by Her Majesty's Government Inspectors, for any reason. Now sit there and keep quiet until we're given the all clear to get back to work.'

Shamefaced, Ginger sat back in her chair, folded her arms and pressed her lips tightly together.

Drina hid a smile. Ginger had only voiced what she would like to do herself.

For the next hour the gathering kept themselves entertained by talking amongst themselves. Except for Olive and Harold. She took a set of knitting needles and some vivid lime green wool out of her capacious handbag and used the time to add some more rows to what could have been a scarf . . . a sleeve . . . it was hard to tell. Harold sat quietly with his own thoughts. He knew the tax inspectors wouldn't find anything suspicious in his meticulously kept books, but that didn't stop anxiety from gnawing away in the pit of his stomach.

It was approaching twelve o'clock and the inspectors

had been carrying out their audit for almost two hours when a barman came hurrying over to speak to Drina. 'Excuse me, Mrs Jolly, but we've just had a telephone call. You've all been asked to go up to the office.'

She smiled at him. 'Thank you, Robin.' As he returned to the bar, looking relieved, she said to Harold, 'This must mean the inspectors have done enough of an audit to satisfy themselves that any information they've received is a hoax and this has all been an utter waste of everyone's time. Hopefully it's not too late for me still to have my meeting today.' She clapped her hands to gain everyone's attention and announced, 'You'll all be pleased to hear we can return to work.'

Rhonnie said to Jackie, 'Danny is due a feed so I'll come back to the office, give him his bottle and change his nappy, if that's all right?'

Jackie looked aghast that Rhonnie was asking her permission. 'Yes of course it is. And you'll still come with me on the walk around afterwards?'

'I'd love to.' Then it became apparent that Rhonnie's terrible bereavement and new motherhood had not diminished her abilities to sense when something was up with the young girl she had befriended and helped to transform into a sophisticated young woman. 'I've a feeling you've had some suffering of your own to deal with while I've been away. When we're walking about, if you want to talk about it and I can help you in any way, then please feel free.'

Jackie smiled at her by way of acceptance.

As they all trooped out no one noticed Olive was still sitting knitting, oblivious to what was going on around her.

CHAPTER TWENTY-SEVEN

They found the door into reception had been unlocked already in readiness for their arrival and several bewildered campers were already standing at the counter wondering where the staff were. Ginger and the other receptionists immediately went to deal with them, while Drina, Harold, Rhonnie and her son, and Jackie all went upstairs.

Drina entered the general office first, expecting the two inspectors to be waiting for them, and was surprised to find just one man perched on the edge of Jackie's desk. He was tall and slim, dressed in a smart grey striped suit, expensive shoes on his feet. His dark hair was fashionably long, touching the collar of a white shirt. A heavy beard obscured the lower half of his face, and his eyes were hidden behind black-framed spectacles.

Standing beside Drina, Harold looked at him quizzically. This wasn't one of the inspectors he had encountered before. Jackie too was eyeing the man with bemusement.

Unaware of this, Drina held out her hand to him, announcing, 'I'm Mrs Jolly, the owner of the camp.'

Expecting him to respond politely, she was stunned when he didn't attempt to take her hand but instead replied in a sardonic tone. 'I know very well who you are. We need no introduction.' He then took off his glasses and the eyes staring fixedly at her held malicious amusement.

She stared at the man for a moment. She was sure she had never met him before . . . but somehow he was familiar to her. Then it hit her and she issued a shocked, 'Michael!'

At this announcement, Jackie clamped a hand to her mouth, Harold's eyes filled with alarm, and Rhonnie, who was holding her son in her arms while concentrating on getting ready what she needed to feed and change him, stopped what she was doing and walked across to join the others. The four of them were well aware that Michael's unannounced visit was not a social one.

He smirked nastily at Drina. 'So you do recognise your son after all, Mother? I don't know why you're looking so shocked to see me. After all, I did warn you the last time I saw you that I would some day get what was due me. I was in a position to bring my plan to its conclusion a while ago, but what fun would that have been in your absence? No, I wanted to see your faces . . . especially yours, *Mother* . . . when you discovered what I've done. You might even, for once, be proud of me.'

Rhonnie demanded, 'And just what have you done, Michael?'

He turned his attention to her, shooting her the same nasty smirk as he had his mother. 'Oh, the Merry Widow. I can't offer you my condolences for your loss because my father's bastard son meant nothing to me.'

Jackie then spoke up. 'Those men weren't tax inspectors, were they?'

He settled his malicious eyes on her then. 'Oh, the little girl speaks.' He then shot a derogatory glance at Harold, standing mutely by the side of her. 'Cat still got your tongue, I see. Still jump a mile if anyone sneaks up on you? Oh, how many laughs I had doing that to you when I had the misfortune to work under Mr Green in the accounts office and you were just his clerk, you pathetic creature.'

Harold desperately wanted to show this odious man that he was no longer the same timid individual that Michael had relentlessly teased at every opportunity, before he'd fleeced his parents out of a considerable amount of money one too many times and they had seen no other option but to banish him. But then Harold thought it might be better to let him carry on talking, believing Harold to be that same timid man. That way it might be possible to take Michael off his guard and render him incapable while they fetched the police to deal with him. Whatever he had done, Harold had no doubt it would be illegal, knowing Michael's past criminal activities.

Having returned his attention to Jackie, Michael said to her, 'To answer your question, no, those men weren't tax inspectors. They did a damned good job of making out they were, though, enough to fool you all.'

'Michael, what have you done?' Drina demanded.

He appeared to ignore her as he jumped up off the desk and went to lock the door, using Jackie's spare set of keys from the bottom drawer of her desk. The door safely locked, he then returned to perch on the edge of the desk and informed them, 'Just a precaution, in case any of you try something stupid like slipping out to fetch the police.' He then fixed his eyes back on Drina.

'So, Mother, you asked what I'd done. I'll give you a clue. A certain Mr Hewitt might not be very happy if you continue introducing yourself as the owner of this place. You might have heard of him? He owns several successful camps down on the south coast and now believes he's just expanded his empire by buying this one too. He's on his way back down south as we speak, planning to celebrate his new acquisition with his family, though I know very shortly he's going to be drowning his sorrows. Stupid man.'

Drina gasped in horror. 'Are you telling me you've sold this place to Mr Hewitt? But how could you have? It's not yours to sell.'

Michael's eyes darkened and he jumped off the desk to stand menacingly before her. 'No, but it should have been. My father had no right to leave everything to his bastard son and nothing to his legitimate one.' He smacked one fist forcefully into the palm of the other. 'Well, Father and you might have made sure I haven't received a penny from Jolly's, but you couldn't stop me using the place to make up for what I should have had from it.' He thrust his hand into the inside pocket of his jacket and pulled out a folded piece of paper. 'A banker's draft for a million pounds. Payable to the bearer.'

Michael took a glance at the clock on the wall opposite. 'Oh, how time flies when you're enjoying yourself. I'd best get on with this as I have a plane to catch. I'm off to sunny climes where I'm going to live the rest of my life in luxury under a fictitious name. Don't bother looking for me because I don't plan to be found. It wouldn't be fair of me, though, to leave you all in suspense as to how I did it.'

He took a deep breath and proudly reared back his head. 'It was very simple really. When you know the right people, obtaining forged documents good enough to fool solicitors and accountants is easy, for the right price. I certainly met the right people when I was serving time at Her Majesty's pleasure just for trying to make enough money to live after you, *Mother*, saw me on the streets without a bean to my name.

'Actually some of the credit for the plan really belongs to two old timers I overheard bragging to each other about past jobs one day, but I prefer to think that as I honed the finer points of it then I've a right to claim most of it. All I had to do was find the money to pay for the documents I needed and two men to play the part of the tax inspectors, then play solicitor and accountant. I also needed some new clothes and decent transport as I couldn't very well present myself as the son of the owner of a lucrative business looking like the tramp I was when I got out of prison.' He issued a small laugh. 'I got that through donations from a few very nice old ladies, I'm sure you get my drift?

'Finding a sucker to fool into thinking he was buying this place took a bit of ingenuity, but a carefully worded advert in *Dalton's Weekly* about a holiday camp for sale brought Mr Hewitt to me. He'd been after a camp here for a while but hadn't found the right place to buy until I offered him Jolly's at a very tempting price. He fell hook, line and sinker for the story I spun him. After the death of your dear husband, and coming so soon after the tragic death of your eldest son . . . well, he didn't need to know that Dan was not your son but my father's bastard . . . my mother had lost heart and gone off to live abroad in a place that held no painful memories, passing Power of Attorney over to me so that I could handle the sale on her behalf.

'Of course, he wanted to have a tour around the place before he went any further so he came up and I personally showed him, his accountant and solicitor around, right under your very noses a couple of months ago. I wasn't afraid of anyone recognising me because I'd lost so much weight during my time inside, and a beard and glasses did the rest. Of course, Mr Hewitt was very understanding about why it had to be a secret visit. We didn't want the staff to get wind that the camp was being sold in case they started to fear for their jobs and left to take up others, leaving Jolly's in the lurch. He himself didn't want it getting out that he was interested in case someone else should come along and outbid him. His people thought the price very reasonable after seeing the set of fictitious books and Fiscal Reports I gave them.

'With Hewitt now champing at the bit to seal the deal, which of course he expected to be done here in Jolly's offices, all that remained for me to do was get them cleared of staff temporarily so that my so-called solicitor and Mr Hewitt's could complete the transaction and he could hand me my money. Of course, the fact I kept stalling him while I awaited your return made him even more eager. I think my way of clearing the office was a stroke of pure genius, don't you? Hewitt did turn green around the gills when I insisted payment be made by banker's draft, but appreciated the reason for that when I explained that we planned to bank it abroad to avoid paying British tax on it, hence the knockdown price he was getting. Oh, in case you're wondering, while you were all being herded out through reception, I made my way in via the fire escape around the back and was sitting behind the desk, ready and waiting to welcome in Mr Hewitt when he arrived in his chauffeur-driven Rolls. So I might not have fleeced the money out of you directly, *Mother*, but I've left you with one hell of a mess to clear up, and the newspapers are going to have a field day with this. It's not going to do Jolly's reputation any good, is it?'

He paused for a moment before adding, 'I don't think I've left anything out so now I'll be off to begin my new life.' He blew a kiss to Drina. 'We won't be seeing each other again but I doubt you'll lose any sleep over that as you made it clear long ago how you felt about me. I certainly won't care because why would I want to see anyone I hate as much as you? Oh, and you won't be able to telephone the police from up here as I've pulled out the telephone wires, and I shall be barricading the fire-escape door too, so by the time you are in a position to call them I shall be long gone.'

Michael's parting gesture was to wave the banker's draft at them once again before he made to depart via the fire escape.

Drina was staring frozen-faced at her son, still having terrible difficulty taking in the fact that she had given birth to such a wicked, callous man.

Harold was feeling hopelessly inadequate for not yet having come up with a plan to overcome Michael and stop him from escaping with his ill-gotten gains. Now it seemed it was too late.

Throughout Michael's bragging, Jackie too was desperately trying to fathom a way she could put a stop to his despicable plan, but she was standing directly in his eyeline so she'd no chance of that. But just as she thought there was nothing she could do but watch Michael Jolly walk away scot-free, she saw an opportunity to thwart his departure. After he'd blatantly waved the bank draft at them and made to turn and walk away, Jackie made a lunge for it, snatched it out of his hand and had leaped over to the locked door leading to the stairs before Michael even realised what had happened.

By the time he did, she was holding the banker's draft in such a way as to warn him that should he make another step towards her she would rip it up.

The roar of anger he issued was deafening. The shock of hearing it woke the sleeping baby in his mother's arms and he broke into terrified screams.

Danny's interruption gave Michael an idea for a way to turn this situation to his own advantage. He made a lunge for the child, snatching Danny out of his unsuspecting mother's arms, then dashed for the other side of the room, stopping just before the door that led out into the corridor with the fire escape at the end of it. Michael was about to demand the return of the banker's draft in exchange for the safe return of the child when he realised he needed to show them he meant business. He must put the child in a life-threatening situation to achieve that. He ran for the door, yanked it open and disappeared through it.

Rhonnie started screaming in fear that her baby was being held captive by a man she knew to be single-minded when it came to getting his own evil way.

Jackie was horrified to realise her actions had landed the baby in such terrible danger and was momentarily rendered immobile, as were Drina and Harold.

Then it seemed to hit them all simultaneously that Michael would only return the baby safely in exchange for the banker's draft, and they dashed after him. Drina was first out and heading for the door to the fire escape which she found wide open, informing her that that was the path Michael had taken.

Reaching the fire escape, Drina stepped out on to the metal landing, the baby's screams from above immediately alerting her to the fact that Michael had gone up instead of down. She automatically raised her gaze and saw him climbing on to the flat roof, the hysterical baby clamped firmly under one arm. She wasted no time in following him.

They all arrived on the flat roof one after the other and froze in terror at the sight of Michael over at the other side, standing an inch or so away from the edge, holding the baby upside down by one leg over the sheer drop. He was so desperate to get his hands back on the banker's draft that he was unaware that the screams of the baby had drawn a gathering crowd down below, all looking up and wondering what was making a baby cry like that.

Michael frenziedly bellowed, 'I get the draft back in one piece or I drop this fucking kid!'

Jackie screamed back at him, 'I'm bringing it right over.'

An ashen-faced Rhonnie had collapsed to her knees and was sobbing, 'Please don't hurt my baby! Please, Michael, please, I beg you!'

Fearing Jackie would be putting herself in danger with what she was about to do, Drina grabbed her arm, snatching the draft from her hand and telling her, 'I'll take it.'

Harold meanwhile had seen a way he could prevent Michael from profiting from his ill-gotten gains while at the same time retrieving the baby safely. He felt his plan was good enough to risk. The worst that could happen was that he failed to prevent Michael from getting his hands on the draft, but at least the baby would be safe and that was the most important thing.

To Drina's shock, he snatched the draft from out of her hand, telling her, 'No, I'll take it.'

The three women's hearts were in their mouths as they watched Harold walk slowly over to Michael, holding the draft out for him to see. He stopped just short of the other man, holding the draft towards him, just out of reach. In a quiet, calm voice, Harold said, 'Now please hand me the baby, Mr Jolly, and at the same time I will give you the draft.'

Michael's eyes were filled with amusement when he responded, 'As if I need to warn you, you coward, that one false move and it'll be *you* who goes over the side along with the kid – but then, you haven't the balls to try anything, have you?' He swung the arm holding the baby in Harold's direction, bringing it to a halt just out of his reach. 'Together on my three.' As he counted Harold momentarily shut his eyes and said a silent prayer for the success of his plan. He opened them just as Michael reached three. As Michael then swung the baby all the way over to him, Harold, as ordered, extended the draft towards Michael. The second the baby was within a hair's breadth of Harold's reach he made a sudden grab for the child, managing to get a tight grip on him, while Michael simultaneously made a grab for the draft. As Harold saw Michael reach for it he tossed the draft into the air, the wind caught it and began to blow it over the edge of the roof, just as Harold had hoped would happen.

With a look of utter shock on his face Michael made a desperate snatch for the piece of paper. The wind blew it further away from him, he lost his balance and toppled over the side. A moment later a sickening thud resounded as he reached the ground below.

CHAPTER TWENTY-EIGHT

It was just after four o'clock on the last day of the season. The few remaining campers had been waved off hours before and already the bars and shops had been cleared of their stock, given a thorough clean, shutters pulled down and doors locked for the next four months. Chalets had been checked for forgotten belongings, all bedding removed for washing, mattresses taken into storage. The camp was in the process of turning once more into a ghost town. All of the seasonal staff were in their chalets packing up their belongings ready to depart for home tomorrow. But all of them were excited at the thought of the fun that still lay ahead for them at the end-of-season party in the Paradise ballroom.

For Jackie, though, and a dozen or so other permanent staff, work did not stop. They all continued to beaver away to ensure the campers had a safe and well-kept camp to return to next year.

She was on her own in the general office as yesterday had been Olive's last day with Jolly's after landing herself a permanent job as a filing clerk at the local hospital. How long she would keep it remained to be seen. As yet the agency hadn't found a suitable candidate to replace her. Harold was in his office with the door closed as he assessed tenders from potential new suppliers for goods next year, checking whether they offered more value for money than the present suppliers did.

It wasn't like Jackie hadn't plenty to keep her occupied, but her mood was low and she didn't feel like working, so was sitting at her desk, head in her hands, staring into space. Like the rest of the staff, she should have been feeling very excited at the thought of the fun to come at the end-of-season party, but for two reasons she wasn't.

The first reason was that, having been under the mistaken belief she had suffered and dealt with enough personal trauma to last a lifetime, last night she had received yet another blow and in its way it was proving to be the most devastating yet. She was losing her best friend as Ginger was getting married. Three days ago, out of the blue, Paul had proposed and a madly in love Ginger had instantly squealed her acceptance.

The reason for the sudden proposal was that before he had met her and fallen head over heels in love, Paul had applied for a job with the force in Birmingham. He hadn't liked the idea of working for the bully of a man who was reported to be in line to take over kindly Inspector Clayburn's place on his retirement at the end of December. A few days ago Paul had received a letter telling him the job was his and the start date was in four weeks' time. He couldn't stand the thought of heading off for pastures new leaving Ginger behind, so she was going with him as his wife and they would be living in a police house. In the meantime she was going to be staying with his parents in their spare room while she and Paul made arrangements to be married in Skegness Register Office at the first available date.

Jackie was sincerely thrilled for Ginger, thrilled also to be asked to be a witness at the wedding, but sad for herself that she was going to have to learn to do without her friend on a day-to-day basis. This meant that tonight would be the last end-of-season party she would go to with Ginger, the last she would spend sharing the chalet with her and having to tell her to shut up so she could get some sleep, and the last time she would see her friend's crooked smile beaming over at her from behind the reception counter.

The second reason Jackie wasn't looking forward to the party as much as she usually would have been was that she felt it wasn't right she should be having fun while the woman she thought so highly of was bound to be suffering greatly after the death of her only child. Not that Michael had proved a good son to her, but he had still been Drina's son when all was said and done. She hadn't seen Drina or Rhonnie either since that awful day just over two weeks ago. They had been whisked away by Artie just after the police had left, having taken their statements and been quickly satisfied that Michael had been responsible for his own demise. An ambulance had taken away his body.

The banker's draft had been found by an eagle-eyed camper who had been one of those gathering below at the time of the fall. He'd astutely realised the piece of paper was very important if a man had lost his life in a desperate bid to get his hands on it, so had carefully followed it with his eyes until he observed it come to rest on top of a pile of rubbish in a bin by the tennis courts. He had been shocked to discover just what the paper was, but immediately handed it straight over to the police when they arrived on the scene.

Jackie was intrigued to find out, but wouldn't until she saw Drina again, just how Mr Hewitt had taken the news that he'd been swindled out of his money and was not in fact the owner of Jolly's. But at least he had got his money back whereas most other victims of swindlers never saw theirs again, and were left with nothing but their complete humiliation at having allowed themselves to be conned in the first place.

Jackie was aware that Michael's funeral had taken place two days ago. On Drina's orders only she had attended. His mother did not believe it right that people should feel obliged to attend the funeral of a man who had treated them like dirt under his shoes. Out of respect for Drina, Jackie had complied with her wishes. She supposed that in light of what Drina was going through, her plans to develop the business had been shelved for the time being. Whether she would have the heart to resurrect them in future remained to be seen. Drina, though, had indicated to Jackie that the plans she had made included her in some way, and she still wondered about that.

She heaved a huge sigh. Close friends and other staff she had grown very fond of this season were moving forward in their lives. Rhonnie was a mother now, Ginger getting married, Al had moved to London and was working away in his fabulous new job, and lots of the other seasonal staff would not be returning next year as they all had other avenues they planned to explore. Her relationship with her mother was slowly being rebuilt and was better than most would expect it to be in the circumstances, but the close bond they had once shared would never fully repair and Jackie was learning to do without her mother's day-to-day support. Gina was happy, though, with her new love, something Jackie had always wished for her, and that made her happy too. She had been at Jolly's since leaving school at fifteen and was now nearly twenty-two. She wondered if she should consider moving on too, finding new avenues herself, new challenges to face. Trouble was she loved her job and knew that finding another with such a variety of duties, no day ever the same, meeting the many different characters who came and went through the camp's gates, would be nigh on impossible.

Her thoughts were interrupted by the buzzing of the switchboard announcing an incoming call. She got up to answer it. She was surprised to hear the caller's voice was Drina's, checking whether Jackie and Harold were both in the office as she wanted to come over and speak to them both. On Jackie telling her that they were, Drina asked her to make tea for them all and informed her that she would be with them in ten minutes.

Tea made, Jackie was sitting waiting patiently with Harold in his office. He had respectfully vacated his chair to allow Drina to take her rightful place behind the desk and was sitting in front of it next to Jackie. Neither of them had a clue what Drina could be coming to say, but both of them guessed that after recent events she had decided to sell the business and, as her senior staff, was affording them the courtesy of advance warning before it became public knowledge.

They both expected Drina to arrive showing signs of her recent bereavement so were astounded to see her walk in jauntily, a wide smile on her face, wearing a smart green tweed skirt and pale green twinset, a row of pearls around her neck under a woollen winter coat. She greeted them both with a hearty good afternoon.

Having taken off her coat and settled herself in her chair, Drina smiled at both of them in turn before she began, 'First, may I explain to you my mood, which I noticed shocked you both when I arrived. I know you were expecting to see me grieving for the recent loss of my son, but I hope you won't judge me too harshly when I tell you I have shed so many tears over him in the past that now I have reached the point where I have none left to shed.'

Drina took a deep breath before she went on, 'Now I know you will both be intrigued to know why I wanted to speak to you in particular.'

Jackie could not contain herself any longer and burst out, 'Please tell us you're not selling the camp?'

Drina smiled at her. 'No, dear, I'm not. I would never sell Jolly's, the place means far too much to me. Besides, it's not really mine to sell as it now belongs to Rhonnie and young Danny and I am just caretaking it for them until Rhonnie feels she's ready to take the helm. While I was nursing Rhonnie through her bereavement, then her pregnancy, I had plenty of time to think and I came up with an idea that I thought had some merit to it. I discussed it with Rhonnie and Artie and they both thought so too, as does my bank manager.

'This camp caters for working-class people. We offer them an all-inclusive holiday at a price they can afford on the money they earn. Where, though, do better off people go for their holiday where they can find everything they want in one place? Well, that's what I aim to provide for them. Instead of our basic wooden chalets, my new camp's chalets will be built of brick, have a lounge and separate bedroom . . . some of them two bedrooms . . . and a bathroom and heating in them too so we can open all year round. Instead of one big restaurant serving the same food to everyone, several smaller ones will each offer different food, cooked by professional chefs, and diners will be able to order what they would like to eat not what we dictate to them, and will be able to dine when they wish to and not when we say so.

'There will be shops selling quality goods, and a beauty parlour offering all manner of treatments; children will have their own clubs providing them with all-day entertainment, leaving their parents free to spend their days as they wish, and the use of a night babysitting service; there'll be an eighteen-hole golf course with several professional golfers offering coaching, and tennis courts offering the same. We will be putting on a cabaret show with professional dancers in a luxury theatre every night along with a variety of top entertainers making guest appearances. At this camp there will be no knobbly knees competitions, no egg and spoon races, no donkey rides on the beach. Sunbathers around the outdoor pool will have their every whim catered for by attentive staff. A professional swimmer will be on hand in the indoor pool to give lessons to those who wish to take them.

'I could go on but I think you now have an idea of what my new camp will be like. I don't intend it to cater for the same numbers that this one does. It's to be smaller, more exclusive . . . two thousand people at a time. And they will pay well to holiday with us. I have found a site on the Devonshire coast that is the perfect setting for what I want. It is in beautiful countryside, by the sea with a private beach. I have just returned from a meeting with the bank, and the board there love my idea. I am pleased to tell you that they have agreed to the loan I asked them for and two private investors will put up the rest. I now have the funding to bring my plan to fruition.

'Now to come to my proposition to you both.' She first looked at Jackie. 'My dear, I will be moving down to Devon and personally overseeing every aspect of the build and refurbishment. Of course Artie is coming with me. He will be site manager. Rhonnie is coming too and will play a back seat role while she raises her son, becoming more involved on a day-to-day basis when he goes to school. So I will be needing a personal assistant. The job will be varied and very demanding and certainly not nine to five. I couldn't think of a better person to offer it to but you, Jackie.'

'Me!' Her mind whirled frantically. A very short while ago she was wishing for a change of scene and a job that offered her new challenges. Now here she was, being offered that very job. The Three Musketeers were back in business again. Did she need time to think about it? No, she didn't. 'When do I start?' she excitedly asked.

A delighted Drina told her, 'As soon as we find a suitable replacement for you here.'

Then she turned her attention to Harold. 'I never thought I would be offering you such a position because it requires a person who is good with people, has the acumen to deal with all manner of problems, and can make snap decisions in emergency situations. Several months ago you were not that man, Harold, but it seems while I was away a miraculous transformation has taken place. I would like you to consider accepting the role of manager of this camp. Of course we will make sure you have the right staff to support you, but what do you say?'

Harold stared at Drina dumbstruck. Not because he was doubting he had the ability to do this job, but because he was having such difficulty accepting the man Drina Jolly believed him to be. He felt himself swell with pride. He was no longer a shy, easily intimidated man with no self-belief, but a force to be reckoned with. With his head held high, he responded with conviction, 'You have made the right choice in asking me to do this job for you, Mrs Jolly. I am honoured to accept.'

'Good,' she declared. 'You've both made me very happy. I now have the perfect staff on board to move the business forward so it's a thriving and successful one for the next generation to take over in due course.' She rose and put on her coat. 'Right, I have a party to get ready for and so have you. We have much to celebrate tonight. I'll see you both later.'

She left them staring at each other as they both digested what had just transpired. It was Jackie who first found her voice but all she could think of to say was, 'We haven't closed and locked the entrance for the winter. I'll go and see to it.'

A while later she pressed her back against the closed iron gates and looked back into the deserted camp that only a short time ago had been teeming with people. This time next year it would be someone else who would be closing these gates and she'd be closing those of another camp. She knew without doubt that whoever took her place here was in for a roller-coaster ride as they dealt with all the trials and tribulations, tears, heart-ache, fun and laughter that working for a place such as this would bring them daily. She would be taking with her numerous memories of her time here, some very happy, some excruciatingly painful, but one thing was for certain: where she was heading she couldn't wait to begin making new ones.

The Time of Our Lives

Lynda Page

When Rhonda Fleming runs away from home the last place she expects to end up getting a job is at a Jolly's holiday camp in Mablethorpe. Thrown in at the deep end, Rhonnie discovers there's never a dull moment – particularly with gorgeous staff like Dan around. From the beauty contest by the pool to jiving in the Paradise dance hall and from the rollercoaster at the fair to donkey rides on the beach, the holiday-makers are guaranteed to have the time of their lives. But it's not all fun and frolics and Rhonnie has to deal with situations she would never have imagined, particularly when the boss's son surfaces to claim what he believes in his . . .

Praise for Lynda Page's previous novels:

'All manner of page-turning twists and turns. Expect the unexpected' *Choice* magazine

'Filled with lively characters and compelling action' *Books*

'Inspirational and heart-warming' *Sun*

978 0 7553 9845 4

headline